THE
GAME
OF LORDS

THE GAME OF LORDS

SANDRA D. JOHNSON

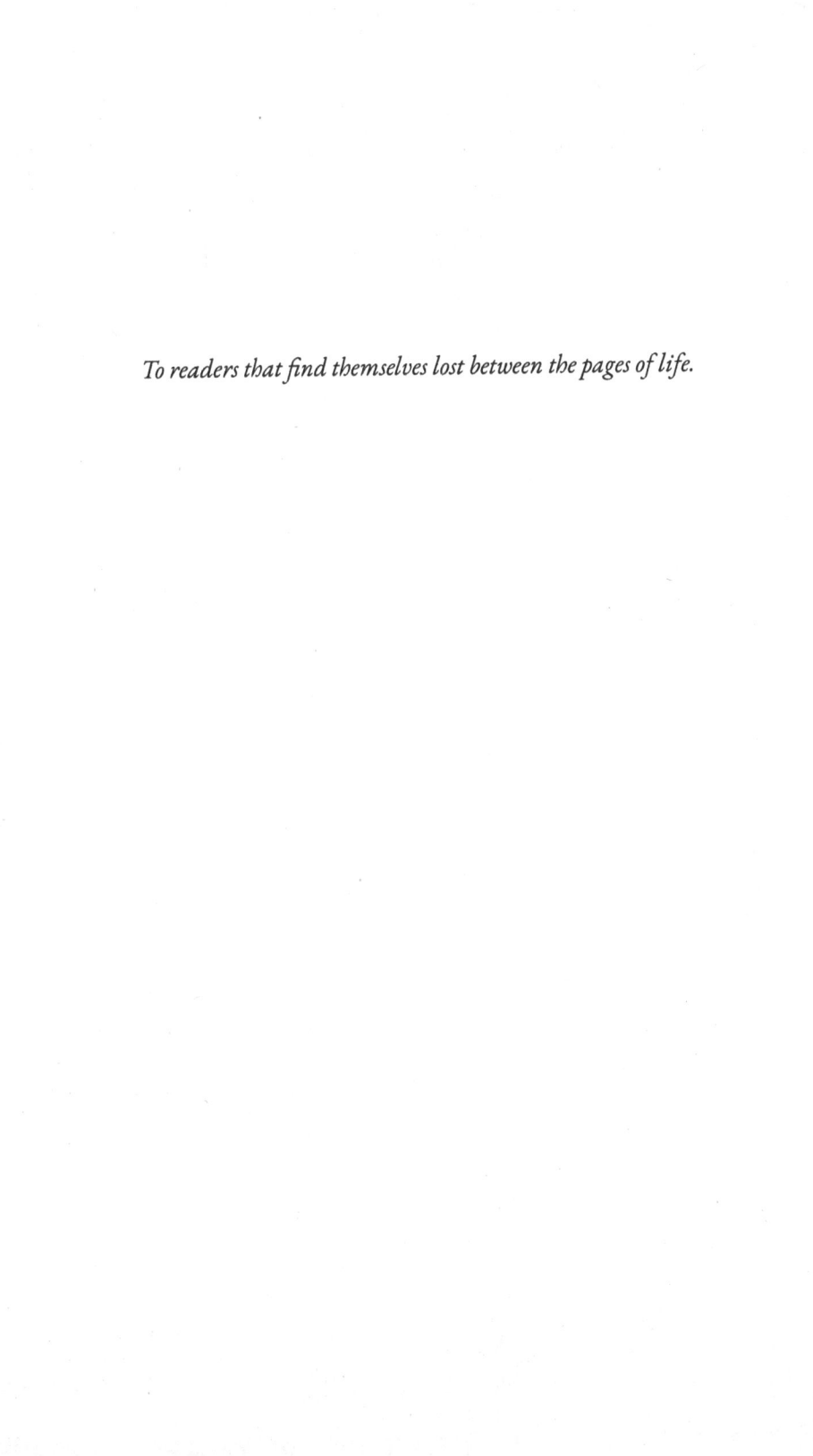

To readers that find themselves lost between the pages of life.

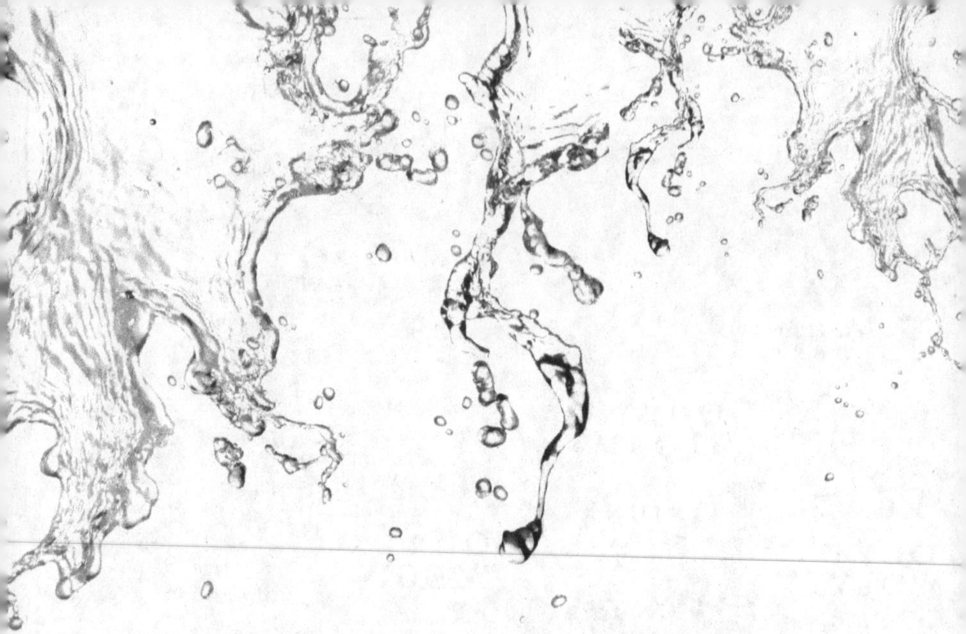

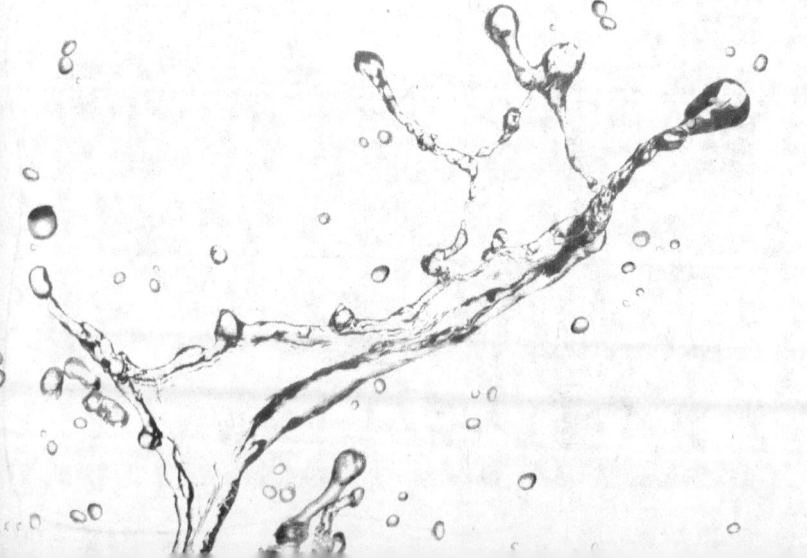

ONLY ONE MAY
WIN, AND THE
REST MUST DIE.

THE FIVE COURTS OF
LATERRA

COURT OF MAGIC
RULED BY:
LORD OF ILLUSION,
LEADER OF HOUSE OF CARDS

COURT OF WIND
RULED BY:
LORD OF SKY,
LEADER OF HOUSE OF AIR

COURT OF SMOKE
RULED BY:
LORD OF FIRE,
LEADER OF HOUSE OF FLAME

COURT OF STORMS
RULED BY:
LORD OF THUNDER
LEADER OF HOUSE OF RAIN

COURT OF WOLVES
RULED BY:
LADY OF WOLVES
LEADER OF HOUSE OF THE WOLF

PART I

A Game of Vanishing

I

Valeria swallowed, lifting her head to examine the stone walls that encased the House of Air. Her sister, Lilith, strode ahead, eager to enter the tall archway. Valeria had never seen the Lord of Sky's castle up close. Her father warned her about the powerful lords and the immortal king, and for good reason.

She used to listen to Eddard, the elderly man who visited her father's antique shop every other day—the only man old enough to remember the most recent Game of Lords competition that occurred five decades ago. He would tell her about the king, how he would stand on his dais, ordering death upon anyone who looked him deep enough in the eye.

The king made the five lords file through their townsmen before settling on a final four that would then be vanished and thrown into the games to compete. Making twenty contestants in total. Twenty throughout the entire land. *Only one may win, and the rest must die.* She shuddered at the old saying.

After the tedious walk up the gravel pathway, and traveling through the chatter-filled hallway, Valeria followed Lilith into the noble House of Air. Locking her arm around her older sisters, she asked, "Now that you've dragged me here, what is your plan?" She let her eyes skim over the crowded ballroom while she waited for Lilith's response.

The walls towered three stories high. A dazzling crystal chandelier hanging far above the troupe of dancers that twirled around on the hardwood floor. Their tapping feet and twisting gowns were silenced behind the melody of the calm piano playing in the corner of the ballroom.

Lilith squeezed Valeria's arm, dipping her head, a piece of her chestnut-colored hair falling from its place behind her ear as she smiled. "I need to find Jonathon. Come with me." Lilith paused when she recognized the hesitant look on Valeria's face. Frowning, she took a step closer. "Wouldn't it be grand if the Lord of Sky noticed us? I mean you, of course."

No, it wouldn't. Valeria stepped around a sticky-faced child. Reality settled in as she noticed the absence of a mother or father to keep an eye on the boy. Why would someone bring their child to the celebration of The Vanishing?

Lilith whirled her head around, searching for the brown-haired man she had fallen madly in love with. While Valeria stole a moment to investigate the room.

A group of officials walked past in their silver armor, flaunting their green and gold colors with pistols tucked underneath their arms. Ducking behind Lilith, Valeria couldn't risk being seen if she wanted her plan to fall through without any worries.

All she needed to achieve was a brisk escape from her sister's attention. Then she could search for the Lord of Sky's office and the card she hoped would be hidden somewhere within the drawers of his desk.

Immediately, her eyes locked onto the floating candles that created glints of light against the towering walls. Forcing her attention away, she gazed past the dancers dressed in pastel gowns of all colors. She examined the farthest wall, where a grand double staircase led up to a marble statue of the powerful Lord of Sky. Dropping her eyes, and swallowing the lump in her throat, she stared at the hall between the double stairs.

If the Lord of Sky caught her rummaging through his things, searching for the Card of Contestants, she'd never get the chance to run away and choose her own ending.

A forbidden temptation filled her body, as if telling her to go. It demanded she walk closer. The card was hidden somewhere down that hallway, and despite how badly she wanted to turn around and leave, she couldn't. *Not yet, at least.* Quickness was necessary if she intended to flee before The Vanishing began at midnight.

Before Valeria could take a single ill-advised step, Lilith tugged her across the floor and through the valley of dancers. Their elegant gowns, pearly hair, and pasty skin blurred together with her movement. Though, the faintest moment seemed to slow everything around her when she spotted a man with raven black hair grinning at her. A warmness spread on her cheeks, only growing hotter when her eyes lingered on the silver chains that dangled from his neck.

"Lords, who's making you blush already?" Lilith prodded, batting her eyelids and lifting her chin to search the room again. "Where is he?" She muttered.

Torn away from the raven haired man's entrancing gaze, Valeria sighed and asked, "Didn't Jonathon say he would find you?"

Lilith scoffed, but continued her thorough search throughout the room filled with pointy eared dancers. "Yes, but don't you know how impatient I can be? I'm eager to see him."

"Lilith!" A familiar voice shouted, stopping the sisters in place.

Lilith turned her face, raising her brows in excitement when she spotted her friend. "Alexa? I thought you were helping your mom tonight?"

Biting her lip, Valeria watched Alexa's long black hair swing back and forth as she sauntered toward them. The elegant red gown complimented her tan skin and dark eyes.

"She let me off earlier than expected." Alexa glanced at Valeria, a smile blossomed underneath her pert nose. "I apologize, Lilith must have bothered you about coming all week."

Valeria chuckled, because yes, once Alexa informed Lilith she wouldn't be able to make it to the ball of The Vanishing, Lilith had decided to harass Valeria until she finally agreed.

A copper red strand fell into Valeria's face and she brushed it away. "You're not wrong."

Lilith playfully slapped Alexa's arm before her attention was abruptly pulled away by Jonathon, who now stood at her side.

Grabbing Lilith by the waist, he spun her around before placing a gentle kiss on her flushed cheek. "There's my darling. I was looking everywhere for you."

"You were?" Lilith feigned indifference. "We arrived a few moments ago."

Valeria barely stopped her eyes from rolling, but she did offer Jonathon a smile when his humored gaze landed on her. Alexa patted Lilith's elbow before whispering something in her ear and scurrying across the floor to a table piled with glass flutes and liquids of all sorts.

"She was looking for me, wasn't she?" Jonathan asked.

Valeria chuckled, managing a nod. "Of course she was."

Jonathan dropped his hand to Lilith's, examining her gown as he said, "I'm glad you decided to come, Valeria. Your sister couldn't stop ranting about it all week."

Pursing her lips, Valeria shot a look at her sister. "I didn't really have a choice."

Jonathan squeezed Lilith's side. "You shouldn't have made her come if she didn't want to. This isn't an entirely enjoyable event. Most of the people here have come to beg for their lives and freedom." He pointed a finger at the dancers. "The performers were hired to keep the ruckus of angry citizens at bay." Lowering his voice, he leaned next to Lilith's ear, who frowned and watched the performers twirl across the floor. "What is there to celebrate for the people? Nothing. This is all set up to entertain the king."

Valeria's eyes landed on a red velvet curtain that draped to the floor into a puddle of fabric. After admiring the beautiful room, she faced Jonathon again. "Do you think the officials will vanish the first contestant for the games here? What if they don't wait until midnight and they do it now?"

Jonathan crossed his arms. "They won't. They never have," he paused, regathering his thoughts before proceeding. "Besides, what if the four contestants didn't come to the ball tonight?"

She nodded, trying to ignore the way her hands trembled at the title of the less-than-ideal event.

He stepped closer to Valeria, and pressed a comforting hand onto her arm. "I promise once the king arrives and announces The Vanishing, we can leave." Lilith sneered at his promise, but all she got was a pointed look in return. "Your sister and I will take you home."

She knew that The Vanishing started at midnight and would end at sunrise, only to begin at midnight the next day. It's how The Vanishing worked for the past two-hundred and fifty years. Nothing had changed. *Nothing would ever change.*

Even if it was a new year that would bring a new court and immortal lord or lady. The Game of Lords and its beginning and end would always stay the same. Nineteen deaths, leaves one winner. Another immortal highlord to rule over the fresh lands of innocent citizens.

Valeria's heart thundered as she considered every possible outcome for the night. The thoughts reminded her of why she had even agreed to come to the ball in the first place.

Nevertheless, she gave Lilith and Jonathon a polite curtsy before they turned and sauntered onto the ballroom floor.

Lilith gripped the skirt of her crystal gown, lowering herself into a proper curtsy. Jonathan bowed, and then Valeria watched as they danced between the performers. Valeria settled her gaze on the hallway between the double staircase, observing a couple who stumbled out of the powder room. She smiled at the two, lifted her gown, and strode across the wooden floor. Closing the distance between her and the hallway.

Dodging a giggling woman who bursted out of a dark room, Valeria swiftly pressed herself against the wall, leaving room for the woman to pass. She didn't have the time for laughter and boys. Everyone was acting as if they were fine– okay with the events that would occur throughout the next few days. Being outside was a risk, especially tonight. And yet, here everyone was. Filling the walls of the enormous House of Air.

When she entered the hallway, she peered around the corner into the ballroom to make sure no one had noticed her absence yet. Then she opened the nearest door and stepped inside.

She leaned against the door until it clicked shut and released a breath.

Darkness filled the room, covering every corner in shadows. There wasn't a single light to guide her. Dropping her hand from the doorknob, she felt something sharp cut into the tip of her finger. A hiss fell from her lips as she squeezed the injured hand to her chest and searched for a candlestick with the other.

What felt like a wooden handle of a dagger spun on the table after the back of her hand skimmed against it. She would have groaned in frustration if it weren't for the metal base of a candle holder that rubbed against her palm. Fortunately she soon felt the thin length of a spare match lying beside it. Scraping the rounded tip of the match against a small stone she found on the table, Valeria set flame to the wick, and waited for the flickering light to fill the room.

Quickly, she was distracted by the large mahogany desk that took up the entire middle of the room, a map of the Court of Wind hung on the wall behind it.

Her heart stopped.

Could it be?

She planned on searching all night. Had she already found the room she was looking for?

Valeria swallowed and stepped closer to the desk, getting a clearer view of the images on the wall. Directly underneath the large map was a smaller, less intricate one. Instead of the farmlands and neighborhoods of the Court of Wind, the smaller map marked different rooms and hallways; it was a map of the house she currently stood in– the House of Air.

Relieved, she freed a much lighter breath than before. The map could lead her straight to where she needed to be. Dragging her uninjured finger along the rough paper until she stopped on the small square tracing of the room she currently stood in. Valeria grinned. She had, in fact, found the room she was searching for. The Lord of Sky's office.

The sound of chuckling and rushed footsteps echoed through the crack of the door she entered only moments ago, cutting her celebration short. Swiveling on her toes, she rushed across the room and locked the door, choosing to ignore the couple that had snuck back into the hallway to do Gods knows what to each other. A small bit of red captured her attention after the lock clicked underneath her fingertips.

Glancing down, she examined her swollen finger, watching as a drop of blood dripped from the open flesh and fell to the floor. Lords. It needed to be wrapped. She couldn't leave her blood all over the place, not unless she wanted to be caught and thrown into the games to die.

Her gaze landed on an unopened letter that was lying on top of the oval shaped table beside the door. The sharp blade of the dagger rested on top of it, staining the white paper with splashes of her red blood.

Cursing, she grabbed the letter and debated opening it to discard the unclean envelope, but the urgency to find what she needed and flee the House of Air forced her to stash the letter into the pocket of her evergreen skirt.

A strand of her copper red locks fell into her face as she blew out a long breath. She couldn't afford to leave any evidence of her being there.

With haste like never before, she positioned herself behind the desk and began rummaging through the files on top of the sleek wood. Pens and paper clips scattered across the hard surface after she bumped a bowl with a frantic hand. Valeria cursed under her breath and grabbed a tissue to wrap around her finger.

Though she had blazed through drawer after drawer, tossing quills and ink pots, she then carefully placed the nibs and parchment back inside.

After combing through the last drawer filled with envelopes and unopened letters, she reached the bottom of the pile. Eyes widening when she picked an opened letter up and held it toward the flickering light. Even though it was exactly what she was hunting for, her body began to shake. Fear soaked through every rational thought of hers.

The card read,

Court of Wind Contestants

Those exact words haunted Valeria's dreams for the past nine years, ever since her father had filled her head with terror of the games. Shoving down the temptation to run into the forest and never be seen or spoken of again, she realized that her fate and Lilith's now lay in her hands.

Gods, she prayed that they weren't on the list.

Inside the envelope are the four names of the future contestants from the Court of Wind—villagers who would be vanished, taken from their families and homes and forced into the Game of Lords.

When Valeria opened the envelope, a small black card slid into the palm of her hand.

She hadn't fully grasped what she would do if she was successful with her plan. The Court of Wind Contestants card was in her hands, but how come she couldn't force herself to read it?

Lifting her eyes to the ornate ceiling, she flipped the card around in her hands as if she were weighing her options. If her name was on the card, she would never come home. She would never grow old. Win or die, she would always remain young.

Releasing a sigh, Valeria closed her eyes. Before she had the opportunity to lower her gaze onto the card and behold what her future might include, the lock clicked and the door swung open.

The Lord of Sky stood underneath the threshold.

2

V aleria stood frozen in place, only able to observe the Lord of Sky as he stared down at her. His brown eyes lowered to the card in her hands prior to examining the mess she made on his desk.

Ballroom music flooded into the room behind him. Without removing his focus from her, he turned and closed the door. She scanned his coffee brown hair, noting the way he slicked it back when he faced her again. She dropped her arms, along with the empty envelope, but tightened her fingers around the black Card of Contestants as he neared. Unable to tear her eyes away from his piercing one, Valeria took the time to observe the blackness swirling in his irises.

From across the desk, the Lord of Sky cocked his head and opened his hand, exposing his palm.

"I'm sorry. I was just—" Valeria stuttered, unsure of how he might react.

She did not receive a response.

Begrudgingly, she handed the card over. Watching as he tucked it into his black vest pocket, keeping his firm eyes on hers. It was Valeria's first time seeing the immortal lord in person. Unfortunately, he was far more attractive than the posters around the Court of Wind captured in their paintings.

Although he was currently glaring at her, as if he wanted to throw her in the dungeons beneath the House of Air, and let her rot there for Gods knows how long, Valeria couldn't help but think it was a shame he never left his home to wander the village. There were never any known sightings of him in the papers. Any news about the highlord had been about the plans he had for the Court of Wind.

He crossed his arms over his chest, watching her struggle to find a decent explanation.

It wasn't a common occurrence for Valeria to be caught rummaging through someone else's belongings, let alone their home. She never found a good enough reason to snoop around and seek anything other than the card that was resting comfortably in the Lord of Sky's vest pocket.

She took a step back, her legs bumping into the leather black chair that was tucked underneath his desk.

"You're not supposed to be in here," he said.

Valeria felt her cheeks flame with embarrassment. "I'm aware, my lord. I apologize. It's just that—"

"You were looking for the Card of Contestants. This." His finger tapped against his chest, right where the card was sitting. "And you wanted to see if your name might be on it," he concluded, leaning over the desk to take a glance at the now empty envelope. Before Valeria could respond, he turned for the door. "However, Valeria Rox. This is not the way to do so."

"But—" she tried, flinching when he said her name. *How did he know her?* Her chin wobbled as he faced the only exit. She could find another card. There had to be another one. Especially with so many officials wandering through the Court of Wind the last few days.

Opening the door, he gave a quick hum. "I suppose you're lucky tonight. If it weren't for more important matters at hand, I'd have called a few officials in here to deal with you." His tone was hard and plain, exactly what one could expect from him. "I recommend leaving before the night ends. Enjoy the rest of the ball, and please... refrain from touching anymore of my things."

She sighed and slowly made her way around the desk, her hands wet and clammy ever since he had walked into the room. When she looked into his dark eyes, she wondered if she had been the only one to attempt such a thing, sneaking around inside the House of Air in hopes of finding the Card of Contestants to learn if they would be vanished or not.

The Lord of Sky moved, giving her room to slip past him and into the sky blue hallway. She jumped when the door slammed shut. Then she left the hall, and entered the ballroom once again.

Hopes dwindled down to nothing as she glanced around.

When her attention drifted toward the crowd surrounding the stage that had been hidden behind the ruby curtains before, Valeria failed to notice the Lord of Sky stepping out of the office and cutting past her, then sauntering through the crowd.

She pushed farther into the room, unable to remove her gaze from the nine people who stood on the stage, ten once the Lord of Sky joined them.

All five lords stood over the crowd, faces neutral as they looked upon the townsmen of the Court of Wind. Her warm blood ran cold when she finally saw the king and his four children standing front and center.

Her breath got caught in the back of her throat when the immortal king began to speak.

15

"As you all may know, today is the final night of the sixth Game of Lords ball."

A deep craving to leave before the king could finish his speech fled through Valeria's body. After tonight, everything would change, and she had yet to find out if she and Lilith were one of the four contestants chosen for the games, thanks to the damned Lord of Sky.

She was so close, and failed despite all of her scheming.

But there was still a lingering chance to run—to hide. To flee the cursed lands of Laterra and live in the outskirts of the kingdom. Perhaps she and Lilith could sail to another continent, settle down on a farm and raise chickens, goats, cows for milk. Even if she loved her home and its people, Valeria would do anything to keep her and the ones she cared for away from the Game of Lords.

But it was already too late. None of that mattered.

They were already here, at the ball of The Vanishing, and it was going to begin at midnight. Time had run out, they could no longer leave the Court of Wind without being stopped by the armed officials who stood watch outside the city gates.

Valeria spotted Lilith's dark hair over the crowd of people and proceeded to push through thick gowns filled with trembling bodies until she reached her. Latching onto Lilith's silver dress, Valeria gave it a yank, watching as a sprawl of sparkles fell to the wooden floor.

Lilith frowned when she noticed her younger sister. "What is it?"

"Come with me," Valeria pleaded, glancing at the stage where three officials stood behind the king. Their glares barely visible beneath the silver helmets.

Lilith sneered, annoyed, she tried to pull out of Valeria's grip. "The Vanishing hasn't started yet. Please, wait until Jonathon and I are ready. We'll leave soon, I promise."

Valeria started to argue, but was drowned out when the king's deep voice boomed over the crowd. She turned her attention to the stage.

"For the coming midnights, four of you will be vanished. When the final contestant is collected, our glorious challenge and all of its twenty contestants will be together, and the sixth Game of Lords will begin."

Eager whispers and muffled cries echoed around the room. The king grinned from ear to ear as he listened to his people beg to have their lives spared from the game. This was why everyone had come to the ball. To beg. To plead. It wasn't for the expensive drinks and unique treats... it was to bargain for their lives.

"Please!" A lady shouted above the cries, her voice breaking as she raised a young child high above the crowd. "Spare me! Spare us!"

Valeria yearned to beg with them.

Choosing to ignore the woman and child, the king turned toward the prince, collecting a scroll from his eldest son before he spoke, "Now, I will read from the list of names that have already been pulled and competing."

Valeria swallowed. Names. Objects. Play things. That's all they were. That's all they would ever be underneath the king's command.

"From the Court of Smoke; Ridoc Cadence, Albert Cooper, Shane Newton, and Rob Johnson. From the Court of Magic; Ruby Easton..."

It took everything for Valeria to refrain from screaming as he continued to read each name. Sixteen of them in total. Four names from each court.

Once the king was done listing the names, he motioned to the lords that stood off to the side of the stage. Valeria allowed her gaze to skim over the tallest one, the man who had grinned at her earlier with those sparkling turquoise eyes and raven black hair. He was the Lord of Illusion. She hadn't recognized him before.

When his eyes locked with hers, she shifted her focus onto the other highlords.

Ignoring the burning sensation on the side of her head, she examined the magnificent Lady of Wolves.

Valeria always despised the games and what they represented—to serve a lonely and arrogant king, who had lived for far too long. He decided loneliness was tedious after the queen's death, and created a competition to fulfill his growing boredom instead of mourning like any normal person would.

He is a selfish king.

The Lady of Wolves changed the games and what they represented to Valeria, because she is the only woman to win. As the most recent victor—winning five decades ago, she is living proof that immortal lords do not have to be men.

Valeria usually didn't bother to keep informed with the five lords and their power-ridden courts. Though she sometimes read about them in the many newspapers and articles that were delivered throughout the vast land, she had hardly taken any interest in their stories.

Lilith nudged Valeria, making a point to listen to the rest of the king's speech. But Valeria didn't want to listen, not after her eyes had strayed over to the three officials beside the king. She glanced at the onyx clock above the stage.

An hour before The Vanishing.

Valeria gulped, wanting to leave.

"The trials this year have been designed for someone who truly deserves the title of becoming our new highlord. Whoever wins will be granted great—and I mean *great* power." The king glanced at the lords standing beside him. Not one dared to meet his gaze, none except the Lady of Wolves.

The king continued, "Again, I must repeat myself every year, because too many of you have a passion of dying off before informing your offspring... Once the final midnight has passed and the contestants have been vanished, do not expect to see them again. There will be no time for farewells and hugs. The games are vicious, and might I add, quite cruel." The king's lip threatened to curl upward as the room cried. "Only one may win, and the rest must die." His voice dripped with venom. Swirls of black magic flickered in his dark green eyes.

Valeria's breath hitched when she saw the time.

Five minutes had passed, it wasn't midnight yet.

Relief fled through the open doorways when the king spoke again, "Let The Vanishing *begin*." A wide smile spread across his cheeks, and he laughed.

Panic burst inside the ballroom.

3

Focusing on how to breathe proved harder than she remembered as Valeria and Lilith rushed out of the carriage and toward Jonathon's massive estate. In order to avoid the officials, they had to find the nearest place to hide, which was Jonathon's home.

Why would the king start The Vanishing early?

The panic Valeria witnessed lingered in the back of her mind, so she let her attention drift to the white building that towered ahead.

She had never been to Jonathon's estate. Lilith always visited him on the days that she didn't have to run their father's antique shop. Out of genuine goodwill, Lilith extended multiple invitations to her younger sister, but Valeria couldn't shake the feeling that she would be encroaching on their privacy.

She always wondered how large of a home Jonathon owned, but she didn't expect it to be so grand. Jonathan was wealthy. She just hadn't realized *how* wealthy.

Flower bushes and magnolia trees lined the gravel pathway as they walked, Jonathan pressing his palms against their spines, rushing them along. Valeria nearly rolled her ankle in her heels as she gazed at the sloped windows and intricate detailing of the stone pillars above the door.

"It's wonderful. Isn't it?" Lilith whispered after catching Valeria admiring her soon-to-be home.

Valeria glanced at Lilith and nodded. Even though her veins throbbed, joints ached, and her head was running with uneasy thoughts, she couldn't help but be in awe at what Lilith's future would hold.

Before they could reach the front door, Jonathan steered them away, leading them toward the small stone trail that wrapped around the side of the house. Once they rounded the back corner, an extravagant garden bloomed across the yard. From what little she could see through the dark night, she examined the purple, yellow, and red flowers. Flowers she'd never seen before dotted the spaces between grass and cobblestone.

She didn't have the chance to admire the garden like she wished because Jonathon opened a door that was hidden behind a trimmed topiary tree on the backside of the house. Valeria entered the dark passage first. The stairs descended into a bunker of blackness. Jonathan and Lilith's footsteps made the walls shake as they trailed behind. Valeria stopped, following Jonathon's shadow as he reached over her shoulder, flicked a match against the stone railing, and lit a wall sconce.

The entire room was stone, the floors, walls, and even the ceiling. Only a brown carpet covered a majority of the floor. Valeria stepped closer to the tan leather couch. Aware of Lilith's eyes on the back of her head as she took a seat on the stiff cushion.

"I hope this is okay?" Jonathan asked.

Lilith caressed his arm. "It's perfect, my love. I just hope father will be okay." She focused on the locked steel door at the top of the stairs.

Their stubborn father had always been the first to protect them, especially since he knew that they could be one of the four contestants for the games. He dedicated his life to guarding Valeria and Lilith. If it weren't

21

for Jonathon and Lilith's new engagement, then Valeria knew that they could rely on their father for a safe place to hide.

The house their father built was practically made of iron and steel. The windows, the doors, anything that could potentially prevent the officials from breaking in and taking them away.

"I'm sure he will be," Valeria offered as comfort.

Before, Lilith had seemed undisturbed, even excited to be at the ball. But now, after witnessing the burden of the king's speech, and the panic of the Court of Wind, Lilith's blue eyes were wider than before... darker. Her breathing had sped up, Valeria was sure it was in fear of the officials knocking down the door and taking one of them away.

It was certainly known throughout the five courts that the king had his own mysterious ways of watching The Vanishing. Some had even theorized that he could see through every statue's eyes. Though no one could figure out how he would be capable of doing so. Could it be a spell that he bound to the stone? Were there secret devices that recorded events for the king? No one knew, and perhaps that's what made Valeria's chest shake.

Jonathan rubbed Lilith's shoulder as he gazed down at her. "If you want, I can have someone bring your father here. This bunker is safer than most. No one knows about it besides the both of you now."

Valeria glanced away when Lilith gave Jonathon a loving smile in return. She'd recognized that look many times before from her sister—toward plenty of other boys. Lilith was the beautiful one, she could blend in with a crowd of princesses if she so wished. As for Valeria, she had more of an old, elegant beauty. Gifted to her from her mother. *The only thing her mother had given her.* She knew she wasn't repulsive. In fact, she quite liked the way her copper red hair curled at the ends, and the roundness of her green eyes.

Lilith was far too open with boys and their flirtatious behaviors. Valeria, however, was different. She preferred picking flowers in the meadow past the gates on the days she wasn't required to dust the shelves of their father's antique shop. While Lilith enjoyed sneaking boys into her room window while their father slept peacefully unaware on the parlour room couch.

Valeria almost considered leaving and hiding with her father, but that would mean going outside and possibly getting vanished before she could make it home. She just hoped that Lilith would be decent enough to avoid making Valeria uncomfortable.

A small buzz sounded inside the room, not hard enough to shake anything, but enough to make Valeria's heart drop into her stomach. Jonathan sauntered over to the side table beside the couch and slapped the top of the ringing golden alarm clock.

"It's midnight." He said. Fear filled his eyes as he looked up, watching the door at the top of the stairs.

Even he was terrified of the officials.

The bunker fell silent as they sat frozen in their seats, eyes on the door. The only sound was a tree branch bashing and scratching against the steel door from outside. Every time it scratched, she flinched. The current time meant the officials had to be close to the first contestant on the list.

Twenty minutes passed too slowly.

Chills coated Valeria's arms. Lilith chewed on her bottom lip as she curled into Jonathon's side. He glanced down and squeezed her shoulder.

23

"I'll grab some blankets." He said before stepping away, opening the small closet underneath the stairs. Valeria never tore her attention from the door. She imagined the officials busting it down, dashing down the steps, and tearing her off of the couch.

Gulping, she focused on Jonathon as he closed the closet and walked back to the couch. He offered her a blue knitted blanket before sitting beside Lilith on the loveseat across the room.

"Let's get some sleep." Lilith muttered, cuddling into her fiancé's side.

Valeria settled in and closed her eyes. Yet the lights stayed on, and her mind continued to race.

Hours after the sun rose over the cloudless sky, Valeria awoke to find herself alone inside of Jonathon's bunker. The door at the top of the stairs was swinging wide open. First she panicked in fear that Lilith or Jonathon had been vanished in the night while she slept. Then the terror dissipated into relief when she found them in the garden, where Jonathon was hunched over, comforting a teary-eyed Lilith.

That was when Valeria beheld the note laying in the grass beside her feet with Alexa's name written in gold print.

Alexa Santiago was the first contestant from the Court of Wind to be vanished.

Valeria loosened a breath. Alexa was only two years older than her. They'd grown up together. She considered Alexa another sister since she was always around.

Lips trembling, Valeria tried to hide her building tears when she realized why Lilith was so distraught. Even though the sun was shining, and they had survived the first night of The Vanishing, a darkness filled the breaking cavity in her chest. Lilith and Alexa... they were each other's everything.

Why them? Why not someone else? *Anyone else?*

Lilith wailed, crumbling in the grass, and Valeria nearly fell over beside her in tears.

So this is what it felt like? This was the reality of the games and what it meant. Never knowing if they would see Alexa again. Knowing that if they did, she would be immortal. Being so would mean a lifetime of loneliness and heartache. How could anyone manage to live happily after witnessing everyone they love turn gray with age? How could anyone live after everyone they loved had passed on to the second life, and there was no one left for them in this one?

Once The Vanishing was over, all news of the Game of Lords would vaporize into thin air, as if it didn't exist. As if twenty people hadn't vanished from their homes and been forced into the games to die. None of the townsmen or mortals would know who won the competition, not until the last man or woman was standing.

She was about to leave Lilith to mourn when Jonathon's brown eyes met hers. He nodded toward the pathway and pulled Lilith closer, whispering something in her ear.

"Are you going home?" Lilith asked.

Through the prickly bushes and flowers, Valeria nodded.

Lilith stood, wiping at her face with a sniffle. "I'll come with."

"Are you sure?" Valeria asked. Unsure if her sister needed more time to mourn, although their father was probably the only person in Laterra that knew what to say to comfort Lilith.

Lilith sniffled again and wiped her nose with the back of her hand. Jonathan frowned. His arms were wrapped tightly around her, as if afraid to let go in case she might crumple to the grass again. "Yes, I'm sure." She turned to look up at him. "Would it be okay if we take the carriage?"

Jonathan easily nodded, pecking a kiss on her forehead. "Anything for you, my darling."

Valeria started for the trail that led to the front of the house. She could hear Jonathon and Lilith following shortly behind. The carriage was sitting in the driveway.

"Do you want me to join?" Jonathan asked.

Before Valeria stepped inside the carriage, she swiveled around just in time to notice the knowing look Lilith was giving her.

"I think it'd be best if we went alone." Lilith said. Then she looked up at Jonathan and rubbed his arm. "Our father is very... protective, and considering Valeria and I didn't come home last night, I don't want him to take his anger out on you."

Jonathan stepped back, but briefly nodded his head. "I suppose I understand." He muttered. "Don't forget our plans for lunch later, alright?"

Lilith squeezed his hand one last time, placing a kiss on his cheek before following Valeria into the carriage.

26

"I cannot believe the both of you!" Their father shouted after slamming the front door.

Valeria and Lilith shared a glance.

"Not only did you fail to come home last night, but you also went to the ball?" Tugging his fingers through his dark hair, he paced back and forth in front of the door.

Lilith reached toward him, saying, "It's my fault. I begged Valeria to come."

Valeria looked at her older sister with softened eyes.

Their father stopped his pacing. "I don't care whose fault it is, Lilith. I thought I raised you both to know the dangers of the games. Either of you could be on the list and could have been vanished last night."

The stress on his brow made Valeria's heart sink into her gut.

"I'm sorry." She whispered, rubbing her palms together as she examined the wrinkles on his forehead. "But we were safe. Jonathan—" Valeria glanced at Lilith, who was already watching her. "Lilith's fiancé let us stay in his bunker for the night. It was completely safe. He had a steel door and everything."

He scoffed, but his eyes softened by a fraction. "A steel door is just a door," he said while motioning to the one behind him, and the windows above the parlour room couch. "I had these installed because I was—am paranoid." He stressed. "Nothing will stop the officials from vanishing the people on their list. Even if it means bombing down a door, they will find them."

Lilith shuddered.

Valeria glanced away from the petrified look on her sister's face. "I'll stay home for the next three nights. If it will keep you from worrying, that's what I'll do." She watched the lines around her father's mouth vanish. He glanced at Lilith, but she remained silent.

His gaze lingered as if to intimidate her, until he finally looked away. "Thank you." He muttered, turning for the kitchen. "I'm going to make a pot of coffee. Would you like some?"

Valeria walked with him to the kitchen counter. "Yes, please." She peeked over her shoulder at Lilith, who hesitated by the door. Her blue eyes glossed over as she chewed on her lip.

Lilith met Valeria's gaze and forced a small smile. "I actually need to go," she said. Their father tilted his head, but didn't turn away from the counter, "I promised Jonathon that I would meet him for lunch." Lilith finished.

Valeria glanced at the clock on the wall. It was only 10 o'clock.

Lilith rushed toward the door, leaving no time for questions as she said, "I better get going. I love you." Then she found Valeria's eye again. "I'll be safe."

The steel door shut quietly behind her sisters retreating back.

Valeria's father turned away from the cupboard, leaving his half empty cup of coffee. He peered across the counter at her. "Lilith has always been a little more reckless than you. I'm afraid she might get herself into trouble one of these days." He whispered, as if Lilith were still in the room with them.

Valeria laughed.

4

On the third day of The Vanishing a boy from the south-side of the Court of Wind was vanished. His name was Isaac Bushman.

Neither Valeria nor Lilith had ever met the boy. They never ventured to the far side of the court, especially where the air was dirty, and the streets were covered in filth. Yet Valeria's heart still ached for the kid. He had a mere four-year age difference from her, being only fifteen. She couldn't fathom why the king would even consider someone so young to be in the position of becoming a highlord. Let alone an immortal.

It was nearing midnight on the third night. Only two contestants were left to be vanished. With each passing day, Valeria had felt a little more at ease when she woke up inside her room. Safe. *She was safe.* She kept reminding herself.

Her father left at the last minute to run to the market. He had dealt with a striking fever and an irritating cough all day. He called Lilith over before he left, just so she could be with Valeria in case he didn't make it back in time.

It was already an hour before midnight.

Valeria couldn't help the pounding of her heart as she tried to calm her ragged breathing.

If he wasn't back before midnight, they would have to lock the doors and leave him outside, exposed to the officials rough hunting. She didn't want to do that, but that was his plan, and why he called Lilith over in the first place—because her older sister wouldn't hesitate to lock the doors. Jonathan came with, because Lilith didn't want to leave him alone inside of his dark and cold bunker.

Now, they lay snuggled up on the parlour room couch as if there wasn't something frightening going on outside. Meanwhile, Valeria paced back and forth beside the front door, anxiously waiting for her father to return.

With every passing minute, Valeria's pulse quickened.

"Just come sit down, Val," Lilith groaned from the couch. "He'll be back soon. You know how he is, he wouldn't leave us alone while The Vanishing is happening."

Valeria merely glanced at her sister when she stopped in place. Yet she didn't move away from the door. "I just have this nagging feeling in my stomach," she said. "Like I need to vomit."

Lilith sat up on the couch. Jonathan lay silently sleeping, while Valeria's entire world felt like it was splitting into two. Or maybe that was just her stomach?

"You're just having anxiety. Come sit down. I'll grab you a glass of water."

Valeria knew Lilith was right, but the twisting of her gut was causing her throat to close up and her tongue to feel dry. She was desperate to go after her father, even if Lilith disapproved. She glanced at the clock on the wall for what must have been the twentieth time.

Forty minutes until vanishing.

"What if he doesn't make it back in time?" She asked, turning back around to face the large steel door. The market was only a ten-minute walk from the house. If she left now and found her father, they could make it back in time to avoid the officials.

"You're not leaving," Lilith demanded as she stood from the couch with a glare. "He'll be back. Go sit down."

What if he can't make it? What if? What if?

Valeria started pacing again.

"Valeria, please sit down." Lilith begged, crossing the room.

But she couldn't sit down. Her heart was pounding too fast. She needed to move. She needed to vomit. She needed to cry. She needed to do anything to keep the awful, intruding thoughts of her father's wellbeing from her mind.

Copper hair tangled in her fingers as she ran a hand over her head. "Don't be mad," Valeria said without moving her gaze from the door.

Lilith cursed under her breath and tried to block Valeria from the door, but Valeria's hand was already clutching the doorknob, and her decision was already made.

"Valeria!" Lilith shouted.

Valeria turned the knob and pulled the steel door open, but it slammed shut when Lilith threw herself against it, forcing the door closed. Jonathan's head snapped up from the couch as the loud scuffling noise awoke him.

"What's going on?" He asked while dragging a hand down his tan face.

Lilith bared her teeth at her younger sister. Valeria frowned, but refused to take her hand off the door.

"She's trying to leave." Lilith flicked her blue gaze to her fiancé.

"Why?" Jonathan asked. He stumbled off of the couch and over to the door where the sisters pressed up against each other. They stared down at one another, debating eachothers next form of action.

Lilith shoved Valeria back. "She thinks she needs to find father."

Jonathan chuckled, only pushing Lilith's annoyance further over the edge. "He'll be back, Valeria. It's only eleven-fifteen. He has plenty of time."

Valeria glanced at the clock.

He was right.

Jonathan was right. Lilith was right. Why was she acting so foolish?

Valeria dropped her hand from the door and stepped back. Lilith's shoulders fell and she sighed.

"I'm sorry." Valeria mumbled, running a hand through her lock of curls again. Her thumping pulse slowed only by a little, but her stomach was still in knots. "I don't know what got into me."

Lilith frowned at her sister before pushing herself off of the door. Gently, she squeezed Valeria's arm and stepped around her. "It's okay, but we need to stay inside where it's safe. It's already so close to midnight. I don't want to have to worry about you too."

Valeria sighed.

"I'll grab you some water." Lilith gave Jonathon a look full of warning.

Valeria watched, reading her sister's weary expression. She knew exactly what Lilith was trying to convey to her fiancé.

Make sure she doesn't try to leave again.

She'd never felt so daft—so senseless. She glanced up at Jonathan, who stared, studying her every move. He flashed a hesitant smile that she sheepishly returned.

Before Lilith could come back with the water, Valeria trudged to the stairs and made her way up to her bedroom. Jonathan's eyes lingered as she marched up the steps.

Maybe if she laid down until her father got home, it would quiet the rushing anxiety that was biting at her thoughts. But before she could lay her head onto her soft green pillow, someone knocked on her bedroom door, and Lilith didn't wait to enter. Valeria's older sister gave her a look of sympathy. She didn't need sympathy. Nor did she want it. Lilith set a glass of water on the nightstand beside the bed before sitting on the mattress.

"Are you okay?" She asked.

Valeria moved her gaze onto the emerald curtains that hung over the window. She sat up against the wooden headboard and released a breath.

"I'm fine," she lied. "I just think father has worried about the games for so long, and pushed it onto us our entire lives that I can't go a day without thinking about it. Without being stressed about it."

Lilith snorted and leaned back on her hands. "I know what you mean. He really nailed it into our heads. Maybe too much."

They shared a laugh, and Valeria finally felt her stomach untwist. She stared at her sister, suddenly lowering her voice. "I have to tell you something."

She didn't know how Lilith would react, but she needed to get it off of her chest. She hadn't told anyone about it since it happened, and it was slowly eating her alive the longer she kept it a secret.

Lilith's sky-blue eyes latched onto Valeria's emerald ones. "What is it?"

"I went into the Lord of Sky's office while we were at the ball."

"You what?" Lilith sat up. Eyes wide as saucers as she stared at her younger sister.

"I went into the—"

"No. *No*. Shut up. No way!" Lilith yelled before giving Valeria a playful slap on the knee. "Wait how? No, nevermind that... why?"

Valeria chuckled too, before nervously dragging a hand over her freckled cheeks. "I wanted to know who the contestants were," Then she straightened her spine and stood, finding herself walking toward the window. "I needed to know if either of us were on the list. In case we needed to find a safer place to hide, or maybe try and leave the court."

Lilith sighed. "Like father has said countless times before, if one of our names is on the list, no matter what we do, we won't be able to stop the officials from taking us."

"I know," Valeria said. "But I had to at least try."

"Well?" Lilith asked.

"Well, what?"

"Were our names on the list?" Lilith asked while crossing her long legs.

Again, Valeria realized she had acted foolishly. Tonight, when she almost fled the house in search of her father, and again when she had gone searching for the Card of Contestants only two days ago. "I don't know... I got caught." Her cheeks flamed.

Lilith grabbed the glass of water from the nightstand and took a swig. "By the Lord of Sky?"

Valeria nodded, and then she felt a sudden urge in the back of her mind—as if she was forgetting something. Attempting to ignore Lilith's joyful squeal and kicking feet, Valeria peered around her messy room. Eyes landing on the green dress she had worn two nights ago at the ball, she noticed a piece of paper peeking out of the hidden pocket in her gown.

"I almost forgot!" Valeria pounced over to the dress that lay in a crumpled mess beside the long body mirror.

Lilith leaned back and watched as her sister dug out the seemingly trashed piece of paper. A small red stain was smeared across the corner. Valeria held up the note to show Lilith.

"There's blood on it." Lilith frowned, setting the glass of water down and walking over to Valeria, she yanked the note from her sister's hand and examined it. "What is it?"

"I'm not sure." Valeria said. "I accidentally sliced my finger with a dagger and a drop of blood fell on it, so I had to take it in case someone noticed and came after me."

They shared a look before Lilith handed the note back. "Open it."

"What? Are you insane? No. What if the Lord of Sky comes looking for it? He'll know it was me, because I was the only one in the room when he found me."

Lilith shrugged and pursed her full lips. "Then I'll do it." She grabbed the note from Valeria, and proceeded to rip it open with haste. Her blue eyes skimmed across the parchment before her lips parted.

Valeria snatched it from her sister's fingers and read.

Dear Lord of Sky,
The King has decided what this year's contestants will be competing for. I'm sending this in regard to your latest request. The King and I cannot thank you enough for the gifts that you have given his royalty. I am joyful to announce the next highlord will take over the House of Embers. That's right. You're reading this correctly. Our next winner will be the Lord of Dragons. They will live in the House of Embers and lead the Court of Ash. Thank you again for the gift that you have given the sixth winner of the Game of Lords. They will greatly appreciate the gesture.
— your seventh gamerunner, Laurent

"Oh. My. Lords." Valeria gasped. Covering her mouth as she reread every word. She glanced at Lilith who was equally as surprised. "Lord of Dragons?" She questioned, even though she had read it twice. "Do you think they mean *actual* dragons?"

Lilith read the letter again. "I think so... It seems that way."

Valeria froze. Dragons don't exist. *Do they?* At least for the past two-thousand years they didn't. So why was the new lord or lady going to be named after the extinct beasts? And what gift did the Lord of Sky give to the royal family? Was it the eggs? If so, where did he find them? There were so many questions and not enough answers.

"The contestants, Lilith." Valeria reminded. "What if they have to fight a dragon for one of the trials?"

"*Alexa.*" Lilith whispered and dropped her eyes to the floor. Surely remembering her friend who had been vanished only a few days ago.

Shame swirled in Valeria's belly for bringing up Alexa, but the note had been a complete surprise. No one is supposed to know anything about the games. Once the Game of Lords begins and every contestant has been vanished, life is expected to go back to normal. The games are never spoken of again until the final contestant has won, and become an immortal lord.

"What am I supposed to do with this?" Valeria asked as she held the note up between them.

Lilith brought her gaze back onto the parchment and quickly yanked it from Valeria's fingers. "I'm going to burn it." She glanced at the alarm clock on Valeria's nightstand. "Five minutes until vanishing. I'll start a fire and check if father made it back."

Only five minutes until midnight...

Valeria pressed a palm to her forehead and cursed. Her father. How could she forget?

She rushed after Lilith, feet thudding against the steps and making the thin walls shake. Jonathan stood from the couch, his brown hair disheveled as if he had been dragging his fingers through it.

Lilith walked to the fireplace beside the couch and threw the note card inside. She reached up and grabbed a match from off the stove, scraped it against the stones and tossed it into the fire pit.

Flames lit immediately, and they all stood, watching as the note shriveled up and turned to ash.

"I'm curious, but I'm also getting the idea that I shouldn't ask what that was." Jonathon mumbled, crossing his arms.

Lilith shook her head, frowning before stroking his arm.

Valeria glanced at the clock above the stone fireplace and watched as the clock hand ticked, striking midnight inside the Court of Wind.

Feet scuffled outside the steel front door.

She released a breath of relief. *Thank the Gods.* Father made it home just in time.

"What was that?" Jonathan asked. Noticing something that Valeria failed to hear.

But before she could answer—to let him know that it was just her father, the front door swung open, smashing against the wall.

Valeria whipped around, expecting to see her father. Lilith screamed, and Jonathon threw himself in front of her before the officials in green and gold armor could snatch her away.

They rushed inside, a white cloth dangling from the first official's hand while the other official gripped a large brown pouch. Valeria tried to stand still as stone as they prowled toward her. She'd rather be attacked by a storm of furious gnomes than the officials who marched closer and closer.

"This is her?" One of the officials asked, though his eyes lingered on Jonathon, who was trying to comfort Valeria's frantic, pale sister.

"Copper hair. *Striking* green eyes." The other official muttered. "This is her."

"What?" Lilith panicked, clawing at Jonathan's arms. "No."

But Valeria was frozen in place. She couldn't move. Not as the officials grabbed her arms and yanked her toward them. Her head whipped back with the harsh movement, then finally she screamed. She thrashed, and she punched, but nothing stopped the king's officials from holding her down.

While the first official held her arms against her side, strapping them down, the other peered into her eyes.

"What are you doing?" Lilith's lips trembled, her eyes pleading. "No. Don't take her. Please. *Please, no.* Don't take my little sister."

Lilith's voice was all Valeria focused on as she watched the official search her face with empty black eyes. He leaned in, examining something she didn't know of. It was as if he was talking to someone inside his mind, letting another use his vision for the moment. But that couldn't be possible...

Then, when she thought he was close enough, Valeria swung her neck back and smashed her forehead into his.

An ache like never before spread across her face, liquid ran down her nose, and tears filled her eyes.

Someone yelled, and then her sister's screams filled her ears. As her head lolled to the side, Valeria watched Jonathon hold Lilith back. Her green eyes remained on Lilith's blue ones. Even as Lilith tried with all her might to free herself from Jonathon's tight hold.

"Let me go! Let me go, Gods dammit!" Lilith yelled. Her tear-filled eyes never left Valeria's.

A white cloth came closer to her peripheral vision. The official she head-butted clenched his jaw, rubbing at his forehead with a grimace.

"I was told to be nice with this one." He growled.

Jonathan shot a glare over his shoulder. "You *will* be nice with her."

Grumbling underneath his breath, the official lifted the cloth over her mouth, pressing it hard enough to make her teeth sink into the inside of her lips. He smirked, lifted his chin and said, "Breathe."

SANDRA D. JOHNSON

Valeria inhaled the lavender and lemon fragrance with a shudder. The last thing she did was blink at her screaming sister before her eyes fell shut, and everything went black.

5

V aleria Rox was the third contestant from the Court of Wind to enter the Game of Lords.

A pounding inside her head woke her before she could even open her eyes. She wasn't entirely sure where she was, or where she had been taken as she scanned the small room. The walls were an old tan color. Perhaps once white, now brown with age. Valeria's stomach twisted. She gulped down her bile before pushing herself up.

She looked around the unfamiliar room, gripping the thin mattress beneath her. The scratchy material was far too hard for comfort. Though it appeared to be mostly clean, even without a sheet. Rubbing the back of her neck, she moved the only pillow to the side and clutched the thin towel that covered her. No wonder she was shaking. It was freezing.

As Valeria averted her attention away from the bed, she spotted a steel dresser across the room. She stumbled off of the bed, but had to catch herself against the wall when the room spun.

Right.

She had smashed her head into the officials. How long ago was she vanished? How many hours—days—minutes have passed since?

Valeria swallowed the thick lump that was sprouting in the back of her throat. Would she ever see Lilith again?

41

No. *No*, and that was the utter truth.

Because she had been vanished, and now her uncertain future was in the death grip that was the Game of Lords.

Tears threatened to fall, but she blinked them away as she found her balance and trudged toward the dresser.

There had to be something in here. She had to escape, if it was possible. These games were not designed for girls like her. Valeria Rox was not a fighter. She hadn't wielded a weapon, let alone fought anyone ever. She was not designed nor raised to be a highlady of a court. Especially one that ruled alongside dragons.

This was her death sentence.

She opened drawer after drawer and was left with disappointment each time she came across nothing. Empty. Empty. *Empty*. The only thing that filled the room was the dresser, bed, and a circular window just above the foot of the mattress.

Valeria walked over to the window, stood on her toes, and smashed her nose against the glass to get a better look at the outside world.

Beds of soil lay across the side of the stone building she stood in. Flowers were full of life, exploding in colors to fill the grayness of the sky. There was one pathway that led into a white gazebo, covered in vines and white blooming petals she didn't recognize.

Past the floral stood an extravagant courtyard. Inside sat a few stone benches and one giant oak tree. To the east, there was a hill that sloped down into a vast field. Then, past the field, was the largest forest Valeria had ever set her eyes on.

Where had they taken her?

It was nothing like the Court of Wind. There were no buildings, no shops, and no village of people.

It was vacant.

Valeria stepped back, though before she could turn away, something shimmered against the glass. She squinted just enough to spot a large, illuminated lake. The water looked as though it expanded farther around the stone building. The depths could swallow an entire castle from the looks of it when the waves sparkled against the sun's reflections. If there was a bottom she would have been able to see it.

When the door to her room opened, she jumped, holding her fist up in case she needed to defend herself. Spinning on her toes, she spotted a woman with long braids that cascaded down to her hips. The woman stared back, standing in the doorway holding a folded gown in her arms. Her skin was like liquid brass. She was beyond beautiful.

"Hi, hun." The woman said, stepping farther into the room.

Valeria moved, pressing her back against the window. "Who are you?" She asked.

"Alrighty, then. Straight to it, I suppose." The woman chuckled, set the gown on top of the dresser and put her hands on her hips. "I'm Jacky. Your help."

Valeria's eyebrows knit together. "What is that?" She asked, tilting her chin toward the blush pink material on the dresser. She had so many questions, but had no idea where to start.

Jacky crossed her arms. "Your gown."

"Yes," Valeria said hesitantly. "But for what? I'm not going anywhere until I know what's going on."

Jacky chuckled again, leaving Valeria even more confused. If this was the Game of Lords, then why didn't Jacky look terrified? Frightened even?

"You're a contestant, hun." Jacky said, examining the way Valeria remained pressed against the window. "Whether you want to play or not, you're in the Game of Lords. If you don't want to participate you will unfortunately be left with one outcome." Jacky's pert nose turned up at her with a sharpened tone. "Of course, that is death."

Before Jacky turned for the door she shot one last glance over her shoulder. "Now change into your gown. Once you're done, I'll be waiting right outside." She tilted her head toward the only exit. "Any more questions?"

Valeria stepped away from the wall and lifted her chin. "Where am I?"

A slow smirk spread across Jacky's face. "Azrael estate."

Azrael estate was a mansion, or castle. Valeria didn't have a single clue. The little information she got out of her help, Jacky, was that Azrael estate was outside the five courts and hidden deep within the lands of Laterra. When she asked a few more questions, Jacky only narrowed her eyes and pursed her lips before ushering her to follow along.

She'd never been in a building with so many hallways before. And she thought the House of Wind was huge... but it was nothing compared to *this*.

As Valeria scurried behind Jacky, dressed in the simple pink gown she was provided, her eyes latched onto every detail possible. Which wasn't much until they left the hallway behind and the flooring shifted from old stone to a pristine black and white marble tile. A red rug led them toward a grand curved staircase. Valeria gazed at the ceiling as the walls opened up into a tall wide room.

Her jaw unknowingly dangled open as she examined the stained-glass windows that lined the walls from floor to ceiling, all had intricate wood detailing surrounding them. Valeria's eyes melted into the painting above the crystal chandelier. The art told a story of angels turned evil, Gods falling then rising to the heavens, and kings turned to dust. Black murky swirls flowed throughout the entire work of art. Her throat bobbed when her eyes lingered on a black dragon.

After staring at the paintings, they began to move, swirling and twirling together. Angels fought, Gods rose, and Dragons raged war.

"This way." Jacky muttered before she started down the stairs. Though she began to speak again, Valeria had a difficult time focusing.

She made sure to watch her steps before following behind. The dress was tight around her bust and waist, but flowed out into a beautiful waterfall of pink. Luckily it was just long enough to reach her ankles. She didn't need to be tripping over a skirt all day. Not if she was going to try and at least stay alive.

When they reached the bottom of the stairs, Jacky made a right turn down yet another hallway, however this one was much shorter than the one upstairs. "The estate has many amenities available to you such as the training wing, study hall, dining hall, gardens, and field for activities of all sorts. Training, praying, whatever it is you must do in order to win. The gamerunner will inform everyone about the games and all that they entail when it comes closer to the first ball."

Valeria took in the information as she examined the old paintings of landscapes lined along the wall. She faltered for a moment when her eyes landed on a painting of the Court of Wind.

The sparkling lights of the small village, buildings, and homes scattered about.

She imagined her father inside the painting, smiling proudly as he stood in front of his little antique shop in the market. Then her sister, Lilith, standing tall and happy alongside Jonathon as they held each other outside of his estate.

Valeria's heart ached.

Everything happened entirely too fast. The officials didn't show any mercy, not enough to even let her say goodbye. Why? *Why are they so cruel?* The images of Lilith flashed through Valeria's mind, forcing her to remember the way her older sister begged, pleaded, and screamed for them to let her go.

"Come on, hun. We don't want to be late." Jacky said from beside her, pulling her from her churning thoughts.

Valeria hadn't even noticed she stopped.

They started walking down the hall again, and Jacky quickened her pace as they rounded a corner.

"Where are you taking me?" Valeria asked.

Jacky turned so that Valeria could only see the side of her russet face. "To breakfast, of course."

Breakfast?

The double doors at the end of the hallway swung open, two people rushed through, passing Jacky and Valeria on their way. They were dressed in black buttoned up and collared shirts with a matching short black apron tied around their waist.

Servants, Valeria realized.

Jacky didn't falter as she stopped the doors from swinging closed, and pushed them open. Brightness stung Valeria's sore eyes as they stepped outside, and walked across a small courtyard. Once across the courtyard, Jacky pushed another set of double doors open and ushered Valeria through.

Chatter filled Valeria's ears before she was able to focus on what sat right in front of her.

"Welcome to the dining hall." Jacky said.

The voices came to a halt upon the doors slamming shut behind them. Valeria's lips parted as she gazed at the faces and a few backs of the eighteen other contestants.

She was the nineteenth one. The second to last.

"Find a spot to sit. I'll have someone bring you a plate."

Valeria wanted to decline. She wanted to turn around and go right back outside those doors. There were too many of them. Too many men, and not enough women.

A long table took up the middle of the room. There were only two more seats available. One next to a male who looked to be around her age, but he already seemed to be glaring at her when she met his brown eyes.

The contestants were dressed in all different colors and fashions of clothing. It was a mix of creams, blacks, reds, even whites. Then she noticed the embroidered emblems on the few backs that faced her. Four wolf heads for the Court of Wolves, four flame wrapped swords for the Court of Flames, and one wind emblem for the Court of Wind.

Valeria looked away as she folded her hands together in front of her. Her mind was too rattled to find Alexa throughout the crowded table.

The other empty seat was diagonal from the auburn-headed male who kept staring at her. Valeria hesitated as she stepped closer to the table. The remaining people that were speaking, stopped as soon as they saw her pull the seat out next to a smaller male who kept his head down. His shoulders were hunched, he refused to move his face from his hands.

She hadn't failed to notice the wind emblem on the back of his jacket before she sat down. Glancing around the table, she looked over her shoulder to find Jacky, but found an empty space instead. Jacky had already left the room.

Strangely, Valeria felt worse without her presence.

It wasn't long before a servant appeared at her side and leaned over the table to set a plate of eggs and bacon in front of her. Valeria nearly gagged. Her stomach was in knots. There was no way that she could eat. Her whole life had just changed. She wasn't even sure if anything was real or not.

"So, you're what? The competition?" The male across from her asked, shoving a piece of bacon into his mouth.

Valeria stayed silent.

He didn't bother swallowing his food when he spoke again, "How pitiful." She examined his buzzed-auburn-hair while he finished chewing. "Look at her, Ridoc." He nudged the scraggly looking male beside him, but Ridoc wasn't concerned with any menacing antics, only giving Valeria a mere glance. "She doesn't even look like competition." Leaning over the table, the auburn-haired one whispered, "I could kill you right here and no one would bat an eye."

"Knock it off, Lance. Let the girl settle in before you start harassing her." Ridoc said, tilting his lips as he ate.

She chewed on the inside of her lips and leaned back in her seat, giving Ridoc a nod as she fiddled her fingers together underneath the table.

"Ignore him. Lance wasn't shown any love as a child, and that's why he's such a bastard now." The smaller male muttered from beside her.

She glanced at him as he shoved a hand through his curly black hair. "Oh." She whispered loud enough for only him to hear. "I can tell."

He raised his head and looked at her as if surprised she had spoken to him at all. A small smirk danced across his face, but he quickly frowned it away before resting his head back into his hands. "Isaac." He said.

Valeria's eyes widened when she recalled reading his name on the slip of paper only two days ago. He was only fifteen, and from her village. She dropped her eyes, and felt her stomach fall.

"Nice to meet you." She offered, but he slightly nodded his head in reply.

It wasn't nice. Nothing was nice about this. Everyone in this room would be dead in only a matter of time. Only one would remain at the end of it all.

Valeria pushed her plate of food away as she tried to get a better view down the length of the table.

She longed to find Alexa, her sister's friend, but she couldn't spot the familiar black hair of hers. All she could see was the few bigger men that blocked the rest of the people that sat at the table.

Footsteps clacked on the marble floors, and then the sound of a door shutting. That was when she looked up from the iron table and watched as a man dressed in a shiny black and red tux saunter toward the front of the room.

Everyone raised their heads from the table to watch as the man turned around and faced them. His grey hair was tied back in a slick ponytail. There was a matching mustache above his thin upper lip as he smiled down at the contestants.

"I see our nineteenth contestant has finally joined us." He eyed Valeria over the table. She glanced away. "Welcome to Azrael estate. I hope you enjoy your stay."

Valeria bit her lip, keeping the awful curse from spilling out. She wanted to lunge across the table and punch him in his smug face, because how dare he? How dare he act as though everything was okay? Like her life wasn't on the line if she didn't win the game?

When she finally looked back up at him, his eyes were no longer on hers, but on a card he must've pulled from his pocket. He read from it before shoving it back into his tux.

"Tonight is the last night of peace." He started again. "Our last contestant will be joining us tomorrow in this very room. The first trial will begin shortly after, but of course we will let you gather a few weapons and armor beforehand." The gamerunner turned and started for the door he entered a few moments ago. "If you follow me, I will take you to the armory."

Chair legs scraping against marble pricked Valeria's ears as the contestants stood and hurried after the gamerunner. Valeria was slow to stand from her seat that was in the back of the room. She didn't see a reason to rush. Sure, having a weapon would come in handy, but if someone were to hurt her for merely having one? She'd rather steal one later on.

Isaac joined her side as they followed the crowd of contestants through the small doorway.

"You're from the Court of Wind?" He asked.

Valeria glanced at Isaac, noticing the way he stared at the floor as they marched into another part of the estate.

"Yes. From the east side." She said and let her eyes scan the contestant in front of her. Her heart skipped a beat when she caught sight of familiar black hair cascading down the back of a petite girl.

Isaac's voice sounded much quieter when he spoke again, "I'm sure you read my name in the paper."

A pang of sadness fled into Valeria's veins. But she stayed silent when they stopped in front of a tall iron door.

"Now, take whatever you can hold. I will provide the rules tomorrow when all of you are here." The gamerunner's voice boomed over the eager yelps and chants of the other contestants. "Remember, the games have yet to start. So remain patient, my future lords and ladies."

Valeria and Isaac scoffed, sharing a glance as the both realized they would be getting along if they shared that same distaste for the well-dressed gamerunner.

The ache in her chest lifted, but only by a little.

She was used to being the younger sibling—the one that was always looked out for. Not the one that someone else looked up to. If Isaac was competition, she wasn't going to let him be hers. He was too young, and perhaps she was too. But he needed someone to have his back. He would need someone to rely on, and she could be that for him if he wanted.

When she looked at him, all she saw was herself at his age. Lilith had been the one to protect her when Valeria had gotten her heart crushed by a boy. Or after their mother had left and Valeria cried about it at night. Lilith was *always* there.

She decided just then that she would be Isaac's Lilith. Even if it meant getting hurt in the process.

By the time Valeria and Isaac entered the armory, all of the weapons were gone. The only things left were a few leather straps for daggers that they did not find nor have.

Scuffs sounded beneath the door as Valeria laid awake atop her new bedsheets. It was covered in soft tan sheets after she begged Jacky to bring her an actual blanket. Jacky merely rolled her eyes and tossed the silver nightgown on her bed before she left and returned with the new bedding.

Valeria sat up as the bustling footsteps drew closer. There were two of them. Maybe three if Valeria was hearing correctly. She scooted off of the mattress and tried her best to remain silent as she tip-toed over to the door.

A muffled shout sounded down the hallway, only getting louder as the footsteps neared.

"Get off me!" A deep voice shouted, the words echoing down the hallway.

Valeria frowned and pressed her ear up against the door. Hoping that her shadow wasn't visible as she leaned in closer.

There was scuffs, shouts, and cursing, and then a bang as the wall shook beneath her head. She leaned back for only a second, before listening closely again.

"I said don't touch me!"

The man's voice was right next to her door. She stepped back and stared at the old tan wood and chewed on her bottom lip. Someone was being dragged by a few officials.

It must be the final contestant.

There was a slam as if an official had closed the door across the hall, and then muffled shouting and multiple bangs as the newest contestant racked their knuckles against the door from inside of the room.

Valeria's heart raced inside her chest.

A vibration against the walls, and then a quiet voice that she couldn't quite decipher sounded, ringing down the hall.

Chuckling, the official said, "He's here, sir. The twentieth contestant has been placed."

A throaty groan across the hall and inside the other room caught Valeria's attention. She wondered who it could be. He was obviously from the Court of Wind. *But who was he?*

Another buzz went off as the official stepped farther away from Valeria's room and deeper into the depths of the estate. Although Valeria's pulse was thrashing inside of her head, she still heard the darkly spoken words echo through the cracks of her door as they replied to the quiet voice. *"Let the games begin."*

6

The last night of the vanishing was over, and the twentieth contestant had been taken into the Game of Lords to compete against nineteen others.

Valeria listened to the cursing, slamming, and thrashing that the twentieth contestant had done in the room across the hall. She listened to the man all night and failed to rest for a single minute.

She couldn't blame him. Valeria was angry as well. She wanted to trash her room—scream at the darkness lurking, teasing her uncertain future.

Now, as she entered the dining quarters and sat next to Isaac, all she could manage was a yawn. How was she supposed to compete like this? How was she supposed to stay alive?

It wasn't long before every seat at the dining table was full, besides the empty one that sat across from her. The twentieth contestant would enter soon, and she had wondered all night about who it could be.

She was glad it wasn't her sister or father or even Jonathon, certain that the voice from last night was one she'd never heard before.

Six servants appeared from the far doors with large gold platters in their hands. She watched as they walked in a straight line, one after another, to the front of the room. As if it were a routine performance, they all stopped and faced the contestants before separating and coming around the table.

An arm reached out from behind Valeria as she leaned to the side and let the servant place a steaming plate of oatmeal in front of her that was garnished with berries and one single orange slice.

She groaned.

If they were going to force her into these games, why couldn't they at least provide something better to eat?

But the question vanished as she watched Isaac bow his head and dig into his plate. She felt guilty for not appreciating the food. Isaac had grown up on the south-side of the Court of Wind, and there wasn't much in that part of the village. Valeria knew that there was little income to be made there. As for her, she'd been lucky for her father and his business that he built all on his own on the east-side. If he hadn't—she would be just as hungry as Isaac was.

She wrapped her fingers around the golden spoon. Her stomach rumbled. She hadn't eaten since the night she'd been vanished. To her surprise, the oatmeal wasn't all that bad. It had a hint of sweetness and a bit of a crunch. The oats melted in her mouth as she chewed.

A door slammed just as she finished swallowing her bite. Valeria turned, expecting to find the newest contestant, but it was only the gray-haired gamerunner. He was wearing an emerald vest over his white shirt and pants to match.

She held back a grimace as she watched him stand at the head of the table. The gamerunner tucked his hands into his pockets and peered down his nose at everyone.

A clap vibrated against the walls when he brought his hands together. His deep voice echoed around the room, "Today we have something planned that will help every one of you with the first trial of the games."

A soft click sounded from behind Valeria, interrupting the gamerunner. She turned her head just in time to spot a male who appeared to be only a few years older than her standing by the courtyard doors. Slowly, he met her gaze and moved toward the table. His eyes were as blue as the crystal lake, shimmering and full of deep, deep annoyance.

A piece of his messy blonde hair flopped onto his forehead as he sat in the empty seat across from her. He let his gaze drag on to the gamerrunner. Valeria examined the dirty blonde hair that hung in front of his eyes, noting the way it was neatly trimmed at his neck.

Unkept, yet the male was oddly handsome. She knew the tiredness behind those blue eyes was because he had been up all night and had kept her up with him. Valeria looked away, letting herself focus on the gamerunner instead, whose attention was already on the male seated across from her.

"Thank you for finally joining us, Flynn. As I was saying, today there will be hints and clues scattered around the estate. Both inside and outside, if you think you've found one already, congrats. If not, then I recommend you finish your meals and start as soon as possible."

The table shook as Lance and a few others pushed themselves onto their feet and bolted for the doors. The gamerunner smiled when they brushed past him.

Valeria watched as Alexa stood from the other end of the table and sauntered after another group of males. From what little Valeria could see, there were only five girls including her.

That meant there were only six women and fourteen men.

How encouraging. Valeria grimaced and swallowed the thick lump in her throat.

She frowned after counting the remaining contestants in the room.

Isaac finished his oatmeal and lifted his gaze to meet hers. "Are you going to eat that?" He asked.

Glancing at her barely touched food, Valeria nudged it toward him. "Have at it." She said.

Isaac thanked her before he shoveled a spoonful of the liquid oats into his mouth.

An older man sat midway down the length of the table, five seats away from her. Valeria watched him lean back in his chair, cross his arms, and close his eyes. A single tear threatened to slip, but he smeared it away with his thumb, blinking as if he hadn't been lost in his gruesome thoughts.

Something thrummed and thrummed then cracked in her chest. A wave of emotions crossed her face, flooding into her bloodstream.

The contestants that filled the table had lives. All of them taken for no reason. She didn't understand the games. Perhaps she never would.

Why couldn't the king alter the rules of the game? Why couldn't people volunteer to compete instead of using force?

None of it was fair.

Someone stomped, causing Valeria to tear her gaze away from the older gentleman and let it fall onto the golden-haired stranger across from her.

Flynn.

If the gamerunner hadn't mentioned the male's name earlier, she thought that she might have never known it. She wasn't going to take the time to be friends with anyone. Not if they were going to die.

She couldn't handle any more loss.

Her emerald eyes locked with his crystal blue ones when she caught him staring. Oxygen fled down her throat and she choked on a breath. Before she could say anything, he pushed his plate away and stood. Then Flynn glanced at the gamerunner who still lingered at the front of the room. He glared, turned, and stormed for the courtyard doors.

The gamerunner shrugged his shoulders at Valeria, but she glanced at her hands and began to pick her nails. She'd be patient and wait for Isaac to finish his meal before they would leave and search for the ridiculous hints and clues.

"What a pity they left so soon." The gamerunner said. Valeria snapped her eyes up, focusing on the gamerunner's sparkling gray stare. "I was just getting to the good part." Valeria glanced at Isaac, who was also watching the gamerunner. "For those of you that decided to stay a bit longer, I have splendid news."

Her spin straightened. There were only five contestants in the room, including her.

"The first trial will be a night spent in the Forest of Angels. You have all day, and then the next until nightfall. That is when the first trial will begin." He patted his vest before tilting his head. "Feel free to keep the news to yourselves. I have a wondrous feeling that the others will be quite surprised when it comes time. Good luck."

Valeria stumbled over her feet, rushing through the courtyard doors as she tried her best to avoid running into Lance and his friends. They had entered the dining room, prominent anger on Lance's flamed cheeks as he shouted for the gamerunner.

She wasn't sure why Lance needed him, but she didn't care to find out. If Lance had spotted her, she feared he might let his rage out on her. Lance didn't seem like the kind of male to care about who he attacked, whether they deserved it or not.

Isaac fell into step beside her as she raced across the brick courtyard and out onto the grass. No one would find them out here, she hoped. There were bundles of brush and bushes that covered the entire backside of the estate. She followed the outside walls of the castle until they came around a shadowed corner where Flynn stood, leaning against the stone.

His golden windswept hair fluttered against his forehead as he puffed out a cloud of smoke. The white long sleeve of his undershirt was hanging over his pants as if he had ripped it out. Although his black vest still appeared to be clean and unwrinkled, Flynn looked as if he had just woken up.

Isaac froze behind Valeria, she glanced at him once, only for her focus to return to the disheveled male in their path.

Dropping her eyes, she tried to step around Flynn, while Isaac latched onto the skirt of her yellow gown.

When Valeria awoke to find the hideous thing on her dresser this morning, she couldn't roll her eyes hard enough. Yellow was her *worst* color. But there were far more serious things to be frustrated with, so she put it on and went about her morning.

"Valeria Rox, correct?" Flynn muttered her name, tasting the flavors of each syllable as he stared down at her.

She stopped. Her head snapped toward him, and she watched as he lifted the corner of his lip around a cigarette.

At least she hoped it was a cigarette.

"Yes." she answered, voice shaking as she tried to find her breath. Lance had truly frightened her inside the dining room. "How do you know my name?"

Flynn kicked off of the castle wall and took a step forward, tossing the cigarette to the grass and stomping it out. "Your name was in the paper the morning after the third vanishing."

"Right." Valeria dropped her head with a sigh. He was from the Court of Wind. Of course he knew her name. Everyone must've known her name now. "And you're Flynn." She added.

His eyebrows knitted for a split second before he glanced at Isaac and nodded. Valeria followed Flynn's gaze and stepped back, blocking Isaac from him.

"You're the kid." Flynn said as if the words tasted bitter. "The fifteen-year-old."

For some reason she felt relief knowing Flynn was angry with Isaac being here. He was too young—far too young to be here.

Flynn frowned when Isaac stayed quiet. His brown eyes were hollow and dark as he shifted around on his feet.

Valeria hesitantly placed her hand on Isaac's back and nudged him forward. Hoping he'd take the hint to keep walking. "Well, we must be going."

Before she could take another step, Flynn moved closer. "Wait." An icy hand brushed against her arm. Instantly she stiffened. "If you can, stay away from the others."

She turned to meet his dark blue eyes. They were red and bloodshot. She didn't know if it was because he hadn't slept, or if it was because he was smoking something more than just a cigarette.

"Why?"

Flynn shoved his hands into the pockets of his pants. "They'll try to make an alliance with you, but don't do it. It's all a lie. The only thing they want is to live. They'll do anything to win. Even kill."

Valeria's heart sank into her gut. She managed a nod.

Just moments ago, Lance's angry brown eyes had no thoughts, only action. Pure wrath. What would Lance willingly do in order to avoid death?

Then she wondered what she would be willing to do if it meant she could see her sister again.

She would never kill someone. *Never.*

The wind blew a lock of Valeria's copper hair into her face as she stood in the garden beneath her bedroom window.

Now that the sun was beneath the mountains, the stars shone brightly over the liquid night sky. She crossed her arms as she stared out past the fields and into the forest. She and Isaac hadn't found a single hint or clue throughout the entire day. They searched every last nook and cranny of the estate, even the damned tower. Still, they remained empty handed.

She wondered what was in the forest that was so bad as to be the first trial in the games. The gameunner said it was the Forest of Angels. Weren't angels supposed to be good and righteous? At least that's what it said in the book of fairy tales Valeria had read as a child. But nothing seemed to make sense anymore. Surely there weren't any angels in the forest.

Dropping her arms, she lowered her eyes and kicked a pebble into a rosebush that was the same color as her bright yellow dress.

Tomorrow afternoon was the first ball. Then after that, the trial would begin. Valeria snarled and kicked at the gravel again.

She didn't want this. She didn't ask for it... any of it.

She wanted to run and hide and never see this damned place again—she wanted to go home. But her wants and dreams and hopes were no longer an option. Valeria was going to have to fight her way out of the games if she wanted to see her family again.

Laughter ripped her out of her thoughts, she lifted her head and peered out past the garden. When she spotted Lance's buzzed head and tall form in the shadows beneath the courtyard, she ducked behind the flower bushes. The group snickered as they trudged toward the lake.

What were they doing out here so late? She assumed everyone had already gone to bed. That's why she had come out here in the first place—to find a moment alone with her thoughts where she didn't feel trapped inside a small room.

The four shadows disappeared behind the corner of the castle. Valeria hesitated before deciding to follow after them. If they were talking strategy, then it would be best for her survival to know what they were planning.

She needed to know who to trust, and clearly it wasn't going to be Lance and the others who were in his alliance.

Valeria peered around the stone corner as she tried to listen to whatever they were saying, but the wind and lapping water were too loud to understand anything. She slowly stepped out from the shadows, hoping that none of them would turn and see her silhouette as she stepped closer.

When an arm wrapped around her collar bone and yanked her back around the corner, she tried to scream, but it was muffled. A cold hand pressed against her mouth, silencing her.

"Didn't you listen to anything I said earlier?" A deep voice whispered in her ear.

Valeria scratched at the icy hand on her mouth, and when he didn't move fast enough, she sank her teeth into his palm. The man hissed in her ear before letting his arms fall away.

Swiveling on her toes, she found Flynn examining his palm.

He lifted his gaze in disbelief as if he wasn't the one who attacked her first. "You *bit* me."

Valeria nodded, staring at him as she wiped the wetness off of her lips. "You manhandled me."

"Manhandled?" Flynn huffed. "I did not *manhandle* you, Valeria. I was protecting you."

"From what?" She snapped. Her blood pounded through her veins. She didn't care if she looked crazy. The makeup that Jacky had applied on Valeria's face earlier this morning was most likely smudged, if not already completely gone.

He sighed and motioned over her shoulder. When she quickly glanced around the corner, she saw four shadows looking toward them.

"Whatever." She whispered as she faced Flynn again.

"Whatever?"

Releasing a breath through her nose, Valeria rubbed the irritation out of her temples. "Yes." She dusted her skirt off and started for the castle door. Flynn followed shortly behind. "I was trying to listen to them." She admitted.

"Why?" He asked, sounding uninterested.

She peaked a glare over her shoulder to see him shoving his hands into his pockets. "To hear about what they might be planning." When he didn't answer, Valeria shoved the door open and entered the main quarters of the castle. "I have reason to believe that Lance is out to get me."

Flynn matched her pace as the hallway shadows embraced them. "He's the skinny one with the buzz cut?"

She nodded, and he chuckled.

Valeria stopped and spun on her heel to face him, her eyes narrowed to a slit. "I'm sorry. Is that amusing to you? That somebody could possibly be planning my murder?"

The smile immediately slipped from his face, but she could still see it dancing in his blue gaze as he replied, "What? No. I just don't think he's much of a threat."

Valeria rolled her eyes and started for her room again.

Flynn followed. "Look, if you're truly that worried about him, I'll keep my eye out."

"And why should I trust you?"

Valeria came to a stop when they reached their rooms.

He crossed his ankles as he leaned against his door across the hall. "Because I want an alliance."

She chuckled, but when she looked up and saw the humor wiped from his face, she scoffed. "I don't even know you."

He shrugged. "You don't know Isaac, yet you two seem to be inseparable already."

Her eyes widened at his arrogance. "*He's fifteen!*" She tried to remain quiet as her arms flew outward. Flynn only smirked and found entertainment in her small outburst. Finally, Valeria dropped her annoyed gaze from his and turned toward her door. "It's not happening. Try someone else."

"I don't want someone else." Valeria ignored him, reaching for the door handle when he spoke again, "I only want an alliance with you."

"Why me?" She was caught off guard. Seconds from entering her room and ending the night, when this strange man had rattled her mind.

Flynn pushed off his door. "Because..." He paused, lost for words. "Because you're fierce. Because you're the only one who made an alliance with a fifteen-year-old. Because you're quite attractive, and also because I simply don't need a reason."

Valeria swallowed the heat that burned up her throat. Her heart pounded for a moment before she finally found her previous thoughts. "I don't want an alliance with you."

She heard his deep chuckle before she closed the door behind her. After listening for the door across the hall to close, Valeria huffed and threw herself onto her bed.

7

S omething dark crept over Valeria's presence.

Her heart was racing when she opened her eyes and sat up, but nothing was there. She was the only one in her bedroom. Although, as her eyes scanned the emptiness of her room, they landed on a sparkling gown folded on top of the steel dresser. Jacky must have just left before dropping off her dress for the day.

Valeria wondered if she would get a pair of pants and shirt when it came time for the first trial. It didn't seem fair if she would have to spend an entire night in the Forest of Angels wearing a gown, while all the men got to wear pants that were much easier to move around in.

When she stood and made her way over to the dresser, she could've sworn she heard Flynn's door open across the hall, but there were no footsteps to follow.

She lifted the gown in her hands and watched as it draped to the stone floor in a puddle of diamonds.

Valeria gasped, nearly dropping the piece of art in the process. How much could this have cost?

She didn't want to put the gown on. She didn't want to ruin it before the ball, but there was nothing else for her to wear, unless she spent the entire morning in her silver nightgown.

A sigh escaped her lips before she set the sky blue dress on the dresser and slipped out of her nightgown.

"Good morning to you, princess of the sky."

Valeria rolled her eyes as she took her seat across from Flynn at the dining table.

Underneath the sunlight, the diamond dress lit up like the sky on an early summer morning. She assumed that everyone else was supposed to be dressed in a way that represented their courts. Yet as she examined Isaac and Flynn's clothing, she noticed they were only wearing different creams of colors with small hints of black on their shoes and vests. Along with the Court of Wind emblem patched on their shoulders.

She hadn't bothered to look where hers might be. Perhaps the dress was enough to state which court she was from?

Today, Flynn was wearing a tan vest with another white collared shirt underneath. Isaac's wardrobe was similar, except his vest was a darker tan than Flynn's.

She hadn't seen Alexa around to know what she was wearing. It seemed as if Alexa had hardly even noticed her ever since she joined the Game of Lords.

Back when Valeria had been in the Court of Wind, Lilith would either visit or have Alexa over almost every other day. She had almost always stopped and had a small chat with Valeria each time she was over.

Now she wondered if Alexa was avoiding her, and for what reason?

Could it be for her own game? For her own alliance or strategy?

Valeria leaned over the table and peered over the heads of many men before she spotted Alexa's dark hair. She tried to wave and capture her attention, but Alexa only shot her a quick glance before tilting her head and turning away. She started a conversation with the boy beside her, ignoring Valeria's emerald eyes on the side of her face.

Someone whistled, and Valeria sat back in her seat with a frown.

Flynn smirked across the table. His hands were tucked behind his head as he leaned back in his chair and stretched. "You know her?"

Valeria simply ignored him, dropping her eyes to the table instead.

"So you *do* know her?" He tilted his head. "That was rough, huh?"

Valeria could only scoff and shake her head. "Are you done?"

Flynn went on, "See what these games do? They change people. They make people turn their backs on the ones they love. Most of the time, at least. Not always."

Valeria bit her tongue.

Flynn dropped his hands to the table and drummed his fingers. "But hey, don't fret. I'm sure she'll come around."

It was only when the servants entered the room and spread plates of waffles and fruit along the table when she removed her glower from his sparkling blue eyes.

Her stomach growled before she dove into the buttery goodness.

"So." Flynn said. He had yet to touch his food as he watched her take another bite. "About this alliance of ours."

She slapped her fork onto the table, chewing, she sent a piercing stare at his annoyingly handsome face. "Not happening."

"Alliance?" Isaac asked from beside her.

The grimace on her face fell as soon as she looked at him. Grabbing her fork again, she stabbed a thinly sliced strawberry. "There's no alliance. At least, between Flynn and I." Flynn kicked her leg from beneath the table. She sighed and shoved the fruit into her mouth, shooting another glare at Flynn. "He just happens to think that he can intrude on ours."

"Well... Why can't he?" Isaac asked.

Valeria bit the inside of her cheek and closed her eyes. She swallowed before responding with a heavy breath, "Because he's too arrogant—"

"Insanely attractive is what she meant." Flynn leaned toward her, caressing the back side of her leg with his shoe.

Isaac snorted, and Valeria rolled her eyes before moving her feet underneath her chair.

The moment seemed to freeze over as soon as Valeria spotted Lance entering the room. Her gaze followed the auburn-haired male as he stalked across the floor and sat in the chair beside Flynn.

His dark eyes examined the plate in front of him before he lifted his gaze to hers. Valeria quickly looked away.

"You know something," Lance stated rudely.

She pretended she hadn't heard him as she focused on her nails and picked at her cuticles. Isaac lowered his head as if he wanted the table to swallow him whole.

"I'm talking to you, sunshine." Lance tried again. This time gripping the iron table between his hands as he leaned forward.

Valeria kept her eyes down, picking at her nails until a pool of blood formed in the crevice between skin and nail.

A high pitched bang made her jump, and her plate of food rattled as Lance pounded his fist on the table in front of her. "You found a hint, didn't you?" Lance stood, a growl grumbling from between his bared teeth. "Give it to me."

She whipped her head up just in time to see Flynn grab the back of Lance's shirt and force him to face his stormy eyes. "She doesn't want to fucking *talk* to you, you bastard. Leave. Her. Alone."

Lance yanked himself from Flynn's grip and spit at his feet. "You're sticking up for the wrong person, *blondie*. Just wait for the games to officially start. I'm going to fucking–"

Before he could finish his sentence, Flynn's fist smashed into Lance's jaw.

Isaac jumped out of his seat. Valeria copied and grabbed his hand before pushing him toward the courtyard doors. Her eyes remained on Lance as he regained his balance and launched himself at Flynn.

She turned away and hurried after Isaac.

An hour later, the gamerunner had gathered everyone inside the main room of Azrael estate. Valeria watched as he held his arms behind his back and tilted his head at the two males in front of him. The rest of the contestants stood farther behind, facing Flynn and Lance's backs.

Isaac sat on the black-and-white checkered steps beside her. She wished she could climb up the stairs and enter her room just to get out of this mess. She wasn't sure if there was a punishment for beating another contestant to a pulp, and she didn't want to find out.

Flynn and Lance looked as if they had both done the same amount of damage to each other. If Lance had longer hair, she assumed it would be just as messy as Flynn's was now.

The gamerunner stepped forward and examined both of the males. To her surprise, his face lifted into a smile.

"Just what I love to see on the day of the first ball. This will definitely catch the king's attention if it hasn't already." Valeria's chest flared. "Way to start the games, gentlemen." He stepped around them and faced the small crowd of contestants. "Tonight, you will have a chance to meet the king and his children. In the past games, the king did not have any—this changes things for you, and how you choose to play the games. Now he has four children, and two of which are of age. So here's the good news for some of you." The gamerunner quirked his lip as he scanned the crowd's reaction. "As contestants in the Game of Lords, you must do anything to win, and however you choose to do so, is up to you. If you wish to seduce and bed one of the king's children, you may do so."

Valeria frowned as the other contestants grimaced and threw insults.

The gamerunner noticed his mistake and chuckled. "Excuse me, two of the king's children are off limits, given that they are not of age yet. The oldest twins are up for grabs." Only a few murmurs were heard before he began to speak again, "There is a chance of surviving the games if you do not win, and that is only if you are able to wed either the prince or princess."

Isaac lowered his head into his hands and sighed. Valeria lifted her palm to rest it on his back. He wasn't of legal age to be married yet.

If he needed comfort, she would provide it. She felt as if she needed a shoulder to rest her head on too, but at least she was old enough to try and seduce the prince. Though she wasn't any good at seduction, if she didn't, the only way to live would be to win. And there was already a very low chance of that ever happening for her.

Too many men surrounded her. And the thought of possibly fighting a dragon?

Valeria shuddered. She wondered if she would even make it that far into the games without dying.

The gamerunner clapped once. "There will be bets placed on how you present yourself at the ball tonight. If a bet is placed on you, it is because someone very important thinks that you have what it takes to become the next lord or lady. You will be given something very valuable at the end of the night. If not, you will remain empty handed."

Curses and muffled whispers chimed around the vast room. Valeria glimpsed up at the ceiling, where she found the painting of the fire-breathing dragon looking down at her. She sighed and wrapped her arms around her knees. Diamond scratched against her pale skin as she moved her eyes onto the gamerunner.

"Tomorrow night the first trial begins."

A few of the contestants panicked and cried, glared and spat as they watched the gamerunner bow before making his exit.

8

I f the ball had already started, Valeria wouldn't know. She was too busy watching Jacky tighten the corset around her waist.

She was more than fine with wearing the sky-blue dress she had put on earlier in the day, but when Jacky came into her room after dinner only to find that a few of the diamonds had fallen off of the gown, she ran out of the room in a full-blown panic.

After an hour or two, Jacky returned with a long white and lace dress. The frills along the skirt had pink detailing, and the corset had small pink flowers sewn in to match.

She thought it was beautiful—quite feminine, if she had to admit. Though it was much better than the uncomfortable diamonds that dug into her skin all day long.

Jacky finished her knotting and stepped away from Valeria's back to examine her work.

"This dress wasn't made specifically for you, but now that you're wearing it, I want to pinch myself for not thinking of it sooner," Jacky said as she grabbed Valeria's hand and spun her around.

"Who was it made for?" Valeria asked. She grabbed the light tan pair of heels from off of the mattress and sat to put them on.

Jacky waved her hands around as if she had forgotten. "I think the other girl from your court. The one with the raven hair." Valeria nodded and stood to her feet before dusting the skirt of her dress down. "Her Help will be furious when he sees you wearing his gown."

Her eyes widened as she stared up at Jacky. "You stole it?"

Jacky nodded. Her long caramel hair was tied up in a sleek bun, and a deep shade of red on her lips complimented her dark skin. "He had an extra gown on hand in case the girl hated the one he made for the ball. She's been a handful for him, you know?"

Valeria knew it was true. Alexa and Lilith were all about their clothing. A gown could be the most beautiful thing in the world, but if it didn't compliment Alexa's eyes or hair, then she would refuse to wear it.

She grabbed two crystal earrings from Jacky's outstretched hands before placing them in her ears. "So, do you know what I should expect tonight?" She asked.

Jacky smirked and leaned her hip against the dresser. "It's not about what you should expect, it's about what you should do."

Valeria sighed and dropped her shoulders. "And what is that?"

Jacky stepped toward her and dipped her chin. "What would you do to win? What would you do to survive the games?" She snapped her gaze to the door when they heard Flynn exit his room across the hall.

His footsteps froze beside Valeria's door before he walked away.

Jacky continued, whispering unlike before, "I heard the young prince is your age. If I was in your position, I'd be down there already trying to seduce him into my quarters." Jacky took another step toward Valeria and gently grabbed her painted fingers. "Make him fall in love with you, hun. Make him slide a ring on your pretty little finger. I fear that—that is your only way out of the games alive."

The music of Laterra shook the floorboards as Valeria dropped her hands from Jacky's. She already knew what she had to do. She was just afraid to admit it to herself.

Valeria was going to have to seduce the prince. And if that didn't work... she shook her head and walked for the door.

It was going to work. She was going to *make* it work.

The only light inside the ballroom were the candles that hung from the ceiling and reflected off of a large crystal chandelier. It reminded her of the last night of the ball in the Court of Wind. When she had snuck into the Lord of Sky's office.

Where would she be now if she had read the card before the Lord of Sky took it from her?

She would have seen her name—Alexa's name, and could have found a better place to hide from the officials. She could have run away. She could have left the Court of Wind behind, and ran out of the village and into the forest where no one could have found her.

Valeria stood at the entrance of the ballroom, pushing the aching thoughts away.

She needed to find Isaac.

With shaking legs, she walked along the wall and farther away from the platform where she assumed the king and his children were sitting. Bodies and gowns blocked most of her view of the throne. She could only see parts of the king's legs and the golden crown on top of his head reflecting the chandeliers' sparkling lights across the cream-colored walls.

The king's throne in Laterra city was probably much larger in size, and bejeweled with the finest diamonds from the lands. The one he sat in now was plain and simple, yet still had the authority to remind Valeria how much power the king held.

She spotted Isaac's smaller form standing in a dark corner beside a group of other contestants. She stepped around a mass of selkie men and women, who must have been hired as performers in their elegant suits and gowns. Joining Isaac's side, they sent nervous looks toward the front of the room where the king sat at his throne. Isaac only looked at his shaking hands before he glanced up to find Valeria making her way toward him.

"What's going on?" She asked after stopping in front of him. "Why are all the contestants over here?"

She scanned the contestants in front of her. She didn't spot Lance, only the three males that were usually attached to his side. Flynn wasn't around either.

Isaac straightened his spine and gave her a small, uneasy smile. "We have to wait here until the king wants to speak with us." He nodded his head in the king's direction. "Flynn is with him now. Lance just got done meeting him."

Of course, the two males who had black eyes and dry blood on their lips caught the king's attention first. Valeria wondered if that was the reason Flynn had started the fight in the first place. Not to defend her, but only to attract attention from others at the ball.

Maybe he was trying to have bets placed on him?

She couldn't blame him. Not when she was minutes away from beginning her own game with the prince. She just didn't know how she was going to do so.

Valeria stood on her toes and tried to get a better view. Then she spotted Flynn's ragged blonde hair over the crowd as he faced the king and bowed his head. She watched him step to the side and lean over to take the princess's hand, planting a soft kiss upon her skin with what Valeria was sure was a devilish grin.

Her blood chilled. Flynn was playing the same game as her.

The princess stood from her seat beside her father. Letting Valeria finally get a good look at her face as she did so.

Utter beauty greeted Valeria's eyes. The princess was unnatural. She was extraordinary. She was a diamond in a room full of stones.

Her long chestnut hair fell in spirals to her thin waist that was covered in the most magnificent golden fabric that Valeria had ever seen. From across the room, she felt unworthy, almost nauseous while examining the spark in the princess's hazel eyes as she gazed up at Flynn.

Lords.

Whatever he was saying... It was working.

The princess was entirely enamored by him.

"Looks like Flynn might be surviving the games, whether he wins or not." Isaac muttered after following Valeria's stare.

She glanced away before dragging Isaac forward to fill the space between them and the other contestants. She watched as the next contestant was dragged away by an official. The man's shoulders fell before the crowd parted for him.

There sat the king. Watching the man shake with nothing but pure malice in his eyes.

Valeria's jaw clenched unknowingly.

She looked behind only to find that she would be the last one to meet the king.

Great. If any of the girls were to take a chance with the prince, they would get to do so before her, and if they caught his attention, she feared he would have little left for her.

"Don't worry." Isaac must have seen the fear in her eyes as he gave her a mere glance. "I don't think the prince wishes to be here. *Look.*" He pointed to the farther side of the king, where a young man glared at the ballroom floor with his jaw resting in his hand.

The prince seemed as if he wanted to be anywhere else rather than here. Chewing on her bottom lip, she tilted her head in thought.

Perhaps he would enjoy a conversation that took place outside of the ballroom? Then she could draw his attention away from the ball and onto her. Maybe she could distract him with her touch... if that was what he wanted.

Valeria swallowed down the nerves that threatened to spill out.

She stepped closer to Isaac as the line continued to move forward. The king must be bored if he was going through the contestants so quickly.

"You look lovely, by the way." Isaac said.

She looked down to see him examining her gown. As he did, she took in his black suit and sky blue bow tie. "As do you."

He blushed and glanced away. "I'm disappointed we didn't meet before this."

Was Isaac finally opening up to her? He had never spoken about their home, the Court of Wind before. The times that she had brought it up, he would fall silent. But now, he must have grown more comfortable with her.

"Me too." She paused and drew her attention away from the ball. "What is it like in the south-side?"

Isaac smiled slightly as he recalled memories of his life from before The Vanishing. "It was wonderful. I know that those who weren't born on the south-side viewed it as poor, and nothing but rubbish, but I enjoyed my life there. My mother always made sure we were fed and had the best clothes. I was well taken care of."

Valeria frowned. "You say we, as in there are more. Do you have siblings?"

He nodded. "A baby brother, Michael. He was born only two months ago." His voice began to shake before he swallowed. Then he waved it off as if it was nothing. "I took care of him while my mother was at work. She had just returned home when the officials broke down the front door and took me away."

Her heart broke as she watched him try to cover his watery eyes with a smile. She grabbed his hand and gave it a light squeeze. "I'm sorry." Valeria muttered. She didn't know what else to say. There wasn't anything else to say.

They both had been ripped from their homes in the middle of the night. But now Isaac's mother had to worry about her baby while trying to balance work and survive on the south-side. To make matters worse, her eldest son was in the Game of Lords.

If she could fly to the Court of Wind and hug Isaac's mother, she would. Instead, she held onto Isaac's hand and hoped that it was enough to comfort the quiet boy.

The line moved forward again. Valeria and Isaac stayed put and let a small space form in front of them. Anything to stay in the back of the ballroom. She was sure Isaac wanted to meet the king just as little as she did.

She lifted her head just in time to watch as Flynn finally stepped away from the blushing princess. When he turned, his eyes wandered the ballroom before he walked straight through the middle of the dancing crowd.

Valeria didn't notice the hallway behind her until Flynn met her eyes and continued to hold them. He smirked before he brushed past her shoulder and exited the room.

The line grew shorter when the third person in front of them sauntered toward the king. Only an older man and Isaac were left besides Valeria.

It didn't help that her heart sank at the same time her mind decided to swim with anxiety.

Hesitantly, she dropped Isaac's hand and excused herself. She couldn't meet the king like this, let alone the prince that she was supposed to be seducing. Valeria stepped out onto the ballroom floor and fled for the doors that she had entered. But before she could reach them, a curtain of brown hair flew into her face as she tripped and crashed into another person.

Valeria caught herself before she could fall over. Her breath was heavy and ragged, even when she lifted her eyes and found the princess standing right in front of her.

Holy. Living. Gods.

There was a red stain on the princess's golden gown. Right where her goblet of wine had spilled when Valeria ran into her.

She pressed her hands against her chest as her mouth parted in shock. "I'm so sorry, your royal highness. I was—"

The princess flicked her long brown hair back before she lifted her hazel eyes and smiled at Valeria. She wiped her hand over the wet stain with little care. "Oh, don't fret. It's nothing. I have another waiting for me after the ball. No worries, seriously."

The words were meant to comfort Valeria, but all she could feel was the blood rushing through her veins and the panic biting at her bones. "No. No. Let me help you."

The princess chuckled and waved her off. "No need." She offered her hand before speaking again. "My name is Helena. And please, there is no need to call me your highness. I absolutely loathe the word."

A servant appeared beside them, and he began patting Princess Helena's gown down with a moist cloth. Helena batted his hands away and furrowed her brows.

Valeria's eyes widened at the slightest. *This was the princess? An heir to the crown?*

She thought that the king's children might have been uptight and selfish. Not this. This was something entirely different. And despite Valeria's surprise, she liked this much better than how she previously assumed the princess might behave.

Helena's cheeks tinged pink as she glanced away. She lifted her empty glass before tilting her chin up. "Excuse me, I must be going." She leaned closer to Valeria and whispered, "Thank you for giving me an excuse to leave."

Then the princess turned and walked away.

She didn't get a chance to reflect on what had just happened because someone grabbed both of her arms and pulled her. Valeria kicked and screamed as she was dragged across the ballroom floor.

"Let me go!" She shouted, voice pounding against the walls.

A sharp yank on her arm made her stop kicking, and she pressed her lips together tightly.

"The king wishes to speak with you." The official muttered in her ear as he finished dragging her.

Instantly, she stood to her feet and let the official guide her instead of using force. Her eyes scanned over the room before landing on Isaac who remained standing in the dark corner. He was alone, but his brown eyes latched on hers underneath furrowed brows.

She looked away when the official came to a halt. Then, when she lifted her glare, she found the king sitting before her on his throne.

"I was waiting for someone to do something entertaining. Although, I hoped it wouldn't involve one of my children."

Valeria forgot how to speak as she stared into the king's black eyes. His blonde hair fell to his shoulders as he leaned forward on his tree shaped throne.

"What's your name?"

Her mind stuttered before she found her voice. "Valeria Rox."

The king nodded as he dropped his eyes and examined her gown. "Not a drop of wine on you. Did you perhaps run into Helena on purpose?"

She began picking at her nails and stepped back. The official lifted his hand to her shoulder to hold her in place. "No. No, I wouldn't do that. It was an accident."

"Hmm." The king huffed and sat back in his seat. Although his swirling black pupils remained on hers. "I'm assuming you're from the Court of Wind, yes?" She nodded, and his lips pulled up into a taunting smile. "That is why I recognize you now, isn't it? You were the girl who broke into the Lord of Sky's office looking for the Card of Contestants."

Her breath caught in her throat. "How did you know?"

The king chuckled. "I know everything." He leaned over, inspecting her gown and copper-red locks for a second time. "I do not expect a little girl to win my games. Try your hardest, dear. But in the end, you will not win. I will not allow it." The king didn't even bother to rid the disgust from his face when he sat back and nodded his head toward the corner of the room. "Bring me the boy."

And just like the old man Eddard had said in his stories, the king sat on his dais, and ordered Valeria away.

Valeria wanted to curse at the king for being so cruel. Though her lips were parted in shock. *Did he just threaten to kill her if she were to win?* Then she watched as a group of officials marched toward Isaac and she growled. He talked about Isaac as if he was nothing more than a piece in his game.

The king was immortal. He had outlived people for hundreds of years. It was no surprise that the games kept him entertained, and adding a young boy into the mix must have brought him such joy.

As the official yanked Valeria away from the king, she wanted to fight back and spit at his feet. She wanted to show him what she really thought about him, but she also didn't want to be killed. So she let the official drag her away.

Everything moved in a blur as the towering official opened a door and shoved her into a room.

Valeria fell onto her hands and knees with a curse. She lifted her head to find the rest of the contestants, besides Isaac and Flynn, waiting inside the room along with her.

Everyone's attention landed on her as she stood and dusted herself off. Now there was a giant smudged stain of dirt down the length of her white gown. Some of the flowers had fallen off and lay on the floor below her feet.

She avoided the judging eyes as she walked toward the wall and picked at her hands.

Where was she? Why had they taken her and the other contestants into this room?

Alexa stood beside her, but made sure to have her back turned away. She was avoiding her, and what for?

Though Valeria couldn't entirely focus on her childhood friend and her silence. She was too worried about Isaac and how the king might treat him.

He spoke about Isaac as if he were his own little toy to play with—to use at his own disposal. Is that all this was to the king? A *game?*

Because it was so much more.

It was life or death.

The door swung open before Valeria could ask the man beside her about what was going on. She turned and watched Flynn saunter inside, Isaac silent behind him.

Flynn's hair was messy, as if someone had been running their fingers through it. His lips, swollen, and face flushed as his dark blue gaze drifted onto hers.

He didn't wait to walk over with Isaac following close behind.

Valeria adjusted against the wall and readied to hurdle a million questions at him. But she wasn't sure what for. Was it because of the king? Or was it because of the way he had wandered off after speaking with the princess?

A smirk grew on Flynn's lips as he leaned against the wall between her and Alexa. "Have any fun tonight?" He asked, letting his eyes drift down her body and linger on the stain on her newly ruined dress.

She narrowed her eyes at him before focusing on Isaac. "How was it?" She asked.

Isaac frowned and shook his head. "It was fine. Probably went far better than it did for you, considering you stained the princess's gown."

Valeria sighed and looked at her hands. "I hate it here." She whispered.

Flynn rolled his eyes and glanced at the ceiling. "At least I enjoyed myself tonight."

Isaac sank behind Valeria when she turned and scowled at Flynn. "Yes, I'm sure having the princess's tongue shoved down your throat was incredibly enjoyable. Though I hate to ruin your mood by focusing on our survival, I just *have* to remind you, *we* are *not* in an alliance. So please, leave us alone."

Flynn pressed off the wall and mimicked her stare. He leaned toward her until their noses were mere inches apart. "*Gladly.*"

The word was liquid darkness as it slid off his tongue.

She was surprised when he spun around and walked across the room, only to face her again. Flynn annoyed her further when he flashed a grin and crossed his arms.

The room felt as if it could spin for eternity when he looked at her like that, but it stopped the moment she ripped her eyes away and found Lance staring at her as well. A sinister smile bloomed on his chapped lips. He was moments away from bothering her when the door swung open and banged against the wall.

Valeria stiffened when the gamerunner stepped inside.

"Bets have been finalized. You may all leave."

9

The day after the first ball passed far too quickly, even though Valeria had tried her hardest to make the time pass slowly. It had only been an hour ago when Jacky stormed into Valeria's room and threw a stack of black clothing at her. A few moments later, she was dressed and standing before the Forest of Angels, facing the gamerunner, who stood in front of the crowd of contestants on a short platform.

When he opened his mouth to speak, Valeria was pulled from the thoughts that puddled in her mind. "Ridoc Cadence was killed last night."

The contestants gasped, their eyes darting every which way, lingering on each other as they gaped in utter surprise. A spell of lights shined down on the gamerunner as if Azrael estate was an arena. She didn't think it was, at least. Her eyes scanned the mountains, trees, and lakes.

She stepped back when her curious gaze landed on Lance, who stood on the other side of the platform from her. His stare searched hers before he grinned.

Ridoc was one of the three males that was always with Lance.

Did Lance kill him? Kill his own friend? His own ally?

She thought back to last night, but didn't remember hearing anything in the contestants' hallway.

Valeria had gone back to her room last night in hopes to find a gift, but wasn't surprised when there was nothing else in her room but her bed and dresser. She had given no reason for someone to place a bet on her. She was a girl and appeared clumsy at the ball. If anything, someone might have bet on her to be the first to die.

She shuddered at the thought and focused on the gamerunner instead.

"We have notified the king of the first death, and send our regards to the Court of Smoke. Of course, we cannot notify the House of Flame due to the king's strict orders, but when the last person is standing and the games have ended, every court shall know who they have lost."

The gamerunner continued, "Now, since we have lost our first contestant, we may move past the existing death as it looms over us. There is much more to come, everyone." He dragged his eyes along the nineteen contestants that stood around him. "Once darkness falls, and night begins, if you are not past that gate and inside the Forest of Angels that stands behind me, you will be killed on sight."

Ten officials stood around them and shifted the heavy pistols in their gloved hands.

Valeria swallowed, but nothing could clear the lump that was lodged in her throat.

"Once you have made it inside of the forest, you must stay under the trees until the sun rises. When the sun has risen, then, and only then, you must exit the gates before they close. If you fail to be inside the gates on time, you will be locked in the forest until death greets you." His eyes landed on Valeria before he moved on. "Understood?"

There were no questions asked. The first trial was going to begin any moment as the sun continued to descend behind the mountains.

Valeria's heart thundered inside her chest, she latched onto Isaac's hand. She did it for her own comfort this time.

What was in the forest that was terrible enough to make it the first of five trials? Why was it named the Forest of Angels?

She couldn't stop shifting her panicked eyes, letting them drift everywhere and anywhere.

Blackness nearly filled her vision. Each contestant was dressed in a pair of black pants, a shirt, and a thin jacket with the emblem of their court on the back. They couldn't have anything else besides the weapons they grabbed from the armory and the clothing that they were provided.

Valeria had little resources for survival. She didn't even have a damned dagger. She cursed, thinking back to the butter knife she used during breakfast. She should have stolen it.

"Now, for the rules." The gamerunner smiled and tilted his head. She stared at Lance as he watched the gamerunner on the platform. A small evil smirk dressed on his thin chapped lips. "There are none."

There was a series of chants and whoops, mainly coming from Lance's mouth as she watched him. But the others stayed silent. Even Isaac was motionless beside her. She glanced at Flynn, who stood a few people away from her. He looked bored, turning, he gave an official a menacing look.

"If you feel like killing, please do so." The gamerunner chuckled. "The trials will only become deadlier, and you'll need less competition if you plan to survive. Now," he clapped, "May the Game of Lords... begin."

Before Valeria could blink, the gates behind the platform began to open with a resounding clang, and groups of contestants pushed and shoved as they ran past her. She watched them scamper through the gates, down the muddy path, and into the forest. All the while she never let go of Isaac's hand.

She glanced at the sky to see that the sun was halfway behind the mountains. As soon as it was gone, she would need to be inside of the forest, if not... she looked at an official, who was already staring straight at her. Valeria gulped and gave Isaac's arm a tug.

He shook beside her. Crippling fear in his eyes as he stared at the forest. "Come on." She said and tugged again. His wide orbs found hers. "Stay with me." She hated every part of herself as she tugged and pulled him toward the gates—toward their deadly fate. His legs went stiff, and his eyes lined with tears. "Isaac, please." She begged.

The sky began to darken when they finally made it through the gates, but they needed to go farther. They needed to be inside of the forest before nightfall.

Valeria pulled harder on Isaac, but he was too heavy. He was frozen in some kind of trance.

Still, she refused to give up. If she couldn't get Isaac into the forest before the sun was gone, then she would stay out here with him. But the thoughts vanished and the weight of Isaac's body disappeared as his body was flung through the air and thrown over Flynn's shoulder.

He met her frightened eyes and nodded forward. "Go." Before Valeria could argue, Flynn took off, sprinting with Isaac over his shoulder. "Hurry!"

She gasped and quickly observed the mountains. The sun was almost gone, only a sliver of it remained.

Together they ran into the forest and heard the gunshots go off for the contestants that failed to make it in time.

10

There were a total of three gunshots.

Each bang sent a blast of chills up Valeria's neck as she ran through the bushes and twigs. Her ears were ringing as she watched Flynn jump over an old fallen log. Isaac latched onto his lower back, trying his best to hold on. His eyes were wide and dark, watching the gates move farther away.

"Keep running!" Flynn shouted over his shoulder.

Valeria picked up on the noise of snapping twigs as she continued to sprint. The forest was too dark—too foggy to see even ten paces ahead. She focused on Isaac's shadow before she tripped and pummeled forward.

"Valeria!" Isaac shouted. He beat against Flynn's back before he came to a stop and dropped to the ground. Flynn turned as if annoyed or frustrated. She didn't care. She just needed to get back up.

"I'm okay. Keep going." Valeria huffed as she stood and grabbed Isaac's shoulder. "Are you good to run?"

He bit his lower lip and scrunched his eyebrows. "Yeah, I'm fine. Let's go."

Darkness invaded the forest. She tried to find Flynn. She couldn't see him through the thickness of the wavering fog. A branch crunched behind her and she swiveled around. "Flynn?"

"Right here." But his voice came from a different direction.

She faced something else. Something large and terrifying.

Valeria squinted and peered through the trees. The shadow moved closer, and its eyes grew brighter. She took a step back, but bumped into Isaac, who turned and latched onto her wrist.

"Let's go, Valeria." He panicked.

The yellow glowing eyes multiplied and formed in the distance. Their shadows only closing in at a faster pace. Valeria's heart pounded.

"What is that?"

Another hand grabbed her free wrist. "Valeria. *Now.*" Flynn pulled her back. "We need to run. I know where to go."

Although they tried to pull her back, she couldn't help but watch as the shadows turned into gray wings and feathers. The angel's eyes were a replica of the sun. Glowing and magnifying. Razor-sharp teeth jutted out of its mouth as the creature licked its pale lips.

Her blood chilled.

Flynn didn't need to pull on Valeria's arm. She stepped back on her own this time and turned around. The angels were everywhere. The tall, feathered beings surrounded them.

Through the fog, she watched the closest angel stand two entire feet taller than her.

"What do we do?" Isaac asked.

The three of them formed a circle and pressed their backs together.

If the past four days were all a dream, Valeria wanted nothing more than to wake up. But as she reached over Flynn's hand on her wrist and pinched herself, she remained in this nightmare.

"We need to split up." Flynn muttered.

"What?" Valeria whispered and tilted her head. Her eyes stayed on the angels that continued to prowl closer. "No."

The nearest angel flicked its large gray wings, taking another step.

"I'm not leaving without you guys," Isaac said.

Words got trapped in Valeria's throat as she fell back and bumped into Flynn's shoulder.

"There's an opening in front of me." He said. "Valeria, you go first."

"Not happening."

What was Flynn even suggesting? If she ran first, she'd be leaving Isaac behind with him.

The forest grew brighter as their eyes grew larger.

Or maybe if she ran first, they would all chase after her and Isaac could get away?

"Valeria," Isaac pleaded as she removed his grip from her arm. "Valeria, *don't*." He tried again.

She gave his hand a tight squeeze before dropping it. Flynn's blue eyes glimmered against hers when she nodded and turned her back to the angels. She faced Isaac, who was already pleading with her with desperation in his expression. Anguished to make her stay. To stop her from risking her own life.

"I'll see you later." She said and dropped her gaze from his. She couldn't look at him anymore. Not when she didn't know if she would ever see Isaac again.

All Valeria wanted was to protect him, and she was putting a lot of trust in Flynn to do so while she was gone.

The demonic angels stopped as they watched her step away from the three-person circle. Only a small amount of light shone from their eyes and lit up the distance that she needed to run. Flynn flicked his eyes away, and Valeria copied.

Just a few feet ahead was a ten-foot gap between two of the towering angels. If she was quick enough, she could get past them. She feared that the overgrown brush might slow her pace, but she threw the thought away and took another step forward.

"*Val.*" Isaac pleaded.

Her gaze landed on an angel who threatened to take another trudge toward her. Its long-muscled legs flashed from beneath its torn black robe. All she needed to do was outrun them long enough for Isaac and Flynn to get away. She could do that.

Her spine stiffened as she released a thin breath through her nose.

"Get him out of here." The words were strict and hard as she muttered them over her shoulder to Flynn. She imagined he wouldn't leave the boy for dead. At least, she hoped.

The angels were seconds away from pouncing when she steadied her breathing and lunged deeper into the forest.

Wind blew her braided hair back as she jumped, ducked, and rolled away from the flying and crawling angels. They came rushing from the canopy of trees as she forced herself not to look back. She needed to keep going. There was no stopping, not unless she wished for her bones to be the only thing left in the dirt and rubble after her brutal murder.

The angels were out for blood, and everything that Valeria had read about them in fairy tales and stories evaporated and was replaced by the vicious beings that chased after her.

The Forest of Angels. Valeria cursed as she flung herself over a fallen log. It should've been named the Forest of Demons.

Sloped hills and thick bushes slowed her down. She came upon a path and didn't have a moment to debate her next move when she skirted to the right and took off down the trail. She was faster on clear ground, now she just needed to outrun them.

Multiple thundering steps thrashed into the ground behind her.

Mind racing, heart pounding, Valeria's eyes were wide as her legs grew numb. She had empty thoughts between her pounding heart and swimming mind, just a clear understanding that she needed to run. Valeria swerved to the left as a black-winged angel flew toward her at an accelerating pace. She glanced back for a moment to see how close the ones behind her were.

She counted eight angels before swiveling her head around and quickening her already swift feet.

The world flew off of its axis when something rammed straight into her side. Her body flung off of the trail and into the bushes. A cry broke out of her throat as something cracked and snapped in her stomach. Bile gathered in her mouth before she rolled to her aching side and spit it out.

A shadow stood to its feet beside her. She hadn't even noticed it was another contestant until she opened her eyes and blinked at the old man. He was frail and shaking while standing over her. He sent her a glance before looking over his shoulder. "Get out of here." He said before he raced deeper into the fog.

Valeria's eyes widened, and she dropped her head back onto the dirt as shadows blasted above her and through the trees. They ignored her hidden body beneath the bushes. The angels chased after the old man.

It was only a few minutes later when she heard his broken scream echoing through the thicket and into her ears. She opened her eyes and listened for footsteps, or flapping wings, but there was nothing.

Faintly, as she pushed herself to her feet, she heard the snapping of bones before a crunch broke through the brush. Bile rose in the back of her throat as she listened to the angels eat the old man's flesh.

He saved her. He sacrificed himself... to save her...

Valeria threw up into the brush, trying her best to cover her mouth and remain silent.

Why did he do that?

The angels seemed to like the chase more than an easy kill. Meaning the angels were brutal and only wanted someone that was willing to fight?

Her thoughts centered around Flynn and Isaac. She prayed that they were safe before she felt her legs wobble. A hand splayed around her ribs as she limped back onto the path and in the opposite direction that the angels had gone.

Everything was pure agony. Her legs, her arms, and her mind. But she pushed the pain away and feigned that her body was numb as she continued to hobble deeper into the dark forest.

An hour passed while Valeria was walking. Not once did she stop and weep over her broken and throbbing ribs. The pain was excruciating, and no matter how badly she tried to ignore and act like it wasn't dragging her down, it was.

Each step was like a knife inching deeper into her bones. She could hardly breathe—could hardly think.

It wasn't until she finally let herself lean against a damp tree that the pressure on her ribs eased, but only by a little as she let a heavy breath flutter past her chapped lips. She swallowed, chin wobbling and looked up at the purple sky through the shadow covered tree branches. Releasing a sigh, she slouched off of the tree and continued forward.

If there were more angels lurking around, she didn't want to find out. To stay away from them would mean to keep moving.

After about a mile into her limping and tripping over the forest floor, Valeria came upon a clearing. A shed sat high up in a thick sycamore tree. Around the base of the tree were four different paths that all led in separate directions into the forest. As if the tree shed was some sort of hideaway. It seemed like a trap, but she was far too exhausted to care, and desperately needed to find rest.

From the way the darkness was starting to lighten around the corners of the wide sky, Valeria wondered if it was nearing the end of the first trial. Maybe she could get an hour or two of sleep before making her way back to the gate?

She clutched her ribs before taking a step onto the first wooden platform that was nailed into the trunk of the tree. Slowly, Valeria climbed up and up until she found herself pushing a trapdoor open. Then she used the rest of her dying strength to pull herself up into the rickety old shed.

The base of the floor slammed closed behind her, and she swiveled around with a yelp.

Lords.

Valeria cursed at herself as she stood to her feet and hurried toward the small-framed windows on the compact wall. She peered out, hoping that the noise she made hadn't lured anymore angels after her.

She watched as the branches and bushes blew against the wind. Her eyes lingered an extra minute before she pushed away from the wall and wobbled over to the darkest corner of the hut.

For what felt like an hour, Valeria sat in the corner and let her eyes rest as her ears listened for any sudden noises. Then finally, as the wind came to a halt, Valeria's mind silenced and she fell asleep.

A scuff and sniffle woke Valeria from her slumber against the wall. She jolted and snapped her neck upward. A shadow sat across from her, hunched over with their head in their hands as they cried.

Black hair draped over the girl's face when she sniffled.

Valeria shuffled to her feet and reached for Lilith's friend. "Alexa, you have to be quiet."

Alexa didn't listen. She continued to cry and rock herself back and forth into the cupboard behind her. Valeria dropped to her knees and noticed the slight hint of sunlight in the room.

What time was it?

She wasn't able to see anything in the shed before she fell asleep, but now it was light out, and she could examine the wooden walls and rickety old kitchen that they sat in. Cupboards lined one wall with windows above them, while behind her was a pantry that she had slept against.

"Alexa." She shook Alexa's shoulders and brushed her raven black hair out of her face. "Please, you have to be quiet. We need to head back to the gate."

At last, Alexa removed her face from her hands with another sniffle, letting tears fall from her eyes. "He's dead." She whispered.

Valeria's eyes narrowed. "Who?" Alexa let out a deafening sob, and Valeria leaned forward, pressing her hand against Alexa's lips to silence her cries. "Who died, Alexa?"

"Henry." She cried.

Valeria didn't recognize the name. She hadn't taken the time to know all the contestants; she didn't see a reason to. For the same reason as to why Alexa was crying. She didn't want to be hurt when the people she learned to care for would be killed.

Now, she had wished she warned Alexa to do the same so they wouldn't be stuck in this situation.

Except Isaac. Valeria would do anything to protect him. She hoped he would be the one to win the games, but at the same time, she didn't want him to become immortal. Not unless he wanted to, not unless it was his choice.

Alexa pushed against the cabinets as she wobbled to her feet. Her black eyes found Valeria's green ones when she wiped a hand down her tan cheeks. "I thought angels were supposed to be kind and godly."

Valeria frowned. "So did I."

A soundless pause occurred between them before Alexa dropped her arms and leaned against the counter. She stared at Valeria with solemn eyes. "I'm sorry." Before Valeria could question her, Alexa started again.

"Don't take offense to my game play, Valeria. I have to ignore you. I have to."

"Why?" Valeria pushed, but her focus was on something far past Alexa and through the windows where the bushes began to rustle. She tried to step closer, but Alexa kept moving in front of her.

"It's the only way to keep you safe. You have the strongest player trying to make an alliance with you, and you're always with the young boy, Isaac. Everyone can see that you should win. If I'm seen with you, one of us will be killed. If not, both."

Valeria heard the words, but her gaze remained on the forest beneath the tree shed, where shadows wandered out of the bushes and onto the dirt paths.

"Alexa." She tried, but Alexa was already turning around when the door on the floor flung open and bashed against the old wood of the house.

Valeria jumped and ducked as a scream racked out of Alexa's mouth. The windows shattered, and Valeria grabbed Alexa's hand before dragging her across the shed and to the large window on the other side.

"We need to go." Valeria slid the glass open and pulled Alexa closer, but Alexa didn't budge. Her spine stiffened when Valeria tugged on her arm again.

"*Valeria.*" Alexa's voice wobbled as she smacked her palm against Valeria's thigh.

She swiveled around and faced the tall, dark angel that loomed over them. Its hair was black and long, a replica of Alexa's. The angel's teeth were like blades, and its skin was pale as if it was a vampire.

Valeria swallowed and strode backwards. The angel stepped closer. Its wings flicked and a gray feather fell onto the wooden floor beside its black clawed feet.

"What do you want?" Valeria hesitated to ask.

Her legs grew numb, and she threw a glance over her shoulder at the window behind her. She could jump. It might hurt terribly, especially with her earlier injuries. But those razor-sharp teeth digging into her flesh would hurt *far* worse.

The angel licked a fleck of red off of its purple lips and grinned. "It's been five decades too long, deary. I'm far too hungry for questions now."

Alexa stepped on Valeria's toes, causing them to tumble against the open window. Valeria almost fell out, but caught herself against the wooden frame.

"Just let us go." She fired out, as if the angel would care. She was too angry—too tired to put up a fight. She was nearly drained.

It had just got done eating another contestant. She could tell from the blood smeared across its feathers, and thin cloak that draped to the floor.

The angel remained silent as it took another step closer. Behind the lanky beast, scaled hands and tucked wings crawled inside from the broken windows above the counters.

Valeria grabbed Alexa's hand and pulled her backwards. Lifting her leg, she flung herself out of the window. Alexa screamed and leaned over the frame. Her black eyes widened at Valeria, who dangled from a branch just beneath the window. She'd only caught herself when she realized that Alexa hadn't jumped out with her.

Sharp claws wrapped in Alexa's thick hair and pulled her back inside the house. Valeria glanced at the dirt beneath her feet. If she let go of the branch, she would fall a good ten feet, and possibly break another rib.

A scream sounded inside the house. Valeria flinched and pulled herself up to peer inside the window.

The angel held Alexa tight against its chest as three much larger ones smiled down at her tear-filled eyes.

Valeria searched for something sharp, anything thick enough to wack at the angels with. Hoping that maybe, just maybe she could scare them off.

Hope was always a fickle thing.

Her eyes widened when she remembered something valuable. The angels had chased after Valeria, one person, instead of staying back and taking Flynn and Isaac. They craved a fight. They didn't want an easy kill...

The angels wanted a meal that they had to work for—a meal worthy enough to hunt.

"Alexa!" She yelled. Alexa's dark eyes latched onto Valeria from above. Valeria shook her head and lifted a finger to her lips. "Don't fight them." She mouthed.

The angels turned and faced Valeria, who sat on the branch outside of the window. She ripped a smaller twig off of the tree, narrowed her eyes at the slender angel that held Alexa, and leaned forward so that she could reach inside the window. She used one hand to hold herself to the tree as she swung the twig at the angels with her free hand.

A pathetic attempt to give the angels what they wanted, but she had done it on a whim. It wasn't going to physically harm anything, but if the angels wanted a fight, that's what she would give them. She had to get Alexa away first.

The twig snapped underneath the claws of a smaller angel with brown wings. Its eyes were red and wide as it frowned at her. "This one's feisty." It purred.

Valeria scoffed, and sat back on the branch before throwing a glance at Alexa, and then at the trapdoor on the floor. She tilted her head. Alexa followed her gaze and nodded.

Then, Valeria ripped a thicker twig off the tree. She grabbed two pinecones and threw them at the angels. They collided with their gray wings, and hung from the feathers. Before the angels could snatch and wrench her back inside, she loosened the remainder of her grip on the branch and fell through the thicket.

II

E verything faded from light, then to dark.

The thicket and sky were swirling around inside of Valeria's head. She tried to blink, and blink some more, but dizziness held her captive as she tried to push herself up.

Her legs were numb, ribs were throbbing, and head felt loose on her aching shoulders. The sound of buzzing filled her ears, before screams and yells blurred over the noise. When she blinked one last time, she rolled onto her side and watched as the world turned sideways. There was the brush of flapping, and then the pounding of boots next to her face as she used her hands to push herself up.

"*Valeria!*" someone screamed over the buzz and flapping that filled her spinning mind.

"*Valeria, get up!*"

She closed and opened her eyes, stood and wobbled. She leaned against something hard before pushing away from it.

"*Valeria!*"

Something firm slapped her face. Valeria shook her head, blinked, and let her fuzzy vision clear.

"Let's go!" When she turned around, she found Alexa snapping her fingers in her face. "Hurry!" Alexa's eyes widened at something behind Valeria before she cursed and started running away.

Valeria watched for a moment before gathering her lost thoughts. *Angels.* Four of them.

She shook her head, then tried to go after Alexa, who was already far ahead. But Valeria wasn't putting up a fight anymore, and four large pairs of wings blew past her face and focused on chasing Alexa now.

Quickly, Valeria stumbled forward and pushed past the pain. She glanced at the sky. It was almost light out. She needed to get to the gate before it closed after six.

As she watched the angels chase after Alexa, she debated on saving herself and sneaking through the trees in the opposite direction. *But Alexa tried to save her.* Valeria's feet quickened. She'd also left her behind at the same time.

Before she pondered too hard over her decision, Valeria sprinted after the four angels. She pounced over the shrubs, grabbed a few pine cones from the undergrowth in case she needed them, and continued after her sister's friend.

It didn't take long to catch them. There were numerous screams echoing around the forest. Which meant the rest of the contestants must have been making their ways to the gate as well. Valeria did her best to forget them as she glimpsed Alexa's hair flowing viciously behind her.

The angels missed Alexa as she pounced into a thornbush and toppled down a steep hill. Valeria faltered. She was far enough behind to observe the angels continue forward, searching for the girl that had vanished from their path.

Valeria hid behind a tree. She peered around it to find Alexa's disheveled form scooting backwards until she was pressed against a mossy log. A headache was growing behind her eyes, threatening to explode her aching mind. She nearly dropped to her knees with relief when the angels struggled to pick up Alexa's scent. Valeria rubbed her temples and squeezed her eyes shut.

The gate. They needed to get to the gate, and then she could focus on the pain taking over her body.

Valeria glanced around the other side of the tree just as another scream echoed around the thicket. All four of the angels sniffed the cool morning air before launching into the canopy of trees and flying far, far away. Leaving Valeria and Alexa behind as they searched for yet another hunt.

When they were surely gone from sight, Valeria stepped out from behind the tree and jogged down the hillside toward Alexa. She was shaking, and her chin was wobbling when Valeria finally reached her.

"Are you alright?" She asked.

Alexa shook her head.

Valeria pursed her lips and offered a hand. "Let's go."

Alexa stayed silent when they started running again. Through the brush, mud, and fallen leaves, they followed the little light that peaked through an opening of the thick forest.

Various footsteps thundered into the ground from every direction. Valeria didn't know if it was more angels or other contestants. She kept her eyes forward as she hastened her feet, jumping over rubble and mounds of the earth. Then suddenly, her mind eased only by a little when the gates slowly entered her line of sight.

"Keep running!" She shouted over her shoulder in case Alexa was growing tired. She wasn't sure how long they had been running. It felt like it'd been hours.

A cry that sounded oddly familiar struck Valeria's ears. She gasped and tripped over her feet, pummeling to the ground.

Alexa stopped beside Valeria and tried to pull her up by her freckled arms. "Come on!" She grunted.

But Valeria wasn't paying attention. She was too busy looking behind where she watched a boy with curly black hair be dragged backwards. A slender angel wrapped its gray arms around his chest, surely suffocating Isaac underneath its strength.

Isaac's name fell halfway out of Valeria's lips when a log smashed into the side of the angel's face, and blood splattered against Isaac's cheeks. Alexa tugged on Valeria once more, but she didn't move. She froze in place when her gaze followed the unconscious angel. It landed on the ground beside Isaac's feet. The log falling beside its sharp claws, released from Flynn's grip, who stood behind Isaac.

She loosened a breath before letting Alexa pull her up.

"We need to go." Alexa muttered. Her attention entirely focused on the gate far ahead. She dropped Valeria's arm, and without another breath, she ran. Valeria nodded, dazed and tired. And partly relieved.

"I'll be right behind." Valeria shouted as another contestant bumped into her back and ran past.

Alexa didn't turn around—she ran out of the forest and up the narrow path to the gate. It was beginning to open just as the sun shimmered over the mountains.

Valeria slowed her pace and glanced over her shoulder to find Isaac and Flynn behind her. Isaac's brown gaze filled with relief, but before they could run past her, he grabbed her arm, and dragged her along.

"Hurry!" He yelled.

The gate opened completely at the same time the sun bloomed across the sky. No longer casting dark shadows across the land.

It was about a half of a mile sprint to the gate. They had only a minute or so until it would close.

Her entire body throbbed as she chased after Flynn and Isaac. Even when another scream broke through the trees, Valeria never turned around. Her half-lidded eyes remained on the gates that wobbled before they slowly started to close.

When the three of them left the forest behind and started up the hill, contestants surrounded them from every direction. Pushing and pulling on Valeria's clothing to get to the gates faster. As if she was a stepping stool to the top.

But Valeria cursed and punched against the others that held her back. She glimpsed Flynn's blonde hair over the crowd, before planting her feet into the mud, and pushed her legs harder up the steep hill.

The climb was brutal and slow. A blast of wind shoved her back, along with other arms and legs. Kicking and pushing.

The gates were right there, she had to make it. *She just had to.*

Lifting her gaze from the muddy ground beneath her, Valeria watched as Flynn shoved Isaac through the gate, and pushed himself through after.

Crying out, Valeria reached and reached—then, as the final alarm sounded, she flung her body through the thin opening of the gate just before it closed completely behind her.

She didn't lift her head from the grass as people screamed and cried behind her. She only moved when their fists began to yank on the steel gates, and then she heard two gunshots go off over her head and she winced.

Darkness invaded her mind when she finally let herself feel the pain flooding throughout her body.

"Wake up, hun." Jacky said while pushing a strand of copper hair behind Valeria's ear.

Valeria snapped her eyes open and tried to push herself up. Panic struck her body as her heart pounded against her ribs. She winced at the stinging pain.

"Careful, now. Don't need you breaking anything else," Jacky teased with a soft smile.

Valeria's eyes widened as everything came back to her. She had survived the first trial. She had *actually* survived.

She remembered being surrounded by angels with Flynn and Isaac, before being lost and hurt by herself in the forest. Then there was Alexa, and then she was falling. Valeria's head throbbed, and she sighed as she recalled how Alexa had saved her.

"What happened?" Valeria asked once she realized she was back inside of her room. She noticed her old black clothing in a dirty pile across the floor. Then she glanced underneath the covers and saw that she was wearing a nightgown. "Did you change me?"

Jacky's smile dropped and she nodded. "You were caked in mud, and I didn't want to ruin your new sheets. I'm sorry, but I also had to check you for any injuries."

Valeria's throat was sore, she swallowed back a grimace. Despite her discomfort with Jacky seeing her undressed, she was thankful to be taken care of.

"How bad is it?" Valeria asked, sitting up with a wince.

Jacky placed her hands on Valeria's shoulders to hold her down. "You shouldn't move too much. You need to heal as much as you can before the next trial." Valeria sighed with a nod, and Jacky continued, "Only one of your ribs is snapped, and you have a concussion, but thankfully someone offered an amplifier for your wounds. So you're healing much faster than usual. In fact, you should be good to go by tomorrow."

"Someone." Valeria whispered, then glanced at Jacky, who hid a smirk. "*Who?*"

"That handsome fellow across the hall."

"Flynn?" Valeria's eyes widened. "How did he get an amplifier?"

Jacky shrugged and she stood from her spot on the bed. "How am I supposed to know? He could have gotten it from someone placing a bet on him. Or he could have snuck it in. Who knows?" Jacky moved across the room and over to the dresser. "All I know is that you have a chance at winning. Keep that boy close to your side, and he'll take you further in the games."

"I don't need him." Valeria knew it was a lie, and that she should be thankful for Flynn. If it weren't for him, she didn't know if she or Isaac would still be alive.

Flynn had protected Isaac through the entire night inside of the forest, and he had given her medicine to heal. She should thank him.

Jacky faced her and grabbed a gown from off of the steel dresser. It was pastel green, Valeria's favorite color, and her mood lightened some. "Now, hun. If you want to live, then you'll need him. I recommend you get over your frustration before it's too late."

Valeria sighed and adjusted into a more comfortable position. "I know. I know." Then she tilted her head and frowned. "Do you know how many are left?"

Jacky dropped her eyes and stared at the gown in her hands. "Twelve, I believe. Two failed to make it into the gates before they closed."

Her heart stopped for a moment as she held her breath. "We lost eight people in one trial?"

Jacky nodded. "Besides, Ridoc. The boy who was stabbed in his sleep."

Valeria shook her head and glared when she remembered Lance's face before the trial had started. She needed to watch her back around the estate.

"What about the girls? How many girls are left?" Although her heart was broken for the ones who had died, she was thankful when she recalled watching Alexa pass through the gate before her. As well as Flynn and Isaac.

"You and the other girl from the Court of Wind, and a girl from the Court of Wolves."

"*Three?*" Valeria gaped.

Jacky's face fell, and she nodded her head before tossing the green gown at Valeria's feet. "If you need to use the bathroom, or get hungry, change into this. Do not leave these quarters in only your nightgown. Now that the games have officially started, murder will become a popular pastime around here. Please, be safe."

12

Valeria finished braiding her wet hair and swung it over her shoulder as she trudged down the checkered, tiled stairs. She sent a glance to the ceiling, only to make sure that the dragon mural hadn't moved. She couldn't help but always feel like something or someone was watching her.

Inside the Game of Lords, none of the contestants received unbroken privacy. The most Valeria had gotten was inside of the bathing quarters when it was her turn to use the showers. Besides, how was the king watching the games? There had to be spells of some sort cast over the estate that let him watch the contestants through a crystal globe.

Valeria rolled her eyes at herself. *This wasn't a fairytale book*. In fact, it was far from one. Surely the king didn't have a crystal globe...

When the dragon seemed to be in the same position on the rounded ceiling, Valeria dropped her gaze and finished her way down the stairs. Only to trip into the wall when her head spun. She was going to puke. Her lower chest ached as she pushed herself up and readjusted the wet braid that had fallen over her shoulder.

A patch of her pastel gown was now darker from the wetness of her hair. She cursed and moved around the corner and into the hall that led to the dining quarters.

"There you are." Flynn muttered from the wall, where he leaned against a painting of the Court of Magic. His ocean eyes landed on where she held a hand to her rib-cage before a corner of his lip drew upwards. His hair was ruffled and messy, as if he hadn't slept. "I'll walk with you."

Valeria pursed her lips and glanced away. "I prefer to be alone. Thank you." She tried to walk past him, but he fell into step with her and smiled.

Flynn clicked his tongue and shoved his hands into the pockets of his black trousers. "Don't we all wish to be alone?" He waited for her to reply as he tilted his head, but she only rolled her eyes and continued down the hall. "That's what's so ironic about it all, isn't it? We'll never be alone. Not here, at least. There's always someone lurking around a corner, just waiting for the next person to die. Not to mention the king watching us through the eyes of the officials."

She almost faltered, but quickly withdrew her curiosity.

So that's how the king watched the games? Through the officials.

"You didn't know that, did you?" Flynn snorted and flipped a black dagger between his fingers. "Well, now you do. You know, if we were in an alliance, I might trust you enough to let you in on a few more secrets about this place."

Valeria sharply inhaled and marched to the courtyard doors. Before Flynn could pester her even more, a servant pushed the doors open and blew right past. Flynn leaned back and watched Valeria shove through the thin opening of the door and hurried across the courtyard.

She entered the dining hall before he could catch up.

She didn't know what to say, or even what to think about Flynn anymore. What was he planning? Why had he given her medicine to heal faster? And why does he want an alliance with her so badly?

She released a breath before her gaze landed on the back of Isaac's head at the large iron dining table. His hands were clenched into fists beneath the table as he bounced his legs. Valeria walked over and took the seat next to him. A nervous smile played on her lips as she brushed a hand down his arm.

Eight contestants were killed yesterday, and their absences left the table nearly empty with their seats underneath the table. Valeria frowned at the quietness and scooted forward in her chair.

The dining-room doors slammed shut and Flynn's footsteps scuffed against the hard floor. Then, slowly, he rounded the table and stared down at Valeria for a mere second before plopping himself into the seat across from her.

She moved her attention onto Isaac, who smiled widely at Flynn. Valeria furrowed her brows and looked between the both of them before a servant placed a platter with an egg sandwich and a small side salad in front of her. Flynn grimaced at his plate and pushed it closer to Isaac.

"You can have mine." He leaned back and crossed his arms.

"Thanks, man." Isaac said before digging into his food.

Valeria wanted to ask about the Forest of Angels, but felt it was too soon. She didn't know what Isaac and Flynn had been through, and they didn't know what she had been through. She almost died... more than once.

Grimacing, she lightly shoved her plate away with her thumb. *How could she eat?* It was as if she didn't have an appetite anymore... She couldn't with the constant trials and nerve-wracking contestants that most likely wanted her dead. Everyone was probably anticipating the day she would die.

Perhaps even Flynn was. She examined his sharp jawline before darting her green eyes away.

Valeria remembered what Alexa had said to her inside the tree shed.

"You have the strongest player trying to make an alliance with you, and you're always with the young boy, Isaac. Everyone can see that you should win. If I'm seen with you, one of us will be killed. If not, both."

Had Alexa been warning her that the others wanted her dead? Just because she was protecting Isaac? And if having Flynn by her side made Valeria more of a threat in the games, she needed to stay away from him. But that was proving to be difficult when he was always lurking around every corner waiting for her.

Valeria gazed at Flynn, who stared at the walls and art structures around the room. He's the strongest player? She tilted her head and sat back in her seat. What makes him the strongest player? Because he got into a fight over her? Or because he captured princess Helena's attention?

She was thrown out of her thoughts when Flynn's blue eyes snapped to hers. Quickly, she looked away and focused on Isaac, who had just finished his first sandwich and was moving onto Flynn's.

Isaac met her stare and flashed a grin over his food. "How are you?"

A hesitant smile graced her lips, but she couldn't help the slight quiver of her chin. She didn't realize how many emotions she had bottled up inside, and somehow a fifteen-year-old boy could pull them out of her with the one question that she simply didn't know how to answer.

"I'm fine." She lied and bit her lip to hide the quivering. "Just a little bruised up is all."

No. She wasn't fine. She longed to scream and cry. She wanted to flip the table and tear the entire estate apart. She wanted to burn the Forest of Angels to the ground and leave everything in its ruin.

But she didn't. She only smiled and nodded at Isaac's concerned expression.

Before he could say anything else, a door slammed, and the gamerunner sauntered to the front of the room. He was wearing a ruby red suit with shiny black shoes this time. She held in her scoff and leaned back in her chair, waiting for his superfluous speech.

Valeria hadn't been down for breakfast in the morning, so she missed whatever was said, but now she hoped the gamerunner had better things to mention that didn't revolve around the next trial.

The gamerunner ripped a note card from his pocket and began reading a list of names. "Henry Newton from the Court of Smoke. Ruby Easton, Clio Gentry, and Linus Barlowe from the Court of Magic. Riley Hart and Sebastion Hawthorn from the Court of Storms. Finally, Shawn Allen from the Court of Wolves."

Flynn winced and tightly closed his eyes before releasing a long deep breath.

Valeria listened until the final contestant's name was read. Each name sent a shudder down her spine. Those names—those people had sat with her at this table only hours ago. They suffered from the angels, or had been shot by the officials.

She removed her eyes from the gamerunner and peered down the length of the iron table where the old man used to sit. A memory of his scream and cries flashed through her mind. He had been the one to break her rib. He let her lay on the ground hidden from the angels as he ran away. Only to meet his end...

He saved her, and she didn't even know his name.

Valeria breathed through her nose and glanced at Alexa, who met her gaze before resting her chin in her hands and nodded at the gamerunner. When she looked back at him, he was squinting his eyes and frowning at Valeria before shoving the card back into his pocket.

"May the killed be rested, and their lives be remembered." She glared at him, but he turned away to face the other end of the table. The room remained silent before the gamerunner spoke again. "I have good news, my lords and ladies. You will have a week to rest and train before the next trial."

Valeria felt nails on the side of her head. She swiveled her neck and found Lance's eyes digging into hers. He sneered and shot a taunting wink. Valeria's lips lifted into a snarl before she glanced away.

The gamerunner continued, "As I've mentioned before, the Game of Lords has officially started. Over the week, do not think that you are safe. You are *never* safe inside the Azrael estate." He smiled. "So, watch your backs, and make sure you're carrying a weapon at all times if you intend to live."

Once he was finished, the gamerunner left the dining room.

Isaac shoved his plates to the center of the table and leaned back in his seat. "I hate that guy," He muttered.

Valeria nodded and stared at his empty dishes. She could still feel Lance's eyes on her, but she tried her best to ignore it.

Flynn adjusted in his chair across from her. "Eh, I kinda like him."

The legs of a chair scratched against the marble floor as Lance abruptly stood from his seat. Valeria noticed just in time to see him knock the young male in the shoulder, who sat beside him. Towering over the table, Lance's brown eyes remained on hers.

"Let's go," Lance said.

Once the male next to Lance followed, only then did he look away.

Valeria watched as they left the room. She couldn't help the chills that sprinkled along her neck and back. She needed to find a weapon, and she needed to find one fast.

The pathway to the garden led Valeria through rose bushes full of thorns and flowers of all sorts. They scattered an array of colors across the bottom of her green dress as she walked.

With gentle fingers, she picked a white lily from a single bush. Her skin skimmed across the edge of a pedal and it shriveled up, turning to dust. A gasp escaped her throat when it dropped from her fingers and fell into the dirt beneath her feet.

Valeria stepped back and held her arms closer to her sides before continuing through the garden.

Azrael estate was full of magic, and not the good kind. Valeria wondered if there even was a good kind of magic.

The Lord of Illusions flashed through her mind. The way he had grinned at her during the ball of The Vanishing. He ruled over the Court of Magic, so nothing about him could be good.

The lords received their own powers once they were granted immortality. It was the king's gift after winning the Game of Lords.

What was the next lord's power going to be?

Then she thought of all the contestants, and the letter that she had opened with Lilith before she was taken away by the officials.

The House of Embers.

She assumed there would be dragons in one of the next trials. She just didn't know when. It would be best if she could find a library and do some research on the beasts before it was too late.

Lance cannot win. That was the one thing she would make sure of besides protecting Isaac. If Lance won, he would be a leader of an entirely new court and its people.

She muttered a curse before walking underneath a white gazebo in the center of the garden.

Lance would be a terrible leader.

A crunching noise had her swiveling on her toes before she leaned against the white wood railing. Flynn stood in the garden holding a blue star flower. It crumpled to ashes in his grip and a frown fell onto his face.

"That's unfortunate." He said. "Why grow flowers when they can't be picked?"

Valeria almost smiled, but couldn't let herself do it. She needed to remain annoyed and frustrated with him in order to protect her heart.

Except he had helped her. *She didn't know.* She was confused on where her relationship stood with Flynn, and she couldn't form an alliance with him. Because if she got close to him, she could see certain feelings sprouting where they shouldn't. *Not here at least.*

He might've realized that as well, because she could see the faint glimmer behind those blue eyes when he looked at her—the hint of a smile on his lips.

He was dangerous. She couldn't let him get closer. Because only one could win, and the rest must die.

Flynn needed to remain as just another contestant. Nothing more. Nothing less. She didn't need anymore pain—anymore loss in her life.

"It's like the game." She said without realizing, fixing her gaze on the flower bushes beside him. Flynn glanced over, waiting for her to continue. Valeria cleared her throat and rubbed the ache in her side. "They grow and bloom, but once plucked from their homes, they die and turn to ash."

Flynn shook his head and dropped the remainder of the flower before walking toward her. "That still doesn't make any sense. We have a chance to live, Valeria."

Her breath hitched when her name left his lips. She turned away and looked at the lake. "No, we don't."

Flynn huffed. "Maybe not all of us, but a few."

"*A few.*" Valeria scoffed and shook her head at his disregard for the others. "There's one prince and one princess, and twelve contestants that are still alive. Only three women are left. The rest are men. If you really think that *a few* of us have a chance at living through this, you're sadly mistaken."

Flynn ignored her rant and leaned against the gazebo railing beside her. "My apologies." A brief moment of silence passed. He adjusted himself to face the glistening lake. "You know, you could at least try to talk to the prince. I heard the women at the ball chittering about how amazing he is in bed."

Valeria's mouth fell open and she snapped her wide eyes onto his. A smirk danced on his lips as his crystal-like gaze sparkled against the sun's reflection. "You're insufferable."

He shrugged and raised his eyebrows. "I'm just saying, give it a chance. At least try to make him fall for you, so you have a second opportunity at making it out alive. It shouldn't be difficult anyway. Look at you."

Ignoring his attempt at a compliment, Valeria asked, "You're saying that you don't think I can win this thing?"

He fully faced her. "I'm saying that I *know* you can't win this thing."

The steady wind shuffled a loose piece of Valeria's braid into her face. She bit the inside of her lip and glared at Flynn. "Maybe I can." She argued.

Flynn laughed. A full belly, hunched over laugh before he pretended to wipe tears from his eyes. "Valeria," He said once he managed to control himself. "Unless you can get Lance's attention off of you, I don't think you'll survive through the night without him trying to kill you."

Lords. She hated to admit that he was right. Maybe she was feeling a bit of annoyance toward him—making her feel weak. She wasn't weak, but she was also aware that she wasn't stronger than most of the contestants here. They could easily attack and kill her if they so wanted.

"I know." She whispered and dropped her head. She could feel Flynn's energy shift as soon as her voice softened. "I hardly survived the first trial. I don't know what I'm going to do for the next one."

Flynn reached toward her before he stopped and placed his hand back at his side. Biting his bottom lip, he said, "Make an alliance with me."

Valeria gazed into his hope-filled eyes before shaking her head. "I can't. The others see you as the largest threat. Besides, Alexa told me that I'm already untrustworthy as well. For some reason they see my relationship with Isaac as a threat. So you and I getting into an alliance will only give the competition more of a reason to team up against us... You shouldn't even be here with me right now. If we're seen together, it will only make matters worse.

"You're wrong." He said, stepping closer. Flynn dragged a hand through his golden hair before leaning down. "If we make an alliance,

I can protect you. You saw Isaac." Flynn motioned to the forest and Valeria's breath halted when she glanced at it. "He came out of that forest scratch-free. I stayed on lookout while he slept throughout the entire night."

"That's not the point." Valeria said, frustrated that she couldn't give him the full truth without embarrassing herself. "Everyone knows that you have a significant chance at winning, *and* making the princess fall in love with you. If we start an alliance, they'll only want to kill me more than they already do. It's not happening."

Flynn sighed and sat on the railing. "You're making a mistake."

"I'm not." She moved away from him and onto the dirt trail in the garden. "And if I am, then that is on me. I made a vow to myself to protect Isaac, so if you want to help me at all, just make sure he stays unharmed."

13

The first thing Valeria noticed inside of Azrael estate's training quarters was the large tank sitting at the back of the room. The space was wide and tall, and the tank took up the entire length of it. From where she stood just outside the entry doors, she examined the contestants on the black mats. Some fought against each other while others practiced throwing knives and building strength.

Valeria watched as Lance flung another male contestant over his shoulder and pressed his knee into the male's spine to hold him down. A satisfied yet vile smile tugged at the corner of his lips before he glanced around the brightly lit room.

Her chest heaved, and she stepped back to hide behind the door. She released a breath before pushing off of the wall and walking down the hallway. She'd been exploring the estate quarters while Flynn and Isaac trained out in the fields.

The hallway behind the dining quarters was unlike the rest of the estate. The walls consisted of red clay brick. The floors were shiny, deep gray slabs of stone that eased the brightness the tall, round windows brought in. Valeria glanced at the small dangling chandeliers leading her through the halls until she came upon a door that was slightly cracked open.

It was utter curiosity that made her press her palm up against the wood until she could see what was inside. All the contestants were training for the next trial, while Valeria wasn't much in the mood to do anything for the day.

The thought of dragons had been tugging on her mind ever since she opened the Lord of Sky's letter with Lilith. Since the gamerunner hadn't filled them in on what the second trial would comprise, she wanted to at least study dragons in case it revolved around them. She'd been hoping to run across a library or something of the sort.

The door creaked when Valeria stepped into the dark room. However, once she was inside, the door closed by itself behind her and a fiery light appeared in front of her. She flinched. Her eyes stung from the sudden brightness before she peered at the small floating flame.

Was it magic? A life spell of some sort?

Valeria reached her finger out to touch it before pulling away upon feeling the heat. It bristled and swiveled until it floated toward the nearest wall. She followed the flame with her eyes and noticed a tall shelf that was overflowing with old crumbly books. A few of the spines stuck out from their proper places and threatened to join a dusty pile that was already lying on the floor.

She walked over and skimmed her fingers along the spine of a history book. A heavy layer of dust stuck to her skin. Valeria frowned and turned around. She motioned to the flame to move, but it wouldn't. How was she supposed to make it light up where she needed it to?

She moved her arms in front of her and walked to what she assumed was the middle of the study. With each step, the little flickering light stayed by her shoulder. Valeria grinned at the fire before taking in the rest of the room.

The furniture was not pure iron and cold like it was throughout most of the estate. She furrowed her brows and let her eyes trace the soft material of two ruby red chairs across the room. A small wooden side table sat between them, a crumbling booklet lying on top. There was a rich mahogany desk on the opposite side of the room with large potted plants towering behind it. Nothing lit up the room, not a single window or lamp. Only the floating flame that followed her around.

She turned back toward the towering bookcases and traced a few of the delicate spines with her finger.

She wondered if there were any books on dragons, but she would need time to scan the entirety of the collection. Unsure if she was allowed to be in here, Valeria chewed at her bottom lip and dropped her hand.

The gamerunner made it seem like the estate was free to roam at any time, but this room seemed so concealed. So private.

The flame jumped as if it had a personality of its own when Valeria faced the desk. Surprisingly, the flame flew over to it and illuminated the top of the mahogany. A jar full of ink and a black feather pen was the first thing that caught her eye.

A memory of the Lord of Sky's office sifted in and out of her mind as her eyes landed on a folded up piece of paper. She hesitated before reaching toward it.

Just before her fingers could skim across the note, the door opened and light filtered into the room. Valeria spun on her heels and fell back against the desk.

"What are you doing in here?"

Releasing a heavy breath, she said, "Lords, Isaac. You scared me." She placed a hand over her thumping heart.

Isaac frowned and kicked his foot into the door to hold it open. The fire light fluttered over to him in a rush. She watched his eyes light up with a golden hue as he smiled at the small light. Curiously, he returned his gaze to her.

"I'm sorry. Flynn ended our training early. I was just coming in here to read." The light rubbed against the leather of Isaac's arm strap and he jerked away. "That hurts." He hissed.

Valeria's hands remained on the desk behind her. She grabbed the note off of the table and surreptitiously slipped it into the skirt of her gown. All the while, her eyes remained on his.

"Have you been in here before?" She questioned.

Isaac nodded. "I come here when I can't sleep. Most of the time, when you've gone to the garden, I'm in here."

Valeria pursed her lips and stepped away from the desk. "What kind of books are in here anyway?"

He scanned the shelves behind her as shadows slowly enveloped his form. Only the side of his jaw was a blazing orange from the firelight. "I've only read a few. But it's mainly a large collection of the history of the games and how they came to be."

Nothing Valeria hadn't read before.

"Hm." She sighed and turned to peer up at the wall of books before throwing a glance over her shoulder at Isaac. "There wouldn't happen to be anything about dragons?"

"Dragons?" Isaac furrowed his brows. He stepped farther into the room and let the door shut quietly behind him when voices sounded from the hall. "Why do you want to read about dragons?"

Valeria licked her lips before facing him again. "Listen, I was going to tell you eventually, but I could never find the right time." Isaac stared, she swallowed. "Before The Vanishing began, I went into the Lord of Sky's office." His eyes widened, but Valeria pressed closer. "I stole a letter and my sister and I opened it. It was from the gamerunner, thanking the Lord of Sky for some kind of gift. It mentioned dragons, and the next winner of the games to become the Lord of Dragons, and leader of the House of Embers."

"Holy—" Isaac ran a hand through his curls. "Valeria. You think dragons will be a part of one of the trials?" He prowled closer with worry.

"Yes." She replied hoarsely.

At this, Isaac ran another hand through his hair. "What do we do?"

Valeria bit her lip and felt for the note in her gown. "I'm not sure. I was hoping I could find information on dragons. We need to know if there is a way to bond with them." She pulled the note out and showed him. "I found this in here. I'd open it now, but I don't want someone to come in and find us."

Isaac swallowed and nodded. "Let me know what it says once you've read it." He trudged to the door and pressed his ear against it. "Right now, we need to get out of here without being seen. Whose ever note that is, can't know that we were in here once they realize it's gone."

She walked up to him and listened for anyone in the hall. It was soundless, not even the training room was loud with vicious activity.

Isaac flicked a look at the small flame that floated beside him. "Don't tell anyone we were here."

Valeria frowned at him, "It can't speak, Isaac."

He shrugged, "You never know."

She smiled and felt for the door handle before turning the knob and pushing it open. The hallway was empty. Quickly, she stepped out. Isaac followed behind and they scurried toward the dining hall doors.

When they found that the usual loud and chatter-filled hall was clear, their shoulders sagged and Isaac released a breath. "I'll return tomorrow and search for a book on dragons. You need to find out what that note says."

They walked around the dining table and to the courtyard doors. When they were outside, Valeria pressed a hand to his arm. "Hold on. I got this for you."

Isaac watched as she pulled a small dagger from out of her brown boot. He grinned and took it before examining the intricate designs on the blade. "When did you get it? I thought everything was taken from the armory before we could even enter it?"

"I took it from one of the contestants while they were training." She shoved his weaponized hand against his chest. "Put it away. Don't let anyone know you have it."

"What about you?"

Valeria lifted her skirt an inch over her leg. There was a leather strap around her calf, and a glinting dagger underneath. Isaac smiled as she looked at him.

"Thank you, Val." He breathed. "Seriously."

Valeria stood and watched as the lake rippled and shimmered underneath the moonlight. After waiting all day for nightfall, she finally allowed herself the access to outside. Earlier, Lance and his friends had been where she currently stood beneath the willow tree. She wasn't sure why they were so drawn to the water, but she wanted to find out.

Although there was nothing unusual or out of the ordinary about it. It was simply just a large body of water. There was a dock a few hundred feet away, but she remained underneath the large willow tree, overlooking the lake.

Anyone could ambush and shove her into the water if she were to stand on the dock. It was too risky. Lately, everything seemed to be.

Yesterday, when she had walked away from Isaac and they went their separate ways, Valeria had stayed in her room and debated on opening the letter. She hadn't. Jacky kept barging in, asking how she was every hour.

Now, as she stood on the cliff over the lake, Valeria let her fingers wrap around the soft paper edges of the letter before pulling it from the inside of her boot. She gazed at the castle over her shoulder and examined the shadows and shrubs, checking to see if anyone might be lurking and watching from afar.

When she found every corner vacant of wanderers, and the flower petals only moved against the warm breeze, Valeria shifted her gaze back onto the letter.

It had to be the gamerunners. She hadn't seen anyone that was as important as him inside of the estate, besides the royal family. Only the servants and helpers. There was no known reason for any of them to enter the study and leave a mysterious note.

The envelope was blank and unsealed. Slipping the notecard out of the envelope and onto her fingers, Valeria blinked and observed the lake. Once she had a grip on the note, she stepped near the edge of the cliff and let the empty envelope be carried away in the wind. She watched as it blew far out over the waters before diving into the foamy waves.

Valeria turned away from the water and paced back to the tree trunk before leaning against it. The wind threatened to rip the notecard from her grasp as it crinkled and wobbled in her fingers, but she tightened her grip and unfolded the paper.

Only two words were written in sloppy cursive on the middle of the card.

Death Lily

The note crumpled in her fist and she squeezed her eyes shut. Using her last restraint from throwing the paper over the edge of the cliff.

"Death lily?" Valeria scoffed under her breath while pushing a lock of hair behind her ear.

What did that even mean?

She stared at the crescent moon before dropping her chin. What in the lords was an uncommon flower supposed to mean? Who had written the note? And could it really be the gamerunners?

As the stars shimmered brighter and brighter, Valeria took it as her sign to leave. It was an hour past midnight. She needed rest.

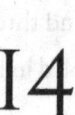

14

T he second trial was two days away.

Valeria was walking through the courtyard when she glimpsed a flash of black from the corner of her eye. Just before the dining hall doors closed behind her, she saw Flynn walking from the garden and through the side doors to the main quarters. His hair was rugged, and lips smeared a blush-colored pink as if he had been doing something that she loathed imagining.

Entering the dining hall, the table was empty and every single chair was pushed in. Valeria crossed the room and made way to the training quarters, where she expected to find the rest of the contestants.

At the end of the wide stone hall was the training room, but she didn't waste a moment to check and see who all was in there. She knew Flynn wasn't, which was well on her part. Running into him now would only make her late to meet with Isaac.

The door to the dark study was closed. Valeria stepped toward it. She pressed her palm against the brass handle and let it creak open, revealing Isaac's shadow sitting on the red velvet chair in the room's corner. His arm was resting on a stack of books as he scanned through whatever he was reading.

The firelight flickered from the side of his face, lighting the pages so that he could see.

Valeria stepped inside and closed the door behind her. The room filled with darkness yet again as the hall light vanished. Isaac looked up and watched her trudge over to the chair next to him.

"Hi," He muttered, leaning forward and marking a page with his thumb. "Did you read the note?"

She nodded and sat at the edge of the seat. Gently, she reached into the depth of her skirt pocket and pulled out the small, crumpled paper. "Do you know what a Death Lily is?"

Isaac frowned and fully closed the book he was reading. "Yes. Why? Did it mention something about them?"

Valeria nodded again. "Look."

Isaac took the paper from her outstretched hand and pursed his lips as the firelight shined over his head. "That's it?" He scoffed.

"Looks like it."

He handed the note back and glanced at the empty desk through the darkness. "Do you have any idea what it might mean?"

She sighed before biting her lip and looking away. "Remember when the gamerunner said something about leaving hints around the estate?" He nodded, and she continued. "I think it might be a hint. I just don't know what it could mean."

Isaac squinted and batted the firelight away from his curls. "I'll go check the gardens for the plant. Maybe there could be another hint where it's planted?"

He was smart. Valeria hadn't even thought to do so.

"Okay, I'm going to do some research. Meet me back here if you find anything."

As he stood from his seat with a concerned look, Isaac stalked to the door and left.

The firelight flew back to her and twirled around her copper hair. She smiled at the small flame before leaning over and snatching two books from the pile Isaac had been reading from.

The titles had captured her attention. One was written in the old language. A language that, thankfully, her father had taught her to read and understand while growing up. The other books' inner pages were written in a language Valeria couldn't decipher, though she could read the title very clearly since it was the common tongue of Laterra.

The Eternal One.

Valeria frowned before setting it back in the pile and focusing on the old, dusty book that had stood out to her instead.

Man and Beast: The Dragon War.

Perhaps this entire study was full of hints? Maybe this was one of them, and the other contestants wouldn't know, because she was the only one who wrongfully read and stole a letter that wasn't hers.

An hour passed as Valeria skimmed through the thick leather book. She stopped in a section titled War Training. Her eyes brightened and she straightened her spine. Hopefully it would tell her exactly what she needed to know if she planned on surviving the games.

Dragons although, rare and disagreeable, require an intense amount of trust and bonding in order to befriend, or ride. It does not come easily for one to gain a dragon's trust. Though there are certain natural organisms and a mentality that a dragon will bow to. However, it is a brutal death if these rarity of possessions are not met by the dragon.

Valeria pulled back from the book and licked her lips. A certain mentality? How would a dragon know someone's mentality? And when was this book even written?

She flipped to the front of the book and found the date. It was written nearly five hundred years ago, and dragons were unheard of up until the night that Valeria had been vanished. Could the book even be accurate anymore?

There were too many questions, and not enough time as she flipped back to the page she was on and continued reading.

If a dragon has chosen to trust you, do not destroy that trust. If one does, they will be burned and eaten alive. Many warriors of our time have taken their dragons into battle, and in doing so have broken their bond, leading them to their ultimate death.

Valeria closed the page and glanced at the firelight that hovered beside her shoulder. She huffed in frustration, because how in the lords would she be able to gain a dragon's trust? *Yes*, she needed a certain mentality and natural organism, but the book hadn't specified what kind. There were so many—too many. Plants, water, wind species, and fire species—basically every court was named after its element or species. How was she supposed to know? How was she supposed to figure it out before it was too late?

There was a tower of books stacked to the side of Valeria's chair. She sat another one on top of the pile she was slowly but surely making. Huffing, she stood from her seat before walking over to the mahogany desk.

The little fire light trailed quickly behind.

As she made her way around the desk, she hesitated on opening the top drawer, but when she finally did, it slid smoothly out, and Valeria peered inside.

Plenty of pens, blank note cards, and paperclips rolled around. But there was something else that caught her eye. She ran a finger across the surface of a small wooden box before she went to pick it up. Black swirls of art covered the sides of the light wood, while the top had a gold emblem of two rings with the letter "A" in the middle.

It took her a fleeting moment to figure out how to unlock and open it. When she did, something clicked and clattered inside the bookcase to her left. She slammed the box closed and furrowed her brows. The curious noise sounded from the bookcase a second time.

Valeria licked her bottom lip and placed the box back into the drawer. She tried and failed to ignore the temptation to open the box again. This time, she made sure her eyes stayed on the bookcase.

She flicked the top open, slowly, unlike before, to make sure she wasn't missing anything or overthinking the small curious device.

Suddenly the spine of a blue leather bound book fell backwards out of its place on the shelf. Valeria was a step away from walking over to investigate when the door unexpectedly opened.

She jolted back to the drawer and slammed the box closed just to be safe. Expecting it to be Isaac returning with news about the Death Lily, but when she looked up and found the gamerunner staring back at her, she gulped and gently closed the drawer.

Why was she always getting caught rummaging through other people's desks?

The gamerunner let the door close gently behind him as he stepped inside. Valeria's eyes traced the tiny smirk that grew on his wrinkled cheeks. His silver hair was tied in a low bun, and he was dressed in a gray suit. Similar to the one Isaac wore to the ball.

Isaac! Valeria remembered. She hoped he wouldn't return while the gamerunner was still there.

"Found my study, have you?" The gamerunner walked to the desk and dragged a finger across the top.

Valeria simply nodded, her lips parted as she tried to take a step away from the desk.

The notecard! Where is it?

Without appearing to be concerned, she felt inside her pockets, but couldn't feel the note. Her eyes peered over his shoulder and scanned the pile of books behind him. She couldn't see through the darkness.

"What court were you from again?" The gamerunner asked as he leaned over the desk and glanced at the shelf of books beside him. Before she could answer, he started, "Oh, yes. I remember. The Court of Wind, correct?"

Valeria cleared her throat and moved her timid gaze back onto him. "Yes."

"I've heard many lovely details about the gardens there, such beauty." Her eyes flickered as she pursed her lips at his casualness. Was she not in trouble? "Anyway, congrats on making it through the first trial. As you can tell, not many make it this far into the games."

She swallowed an insult before lifting her lips into a smile that matched his own. "Thank you. It was tough, but I managed my way through."

The gamerunner licked his teeth as he examined her. "Was it? I remember watching you pass out..." He squinted before moving on. "I've always wondered what the Forest of Angels was like."

Valeria frowned. "You've never been inside the forest?"

He pushed off of the desk and walked over to a bookshelf. Precisely, the one that she heard noises from earlier. "I have no need. I've heard stories." There was a pause when he faced her again. "My father ran the games fifty years ago when the Lady of Wolves won. I was only an infant then, but as he grew older, he told me all about the games, and his position as gamerunner."

His father? Valeria made her way around the desk. "How did you become the gamerunner?"

He chuckled and pressed his hands into the pockets of his clean pants. "My family is close to the king. I was born to continue the legacy."

She didn't know if it was a clever question, but before she could fathom another thought, she asked, "Do you enjoy it?"

From the way his expression dropped, either out of surprise or anger, she wasn't sure. He seemed to stiffen like a rock before shrugging the feelings aside. "I haven't decided."

Then he walked away from her with a snap of his fingers. The fire light above her shoulder hurried across the room to follow him. She cursed when he stopped beside the pile of books she had been reading from. The note sat folded on top.

His back was to her, so she couldn't see his expression when he reached down and picked it up.

It was silent for a moment, then, "Ah, you've found the last hint."

Valeria bit her lip. "The last?"

He turned around, the fire fluttered toward his hands. "The others weren't nearly as important as this one. Trust me."

"How so?" She stepped toward him, tempted to rip the note from his grasp, but she stopped herself. "It's only two words. That's not a very useful hint if I must be honest."

The gamerunner scoffed. "It isn't?" His eyes lingered on the stack of books. "What have you learned about dragons so far? Actually, may I ask *why* you're doing research on dragons?"

Valeria's face paled, and she struggled to find an excuse. "I was curious. They were pretty popular thousands of years ago, weren't they?"

He nodded, but held her stare. Curiosity flickered in his eyes. "Let me give you another little hint..." He dropped his chin toward her, wanting the knowledge of her name.

"Valeria." She said.

"*Valeria*, let me give you a hint. A certain natural organism is known to calm a dragon's flame." He moved his weight onto the opposite leg as he looked at her through narrowed brows. "Now, I'll leave the rest to you." As he walked to the door, she followed. He pointedly held the note out. "I'd also recommend keeping this to yourself. Understand?"

The information clicked in her head as he slid the note into her palm. He opened the door and motioned for her to leave. As she stepped out into the hall, she heard the door snap shut behind her.

Valeria released a breath and shoved the paper into her dress pocket. She knew exactly what she needed to do. But first, she needed to find Isaac.

15

Isaac was lounging peacefully on the small twin sized bed in his room when Valeria burst inside. First, she questioned him about his unlocked door and the opportunity it gave Lance for any potential murders he might have planned. Then she grabbed his brown cloak from off of his metal dresser and threw it at him.

"Come on." She said while crossing her arms.

"Wha—Val, what are you doing? It's nearly midnight." He groaned, blinking tiredly as he wiped at his sleep-ridden eyes.

"I found something."

His curiosity overtook him as he jumped to his feet and slung the ratty brown cloak over his shoulders. "Show me."

After sneaking through the estate with cloaks thrown over their heads, Valeria informed Isaac about the gamerunner catching her earlier. He whispered a silent joke from behind that earned him a slap on the shoulder. Then they entered the dark study together. She sighed a breath of relief once she noticed that the room was empty.

Although, she grew worried when she couldn't find the small flickering flame.

Isaac frowned and walked past after closing the door. "Where is it?" He asked.

Valeria parted her lips and felt for the desk on her left. She ran her palm across the top until she felt something round with an empty center. "Hold on. I think we have to light it."

She couldn't see, but could hear the way Isaac huffed and moved closer.

"He must've put the flame out after catching you in here."

Valeria pursed her lips and nodded as she skimmed a finger inside of the empty circular shape on the desk. She felt a small stick with a rounded end and smiled. "Can you feel anything made of stone?" She asked him.

He clicked his tongue, and she imagined him crossing his arms over his chest as he replied with a hint of teasing, "The walls."

Closing her eyes, Valeria flushed and moved closer to the wall. "*Right.*"

A second later, she scraped the round tip of the wooden stick against the stone wall. The match lit instantly and flamed against her thumb. Valeria cursed and rushed to the gold ashtray where she found the match.

Isaac stood back and watched as she dipped the fiery tip back into the small bits of ash.

"It's not lighting." Isaac said.

She sighed and looked around. "Open the drawer and hand me a piece of paper from the notebook."

He rushed around the desk and did as she said. Once she had the paper, she placed it inside of the tray and waited for the short match to catch fire.

They both released a pent up breath when the ash flamed to life and the little firelight dashed from the tray and over to Isaac's shoulder.

He chuckled and ran a quick finger along the small, bristling flames. "Thought it was a goner for a minute."

Valeria quirked her lip and blew away the smoke from the gold tray. She leaned against the desk and watched Isaac smile down at the creature that couldn't speak. "I thought it annoyed you? Or were you just acting tough all those times before?"

Isaac blushed and batted her away. "Aren't you supposed to be showing me something?"

Rolling her eyes, she walked around the desk and hip bumped Isaac out of the way so that she could open the drawer.

"By the way, did you ever find the Death Lily anywhere?" She asked.

A smirk grew on his lips, he watched her mess with a wooden box. "What's that?" Isaac asked, pointing at the box as she picked it up.

She shushed him and unlocked the black latch on the sides. Her heart raced and she set it back down on the desk. Turning towards Isaac, she pointed at the door. "Maybe we should lock the door first."

He frowned, but shrugged before walking toward the door and examining it. "And yeah, it took me a while, but I found the Death Lily planted just past the gardens. Before going down the hill to the field it should be right by a North Star bush. It has three white petals and a long stem. You can't miss it." He paused and jiggled the door handle. "I don't think—" He lifted his hand. She heard a click, and then watched as he stood to his full height. "There. It's locked."

Valeria sighed and met his brown eyes through the darkness. "Watch the bookcase." She nodded her head to the wall on her left, where the blue book had fallen earlier. She would have to find the Death Lily another time. The mysterious box and bookcase was far more interesting at the moment.

Isaac raised his eyebrows and strode closer to the wall.

Hesitantly, she clasped the top of the box, and opened the lid. Inside was a thick, steel, detailed key with vines wrapped around the handle.

"This wasn't here before." She whispered.

As she examined the key and held it closer to the firelight above Isaac's shoulder, she ignored the sound of him pulling on the blue book inside the bookcase. That was until the entire case swung open, and revealed a dark hidden passage. Valeria tightened her grip on the key and hurried over to Isaac.

Together they peered inside, bones rattled with nerves.

The firelight flickered between the both of them, before flashing away and flying down the unlit staircase.

Valeria and Isaac shared a glance before he licked his lips and followed the fading light. Not a word was spoken when she gulped and went after him.

"I suppose this is what you had to show me?" Isaac murmured ahead, farther down the steps.

She huffed when she nearly knocked her head against the rigid stone ceiling. The path was narrow and ruined. She thanked the Gods that she decided to wear her brown night shoes instead of her daily heels.

"You could say so. I didn't know that opening the box would reveal an entire hidden passageway, but I guess that's better than finding a boring safe in the wall."

"You didn't know?"

"No." She replied. "And look, there's a key."

She tried her best to reach forward for him. He stopped on the stairs and felt for the key in her hand. "It was in the box?"

With a nod, she forgot he couldn't see her as they reached the bottom of the staircase. "Yes. It wasn't there before. I wonder if the gamerunner returned it. And what it might unlock down here?"

Valeria and Isaac looked both ways down each separate hallway, before they saw a trickle of light around the corner to their right.

"This way." Isaac said. He stepped carefully over the gaping cracks in the rocky floor and hunched his back in order to avoid a sharp stone jutting out of the ceiling. "Watch your head."

They rounded the corner and came upon a clear wide space. Her eyes landed on the firelight as it danced across the room in front of a long oval shaped piece of furniture with a dirty tan cloth thrown over it.

"What is it doing?" Isaac asked, wandering around the vacant space, skimming his fingers across old dusty desks and tables.

Valeria refocused her eyes on the flame, instead of looking for a keyhole. She trudged toward the light, doing her best to avoid tripping. And watched as the flame flew up and down, side to side. More anxiously—more quickly as she got closer.

"I think it's trying to show us something." She muttered.

Isaac's footsteps sounded closer as he walked up beside her. They watched the fire dance around for a few seconds before she reached and pulled the tan cloth away from the tall piece of furniture. The fire light blazed a bright white before dashing away, bashing into the wall, and flying back. It stopped just above Isaac's head.

He shook his head and sighed. "This thing is wild."

But Valeria didn't hear him, she was looking back at herself through the large antique body mirror. She stepped closer to it, nearly brushing her nose against the mirror before extending her arm and touching a finger to its thick glass.

A small jolt of pain ran up her arm and into her bloodstream. She jumped back with a curse and grabbed at her shoulder.

"What? What happened?" Isaac worried.

"It shocked me." She winced.

"Could it be static? Or no?"

She drew her bottom lip into her mouth before dropping her arm. "Maybe."

Afraid to touch the glass again, Valeria ran her emerald eyes across every inch of the mirror. Taking in the detail of the wooden swirls, and sharp edges of its corners until her curious gaze landed on an oddly shaped hole at the top of the frame.

"Look." She whispered to Isaac and pointed without touching it again.

Isaac inhaled and eyes widened. "The key. Try it." He urged.

He didn't have to tell her twice. She was already sliding the steel key into the hole before he could finish.

They both took a step back before she could turn the key, because something shuddered and awakened from inside the mirror. The glass became black and murky. It called to her. Repeated her name several times before she closed her eyes and finally turned the key.

"What in the Dead Gods—" Isaac gaped at the world that sat in front of him.

When Valeria opened her eyes, a void of colors greeted her through the mirror.

Her chest ached and burned. She inhaled the smell of burnt flesh before covering her nose and squinting through the brightness.

"What is that?" Isaac asked and grabbed at her arm. With his other hand, he slowly reached toward the mirror.

Valeria slapped his hand down. "Don't touch it."

"It's—" Isaac tried to say, sounding utterly confused. "It's Flynn."

"What?" She asked and widened her gaze. He was seeing Flynn? She was only seeing colors.

"He's inside. He's trying to tell me something."

"Isaac, don't touch the mirror. We don't know what it is."

But her words fell flat when he quickly—like a bolt of lightning, moved his arm and touched his fingers to the mirror. Valeria gasped when his brown eyes rolled to the back of his head. They glazed over, looking like a cloudy gray sky. She watched as the palm of his hand melted into the swirl of colors. It swallowed his dark skin up, then stopped once it reached his elbow. Isaac's head fell back.

Valeria screamed.

She yanked on his arm, snapped her fingers in his face and tried to shove him back. "You idiot, Isaac!" She yelled.

For ten entire minutes, Valeria tried and tried, unrelenting to give up on pulling Isaac out of the mirror. The colors finally vanished, and it was then black and murky again. The blackness threatened to burst through the frame and roll toward her feet, but she only slunk to the floor and waited.

Waited and waited for Isaac to be pulled back into consciousness.

She could not get him to budge. Whatever that creature was saying to him through the mirror, whether it was really Flynn or something else, she hoped it would hurry.

Valeria rested her head in her hands as she closed her eyes and listened for anything. Everything was so dark, too dark. With the firelight refusing to leave Isaac's side, she had nothing to light her way if she wanted to take a look around.

So she sat, and breathed through her nose.

Her ear twitched when something splattered on the floor in front of her. Head pounding, and restlessness tugging at her eyes, she chose to ignore the noise.

"*Valeria.*" Her name echoed around the room, sounding from directly in front of her.

Her breath caught in her throat and her heart started to race.

"*Valeria.*" The voice called again.

Gently, she lifted her head and looked straight up at the now darkly colored room that was inside the mirror. She choked back a gasp and quickly moved to her feet.

"Hello?" She asked, peering into the mirror. Hesitant to touch it.

A voice, strange and deep, wove its way through the glass and into her ears. "*He's okay.*" The man said. "*Your friend. He will be fine. Just give him a moment.*"

"What are you doing with him?" Anger seeped from her tone. She was entirely exhausted. If she had known that the adventure into the passageway would lead to this, she would have never taken Isaac with her.

The voice was filled with entertainment when it replied. "*I'm doing nothing with him. I'm here to speak with you.*"

"What?"

"*Don't act so surprised. You touched the glass, didn't you? You're the one who called me here.*" It purred.

She examined the room, letting her mind absorb every last detail possible in case she were to ever enter a space like it. "Who are you?"

Or rather, what are you? She wanted to add.

Her eyes lingered on the black and white photo over the wide desk. It was of an oddly familiar man with black hair, and tan skin. His eyes seemed to be staring at her through the framed mirror. She would have believed it moved if it weren't for the voice that filtered into her ears, distracting her.

"I can't tell you just yet."

"Why?"

When she blinked, the picture of the man above the desk was gone. She narrowed her eyes and tried to look closer. Had it fallen off of the wall?

"Because you have much to do. Much to focus on." Valeria held in her curse and wanted to kick at the damned mirror, when it spoke again. *"Win the Game of Lords, Valeria. Learn the secrets of the kingdom, and take it down. Take it down. Take it down."*

Her mind scrambled and the frame went black again. The murkiness seeped from the edges of the mirror, and she jolted back.

What in the lords just happened?

"Come back." She shouted, while gripping the back of Isaac's cloak. Hoping the blackness wouldn't drip out and pull him farther into the mirror. "What do you mean take it down?"

There was no reply, only the sound of the blackness dripping onto the rigid stones beneath their feet.

"Take. It. Down." The voice rasped one last time.

Too quickly, Isaac's head fell forward and his hands dropped from the mirror.

"Isaac?"

His back moved up and down as he breathed. He waited a moment to speak, then after shaking his head, he turned around. Eyes wide and wild, breath heavy and uneven.

Isaac's nostrils flared. "We should get some sleep."

Valeria stepped back, surprised and gaped. "Isaac, tell me what happened."

He shrugged and walked past her. "It doesn't matter." He drew in a slow breath, hesitant to say anything else before he spoke, "We need to get back to our rooms though. We've been down here for a while."

Before she could argue and make him stay so that he could tell her everything, he was already rushing down the ruined passageway and back up the stairs.

What had he seen? What had he been told?

The questions filled her restless mind all throughout the night before she finally fell asleep in her bed.

16

The white diamond handle of the dagger dug into Valeria's ankle as she walked past the gardens and toward the hillside that overlooked the field.

The moon was the only light that led to the white plant that she expected to find on the edge of a large North Star bush. Valeria's heart skipped when she leaned over and spotted it on the other side of the brush closest to the hill. She plucked the single flower from its stem and the petals fell apart, landing on the grass at her feet.

"*Lords.*" She gasped and picked the three petals up before shoving them into the pocket of her gown. Without a second thought, she turned and pocketed the stem as well.

As Valeria lifted her gaze toward the gardens, a large dark figure lunged and tackled her to the ground.

She kicked and screamed, but nothing she did made her attacker remove their weight.

"Stay quiet!" A voice from farther away shouted with a hush.

Valeria bit her lip and opened her eyes, trying to identify the shadows above her. But it was too dark, and the two figures had black masks over their heads. All she could see were their beady eyes looking down at her.

The man that was sitting on her lower abdomen put his weight on both of her arms while the other man grabbed her ankles and held her down so that she couldn't move.

She was trapped.

"What are you doing?" She tried to wiggle her way free, but they were quick to elbow her in the rib. She choked on a sob. "Stop! Let me go!"

A hand clamped over her mouth.

All she could do was watch as the masked man moved his other hand to his side and pulled out a shiny dagger. Valeria's eyes widened in fear. She bit at his palm, but the man only grew angrier.

He pressed his hand harder against her jaw until her teeth were cutting into her lips. A muffled cry escaped her throat.

"The more you fight, the longer it's going to take. Let us make it quick, girly." His dark eyes latched onto hers before he whipped the knife behind his head and readied to swing it at her scratchy throat.

She screamed, bucked, kicked, and bit at his hand. The other masked man that was holding her ankles cursed and stomped on her leg, only making her scream louder.

As the dagger came barreling down toward her neck, Valeria closed her eyes and halted her breath. She froze and readied for a quick death.

If she was going to die, she wasn't going to look at the man killing her. She was going to look at the sky. The stars. The moon. Purples and blues mixed and rolled together across the vast plain of the deep, watery sky. A flock of crows flew above just as the dagger began its descent down to her throat.

Valeria always loved the night, but now she despised it.

When the dagger was merely a foot away from her throat, the pressure and weight of the men disappeared off of her body. She dropped her gaze from the sky and hastily shuffled onto her feet.

Both of the men stood with their backs facing her. Their spines straightened to attention, and then as she almost fell back on her hands again, they began to run straight for the hillside.

When they were gone, Valeria stood still as stone. Her bones rattled and shook before she rubbed her arms and turned back for the gardens.

She'd almost died.

Valeria wanted to kick herself for giving up so easily, and why had those men suddenly run away? What had frightened them to do so?

Before she could even take another step, a shadow appeared from behind a bush. She jumped and reached for the dagger in her boot.

Ready to fight back this time.

Although, when she spotted familiar messy blonde hair and sparkling blue eyes, she released a breath and slumped her shoulders. She would have kissed him for being her possible savior if it weren't for the angry look on his sharp handsome face.

She flickered a glance to the hillside and gulped.

"Did you happen to see any of that?"

Flynn trudged closer, letting her examine the dark look in his narrowed eyes. "I did."

Valeria matched his expression and moved a foot away from him. "And you didn't bother to help?"

"I did." He repeated.

Sneering, she jabbed a finger over her shoulder and asked, "Why did they run away from you? Why were they so frightened?"

He tilted his head, and a sinister smirk bloomed on his full pink lips. "Make an alliance with me and I'll tell you."

Valeria scoffed, but then she recalled how he had technically saved her from certain death. How he had protected Isaac in the forest.

Then again, could she truly trust him? At the end of all the games, it would come down to only one winner. Flynn already had a likely chance of winning. How could she make an alliance with someone like him? Someone who could backstab her at any possible moment?

"No." She finally answered.

Flynn's growing smirk fell. He shoved his hands into his pockets and flicked a curious look over her shoulder. "What were you doing out here, anyway?"

Valeria reached into her pocket only to realize that it was empty. Sighing, she turned around and found the petals of the Death Lily laying in the grass where she was tackled. They must have fallen out while she was kicking and screaming. A bumpy line of chills ran up her spine.

She would have died if Flynn didn't follow her.

"For these." Her voice shook as she tried to sound nonchalant. She reached down and picked the petals up before placing them back into her ripped skirt.

Flynn lifted a brow. "Crumpled up petals?" She nodded and watched a smile tug at his upper lip. "Why do you need them?"

With a stutter, she lied, "They're my favorite."

Snagging a glance at her rumpled dress pocket, he released a breath through his nose and walked toward her. "Do you always pick your favorite flowers at midnight?"

Valeria huffed. *Why was he being so frustrating?* She longed to go back to her room, where she was safe and no one would attack her. At least she hoped no one would.

"As a matter of fact, yes. Why? Is that a problem for you?" She shoved past, bumping into his shoulder and stomped her way into the garden. His feet crunched in the gravel behind her as he followed.

He was always following her.

"Not a problem." He muttered. "Just curious as to why it's a dragon's favorite element? Is there something you know that you're not telling me?"

She thought her pulse stopped for a beat, but she swallowed a breath and continued through the castle doors. "No."

Before she could make it to the stairs, Flynn grabbed her wrist and swung her to the wall. Trapping her between his arms, he leaned over her smaller stature.

Valeria flinched and glared into his darkened eyes. "Tell me what you know."

She struggled to get away from him, but he didn't budge. "You're starting to sound like Lance." He growled and only slightly leaned away. Although, his eyes remained locked on hers, unrelenting to her cold gaze. "I don't know anything." She yanked at his wrist. "*Stop.*"

He pressed closer, dropping an arm to her side. Close enough that she could almost feel his breath skim against her cheeks as he said, "You're lying."

"Flynn." She warned, tilting her head off the wall to deepen her stare. "Let. Me. *Go.* I've had enough of this tonight."

Quickly, he removed his gaze from hers. Flynn glanced at the skirt of her gown before he reached into her pocket and plucked a single petal.

When she stepped away, he didn't try to stop her. She swallowed and examined the white petal in his palm before hurrying up the stairs.

When she reached the top, Flynn's icy stare melted into the back of her neck. She could feel it the entire way to her door, until finally, she closed and locked it behind her.

It took a few minutes for him to enter his room across the hall. When he did, Valeria fell back on her bed and rubbed at the chills on her arms until they were gone.

She made a mental note to give one of the petals to Isaac eventually.

Hopefully, one petal would be enough for a dragon to spare her life.

17

The second ball of the Game of Lords had started, and with it, brought the looming second trial that would begin at sunrise the next morning.

Valeria entered the ballroom looking as if she were a princess from the forest. Jacky designed her gown with a tan lace material that clung to Valeria's fair skin. The bell sleeves flowed out past her fingertips, while growing vines swept over her shoulders and swiveled their way down into a puddle of green at her feet. Like snakes, they slithered and looped around her body, complimenting the slight curve of her waist.

She came to a stop in the middle of the threshold beneath the tall ballroom doors. Eyes seemed to watch and stare, taking in her second appearance of the official games.

Valeria felt her skin flush as she met a few wandering eyes. Then she spotted Isaac, who was smiling her way. She swept the gown into her hands and ushered over to him.

"Lovely as always." He muttered into a glass full of a strange pink liquid.

Valeria ignored the compliment and furrowed her brows at his drink. "What is that?"

Isaac swallowed his sip and offered the glass. "Some kind of juice. I'm not sure... but it's sweet. And quite delicious." She nudged it back to him and he frowned before taking another swig. "Why is it that your Help dresses you in something elegant every day, while mine has me wearing the same pairs of vest and jeans?"

She chuckled and scanned her eyes over his casual tan vest and white tunic shirt. "You'll have to make a complaint to your Help."

"I'd offer to switch vests, but I'm afraid that yours might be too tight of a fit for me." Flynn piped in as he stepped beside Valeria. She grimaced when he bumped into her shoulder. And he failed to hide his growing smirk with an arrogant wink.

She scoffed and grabbed the glass from Isaac's hand before taking a much needed gulp.

"Thanks." Isaac smiled at Flynn, but frowned when he threw a wary glance toward Valeria.

She pursed her lips and raised the stolen glass. Before she could take another drink, Isaac whisked it away and clicked his tongue.

Valeria narrowed her eyes before returning her annoyed glare onto Flynn. "What are you doing here?"

Feigning a frown, he shrugged. "What do you mean? It's the second ball. Of course I'm here."

She shook her head. "No, I mean, what are you doing over here with us?" She asked, motioning between herself and Isaac.

Flynn rolled his eyes. "I wanted to spend some time with my friends. Is that so wrong?"

Valeria could see the flicker of entertainment in Isaac's eyes as he glanced between them.

"I think you're confused." She ignored Isaac and gave Flynn her complete attention. "We're not friends. Not after last night."

A small, urgent voice flickered into her head. *But he saved you, Valeria. Give him a chance.*

She pressed her lips together and shoved the intruding thoughts down, never letting them resurface as she watched Flynn's eyes grow brighter with entertainment. Yes, maybe he did save her. But he also used her fear and shock to try and pry answers out of her. He tried to make her feel small, and maybe he achieved that in a way.

For a moment last night he had reminded her of Lance. And she hated it.

Flynn took a step toward Isaac. "Maybe you and I aren't, but Isaac might be? Right?"

She darted her eyes to Isaac, who was still looking at her. His gaze was worried, but slowly lightened with Flynn's words. "Yeah, man. Of course we're friends." Then, when Flynn glanced away for a short second, Isaac shot her a look that said he would be questioning her later.

Valeria only sighed and patted Isaac's arm before walking toward the drink table.

She grabbed a cup for herself and started to spoon the acclaimed mysterious golden liquid out of the dazzling punch bowl when a roaring voice echoed against the tall, curved walls.

"Silence!" The gamerunner's voice filled her ears, "The king has prepared a speech for tonight. Please give him your full respect and undivided attention."

The dancing and lively chatter came to a halt when the king tapped a finger on his throne and stood to his feet. Long blonde hair shimmered underneath the candle light and golden crown as he narrowed his eyes and licked his lips.

"Tomorrow the second trial will be one of courage, strength, endurance, and speed. You will question the person you once thought you were. You might even come to realize the kind of people you thought were your allies. Do not fret, as this is simply a part of the games. I wish to speak with no one tonight, as I do not care for the theatrics. Tomorrow, I will bring the survivors face to face with myself, my children, and the past five winners of the Game of Lords. Seeing as there will be our strongest contestants left. Enjoy yourselves tonight, for this may be your last one alive." He flicked his wrist and four of the officials stepped up beside him, then he sauntered out of the room and left the ball.

Valeria's jaw was locked in place. Her mind racing. *What was going to happen tomorrow?*

She watched as the prince glanced around the room with a look of misery written all over his chiseled face. He pursed his pink lips and muttered something that she couldn't hear, or even make out what was said. Nobody could, given that he was sitting by himself at the front of the ballroom.

The princess glanced his way before saying something to him and then slyly walking off.

Her eyes traced Princess Helena's form before she focused back on the prince, whose gaze was now locked on hers.

Valeria held back a gasp and swallowed. His eyes glimmered for a moment before he shifted in his seat and leaned back with a frown.

"Go talk to him." Isaac pushed. Her hand snapped to her chest and she let out a gasp of surprise. Isaac bit back a chuckle and pressed on her arm.

Flynn was gone from his side, possibly hiding in a dark corner somewhere. She didn't care, nor did she let herself pay attention to the growing pressure in her chest that filled with shaky adrenaline. Why did she care where Flynn was? She didn't want any part of him, nor his offering alliance. She didn't even want him around. She had enough of his mood swings, given his anger last night that caused him to trap her against a wall.

She needed to stay far, far away from him... It was for her own good.

Valeria dropped her hand and smoothed it across her gown as she flicked a hesitant look toward the prince. "What should I say? How does one even talk to a prince?" She followed Isaac's amused gaze and stared at Princess Helena's brother. "He already looks so irritated being here. I feel as if I'll only make him more upset just being in his presence."

Isaac grabbed her trembling hand and gave it a comforting squeeze. "It's worth a shot. Look, if any of the women here could pull his attention away from the ball, it's you. Trust me, go talk to him."

She inhaled deeply and centered her thoughts around winning and finding a way out of the games. She needed to live. She *had* to live.

With another slight push in his direction, Valeria was walking toward the prince. She forced a smile when she threw a glance over her shoulder at Isaac. He lifted both of his thumbs and nodded his head with a gentle, yet playful smirk of his own.

"Okay." she whispered to herself. "Flirt. I can flirt." There were only a few boys back in the Court Of Wind that had ever captured her attention, and she flirted with many of them—even started a short-lived relationship for a week or two.

But a prince?

Valeria swallowed again as she neared his stormy presence.

The energy in the ballroom shifted as she stopped in front of his throne. Slowly, as if he were lifting his gaze in annoyance, the prince examined her gown, hair, and when he was done, finally her eyes.

Without realizing, Valeria clamped her hands together in front of her. She shifted on her feet until she was comfortable under his judging eyes. Then she bowed.

There was a slight shake in her knees as she wobbled back into a stand. "My prince." Her words were laced with a nervous exhale.

"Valeria Rox." The prince drawled while leaning forward in his seat. His dark eyes filled with something exciting. Something that racked her nerves. Something new.

"I hate to question, but may I ask how you know my name?"

He smirked. "I'd never forget the face, nor the name of the girl that ruined one of my sister's precious gowns."

Her smile wavered as the words left his mouth. "Yes, of course... About that, I'm so sorry. I should've been paying more attention—"

The prince sat even further up in his seat and flicked his hand away. "Oh, don't bother. If anything, I should be thanking you. Helena deserved it."

"*Oh.*" She struggled to find words and bit her lip.

A common sibling teasing, yet she couldn't help the spark of comfort that eased a bit of the tension in her neck. Sure they were royalty, but of course, they were still human. Well, mostly human. Were they immortal like their father?

Valeria shook her head and tried to focus on what she was here for. Flirt. She needed to flirt.

Before she could make a ridiculous attempt at a compliment, the prince stood and extended his hand. He was much taller than she anticipated, nearly an entire foot towering over her. "Come. Let's find somewhere else to chat. I feel that if I spend another minute in this room, I'll go insane."

She grabbed his hand and tried to hide the rise of her brows. She turned toward Isaac for a split second, just long enough to see his excited expression.

The prince was warm, and his grip was light. Not controlling as if he were entitled and took whatever he wanted, and when he wanted. Not like she had expected.

Nothing ever was.

The prince took them through hall after hall, then shortly after their walk, they entered a room.

She gaped up at the high ceiling and glass frames surrounded the painted windows. He dropped her hand before trudging toward a set of tall double doors. They swung open and let the cool night air blast a bundle of chills up her arms.

"It's my favorite room in the estate." The prince said from underneath the threshold. His back was turned, and she watched as he stepped out onto the balcony.

Valeria was behind him in seconds. Hesitant to speak. Afraid that she might say something to upset him.

The entire estate could be seen from where they stood out on the balcony. The colorful gardens, wide crystal lake, dark forest, snowy mountains, and more. A hint of a smile tugged at her lips. It was extraordinary. She might've thought her sister would love to spend a weekend at Azrael estate, when she remembered why she was even there in the first place.

To win, or to die. There was no way out of it, not unless she could make the man, whose eyes were currently tracing the dips and lines on her face, fall in love with her. When she looked up to meet his intimidating gaze, he was frowning.

"Is something wrong?" She asked.

He shook his head. "It's just appalling, you know? How my father can kill anyone that he pleases. How he can just take someone away from their lives and throw them into a game that was created to kill and feed the enemies." She tried to search for words, but her mind ran blank. He had taken them right out of her mouth.

"You—you're against the games?" She asked.

The prince threw his hands into the air. "Of course I am! Whoever isn't, is not any better than my wretched father." Valeria leaned against the railing. Her heart was racing with the prince's angry tone. Suddenly, to her astonishment, the prince reached out and pressed a gentle palm against her shoulder. "I don't mean to frighten you, truly I don't. I've just... It's just that..." He dragged a hand down his face. "I hate that there's so much to unload, and so much to keep hidden. That's all."

She faltered while trying to take a step back. Only watching as he stared down at her, eagerly waiting for a response.

Releasing a breath, she asked, "Is there anything I can do to help?"

He only sighed and looked away. Facing the vast lake as he rubbed his palms together. "No. Not really... Not yet at least."

"Oh." Confusion racked against her already disturbed nerves. She needed to flirt with him, but his tense rant had sort of ruined the mood. *How could it be possible?* He was a ball of tension, more wound up than her. "Would you like anything to drink?"

Sending her a curious look, the prince ignored her question and simply stated, "My father doesn't even know I'm to be wed."

She choked on her saliva. "I—I—"

Holding a hand up, he stopped her rambling. "I trust you to do what you wish with the information. My father is blind to the fact, because..." He paused and drew out a long breath, as if the admission eased his temper by the slightest. "Well, simply because I am engaged to a man."

He held a hand out to stop her short-lived stumble. "Woah there. Are you okay?"

Was she alright? She was chatting with the prince, who was giving her insight into his life when she had just met him. Of course she wasn't alright!

"I'm—I'm confused... Why are you telling me this?"

There was a moment of hesitance in his eyes, before he rolled his shoulders and dropped his chin. "I needed to get it off of my chest. I needed a contestant to know, and I saw the way you were looking at me. I saw how you didn't want to speak to me, and how you judged me the same way you judge my father." He stopped. Pressing his lips together, he finished with, "But I am not like him. I will *never* be like him."

Valeria inhaled and swallowed. "I won't tell anyone, Your Highness."

He gave her half of a smile. "It's Luther."

"What?"

"My name. It's Luther."

She and Prince Luther spoke for a few more minutes before she eagerly excused herself from the advantageous conversation.

Valeria stumbled out of the courtyard and stepped onto the embedded rocks that led her across the grassy slopes of the earth.

Isaac was probably somewhere with Flynn, and she didn't bother to search for them with the new information that she had just been given. It felt as if her former plans were falling apart all over again, just to be slowly rebuilt.

She could have run away. She could have left everything behind if she knew a way out of Azrael estate, but she didn't. She and the other contestants were stranded in the middle of nowhere, and even if she did try to run away, the officials would hunt her down and kill her. Or worse; feed her to a dragon.

Neither of those options were ideal. She would have a better chance at winning the games than attempting to flee from them.

As she dragged her feet and slowly moved across the outside walls of the estate, Valeria heard a hushed womanly voice. Seduction weaved through the brisk evening air as the woman murmured something underneath her breath.

Valeria tried listening to what was being said when her skirt got caught on a branch from a nearby tree. She yanked at the lace material of her gown, ripping it to shreds before tripping and almost tumbling forward. The woman went silent at the sudden noise.

She caught the sound of retreating footsteps before a faraway door slammed shut somewhere on the other side of the castle.

"Valeria?" Flynn appeared from around the shadowed corner. His lips swollen, and ocean eyes shimmering underneath the moonlight. "What are you doing out here?"

From her ruined gown and game-breaking conversation with the prince earlier, Valeria's annoyance grew further at the sight of his disheveled hair and unbuttoned pants. "Might I ask *who* were you doing out here?" She bit out.

"I asked first."

She scoffed and straightened her spine.

If she was a mess, she didn't care. It's not like Flynn would when he was clearly messing around with someone else.

"I needed fresh air."

He nodded, then frowned when he caught her glancing at his pants. He furrowed his brows and chuckled when he noticed that they were unbuttoned. "I was chatting with an old friend." He said, zipping them up.

Valeria rolled her eyes. "Having fun with Princess Helena?" The words tasted bitter on her tongue. *Why?* Why did the princess's name sting against her mouth? She pressed the confusion down and crossed her arms.

Flynn smirked and leaned against the tree that Valeria's gown had been stuck to. "Someone sounds a little jealous."

"I'm not." She kicked at a blooming daisy with her lie, "Besides, I was with the prince. Why would I be jealous?"

He left her question unanswered as he prowled closer. "The prince? How was he? Did he meet your expectations?"

She growled and took a step back. "Maybe he did. Maybe he didn't. It's none of your business, anyway." When she turned to leave, Flynn latched onto her arm.

"Wait. Just hold on." He turned her around to face him again. "Yes, I was with Helena, but you're right. None of that matters." He stepped back from the heat of her growing glare. "Listen, do you want to survive the second trial tomorrow or not?"

Instantly, she dropped her attitude, and widened her eyes. "Why? Do you know something?"

He refused to answer, but she could see it in his crystal gaze. The teasing and jeering at each other had vanished so suddenly. Whatever Flynn knew, she wanted to learn. She was desperate for any bit of information that could help her survive at this point.

"I'll tell you... but only if you agree to one thing." Valeria knew where this was going, so she turned on her heels and began to walk away when he said, "You won't be able to protect Isaac tomorrow, and you won't live through the first five minutes if you don't know what you're facing."

Valeria stopped and blinked at the ground. She turned around and faced Flynn again. "Fine. Tell me."

Flynn smirked and stepped forward, "Take my hand."

"What?" She crossed her arms. "No."

He pressed closer, shadows sliding against his face as he dipped his chin. "I'm not telling you anything until you shake my hand and form this alliance."

She pressed her lips into a straight line before dropping her arms and letting out an exasperated sigh. "*Fine.*" Then, swiftly she lifted her hand into his cold one and shook. *Anything to protect Isaac, remember?*

"Perfect." He said. Smiling as if he had won—as if he had sealed the deal on her soul.

Later that night, after Jacky left the room, Valeria stripped from her elegant gown, threw her nightdress over her shoulders and snuck out into the hall. From there, she tiptoed past three other contestant rooms and gently closed herself inside of the bathing room.

It was when she let herself sink into the freezing cold water that she remembered what she had agreed to.

In order to keep herself and Isaac safe, she accepted an alliance with Flynn. The decision may have cost or granted her her life in the games. But it didn't matter anymore. What's done was done, and Valeria closed her eyes, held her breath, and sank into the prickling, biting waters.

She didn't leave the tub for the next five hours. She needed as much practice that she could get before the second trial started in the morning.

18

R ight in front of her, lining the training room walls, was the giant
tank she had looked at every day for the past week.

Valeria thought it was only there for looks. If she would have known
that it was for the second trial, maybe she would have been practicing
every day. But no, there it was. Taunting her, waves thrashing and threatening to break the solid glass that contained it.

Flynn told her the second trial required holding your breath for an
extensive amount of time, all while swimming and struggling your way
to the other side, where, in Flynn's words, "A land hidden far beneath
the estate thrives."

She looked at Flynn, who stood on the boxed platform. The contestants were elevated ten feet above the training rooms floors and facing
the tank. He was already staring at her, a grim expression on his face.

Lance stood between them, his arms crossed and appearing unbothered as the king and his men marched in from the wide double doors.

Valeria heaved a sigh and tried to shake the nerves away.

Doing so caused Lance to snap his attention toward her with a chuckle. "Nervous?" He snickered. "You should be."

"Enough." Isaac snapped from his position, standing three contestants away.

She watched as he tried his best to lean forward and send Lance a threatening glare.

"It's okay, Isaac." She said, "It's not like he knows what's on the other side of the tank."

With that, Isaac smirked, and Lance growled from beside her.

"You're dead, princess."

She ignored the threatening burn on the side of her face, instead she watched the gamerunner walk up the steps to the platform and stand facing the room.

Only the King of Laterra and his children were here, along with the four lords and the Lady of Wolves.

"Welcome, contestants, to the second trial." The gamerunner began. Valeria noticed his silver hair tied back in a short braid as he flicked a piece of dust from his shoulder. "When the clock strikes six, you have twenty minutes to swim through the tunnels, reach the other side, find the crown, and come back alive." He sounded bored, refusing to meet anyone's eyes as he fixed the cuffs of his blue jacket. "If you don't make it back in twenty minutes, you will be assumed dead, and the hatch of the tank will shut, leaving you trapped inside." He clapped, "Now, with that said, the contestant who arrives with the crown will be awarded an advance. They may choose to keep their award a secret or not."

He went on and on about the rules of the game and even made a whole inspiring speech for the lords and lady. The king rolled his eyes before the gamerunner finally stopped and made his way back down the steps.

Valeria inhaled through her nose and closed her eyes. She did her best to ignore Lance's threats and crude remarks as she relaxed her muscles and focused on breathing.

It would only take one mistake. One mistake, and she could mess up everything. She could drown to death in a few short moments if she didn't prepare and slow her stammering heart.

On the gamerunner's directions, she and the others moved forward and climbed the two steps to the top of the tank. She looked down at the lashing water, just below on the far side of the wall. She could see the tunnel. Her heart began to pound against her sore, aching ribs.

"Gods above, if I go today, send blessings and wealth to my family." The contestant next to Valeria prayed underneath his breath. When he opened his eyes and looked up, she gave him a warm, gentle smile.

She tugged on the tightness of the wet suit she was wearing. It was all black and nearly absorbed the ceiling lights above.

"For your sake, I hope you know how to swim." Lance said.

Valeria bit her bottom lip to keep from causing a scene. If he wanted to threaten her, sure, let him. But she would not give in that easily. After being attacked the other night and almost killed, Valeria would do everything in her power to survive.

She wouldn't let the games take her. She would *not* die.

An alarm blasted throughout the room, and Valeria didn't waste a second. She gulped down a large breath, bent her knees, and dove into the deep, freezing cold waters.

Kicking and clawing her way, Valeria swam farther and farther down. When she opened her eyes, the water felt like needles prickling and stinging her brain, but she didn't give in to the pressure to swim to the surface. There were only twenty minutes on the clock. If she wanted to find the crown and get away from Lance, she would need to keep moving.

The dark tunnel grew larger as she swam closer. She neared it in seconds and grabbed the outside edge to shove herself farther inside.

Only a small trickle of light at the end had her pushing against the walls harder and faster.

A pain shot through her fingers when her nail bent backwards from the stone. She grit her teeth but pushed herself to continue.

When she was a little more than halfway through the tunnel, she felt it—or rather... him.

Lance.

His large hand wrapped around her ankle and he tugged.

Losing her grip on the slippery round walls, bubbles escaped her lips as she let out a watery scream.

He crawled his way up her body at the same time she pulled against the curved walls. She slid back, farther away from the other side. There was only a flicker of Lance's sinister white smile before his fist drove straight into her nose.

Everything moved in slow motion.

Valeria blinked to clear her blurry vision. Lance was already swimming past her, but she didn't let the pain stop her. Her lungs were on fire already, and her chest was hammering against her ribs.

Life was better than death inside the tunnel walls.

So she wouldn't give up. She couldn't.

Valeria reached for her arm strap and pulled out the dagger she had hidden inside the sleeve. She barreled through the tunnel after Lance, who was five feet away from reaching the other side.

Within a minute she was behind him, grabbing his foot before lifting her weaponed hand back and slashing the blade through his ankle.

Scarlett filled her vision. His blood was squirting and filling the clearness of the water as he lashed against the tunnel walls.

Valeria took a chance when she heard his muffled screams through the water. She pushed herself up to the top of the tunnel and shimmied over him, as he was too busy trying to figure out what had just happened.

The light returned in front of her, no longer blocked by Lance's lengthy form.

She quickened her arms, pushing and pushing her way through. Lungs nearly empty, lightheaded, and winded, she emerged from the water and threw herself up onto the grassy dirt above.

With a deep inhale, oxygen filled her tightened lungs.

The tank was below ground rather than above it like it had been on the other side of the tank.

She watched Lance's red hair come through the tunnel and she hopped to her feet.

The other contestants were starting to come through. Water slashed and splashed as three others took off running into the trees.

Valeria shot a glance at the dome ceiling before she tried to run, but it was more of a limping jog. Her hand was splayed over her ribs, mouth ajar, trying to catch her breath. She could already feel a bruise forming where Lance hit her, but ignored the growing pain.

She prayed that Isaac would remain safe with Flynn. If Flynn was speaking the truth last night about protecting Isaac. Isaac was safer with him than with her anyway.

As for the alliance with Flynn, they decided it would be best to spend less time together in front of the others. She didn't want them to know that they were now in an official alliance.

"Just wait until I get my hands on you." Lance clawed his way out of the water.

Valeria winced and ducked behind a tree where she could catch her breath and watch as he examined his sliced open ankle. Snarling, his jaw clenched, Lance wobbled and stood to his full height. Instead of what should have been pain written on his face, there was pure, unrelenting hatred.

He was going to kill her.

Valeria lunged away from the tree, bark biting into her hands as she pushed herself. Just like she did in the Forest of Angels, she ran.

She ran and ran until she couldn't anymore.

Until she couldn't hear the sound of Lance's pounding feet behind her.

Until her head was swimming and her heart was racing.

Pushing through the thick brush, she came upon a live oak tree. Its long branches cascading over the forest were covered in wispy chunks of moss. She ducked underneath and hurried over to the trunk of the tree, noticing sparkles that shimmered and waved as she pressed her hand into the bark.

Rustling sounded from the brush, she crouched behind the tree. Her hands were covered in dirt and sparkles when she leaned against it.

"I know you're over there. Your tracks betray you." Lance's voice was thick and haunted.

Valeria's heart sank into her stomach. She shimmied deeper into the shadows.

His feet appeared through the clearing, limping and clearly in pain. "You best hope your little friends find you before I do." He was close enough to hear his whisper.

Quick and quietly, she stood, then started to climb.

Doing her best to remain silent and hidden behind the tree, but she couldn't help when the stitch of her wetsuit caught on the bark and ripped against the skin on her thigh.

Muffling a cry against her shoulder, she pulled herself up.

Upon reaching the first thick branch, she swung her leg around and hiked herself even higher. She sighed a breath of relief when she successfully remained unheard.

The ground crumpled and thrashed when Lance swung at the brush and thicket. The hint of a glimmer revealed the large dagger in his hands. He was undeniably pissed. A snarl on his lips as he dragged his injured foot behind him and limped back underneath the canopy of trees.

Valeria released a long sigh of relief.

There wasn't a timer or anything to reveal how many minutes had passed, but to play it safe, she gave herself ten minutes until she would make her way back to the other side of the tunnels. So she scooted along the branch until her back was resting against the trunk and looked up at the rounded ceiling.

There were no birds, insects, or any signs of life besides the breathing, sparkly tree that she sat in.

How in the Lords had she gotten here? So far away from home, away from her sister, her father, and Gods, she hated to admit it, her mother.

Anger built in her already aching chest.

Her damned mother had left when she was only a child. She had abandoned Valeria and Lilith, as if there was something more important than her daughters out there in the world.

Valeria clenched her jaw and swallowed. Her head fell back against the bark, and she examined the shimmering green leaves of the oak tree.

She didn't care to look for the crown, besides with the time that had passed while she was running from Lance, looking for it now would only get her killed. Lance was still out there in search of her, and if he got his hands on her, she was keenly aware that it would be her final moment alive.

When she blinked to clear the building of tears in her eyes, she saw it. A dark wooden box hidden in the branches higher up in the tree.

She gasped, carefully balancing her trembling legs. Adrenaline coursing through her veins with the newfound hope of finding the crown in the wooden box.

Her arms tensed in pain after she reached and reached, but could not get a hold of the box.

Thinking quickly, she leaned down, ripped a long stem from the branch she stood on, and swung it at the box above. When that didn't work, she took a deep breath and tried again. This time, she poked underneath until it moved an inch. A smile grew on her face. This was it! She would get the crown and advance in the game.

Another poke at the bottom of the box made it fling from the branch and fumble to the ground beneath her.

The twig went flying from her hand as she threw it. Valeria focused on the box, bent her knees and prepared to jump. That was until skittering stomps ran toward her.

She saw a flash of long black hair. Alexa sprinted from the forest and underneath the branches of the oak tree. She avoided Valeria's watchful eyes, lunging, grabbed the box, tucked it underneath her arm, and zoomed back for the tunnels.

Valeria's mouth opened in shock before she jumped from the branch and landed hard on the dirt where the box had been stolen underneath her. She was light on her feet when she dashed through the brush and disappeared into the trees.

Gods above. She was so close to having the crown in her hands—to having an advantage in the game now that she knew there was no hope in seducing the prince and making him fall in love with her.

Valeria's anger grew swiftly as she sprinted for the water filled tunnels. She would not—*could* not fight Alexa for the crown.

She had given herself ten minutes to get back to the other side of the tank, and that time was up. Now she needed to focus on her limited time and even her ragged breaths, all while avoiding Lance.

The wall of the domed room was a hundred feet away. A long tree branch thwacked Valeria right in the forehead before she almost fell forwards onto her hands. The canopy of leaves was no longer above her, she was out of the forest, the tank was fifteen feet away.

But as she zoomed for the water, others were already lunging into its depths. Her breathing was shortened and lungs grasped for any bits of air that she could suck down.

A glimpse of red caught her eye after she watched Flynn dive into the water and swim toward one of the tunnels.

She reached the edge of the ground, the water splashing up on her covered toes as she sent a momentary glance down the length of the room.

There, twenty feet away, dangling over the water, was Alexa's body.

Valeria held in a scream, staring at the blood gushing from Alexa's throat.

She was dead.

Alexa was dead.

The girl she had grown up with. The girl who had taught her how to dress and style her hair. The girl who had been over at her house every weekend. Lilith's best friend. Her sister's *only* friend.

Tears swelled in her eyes, and this time she let them fall.

She mourned the girl she was before her eyes landed on what was left of her friend's body. Her eyes quickly darted away from the pool of blood that bubbled out of Alexa's throat.

Choking out a sob, she wrapped her arms around herself and her bottom lip trembled.

Lance prowled out of the forest, looking torn and bruised, limping forward.

When Valeria scanned Alexa's limp body one last time—to make sure she was truly gone, she noticed the absence of the brown wooden box she had stolen.

Whoever killed her, whoever it was, had taken the crown.

Valeria inhaled and dove into the water. Her tears warmed her cheeks against the coldness of the icy water.

What felt like two minutes later, Valeria emerged from the water, her hair now unbraided and slicked back as she gasped for breath. Tears were still falling when she hurriedly pulled herself out of the tank.

The king was slowly making his way up the steps, a small frown on his lips when he spotted her stepping out of the water, though it grew into a smile when he noticed the lump and bruise spreading across her forehead where Lance had punched her. He even had the audacity to chuckle when she turned and he saw the torn material of her black wetsuit.

Valeria bit her lip and closed her eyes.

She didn't even get a second to comprehend the sound of Lance pulling himself out of the tank behind her, and how much time had passed when she glanced up and watched Flynn hand the box over to the gamerunner.

The gamerunner smirked when he opened the top, pulled out the silver crown, and placed it on top of Flynn's damp blonde hair.

"The winner of the second trial, Flynn Adler. From the Court of Wind." The gamerunner stepped back and let Flynn bow to the royal audience.

Valeria stomped down the hallway after dinner. Her blood simmered and spiked as she stopped in front of Flynn's room. She raised her fist and was about to knock when the door swung open to reveal a smiling Flynn on the other side.

"Come to declare your unyielding love?"

She shoved past him and kicked the door shut.

Flynn blinked at the door and slowly moved to face her. The smile no longer shining in his crystal blue eyes.

"Did you kill her?" She asked.

Frowning, he stammered back. "What? No—"

Valeria smashed her fist into his chest, but he didn't even flinch. "Don't lie to me!"

She went to swing at him again, but he grabbed her wrist and swung her around so that her back was pressed against the door. "Calm down. I didn't do anything to hurt her, Valeria."

She leaned into his grip with a seething glare, her teeth clenched as she snarled in his face. "I don't believe you."

Flynn tightened his grip. "She was dying—she was in pain, and I saved her from suffering."

A match of bristling fire seared over any rational thoughts when she swung her neck back and tried to smash her head into his.

He moved back with an annoying smirk on his lips. Then, slowly, he lifted his darkened eyes to hers. "We're in an alliance. Learn to trust me when I tell you the truth, whether you don't like it or not. Alexa was dying, she was in pain. She was begging me to kill her. To finish her off so that she wouldn't feel anymore."

No... *no*.

Valeria almost crashed to the floor. Her eyes blurred with unfallen tears. "You killed her." She muttered.

Flynn stepped closer, gentler than before. "I only did what she asked of me."

"You killed her." She repeated, letting the words sink into her gut.

He reached down before drawing his hand back to his side. "I did." He sighed. "I'm sorry."

Ripping her hands away from him, Valeria's thoughts swirled and stirred like crazy. She feared that she might go insane. The tears still longed to fall; the anger was still building, and she kicked at his legs, but Flynn was quick to dodge the blow.

"Stop." He tried. Valeria kicked again with a growl. "Stop, Valeria. Just stop."

She did, but only because of the weakness that filtered in and out of her mind.

Fire built and burned, then the watery, dreadful thoughts put it out like a douse of water in her veins. When she looked up, the match lit again, and then all she wanted to do was claw his eyes out. But she held herself back, calmed her steaming blood, and stared into his blazing eyes.

Maybe she was going crazy after all...

"I will never forget this, Flynn."

All he did was stare, only flinching when his name left her lips. He watched as she straightened her rumpled blue gown and trudged to the door.

Before she turned her back, she made sure to let him see the anger in her eyes. He had to know what he had done—how his actions had affected her. He killed the girl who had been like a sister. The girl who had saved her inside of the Forest of Angels.

Even if he wasn't the one to hurt Alexa first, he was still the one to end her life. She could have made it through the tunnel. He could have helped her back to the other side of the tank.

Instead, he chose selfish victory and took the crown.

PART II

A Game of Betrayal

19

Rain splattered against Valeria's scalp as she stared out at the water, watching it ripple against the wind. The scent of wet soil and crawling insects tickled her nostrils as she sucked in a shaky breath.

Alexa had been on her mind for the past two days. She couldn't stop thinking about her. She couldn't stop thinking about Lilith either. Her sister had two people she loved inside the Game of Lords. What more could she take? What if Valeria didn't make it home? And what if she did?

Valeria dropped her eyes and stepped underneath the willow tree. She didn't want to think anymore—prayed that her brain would turn quiet and she could feel only the calm numbness flowing through her veins.

She'd almost forgotten her presence wasn't alone when the other contestants turned away from the lake and retreated toward the gardens, where they would all meet inside for dinner.

Lance was nowhere in sight. He was still healing from the deep wound on his ankle. As for the others, they were out by the lake for a reason—to remember the lives lost in the last two trials.

Three people died two days ago. Albert Cooper from the Court of Smoke, Jack Garcia from the Court of Wolves, and Alexa.

Alexa.

The lump in her throat thickened. She swallowed, but it remained in place.

When she looked back to watch the few remaining contestants leave, she saw Isaac turn his back. Sadness lined his dark brown eyes. Before she could glance away, she spotted Flynn leaning against the castle wall with his legs crossed.

When he met her gaze, he pushed away and trudged after the others. A moment later, he disappeared around the corner, with Isaac following shortly behind.

The small light in the dark pit of Valeria's chest flickered out. She bit the inside of her cheek and faced the lake, moving to sit down. She wrapped her arms around her legs and stared up at the gray sky, letting the tears fall from her eyes.

The dining room was quiet for dinner. Only four others and Valeria showed up, including Isaac, who sat silently beside her. The candle-light flickered as she stared at the place mat in front of her.

She didn't know how to speak. Usually around Isaac, she was able to fake her wellbeing, but now, after everything... How could she?

"He didn't want to win," Isaac muttered, staring down at his folded hands.

"What?"

"Flynn didn't want to win the second trial, Valeria." She remained quiet. He continued, "We talked, Flynn and I. He seemed stressed—so stressed. The night after you left his room, I found him in the halls. He looked miserable."

Him? Miserable?

Valeria scoffed. "He's not the one that lost Alexa, Isaac."

"I know, but—"

"No. Look, I will be in this alliance with him, but that does not mean that I have to get along with him. You don't know—no one does. I grew up with Alexa. Though she was distant toward me here, it was to keep a target off her back. She was basically a sister to me, Isaac. So I don't care to hear about what Flynn was going through. Not now, and maybe not ever. Is there anything else you'd rather talk about other than the man that killed my friend?"

It was an outburst, and it felt good to unleash it. Although, guilt gnawed at her insides. She felt awful that her anger and frustration had been taken out on Isaac, but she couldn't hold it in anymore. She didn't want to hear anything kind or thoughtful about Flynn.

She needed time, *lots* of time, before she could even think about him.

Isaac slammed his palms on the table in front of him. The metal shook beneath her elbows and she leaned back, eyes widened, and looked at him.

His eyebrows were furrowed in frustration when he shot a glare at her temple. "You're not the only one losing loved ones, Valeria. You sit here and act like you're the only one playing the games." He gestured to himself. "Look at me!" The two contestants at the other end of the table lifted their eyes to listen. "I may be young, and yes—I'll most likely die here, but you—you have a chance... and I'm tired of *everything*. I'm tired of you and Flynn arguing. Please, while I'm still alive, try to get along with him... Alexa is dead. I'm sorry, it's awful, truly. But you can live, you can go back to your family and let your sister know in person instead of from some stranger through the mail. I won't get to do that."

She didn't know what to say. Her own frustration had died down, overtaken by his. She hadn't known, she hadn't realized...

"Isaac..."

He raised his hands and scooted back in his chair. "It's fine." He muttered, looking down. "I'm gonna go. I have to train early in the morning."

Valeria sat wordlessly as she watched him stalk for the courtyard doors and leave the room just as three servants entered.

They examined the nearly empty table with frowns that resembled her own. Clearing their thoughts, the servants approached the table and placed a plate of mashed potatoes and steak in front of Valeria and the two others.

Her eyes strayed from Isaac's empty seat. She had been selfish... so selfish to not think about his situation and only herself—to unload all of her baggage onto him when all he was trying to do was stick up for his only other friend in the game.

He was terrified.

His mother and baby brother Michael, he wouldn't see them again.

She only felt emptier as everything piled on top of her shoulders. The weight of her fear, pain, and loss was dragging her down, straight into the hollow part of her chest.

She swallowed before gathering a plate into her hands and stood from the table.

After finding a few lingering servants in the hallway, she asked one of them to bring her plate up to Isaac's room. They agreed once they saw the shaking of her fingers and didn't want their perfectly cooked food to go to waste.

Valeria strolled down the hillside, dressed in a silver nightgown and cream cloak thrown over her shoulders, when she suddenly slipped on a wet patch of grass. Luckily, she caught herself before falling the rest of the way down the steep hill.

When she reached the bottom and stood on the field, only the mountains and trees welcomed her far off in the distance. She wondered what it would be like to escape. She would travel north, up into the lush green mountains, past the forest, and live the rest of her days running from the king and his officials.

Unrealistic. She wouldn't last a week. She had never been hunting, she couldn't properly handle a sword or dagger, and with no food or water, meant a slow death. At least it would be better than dying here, in this death field.

She needed to build strength if she wanted to live. Perhaps she would go to the training room tomorrow and apologize to Isaac, and then they could train together. Only if he would accept her apology.

Valeria huffed and rolled her eyes at herself. Blowing up on Isaac didn't mean she was wrong, but it wasn't right to do it to him. If anything, Flynn deserved her angry words and miserable presence. Still, she needed a day or two without him in it.

Upon hearing the whooshing wind, and snapping twigs from the gated Forest of Angels, Valeria turned and rushed up the hillside before heading for her room quarters.

Tomorrow will be a new day. She could ignore the hammering thoughts about Alexa and Lilith for the remaining time, and focus on the next trial with Isaac.

20

T he next morning, Isaac stood on a black mat in the far right corner of the training room when he swung at Flynn's face, who dodged the blow fluently. Of course he was here. He was the one training Isaac after all.

She stood in front of the entryway, watching Flynn send a sharp uppercut toward Isaac, who was too slow to block the blow. Flynn stopped before he would've actually hit Isaac's jaw. He dropped his arms with a frown.

That's when Valeria realized he wasn't wearing any sort of protective gear for his chest and torso. Because he was shirtless. She didn't know why her cheeks flushed, or why her heart had begun to race, but she didn't like it.

Isaac shrugged his shoulders before shaking his hands and bouncing back and forth on his toes.

Flynn separated his legs, reading himself into a fighting position. He said something to Isaac before he moved his body in a slow-like motion. The muscles in his back rippled, and she may have stared and grown flustered at the sight when he paused and shot a stern glance at Isaac.

That was enough. Valeria removed her eyes from Flynn's athletic form and moved swiftly across the room. She was standing beside them a few seconds later, feeling dumbstruck when they both stopped training and noticed her presence.

"Valeria?" Isaac frowned. "What are you doing in here?"

She forced a small laugh. "What? I'm always here." A joke, and extremely bad timing. She wanted to bang her head into the stone wall when Isaac and Flynn shared a look. She sighed and dropped her shoulders before taking a step closer to Isaac. "I wanted to talk."

He sent a glance toward Flynn, who took the hint and stepped away. "We can talk, but you're also going to train. I can't waste time. Who knows when the next trial will be?"

Valeria nodded and tried her best to duplicate his fighting stance. Before she could even speak, his fist was already flying at her face. She ducked down, hands pressed to the mat and yelped, "Isaac!"

He took a step back, eyes narrowed and focused. "Best start talking."

She stood up, shook the tightness out of her arms, and readied for his next advance. "About last night," she jumped back when he kicked. "I didn't mean to take it out on you. I'm sorry. I should've realized you had your own problems as well, but... well," Isaac stalked around her as if she was prey, jaw clenched as he looked for another opportunity to strike. Valeria slumped her arms and released a breath. "This is ridiculous. Can't we talk like normal? I can't focus."

"Neither can I." He feigned a swing at her jaw and she flinched, covering her face with both hands. "And no, I'm busy training. You picked a bad time."

Without withdrawing her eyes from Isaac's, she could see Flynn watching from the sidelines, his expression just as concentrated as Isaac's. He held a hand to his jaw and examined Isaac's movements. "Separate your feet!" He called out. "Shoulders up, and *watch your toes*!"

Valeria was already crunching down on Isaac's toe with her heel. He shouted and jumped back as she swiveled and landed into her previous position.

It was only good luck that Jacky had brought her training gear to her bedroom that morning. She was growing exhausted by lugging around a heavy dress every day. She couldn't imagine training in one.

Isaac grinned with excitement. "There you go. Not the best attempt at an attack, but it was something."

Flynn chuckled, and Valeria threw him a sharp look. He stopped and glanced back at Isaac.

She bit her lip and blocked another swing from Isaac with her arm. *Lords.* That was going to leave a bruise.

"Nice." Isaac muttered. "Now get to talking so I can get back to training with Flynn."

With a deep inhale, Valeria focused on dodging each kick, hit, and swing as she gathered her thoughts. "I came to apologize, but you're so busy trying to attack me—it doesn't feel very fair."

"How so?" Isaac backed up when she flung a pathetic kick at his legs.

"Because my friend was killed three days ago!" Finally, she let loose and attacked him with everything she had.

Of course, she wasn't trying to hurt him, but her frustration was soaring beyond normal at this point. She just wanted to apologize—that's all she wanted. Whether he would accept it or not, why was he making it so hard for her?

Isaac dropped his arms and let Valeria hit him in the chest. He didn't appear to be bothered by her blows as he watched her with dark empty eyes. "Okay." He said. Valeria stopped and backed away. Panting, she relaxed her spine as he finally agreed. "Let's talk."

A sigh, and then, "Without hitting each other?"

"Yes, without hitting each other."

She glanced at her hands as they throbbed. *Lords, she was weak. Maybe she should train more often.*

Isaac listened patiently to her apology, and he even apologized himself. Claiming that how he worded a few things toward her wasn't right.

First she had felt so confused and lost about losing Alexa, but his excuse and explanation, she now understood that her feelings were real and how she acted was understandable.

Sometimes loss made people act out, and grief was a heavy thing. It still weighed her down, day by day.

Now she sat silently, watching Flynn teach Isaac how to throw a dagger into a target. So far, Isaac was only hitting the shoulders of the target, but it was still better than what she was capable of.

Flynn playfully shoved Isaac aside before he whipped his own dagger at the target. The blade sunk into the center of the head.

Valeria gulped and looked away.

Maybe she should stay on his good side after all.

The doors to the training room swung open, bashing against the walls, shaking and wobbling as Lance appeared from the hall. His eyes were dark and angry when he prowled farther inside, looking as if he was searching for something, or rather... someone.

Her eyes widened, and she lunged to her feet. Isaac glanced from Lance and back to her. Instantly, he was at her side, blocking her from Lance's view.

When Isaac let her speak her peace earlier, she told him about her time throughout the entire second trial, and the events that led her to slicing open Lance's ankle.

The room fell silent as everyone stared at Lance's storming presence. He wasn't limping, and pain was absent in his expression as his eyes searched the room. Finally, his furious gaze landed on Isaac, who must have appeared too tense—too suspicious, before Lance strode across the floor.

The next moment happened quickly. Suddenly Lance's hands were latched onto both of Isaac's arms and he was being thrown to the side.

Torn from her side, and exposed, Valeria didn't get a chance to run after Isaac before Lance was in her face. "You think you can hide after what you did to me?" He seethed. His hair was longer and messier, it almost perfectly matched the color of his angry cheeks. Red, pure red wrath. "People who look like you are all the same, aren't they?"

She tried to duck underneath his arm, but he grabbed her throat and threw her flat on her ass. Valeria coughed, reached for her throbbing neck and felt fire. The look in his eye was cold as he stared down at her.

"Stop!" someone screamed.

"I'm surprised you're still able to walk." Sarcasm dripped off her tongue, but the words scraped against her throat and she winced.

A kick to her stomach had her rolling to her side in agony, but she wouldn't let it show. Why couldn't she just keep her mouth shut? Making him angry was foolish when she couldn't even protect herself.

Flynn lunged at Isaac and pulled him back from aiding Valeria's side.

Good, she didn't need Isaac to get injured by Lance. It would only fill her with even more guilt than she already had.

"I gave you a chance to live," Lance spat, stalking forward. No one dared to move. If they did, his anger would only be redirected toward them. "I could have killed you that day, but I didn't." He laughed, an angry, bitter laugh. "And you fucked up. It's going to feel so good to rip the life out of you when I strangle your fucking neck."

Valeria tried to stand before the toe of his boot kicked her straight in the face. Her nose might've snapped. She wasn't sure. One second she could see everything, then the next the room was flickering in and out of consciousness.

Isaac tried to claw out of Flynn's arms, "Lance, just fucking stop!" He shouted.

Flynn shoved Isaac down so that he couldn't lunge toward Lance and attack him. He pointed a finger at Isaac, thick brows raised before he faced Lance. There was a look of pure darkness in his blue eyes.

However, Lance was far to concentrated on the blood that flowed down Valeria's face, into her mouth, and puddled on the floor

When she smiled, all she tasted was the metallic blood that coated her teeth. Lance was nothing but a blurry wave of red above her when she spit out, "Try me."

The last thing she saw was his fist driving straight into her face before Flynn tackled him to the ground. Then everything went black.

21

The world was a blur of sunlight and brownish haze when Valeria opened her eyes. Everything was dull underneath the pressure that throbbed inside her head.

Jacky stood over her, squeezing a thin tan cloth into a bucket of water by the bed. Valeria flinched against the blinding light as her vision cleared.

She felt the bed dip when Jacky sat beside her. "I've tended to your wounds far too many times, hun. I think it's time for you to toughen up."

Words clogged Valeria's throat from the dryness. She motioned for a glass, and Jacky was quick to lean over, grab the glass of water from the nightstand and hand it to her. It cleared the burning heat beneath her skin as she swallowed.

"How are you feeling?" Jacky asked.

Handing the cup back once it was empty, she scooted until her back was resting against the stone wall. "Awful."

Jacky chuckled. "Well, that's normal when you've been kicked in your freshly healed ribs, and have a knot the size of the king's castle on your forehead."

Valeria gasped and ran her hands over her face, where, sure enough, a lump had formed and throbbed on top of her head. "I should've kept my mouth shut." She muttered.

A wet towel was placed on her head before Jacky stood and crossed her arms, looking down at her with a teasing smile. "I think you proved that you're not going down without a fight. Although, I think you should start training."

She scoffed and wiped a trickle of water from her brow. The rag was dripping down and soaking her face and hair. Valeria felt like shit. She probably looked like it as well.

"How am I supposed to train now that Lance is healed and most likely going to hunt me down every time I leave my room?"

With a shrug, Jacky turned and rummaged through the top drawer of Valeria's dresser. She paused before pulling something black and lacey out and placing it on top of the steel. "You're in an alliance, aren't you? Ask your friends for help."

Valeria sat up and cursed at her aching ribs and head. "Flynn? He's not my friend. Besides, he's already training Isaac."

Jacky shot a look over her shoulder before turning to lean her curved hip against the dresser. "I'm sure he can fit you into his schedule. He seemed more than open to the idea."

"You already asked him?" Valeria shot out of bed, not caring about the pain that filtered through her body. "Please tell me you didn't."

"Oh, calm down. He's just a boy." Jacky strutted to the door. "I don't know what's going on between the two of you, but take my advice... figure it out. He's your only shot at survival." With that, she opened the door.

Valeria sat back on her bed with a thump and sighed before Jacky could fully close the door.

"Speaking of the devil." She heard Jacky say with cheerfulness in her tone. "You have visitors."

The door shut. Enclosing Flynn and Isaac inside Valeria's room with her.

She huffed and spun around on her bed so that she could look out the window and watch the storm soak the vast courtyard garden outside.

"I brought food." Isaac said first. She glanced over just in time to watch him set a tray of waffles and fruit beside her on the bed. "How's your head?"

She chuckled sarcastically, turning so that Isaac could see the swollen knob on her forehead. "I'm not sure I'll ever be completely healed while inside this misery-ridden estate. Not unless I win. So to answer your question, my head's fine. It could be worse."

Isaac didn't know whether to chuckle or worry. He did both and he leaned over, wincing at the condition of her wounds. "I'll get you a fresh bucket of cold water." Was all he said before snatching the rag off of her head, along with the warm bucket before he left.

Valeria's green eyes landed on Flynn, who stood awkwardly watching the door close behind Isaac. His hands were in his pockets and he pursed his full pink lips.

Her fingers fidgeted as she searched for something to say.

Flynn finally replaced the silence with his footsteps that scuffed against the hard stone floor. He pushed himself up onto her dresser and stared.

Valeria's heart plundered into her stomach when she met his narrowed blue eyes.

His throat bobbed. "You look like shit."

Out of everything he could have said, she didn't expect that. Yet, it made her chuckle. "You should see the other guy."

Flynn didn't laugh. His eyes were dark and red around the corners. He looked tired, exhausted even. "Let me train you."

Valeria licked her lips and straightened her spine. "No."

He examined the black clothing that Jacky pulled out earlier. His fingers skimmed over the lace before he held it up between both of his hands. An eyebrow raised as he stared at her black underwear.

She sucked in a breath before lunging off of the bed and snagging them from his grip.

He merely smirked at her flaming cheeks. "I thought you were more of a pastel pink kinda girl."

She bit the inside of her flushed cheek to hold in a crude remark and stalked back to the bed. Chest hammering, head throbbing, she felt as if she was going to explode. "I don't get to decide what I wear." Valeria shoved the black lace undergarment underneath her pillow, her cheeks still hot as she turned around and faced him. "Is there a reason why you came here?"

Flynn's eyes lingered on her plain pillowcase before he pushed himself off of the dresser and glanced around her room. "Train with me."

She huffed out a long breath. "I already told you no. Besides, you're training Isaac."

He shrugged. "Doesn't mean I can't train you. He's already learned the basics. Plus, he's not the one that needs to protect himself from Lance."

Finally, the words didn't stutter from her lips as she locked eyes with him. "I don't want to be around you." His mouth parted the slightest, but she continued, "I don't want anything to do with you. I'd rather *die* than be anywhere near you."

She was a bitch. She knew it. Though she wished she could have been different—wished that she could be kinder, but this world was cruel, and these games were deadly. They made everyone's true colors come out of hiding, and so far, Valeria had grown to hate hers.

She should be thanking Flynn for attacking Lance after he knocked her out, but she didn't.

Flynn blinked, a soft, slow, gentle blink, before he bit the inside of his cheek and stalked over to her on the bed.

Slow and catlike, he leaned forward, hands pressed into the mattress on both sides of her, and clenched his jaw. "And what about your sister? What about your father? You'd give up everything, all because you can't stand the sight of my face?" She blinked up at him in surprise and leaned away. But he was so close—too close. His blue eyes were shimmering, golden hair falling over his brows. Her heart may have pounded out of her chest. "I don't give a fuck." He said slowly, dropping a glance at her hands that lay in her lap. "You've been so indecisive toward me since I've gotten here. You think I care about how you feel anymore? Right now, all I care about is making sure you win."

The glass jar full of previous assumptions cracked inside her mind. "What?" She asked.

Her? Win? It didn't make sense.

Flynn pushed back and stood, he dipped his head and ran a hand through his already messy hair. "Haven't you come to realize it yet? Since I've gotten here, all I've done is follow you around like a lost pup. Did you really think that it was for something other than an alliance?"

"Why would you want me to win? What about you? What about Isaac?"

He shrugged and turned away. "I have plans made for myself. As for Isaac, there is nothing that I can do. It is out of my control." He tried to leave, but Valeria latched onto his wrist and he froze.

"Who are you if you have any control over these games?"

Flynn turned his head slowly so that all she could see was one of his glimmering eyes. "Someone you wouldn't want to know."

She spent all night resting against her bedroom door, listening for any sounds across the hall. Every twenty minutes she would hear scuffled footsteps, a slam, and then a curse. Valeria wasn't sure what Flynn was up to, but she wanted to find out.

When two hours passed, and the estate was silent with sleep, Valeria's eyes fluttered open at the sound of a soft click. Silent footsteps scurried down the length of the hallway.

Turning on her knees, she reached for the door handle. Slowly, she opened it and peered down the corridor, where she spotted Flynn's retreating back. She might have thought she imagined it when he disappeared, but the large shadow that remained had her rushing to her feet.

She yanked her brown cloak from off of the hook and scampered after him.

Once she reached the top of the stairs, she knelt and searched for his shadow again. A flash of blackness moved across the walls before vanishing around a dark corner. Valeria pursed her lips and silently rushed down the remaining three steps.

She couldn't risk being seen by him, not if she wanted to find out what he was hiding.

The latch of a door clicked farther down the hallway she had seen the shadow disappear into. As she walked down the slim corridor, she realized she had never been on this side of the estate. It was where Lance usually hid out and tormented the other contestants during the day.

Before the door slammed behind her as she stepped outside onto the cement pathway, Valeria grabbed it, placing a rock between the threshold so that it wouldn't close. It'd be best to make no noise at all, rather than a little.

Wind plastered her unkempt hair against her face, she threw the hood of her cloak over her head. Attempting to blend into the shadows of the castle walls, she scampered in the direction that Flynn had gone.

Too many questions ran furiously through her mind. *What was Flynn? Why was he even here? Why does he want her to win and not himself?*

Stopping in place, she released a breath. *What about Isaac?*

Valeria turned her head just in time to see the shadow of a person standing out beside the lake. The man faced the water and slowly lifted his face toward the sky before dropping to his knees as if he were to begin praying.

Flynn? No, it couldn't be him. The man was far too short, and not nearly as handsome.

Valeria scoffed and started to scold herself until three bulky dark shadows dressed in all black trudged around the corner of the castle. They were hunched over, as if trying to stay undiscovered by unwanted eyes.

She crouched behind the flower bush and watched as they silently jogged closer to the man kneeling before the lake. She tried to catch a glimpse of their faces, but quickly noticed the smooth black masks that covered them.

Her heart started thundering. She peered closer, nearly falling into the prickling thorns of the white roses. The man didn't hear the three figures approaching, and if he did, he didn't move to let them know.

Before she could react or even mutter out a warning, the three figures lunged at the man and tackled him to the ground. His scream echoed in and out of her ears when he fell forward onto his stomach.

One of the attackers put their weight on the man's legs, while another sat on his back and held his scrambling arms down. The third figure stood by the man's head and slowly pulled out a dagger from underneath his belt.

It all happened just like when she had been attacked, only there were three instead of two.

What was going on?

Valeria stood to her feet and tried to go after them in hopes of saving the man, when an arm wrapped around her waist, and a hand covered her mouth, muffling her broken yelp.

She did her best to bite back a scream, letting the familiar scented man pull her beneath the shadows of the castle walls.

"Be quiet." Flynn whispered in her ear. His voice was hoarse and commanding—protective.

Her eyes widened as the shadow of the attacker slashed his dagger down at his victims throat. "We have to help him." She tried clawing out of Flynn's grip, but he wouldn't relent.

"We can't."

"Flynn!" she whispered harshly against the palm of his hand. "He's going to die if we don't do something."

The two attackers on top of the man's now limp body stood and ran off while the one that made the final blow dropped to his knees to wipe the blade clean on the man's shirt. Then he stood and ran after the other two, who were already long out of sight.

Falling back against Flynn's hard chest, Valeria nearly passed out. Her wounds still needed healing, and the murder she had just witnessed was causing her mind to run frantically.

What should she do? Could she even do anything to help? *Gods*, she wanted out of this place.

The attackers were clearly not contestants. The others were playing the game with fairness, besides Lance and his few other allies. So who was attacking the contestants?

"Why are the contestants being killed?" She asked Flynn, who had yet to say anything at all. She could feel his breathing quicken, his cool exhale brushed against her scalp.

He shrugged, still not releasing her, he leaned against the castle wall. "I suppose whoever is doing it wants the games to end soon."

A silent understanding passed between them.

The king was doing this. Somehow, she knew it was his doing.

Valeria swallowed and pushed away from him so that she could walk toward the murdered contestant by the lake, but Flynn grabbed her wrist again. "Don't go out there. Someone will find the body in the morning and everything will be taken care of."

She stomped her foot and spun around to face him. "How can you be so calm about all of this?" Flynn frowned, but examined her distraught expression. "Someone was just killed!" She snarled softly. "Didn't you see? Or are you too caught up in your own shit to care?"

"The second one." He simply replied, eyes hollow of any emotion.

Her body went rigid with anger. Hot and seething, she thought it might consume her. "You're the worst person I've ever met. I'll be glad if I die in these games if it means I won't have to see your damned face anymore." She turned back to the man and continued walking.

"Good." was all Flynn said.

To her surprise and growing anger, his footsteps crunched on the gravel behind her. "Although I'd love to see you try to save an already dead man, I can't let you risk yourself right now. You need to train with me tomorrow." She growled, but he continued, "Then, once you win, you can try to kill me. I don't care. You won't have to ever see my face again, but I need you to win."

She scoffed at his carelessness, but refused to show him her face as she neared the dead man. "I don't understand you, and I don't think I ever will."

"You don't need to." He said. "Just try to work with me here."

"Why should I? You've done nothing but show me that I shouldn't trust you."

"How so?"

Valeria could only bite her lip to keep the insult from spilling out of her mouth. *How could he be so vain?*

She changed the subject, hoping to chill the blistering blood in her veins. "I'll train with you, only if you find a way to save Isaac."

Flynn stopped in his tracks. "I can't do that."

She spun around, anger still simmering beneath her skin. "And why not? Isn't he your friend? Don't you want him to live?"

Finally, he snapped. "Of course I do! Don't you think I've already tried everything—thought of anything to save his ass! I've tried Valeria. There's nothing I can do for him. I'm sorry."

The brisk wind brushed the cloak off of her head, she looked to her feet and sighed. They stood ten feet away from the body now, and the past adrenaline to rush over and see if there was any saving for the man was now gone. She was filled with a sense of unrelenting dread, a sadness of some kind.

Flynn snapped his head toward the door Valeria had propped open with a rock. Two glowing lights were pointed their way.

Flynn grabbed Valeria's wrist, his eyes wide. "Go back to your room, run. Don't let them see you."

"What about you?"

"I'll be right behind you."

Valeria wasted no time and hurried back underneath the shadows. She ran the long way around the castle until she came upon the garden doors that led into the main entrance. She made sure to listen for Flynn's silent footsteps behind her before managing her way up the stairs.

Once she was at the top and hidden beneath the shadows of the hallway, she turned towards Flynn. "I'll train with you." His eyes lightened and he caught his breath when she added, "But I'm not giving up on Isaac."

22

"I am Valeria Rox, and I can do this." She said before entering the training room. Braided copper red hair swaying back and forth against her spine as she trudged over to the mat to stand next to Flynn.

"Have you heard anything about what happened last night?" She asked. Her eyes skimmed the perimeter of the room. Lance wasn't there. *Thank the Gods.*

Healing was taking much longer than she hoped. Her ribs still throbbed if she moved too quickly, and her head was still sore. Sometimes the migraines would get so bad that she would spend entire days in her room.

Dealing with Lance sounded exhausting, dooming, actually. She didn't know if she would survive through another fight with the auburn-headed boy.

Flynn stretched his arms behind his back, frowning when he faced her. "Nothing. They didn't even mention the death this morning at breakfast. And I checked as soon as I woke up, the body was gone. Someone's trying to cover it up."

"But why would they do that?"

Flynn bit his bottom lip and chewed on it before nodding his head at the black fighting mat on the ground. Valeria followed and took a defending stance.

"I'm not sure." He muttered. His gaze emptied, as if distracted. Then he centered himself and focused on her.

"I don't understand." Valeria dropped her arms and tilted her head. "They ran from you that night they attacked me... how do you not know anything? Why are they afraid of you?"

He groaned and shook his head before lifting his arms, ready to fight, or at least practice. "Enough questions. You need to train."

She sighed and centered herself on the mat again. "Fine. But don't think I won't ask anymore questions. If we are going to be in an alliance together, you must be truthful with me."

Flynn's slight tilt of the lip caused her to grimace before he slowly circled her as though she were his prey. "I've never not been truthful with you, Valeria. I've simply kept my mouth shut."

With that, they began training.

Flynn taught her how to block an advance, and how to throw a punch. Of course, he taunted her about her arms that were flimsy, and explained the need to tone her body if she wanted to win a fight in the future.

She, of course, swung at his face after he insulted her, but he was quick enough to dodge away with an irritating chuckle.

After repeating sharp movements and growling out crude remarks, Valeria finally landed a blow to Flynn's chest. Although her knuckles popped and exploded with pain, she was proud of herself.

A smirk lined her lips when Flynn glanced down at where she hit him.

He raised his eyebrows in surprise. "Nice. Next time, fold your thumb over your fingers, not underneath, and it won't hurt you more than me." He finished with a laugh.

Valeria shook her head, but examined her fist before opening and closing it again, this time with her thumb in the proper position. "Let's go again. This time, don't go easy on me."

He frowned. "Are you sure? You've barely learned how to attack your opponent. That last hit was pure luck."

With pursed lips, she dropped her shoulders and cracked her neck. "I'm ready. It's not like I'll be the best fighter before I'm attacked again. I need to learn how to protect myself more than how to fight, anyway."

Flynn didn't look convinced, but he readied himself across from her and nodded his head. "Very well. Don't be mad at me when you land on your ass."

"I'll be fine."

He tilted his head, a hint of a smirk on his lips, but he shook his arms and bit his tongue before stepping toward her.

Like a tango—a waltz, they continued their dance of swinging fists and high kicks. They circled each other as if their lives actually depended on it.

Flynn prowled around her like a cat, while Valeria focused on any opportunities to make her next attack, but he left nothing open. She dropped her eyes to his legs for a moment before meeting his gaze again. He raised a brow, the corner of his lip lifted smugly.

An invitation to make the first move.

She sucked in her lips before dropping to the ground and spinning with a leg out. Flynn jumped back, dropping his arms. Valeria was quick, like a bolt of lighting when she stood again and launched herself at him.

She swung at his face, at his chest, and when she didn't land any punches, she swung in between his legs.

Flynn cursed and blocked each blow fluently. "Easy now, Val." He said with a dazzling smile. "When we train, we don't aim for the important parts."

She grimaced at the nickname and tried to kick in the same spot as before. Flynn's smile fell, he was quick to latch onto her ankle with both hands.

Her mouth parted, gasping when she landed flat on her ass.

Her head spun as she groaned and looked up at his arrogant face looming above her.

"And to think of what might've happened if I was actually going hard on you." He lifted a hand for her to take, but she shoved him away and pushed herself up on her own.

"I said don't go easy on me, Flynn." Her face flamed and dripped with beads of sweat, annoyance lingered in her eyes.

He crossed his arms. "You won't learn anything if I just attack you. Stop trying to control this lesson, take it slow and listen to me. You might actually learn something."

Valeria sharpened her stare on him before lifting a single finger at his back when he turned around to take a swig of water from his jug.

When he faced her again, Valeria's eyes were on the open doors of the training room that led out to the hall, where she watched Isaac pass by with the gamerunner, who was holding onto his shoulder.

"What's wrong?" Flynn asked before he followed her gaze and frowned at the sight. "Shit."

She left Flynn behind, ran to the doors and called after Isaac.

The gamerunner paused, turned, and lifted a brow. His eyes were sprinkled with amusement, but he forced a tightlipped frown.

"Isaac can't talk right now." He said. Her gaze remained on Isaac's slouched back. The gamerunner sucked in his lips. "He'll be fine. I've just caught him doing something that he wasn't supposed to. I'm taking him to his room quarters, where he'll spend the rest of the day." Valeria narrowed her eyes. "You may go back to what you were doing. I promise you," the gamerunner winked, and she lifted her head in confusion. "He will be okay."

They turned back around and began walking toward the dining hall. Valeria watched as they left. She sucked in a sharp breath and considered following after them.

A warmness caressed her back, like a spring breeze. She sighed and dropped her eyes to the ground. "What was he doing to get himself in trouble by the gamerunner?" She asked.

Flynn stepped beside her. A gentle finger skimming across her own before he grabbed her wrist and motioned back to the training room. "We'll give it an hour or two before checking on him. That way we don't get caught by any lingering officials."

She bit her lip, then released a sigh. "Okay."

Half an hour passed, Valeria's mind was still focused on Isaac.

She wondered if he was okay. Stressed that if he wasn't... what she would do. How drastic she would change her mind about killing anyone and go after the gamerunner first.

The gamerunner seemed amused by her reaction, as if it wasn't anything serious, as if the entire point about being in this place, this estate—was not to kill or be killed. He wasn't a contestant, he didn't get it. He didn't understand that her brain was not functioning right. It hadn't since she'd been stolen from her home and dragged here against her will. *What was he doing with Isaac? What did Isaac even do?*

"I need you to focus." Flynn said, dropping his fist in order to not hit her "I know Isaac's wellbeing is very distracting right now, but learning how to protect yourself is more important."

She scoffed and finally left her troubling thoughts behind before she zoned in on his chiseled, sweating face. She was just as sweaty, if not more.

"I'm sorry, but my friend has just gotten in trouble, and was taken away by the gamerunner, when a contestant was murdered by three people last night that were not in fact other contestants, and you want me to think that my training is more important right now?"

Flynn's eyes brightened with a smile. "There you are. Get out of your head and fight me now."

Valeria groaned, which only made his eyes shimmer with entertainment. "You are infuriating."

"I am?" He questioned, but not really. He was bouncing back and forth on his feet, ready to fight. He cracked his neck. "Come at me then. Take your best shot."

Perhaps focusing on harming Flynn would distract her for the better. There was no use in worrying about Isaac when she couldn't do anything for the time being.

Valeria centered on the mat and held her stance, making sure to cover any parts of her body that Flynn had aimed at previously.

With little to no warning, he pounced at her, throwing a punch at her throat, but she blocked it with her arms and fell back a step before quickly moving back into position again.

"Good." Flynn complimented underneath his breath before launching himself at her.

He swung at her legs, stomach, and head. Each blow blocked by her tiring arms. Valeria released a breath and closed her eyes for a moment too long when Flynn shoved her.

She gasped, her back hit the concrete post holding the solid stone ceiling up. Valeria finally opened her eyes and watched Flynn prowl closer. She pushed off the post, but he lifted his head and shoved her back against it. Trapping her with his arms.

"You're not good at this," He stated.

"You're not very good at training." She growled, trying to catch her shaking breath

Flynn lifted his hand and played with a free piece of her copper hair. "Try harder, Val. Don't you hate me? Don't you want to hurt me?" She frowned at his choice of words, but he remained close. A tired smirk played on his lips as he dropped her hair and closed his hands around her waist. "Someone wouldn't want to be touched like this by someone they truly hated. Show me. Prove to me how much you hate me, and throw me to the ground."

Valeria cursed, but couldn't help losing herself in his crystal eyes. He flicked his gaze to her lips, as if to kiss her. Valeria grimaced and shoved him away.

While he stared at her, biting back a smile, she tucked herself underneath his arm, kicked a leg behind his, and yanked him down.

They hit the mat in unison, his weight bringing them down hard. Valeria's cheek landed on top of his arm, blood pooled in her mouth from where her teeth latched onto her tongue. She closed her eyes tightly to fight away the growing migraine, but the fall was rough, and the mats were far too thin.

Flynn sat up, placing a hand on her head. "The headache in the morning will be well worth it, Val. You actually took me down. Congrats"

"Oh, please." She scoffed and slapped his hand away before pushing herself up to sit. "You were going easy on me."

He chuckled and stood, the glimmer in his eyes was cut short when he lifted his gaze and focused on something behind her. "Val, get up." He offered a hand, and if it weren't for the troubled look on his face, she would have refused his help, but the worry that quickly built in her stomach made her reach for his hand and accept his help.

She could feel the blazing energy enter the room before she even saw him. Lance stood at the end of their mat. A shiny dagger in his hand, twirling it as he smirked at the two of them. "Something the matter?" He asked.

Flynn stepped forward, as if to protect her. "She's training right now, Lance. Let us be, and then you can fight her when she's an equal opponent. Or let her die in the next trial."

Valeria glared at Flynn's back.

"Why wait?" Lance taunted as he took a threatening step toward Flynn, who pulled out a black dagger of his own. Lance's eyes landed on the blade for a second before he glanced at her over Flynn's shoulder. "Found yourself a protector, have you? What did you do to get him to like you, anyway? Blow him? Or give him the full course?"

Before Flynn could launch himself at Lance, the gamerunner stormed into the room, his eyes bright and searching as he scoured the perimeter. "Valeria?" He called, voice echoing off the high ceiling. He spotted her behind the two riled boys, stepping between them to face her. "Someone is here to speak with you."

23

J onathon Clarke. Lilith's fiancé. Valeria's future brother-in-law was waiting for her, leaning against the swirling steps of the tower.

Valeria stumbled back, shocked by the man in front of her.

Why was he here? Rather, how was he here?

The gamerunner nudged her forward. Her jaw slackened as she neared the brunette-haired man on the staircase. Jonathon smiled, a hint of unknown pain in his eyes as he examined her from head to toe.

Reaching toward her, "You're okay." He breathed.

"You—you're—" she stuttered.

He gave a gentle smile and slowly pressed off of the railing. "I know."

She took another step back, despite the gamerunner who stood behind her. "What are you doing here? How did you even get here?"

The last time she had seen him, he was holding Lilith back as the officials dragged her away. Valeria shook her head, wanting the memory to vanish forever—the feelings that the memory imprinted on her. She didn't like them.

"I—" He glanced over her shoulder at the gamerunner, who was still in the room. "Excuse us. May we have a moment alone?" Jonathon asked.

Fidgeting, wondering how or why Jonathon felt even slightly comfortable requesting such a thing from the gamerunner. She didn't need to look behind to know that the gamerunner was leaving. His footsteps were silent, but she still heard him close the wooden door.

Valeria raced over to Jonathon, whose brown eyes widened at her quickness. She latched onto his arms, his jacket gripped tightly beneath her fingers. "Is Lilith okay? Please... tell me she is." She begged. *Because why else could he be here? What was the reason?*

A tightlipped frown grew on his lips. "Yes, she's fine. That's not why I'm here."

She sighed a breath of relief and sagged her shoulders. "Thank the Gods." Valeria muttered. A bead of sweat dripped down her brow before she wiped it away. Jonathon watched the movement and stepped back. She loosened her grip on his arms. "So, how are you here? What's going on?"

He ran a hand through his short hair before dropping it. Glancing away, then back, then away again. He refused to meet her eyes... Why? Valeria examined every movement, every twitch, every unspoken thought that filtered through Jonathon's eyes.

Finally, he spoke. "I work for the king."

Her jaw fell slack, eyes widened, and she took three good steps back, trying to get away from him. To see what she had not before, when she had hardly known him in the Court of Wind.

She trusted him. Lilith trusted him...

"What?"

"I work for the king." He said again, and this time she heard it more clearly.

He's... She swallowed the hard lump in her throat, shaking her head. "You're an official?" Before he could answer, she went on, "It doesn't make any sense. You were with us for three nights of The Vanishing. You were there. How could you work for the king? I don't understand."

Her mind scrambled for the truth she couldn't fully comprehend.

Jonathon took a step toward her, an arm outreached in case she chose to run. "I know it's a lot, and I know you're going to hate me. You're going to hate me, but it's the truth... I cannot, nor will I marry your sister without telling you—without telling her."

Valeria dropped her hands from rummaging through her already messy braid. "You've already told her?"

He bit his lip and looked up at the towering, circular ceiling. "She doesn't know yet. I chose to come here first. In case... well, in case something happens." She knew what he meant... in case she died before he could tell her. "Lilith will know as soon as I get back. Our wedding is in a week. We tried to hold it off, but your father has gotten very sick and Lilith won't be able to run the antique shop when he's gone. So we have to rush the wedding to make ends meet."

Her heart plummeted, knees began to wobble, she felt the tower shake against his words.

Bringing a hand to her throat, she wrapped her free arm around herself and stared up at him. "He's sick?"

Jonathon nodded.

She turned away, trying to calm her shaking chest and rid the water from her eyes. "How long does he have?"

"The healer has given him two weeks."

The tears piled higher and higher over her eyes until she could hardly see the blurry sunlight streaming in through the cracks of the old tower walls.

She didn't get to say goodbye. She would never get a chance.

Valeria crossed her arms, tightly gripping her elbows. Surely, leaving red marks underneath her fingertips. "Is—will Lilith be okay? Does she seem okay?"

How she wished—*dreamed* to be with her sister then.

Jonathon nodded again. He let Valeria sit in the cold silence between them, gathering her thoughts. Watching as a single tear slipped from her eye and down her right cheek before falling and soaking into the blackness of her shirt.

"I—" He started. "There's more you must know. Before I go."

Valeria lifted her chin and raised her brows. The aching in her chest was growing swiftly. So many wishes that would never be granted, because she was here, and she would not leave in time to say goodbye to her dying father. She wasn't sure if she would ever leave at all.

"The shame and guilt I carry, Valeria." His eyes were glassy when he looked down at her.

She only frowned. What more could he say? What more could she take?

"You must know, before I tell you, how sorry I am. If it weren't for the love I have for your sister, you wouldn't be here... and Lilith would."

Valeria swallowed and shook her head. *What in the Gods was he saying?*

He continued, "I—you see... Someone switched the names on the officials tracking list. The list of names of the contestants we were supposed to gather for the games." He sighed and ran another hand through his already messy brown hair. He couldn't meet her eyes. "I saw the first list before it was tampered with. Lilith's name was on it for the third night of The Vanishing. But after the ball, when we ran to my bunker, it switched, and your name was in her place."

An explosion of anger, of sadness, of anything but sorrow flowed through her veins. She grimaced before biting her lip. "Then why are you guilty? If it wasn't you who put my name on the list, then who did? Why are you acting as if this is your fault?"

Dust sprinkled from the round ceiling, falling over their heads as his face dropped.

Jonathon took a silent step forward. "Because I didn't report it to the Lord of Sky—to the kingdom." He went on, "Because I tried to look into it, to see who would do such a thing, and I found nothing. I failed you. I failed your sister, and I failed your father." Finally, Jonathon blinked and a wary look grew over his face. His jaw was clenched as he lowered his voice to a mere whisper. "I'm almost positive that I sent the person who switched your names in here. He's here with you, Valeria. His name... I can't remember... It's—"

The facts piled in Valeria's mind before she quickly began putting them into their certain places.

Valeria was with Jonathon and Lilith for the first three nights, so he couldn't have been involved in those vanishings. If Alexa was the first Court of Wind contestant to be vanished, Isaac the second, and Valeria the third, then that meant...

"*Flynn.*" She muttered, looking at her hands. Lifting her eyes, he only confirmed it with the nod of his head. "Flynn Adler put me in here. He's the reason I'm here."

The door swung open and crashed against the wall. Valeria's world shifted. Her heart thundered like crazy inside her chest, mind reeling, stomach twisting. Valeria brushed past the gamerunner and stormed for the training room. But before she could leave, Jonathon grabbed her shoulder and spun her around.

"Take this." It was a small black notebook. Valeria scratched her head and looked up into his eyes. "Read it all before the next trial. Please, it'll help mine and Lilith's worries, knowing that you have this."

She grabbed the small booklet before being escorted out by the gamerunner, who looked at her with humored eyes.

The tower door closed behind them, Jonathon remained closed inside. She walked with the gamerunner to the main entrance of the estate.

"You're lucky I like you, kid." He said with a wink. The words flew past her ears as she stood and examined the notebook in her hand. "If I didn't, I'd have killed you for interacting with one of the officials. Especially one from your court."

She dropped her arm and met his gray gaze. "Why are you helping me?"

He pursed his lips before answering, "I'd hate to watch a soul like yours die in a game like this."

The gamerunner turned to walk away before looking back, a hand reaching out as if he forgot something. "By the way, if you need to find me, go down the southern hallway." He pointed toward the dark corner underneath the stairs. "Take a left and you'll find a door with a sign that says Laurent."

Despite her circumstances and everything that had just been revealed to her, Valeria felt a gentle smile spread across closed lips. "Laurent... What? Is that your first or last name?"

He smiled back. "First." Then he disappeared into the dark hallway, leaving her alone underneath the large mural of the dragon.

As she began climbing up the stairs, ready to visit Isaac in his room, she flipped through the pages of the small booklet. Noticing elegant handwriting, and cut out newspaper prints glued inside.

Curious, but more concerned for her friend, she gently closed and folded the notebook underneath her arm, setting it aside for another time. Perhaps for a day that her world hadn't completely shifted.

"Look, there's no need to worry. He just caught me sneaking around in the hidden passageway. I wasn't doing anything bad. I just suppose he didn't like that I—whoa." Isaac said when Valeria opened his door and stepped inside. He stopped once he saw the paleness of her face. "What happened to you?"

She pursed her lips and walked over to his bed before plopping onto her back and staring at the gray ceiling. "Too much."

Isaac slouched beside her, giving her leg a soft pat. "Tell me everything."

And so she did.

Valeria rambled on and on for what felt like an entire hour, filling Isaac in on every last thing that happened. How Flynn might've been the one to swap Lilith's name with hers, how her brother-in-law was secretly an official and betrayed her for Lilith's safety, how the gamerunner's name was actually Laurent. Finally, she told him about the small booklet she was gifted.

He sat back and listened patiently, raising his brows when necessary. Although, he interrupted her when it came to Flynn, arguing how it had to be impossible. Finally, he glanced down at the black booklet in her hands.

"Have you read it yet?"

She shook her head. "No, I came straight to you. I didn't know if you were alive or not."

With a scoff, Isaac asked, "Why would I be dead? Only the games and other contestants can kill us."

Then it hit her. She hadn't told Isaac about the murder she and Flynn witnessed the night before.

Valeria sat up and faced him fully. Isaac frowned at her widened eyes. "There are people, maybe officials—I'm not sure yet. Anyway, they are going around in groups at night to kill the contestants." Isaac gaped, but she continued, "They attacked me a few nights ago, but Flynn scared them off."

"Flynn? How did he scare them off?"

"That's what I've been wondering too, but since I think he might be the reason I'm here, I have a feeling he's more important than any of us. Let's keep our eyes on him. If he does anything—and I mean anything out of the ordinary, Isaac, you have to let me know."

His eyes shimmered with worry before biting his lip and nodding his head.

They sat on his unmade bed, letting their crazed conspiracies grow wilder and wilder by the minute. It only sparked more confusion in Valeria's mind.

After a crude joke made by Isaac, she gave his shoulder a slight shove.

"Why were you sneaking around in the hidden passageway?" She teased.

Isaac chuckled and rested his head in his hands. "I was researching something."

She nodded. Of course, he was still researching that damned mirror. She wanted to as well, but the way it had smelled and what it had shown her—none of it sat right in her stomach. She couldn't make any sense of the magical object. It was foreign to her.

"It's alright, I got caught snooping around in his desk when he walked in, but he didn't seem to mind." Isaac frowned, and she chuckled. "He must have something against you."

The room filled with silence as Isaac thought about every interaction he ever had with the gamerunner, before he sat straight. A bright smile now shining in his eyes as he laughed out, "I was giving him awful looks and mumbling insults toward him the first day I was taken here. Maybe he heard and hasn't liked me since?"

They laughed together.

As time passed through the day, Valeria sat in Isaac's room. They told stories about their lives, and the things they enjoyed back in the Court of Wind. There were even a few jokes thrown into the conversation before night fell, and Valeria trudged back to her room.

Flynn walked from the opposite direction, meeting her in between their doors before a smirk grew on his lips. But it vanished once he saw the awful look she was giving him.

"Something wrong? Did I push you too hard today?" He teased.

Valeria bit the inside of her lip, opened her door, and slammed it in his face before throwing herself onto her bed.

24

Every morning Valeria is woken by Jacky at precisely seven am. From there she is asked to bathe and get dressed for the day. However, today, she was woken by two aggressive officials as they yanked her out of her bed. Forcing her brown slippers on her feet, they pulled and dragged her across the floor, not caring for the thin strap of her dress that fell, almost revealing her breast beneath the silver fabric.

They were going to kill her. They were going to take her far out into the fields and slit her throat. Every terrible thought that entered her mind sent her into a frenzy of rapid emotions. Whatever or wherever the officials were taking her, she didn't know.

It must have been five or six in the morning, considering the sun peaking over the horizon outside the windows. Valeria nearly puked when she was pulled down the stairs. Her nerves, thick and pulsing, triggered the memory of the officials busting through her father's front door and taking her away.

Scuffling sounded all around her. That was when she noticed three other contestants in front of her, also being dragged across the floors and out through the garden doors. Valeria looked behind and saw Flynn and Isaac being pulled from their rooms.

What in the Gods was going on?

She didn't have a chance to open the small booklet last night before falling asleep. Did it have any information on this? Was the third trial beginning already?

Valeria panicked. Her arms tensed when she reached the last step, and then someone shoved something cold and hard into her shoulder.

Two officials gripped her arms, moving her in line behind the other three contestants at the door.

Her widened eyes searched frantically for Laurent. Because he would know what was going on. *Wouldn't he?* But she couldn't spot him. He wasn't in the hall or the main room. He wasn't even standing outside waiting for them in the garden.

"Where are we going?" Isaac asked, stress laced his tone. "Where are we going?" He asked again, this time louder and more violently.

Valeria heard a scuffle from behind and thanked the Gods when it ended briefly. Isaac needed to stay calm.

She swallowed back her fear, cleared her throat, and eased the frown off her lips.

"We'll be okay, Isaac." She called over her shoulder. "Just take a deep breath. We'll figure it out."

She was shoved through the doors, leaving Flynn and Isaac behind. The officials tugged her through the garden and out past the courtyard, where a small shed wrapped in old vines and shrubs was waiting for them.

The other contestants stood in front of it, their eyes drawn and confused.

She examined everything in case the need to run came. Just so she would memorize her surroundings and know where to escape.

They came to a stop beside the other three contestants, when finally the officials let go of her arms and took two wide steps back. They held their shoulders straight and high, hands on their pistols and stared ahead at nothing in particular.

"Valeria." Isaac breathed once he and Flynn were pulled around the corner.

"I'm okay." She whispered, trying to hide the shaking in the back of her throat. "Just wait for the gamerunner. I'm sure he'll show soon."

"Enough." An official threatened to pull his pistol from his belt, staring at her underneath his brows. Valeria gulped and looked away before focusing on the flat green grass in front of her.

A breeze shot past, blowing her nightgown to the side. She was quick to hold the silver material in place, not wanting to expose herself to anyone. Her hair must've been a mess, having just woken up.

"Oh good, you're all here." Laurent said before he appeared from around Isaac's shoulder, who stood at the end of the line. Laurent walked in front of everyone until he stopped and stood facing them all.

Valeria and the others waited, their expression blank, all tired from the sudden awakening. Except Flynn, who stood confidently beside her.

"Today we have a guest, and what do we do for our guest here at Azrael estate? Of course, we offer a show, and let them decide how to control your fates," Laurent said with a performer's smile. He looked over their heads and his smile brightened, though, just by a little. "Welcome, everyone, the Lord of Illusion from the Court of Magic."

Laurent's smile fell and his eyebrows narrowed. Then, not even a second later, a tall man appeared out of thin air right next to him.

He jumped and pressed a hand to his chest. "Gods, Saint Nyle. Be less frightening next time." He played off his fright with a chuckle. Although Valeria saw the prick of irritation in his eyes.

The Lord of Illusion, who Valeria could now put a better name to, Saint Nyle crossed his arms behind his back and began walking in front of the line of contestants.

His hair was black as midnight, blue eyes pierced straight through her as he passed. He may have been attractive in a dark, brooding kind of way, but the energy that poured off of him... it was taunting, and irritated the Gods out of her.

Did he remember her from the ball?

"That was the least frightening thing that I have planned for today, Laurent." The Lord of Illusion said, skimming his eyes across the remaining eight contestants. "What a pity." He frowned. "It looks as if my very own court of contestants has only one man left. Shame... I had been placing bets on myself sadly." He passed Vincent Brooks, the last Court of Magic contestant, and walked back to Laurent. "You may speak now."

Laurent glowered at the words spoken to him, as if he was nothing but a performer in a play.

Pressing his hands together, he rested his gaze on Valeria for a moment before beginning his speech. "When you are inside of the Game of Lords, haven't I always said to expect the element of surprise?" He asked, but no one answered. "Of course, it is always what a future lady should expect, and nothing less. Today we are starting the third trial, one that will test your abilities in judgment... With that," Valeria's blood ran cold at the chilling smile on Laurent's lips. "Let it begin."

The world flickered around them; the sky went in and out of darkness, and the grass turned gray as stone. Then, all at once, the small grassy field they stood in turned into a large dark room. The floors were of a dark oak, a blood-red carpet covered the length of the halls that extended farther and farther out the longer she looked at them. Multiple doors flashed onto the growing walls.

All of it was magic. A powerful performance made by the only lord that could do so.

Valeria struggled for a filling breath as she glanced around. She was alone in the room, the other contestants, gone. Laurent and Saint Nyle, gone.

The stage lights continued to flicker above her head, as if the illusion hadn't completely settled in.

She wondered if she was really inside of the building, or still standing outside on the grass. The illusion was too strong, and the details of the room—too intricate.

It took a few moments for the illusion to complete, and when it did, Valeria slowly walked toward the first door on the left. She pushed it open, gasping when she discovered a body laying on the red carpet. The dirty blonde hair made her place a trembling hand to her mouth.

Flynn. He was dead... or was he?

She crouched beside his body and examined him for any wounds, then his mouth to see if he had been poisoned, but there was nothing.

His eyes lightly flickered, and chest caved in when a filtered breath left his lips. It had to be another illusion. He wasn't hurt. He was in some kind of sleeping trance.

She lifted her head. He won the last trial... Laurent never told the other contestants what the reward was, and Flynn had kept it a secret. Was it this? Was he not competing in the third trial?

Valeria stood and released a tightened breath. Whatever she was supposed to do in here, it was going to be based on her judgment. Finding the other contestants and spying on them to see what they were doing was her best shot at judging anything. But the question of why Flynn was lying dead—well, partly dead... was it supposed to be some kind of clue?

Laurent didn't give them any information as to what the trial would consist of.

"Valeria!" a voice screamed from afar. "Valeria!" It was much closer this time.

"Where are you?" She yelled back to Isaac, leaving Flynn's body as she ran through another door she hadn't been through yet.

There wasn't any time to take in her surroundings, because a shadow ran underneath the door from the hall she just passed through. She narrowed her eyes and hurried over, opened the closed door, and saw Isaac bent over, hands on his knees, huffing.

"What's wrong?" She asked before grabbing him by the shirt and pulling him inside the room she was in. Once he was inside, she slammed the door and looked over his features in search of any signs of pain.

He was fine. His eyes were wide and wild, but... he was fine. She released a breath through her nose.

Isaac was still panting as he tried to answer her. "Lance, he—" He took another breath. "He was chasing me through a maze of doors and rooms. I got away, but I'm sure he's close behind."

"Do you still have your dagger?" She asked.

"I didn't have time to grab it when they woke me up." He said.

Valeria bit her bottom lip and yanked hers from out of her corset. "Take mine."

He frowned and stepped back. "No. No, I can't do that. I'm a better fighter than you. You need to keep it."

Dropping her arm, she silently agreed. It would be brainless to give away her only protection. Instead, she motioned toward the hall. "Flynn's in the room across the hall. I don't know if it's actually him or if it's another illusion."

Isaac grimaced and walked for the door. Valeria stayed close behind. He opened the door a sliver and peaked. Thankfully, she hadn't closed the other door on her way out. When he got a good enough glimpse of Flynns limp body, he backed away and pulled the door shut.

Another disturbed frown was on his face. "I don't understand. What are we supposed to be doing in here?"

Valeria shrugged before trudging over to a long velvet curtain and ripping it open. A blank wall, there wasn't even a window to see where they really were. "Did they say how long this would take?"

"No, I wonder if they're watching us."

"And how." She added.

More footsteps came pounding down the hallway, closer to the room they were in. Valeria searched for a place to hide. There was only the bed, dresser, and the curtains she had ripped open.

She grabbed his shoulder and threw Isaac against the wall before covering him with the navy-velvet curtains. "Keep quiet. I'm going to hide underneath the bed."

Isaac could only nod, tightly pressing his lips together in order to not make a sound when she walked on her toes to the bed. Grabbing the bed sheet, she dropped to her knees and shimmied between the wooden bed frame and floor. Her nightgown rode up, and she begged the Gods that Isaac couldn't see her.

When she was well-hidden, she fixed her gown and anxiously watched the gap at the bottom of the door, where shadows passed underneath.

"Where's the boy?" Lance's voice filtered in through the cracks of the door, then, whomever it was that he was talking to must not have had the answer he was looking for, because there was a yelp, and then a smash before footsteps stomped nearer.

A door opened close by, and then Lance groaned annoyedly. "Magical bastard." Lance seethed inside the other room. "His illusions aren't even convincing."

Something thudded, and then another door opened. This time into the room Valeria and Isaac were hiding in.

"I know you're close. I saw you come this way." Lance's feet prowled over to the bed and Valeria's breath hitched. She covered her mouth with a hand and watched his slippers stand beside her face for too long of a moment. "Hopefully your little girlfriend is with you too. I'll enjoy killing you both."

End the trial! End the trial! She chanted inside her mind.

Lance was slowly making his way farther away from her, yet closer to Isaac. She began scooting to the other side of the bed.

Hoping—no. Praying that the trial would end.

When she was free, she knelt behind the mattress and waited for the moment to strike. Lance sauntered toward the wall, light on his feet, before he paused. His back was to her, but she could already see what Lance was gazing at.

A black slipper was poking out beneath the navy-colored curtains.

She sucked in a breath, preparing to launch herself across the room—to stick her dagger into his back.

Lance raised his arm, gripped the velvet, and before he could yank it open and find Isaac hidden underneath, Valeria was already sprinting around the bed, dagger in hand.

The blade was two inches away from Lance's neck when the room evaporated into nothingness, and Lance disappeared.

As she fell forward into what used to be Isaac and a wall, her knees landed on hard cement.

When she opened her eyes, wincing away the pain, she found a pair of shiny black shoes next to her face. She lifted her gaze to find the Lord of Illusion standing before her.

He tilted his head with a vicious smirk. One that made chills run up the length of her arms.

Her nightgown was tucked underneath her feet, holding her down when she tried to stand. She adjusted and tried again. Once standing, she struggled to look him in those tormented blue-green eyes.

"Give me a name. Any living contestant's name to cast your vote."

Her vote? Valeria licked and bit her lip before questioning him, "What am I voting for?"

The Lord of Illusion adjusted his stance and stood proud, "You will be voting for whomever you think was the killer. If you failed to find the body, and the killer, then vote however you wish."

Oh, Gods. Valeria threw her hands into her hair and pulled. She knew who she would be voting for. It was easy. Lance. But what about her? What about Isaac? And how was Flynn supposed to vote? Was he even competing in this trial, after all?

Valeria swallowed before placing her vote. "Lance Whitlock. From the Court of Storms." She nervously played with her fingers and waited for the final result.

"As I wait for your votes," Saint Nyle said and continued, "I will have you know that the person with the most votes to their name will die immediately."

Her mind played tricks as she struggled to make sense of his words.

He was showing himself to all the contestants—presenting himself to everyone individually, yet all at the same time. She wondered about the room she was in. How strong was his power to alter the environment so easily?

As Valeria prayed to the Gods for Isaac and her self's safety, a timer clicked throughout the room. One, then two clicks. She began counting.

Finally, an eighth click sounded, ringing off of the walls.

The final vote was in.

Valeria held her breath and waited. She studied Saint Nyle and the way his body faintly flickered underneath one single bright stage light. He glanced around, never meeting her gaze before checking the watch on his wrist.

"The contestant has been chosen." He said, and her heart dropped. The entire room shook, or maybe she was the one shaking? She wanted to yell, to scream in his face, but she didn't. She waited as patiently as she could before he spoke again. "Isaac Bushman."

The world shattered into pieces at Valeria Rox's feet.

25

The walls of the room crumbled to pieces.

Isaac.

No.

Valeria struggled to come back to reality when the illusions fell and every contestant was exposed from behind the fallen walls. Her lips parted and she glanced around, desperate to find him, desperate to find her friend before it was too late.

She felt a presence at her back. Flynn stepped beside her. "Look at that. You made it." He said.

He didn't know.

Valeria's eyes were already filled with unfallen tears. She didn't look at him, she couldn't. There was too much commotion. The other contestants were in her way. She needed to get to Isaac before... She turned in every direction, frantic now that time ticked on and Isaac would be gone at any given moment.

"Valeria?" Flynn asked. He tried to grab her arm, but she was quick to move away and push past another contestant in her way.

"Isaac?" she rasped, her throat swollen and thick with despair. "Isaac!"

Every muscle in her body thrashed and tensed when she finally saw him. Lying there in the grass on his side, eyes open, mouth agape, a single tear falling from his dull brown gaze.

She screamed.

She screamed at the Gods, at Flynn, who kept calling her name until he too also saw his friend lying there dead in the grass.

Valeria rushed over to the fifteen-year-old boy. Too young to compete in these games—too kind for this to be his end. He was her friend, and he was gone.

She fell to her knees beside his still warm body and cried.

"Isaac." Tears blurred over her vision. Her heart thundered, sloppily beating inside her chest, hard enough to make her dizzy. "Isaac, I'm sorry. I'm so, so sorry."

She recalled telling him everything would be okay—that they would figure everything out and be okay... but nothing was.

Not anymore. She was supposed to protect him. He was supposed to live. She was going to save him and he was going to see his family again.

"Please," she choked. "Please, get up Isaac. Come on." A cry bobbed out of her throat, and she collapsed on his unmoving chest. "You were supposed to live." He didn't move. "You were supposed to go home."

Still, he never moved. Never breathed. Never laughed and told her it was fake—that he was joking.

Because he was dead.

Valeria placed a hand over his face before gently closing his eyes.

"As everyone can see, this is why we do not make close connections while staying at Azrael estate." It wasn't the gamerunner who spoke, instead, it was Saint Nyle, the Lord of Illusion.

Valeria's blood simmered and bubbled. It heated into flames as she closed her eyes, took a deep breath, and stood to her full height.

Slowly, she turned toward Saint Nyle's infuriating voice.

Before he could continue, she prowled closer and said in a low, dark tone, "I will win the Game of Lords, and when I do, I will stop at nothing to have your head at my feet." She hissed, now standing in front of him. "When I win, and when I am free—I will kill you... I hope you and everyone you love can outrun a dragon."

His eyes widened, and he took a step back. Flicking a glance at Laurent before turning around, Saint Nyle met her fiery gaze again.

They stared at each other. Her eyes flamed with anger, his with confusion.

Sending a quick nod toward the gamerunner, he said, "I need to speak with you... now."

They sauntered off, through the gardens and back inside the castle walls. Valeria watched until she could no longer see them.

Once they were gone, she walked on shaky legs back over to Isaac. Instantly, her anger boiled down, and agony filled her chest at the sight.

Flynn was already on his knees before him, hands on Isaac's chest, bowing his head into a prayer. She only heard the last of it when she neared, and Flynn lifted his head to glance at her. His eyes were red and lined with a glossy silver.

Valeria put her hand on top of his and nodded before returning her gaze to Isaac's lifeless form.

"I'll get out of here, and find your family. I'll bring them somewhere safe, somewhere where they'll never have to worry about another coin." Flynn listened as she continued, "I just wish it could have been me. You deserve life more than I do, Isaac. You deserve so much more than what this place has taken from you."

She stayed there as the others left. Even when night fell, and Flynn said his last goodbyes. Even as the officials stood over her shoulders, complaining about how long she was taking. She stayed there.

Praying for him—for his family. Because she knew that once she left, once his body was taken away and buried underneath the soil of Azrael estate, that she would never see him again. She would never hear his corny jokes or childish banter.

She would have to continue playing the game.

The first day after Isaac's death, she sat in bed and stared out at the garden. The sky cried with her, and even when it wasn't raining, tears continued to fall from her eyes.

On the second day after his death, she locked Jacky out of her room. So far as to shove the metal dresser in front of the door. Jacky had been insisting that Valeria should continue her training with Flynn and that was enough to piss her off.

She wanted to mourn, for God's sake.

Then came the third day, when Flynn had tried knocking on her door. Valeria hadn't left her room for those three days, and he'd grown concerned she supposed. Thirty minutes passed before he finally gave up and let her be alone again.

An hour after he left, she heard a shuffle of feet, and then a pause before the sound of porcelain sliding against stone alerted her.

Out of nothing but curiosity, Valeria stalked to the door and gently peered outside only to find a plate of chicken and rice at her feet. She would have ignored it if it weren't for the grumbling of her angry stomach.

Her hunger won over her annoyance as she snagged the plate from the floor.

When she was back on her bed with a nearly cold plate of food, she discovered a note stuck to the bottom side of the plate. With one hand, she unfolded and read the surprisingly neat handwriting.

I'm giving you one more day to grieve. After that, we're training. Even if I have to force you out of that tiny room.

—Sincerely, the most handsome man you know, Flynn Adler.

Valeria glared at the paper and threw it across the room before slicing into a piece of chicken on her plate and shoving it in her mouth.

Like hell he would force her to do anything.

26

A crisp breeze blew through the window, brushing Valeria's loose hair into a tangled mess. A shudder ran down her arms and she lept up to slam the metal closed, shutting the coldness out.

Something fell to the floor when she sat back on the bed. Peering over the edge of the mattress, she spotted the notebook that Jonathon gave her. It had opened as it landed, the black spine now cracked.

She sighed and leaned over to pick it up, but a page fell out. Her eyes scanned the ripped piece of newspaper, a picture of a familiar building with a few printed words underneath. A curious frown graced her lips. Valeria reached down for the paper while placing the notebook to the side.

An anxious heartbeat later, she read the words underneath the picture of her father's shop.

Antiques of History, now closed. Business owner Samuel Rox shut down his small business last week due to a cruel illness that has kept him bedridden. The Court of Wind wishes him well at this time of healing.

The rest of the article was unreadable, due to being ripped from its page. She stared at her father's proud smile in the picture. It was an old one, taken many years ago when he had first opened up. His hair was fuller, smile wider than usual, and eyes much brighter. She almost wished he could have stayed that way forever, but he had Valeria and Lilith to take care of after their mother left. Everything was left in his growing pile of responsibilities. The stress had made his hair thin, and with his age, wrinkles quickly spread across his fair skin.

Now, to think that he was sick? Valeria's stomach twisted into knots.

When she finished staring at the picture and article that made her nauseous, the notebook caught her attention. She picked it up and flipped to the first page.

The book was full of article after article, some about her father and his business, others about her sisters near wedding. As she flipped through the pages, her eyes skimmed across what must have been Jonathon's handwriting. The sentences were short and choppy in order to fit on the paper.

A grin grew on her lips as she read about Lilith and the things that she had been doing since Valeria was vanished.

Lilith seemed happy mostly, but it was all from Jonathon's point of view. So, she didn't truly know.

He wrote on and on about how her older sister was stressing about the plans for the wedding. Valeria laughed at a small drawing he drew of her frantic sister.

But the smile fell when she flipped the page and read his next sentence.

Lilith is gone. I can't find her anywhere. I'm afraid she has run off to try and save you. She can't seem to let it go, or live with what happened. She cries every night.

The words cut off. Valeria flipped the page in a hurry.

She's done so much research. Disappearing into the study for hours upon hours in search of anything.

His writing ended there. She frantically flipped through a few more pages, article after article, a few words of advice until she landed on another page with Lilith's name.

> Lilith finally stopped stressing so much
> about her research. She's moved onto
> visiting the family's of the Vanished.
> She hopes Alexa is alive and okay, you
> as well. There is a family that lives on
> the south-side, Lilith seems to visit
> there frequently.

A tear dripped onto the page as Valeria sniffled. She wiped her face before flipping the page to read some more.

> She stays there for hours when she
> does visit, claiming the mother has a
> three-month-old that she needs help
> taking care of. The other day, Lilith
> asked for a large amount of coins. I, of
> course, didn't object. Given she's soon to
> be my wife.

She flipped the page again.

> Lilith gave the coins to the mother and her child. We had them over for dinner. The mother is such a joy. I hope her son is okay, and that you've made a friend out of him.

The tears didn't seem to stop. Valeria dropped the book and flung her head back, a small, pitiful smile on her face. She loved her sister, she always would. But for Lilith to take care of Isaac's family when that was his only worry...

Valeria grabbed the booklet again.

The Lord of Sky has been out more than usual, and his court has no idea why.

A picture of the lord was glued beside the writing. She brushed a thumb over his rugged face. He was standing outside a neighborhood, eyes wide, yet oddly sharp and intimidating.

They say he is looking for something, or someone. We are not sure what it could be, but we're glad to see his face again. Our Lord of the Court of Wind has never shown his face in public this much before. We hope he finds whatever it is he is looking for.

When she was finished reading the article, Valeria flipped through the remainder of the pages. She'd read all of it. There was nothing left. It was like being back in her court with her people for a short time, seeing those things, being able to know what was going on outside of the games.

Her eyes were dry once she closed the book and stood. She lifted the mattress and gently set the notebook underneath. If anyone were to find it, an official, or perhaps even Jacky... She didn't doubt that they would kill her.

There was one thing that Valeria liked to believe she was good at. Sneaking around.

She'd only been caught a few times. Once by the Lord of Sky, and another by Laurent, the gamerunner. Her feet were quick and quiet when she rushed across the hall and tapped on the door in front of her.

There was no response. It was empty.

Valeria looked down the hallway before gripping the knob in her hand and giving it a twist. Flynn's door opened with a creak.

It was cold and dark. A faint smell that reminded her of a warm spring breeze lingered in the air. The slight distraction made her almost forget what she was even doing there.

The bed was disheveled, pillows tossed on the floor, and the blanket thrown to the side.

What a mess.

Valeria walked over to the dresser. The top was wiped clean, and vacant for the most part. Only a few pieces of clothing sat unfolded on top. Hopefully, his Help wouldn't walk in and catch her since Flynn was already gone for the day.

She began opening the drawers, searching for nothing in particular. Only anything that would give her a clue about where his head was at in the games, and who he was exactly.

The first drawer was nearly empty. A few shirts were folded neatly inside. Her eyebrows tugged together and she bit her lip, gently lifting the shirts.

If she hadn't checked, she would have missed the folded note tucked underneath one of his many white tunics. Valeria hesitated before reaching inside and pulling the paper out.

Flynn's name was the only thing scribbled in neat cursive writing on the note. She pursed her lips and shoved it back where she found it.

A glimmer of a brown medication bottle flickered from farther back inside. She pulled it out.

The bottle read, *Healing Amplifier.*

There was no specifics or legal printing elsewhere on the bottle. It seemed to be mostly empty as well. Tilting her head, she remembered that Flynn had given Jacky some sort of medication when Valeria had been injured inside of the Forest of Angels.

A Healing Amplifier was only made and sold by the best healers in Laterra. It must have been expensive—something only immortals could afford.

So, why did Flynn have it?

After placing the bottle back in the drawer, she backed up and faced the bed. Everything smelled like him. She imagined his pillows did the most. And then she scolded herself for thinking those things. Sure, Flynn was—no—*is* attractive. In an unkept, careless kind of way... at least to her.

But she could never let herself think or even feel anything else for him.

Even if he was always around every corner. Constantly following her. Constantly bothering her. He left little room in her mind for anything else.

As she was busy searching for anything else that seemed out of place, her eyes landed on his mattress. Precisely where the sheet was draped over the floor, not tucked in like the rest of the cotton material.

Valeria briskly walked over to the bed, dropped to her knees, and flipped the loose end of the sheet over the top of the mattress. Then she proceeded to lift it up and reached underneath. She was met with the coldness of the unused side of his bed. There wasn't anything besides a few dangling strings where the rough fabric was torn open.

Before she could fit her fingers into the gaping hole, footsteps scuffed outside the door down the hall. The voices that followed shared a few sentences before she realized that one of them sounded far too familiar.

Valeria lurched to her feet, sauntered for the door, and pressed her ear up against it.

Her heart thumped inside her chest. The rush of being somewhere she wasn't supposed to be made her blood surge. She didn't have a craving for it, but the way it made her feel more alive—more awake. She supposed somewhere along the way, her body started to like it.

The footsteps came to a halt. They still sounded far away. So she took the only chance and ducked outside of the room.

She didn't spare a glance down the hall when she threw herself into her room and released a breath.

27

Hours later, when the moon was sitting pleasantly in the sky outside her window, Valeria's door opened to reveal a wide eyed Jacky, who shut the door behind her with a click.

"It's late." Valeria said bluntly. She was tired, and desperately wanted sleep, even though her thoughts kept her from doing so.

Jacky didn't move from the door, she only wrung her hands together. Eyes wide, mouth ajar, she spoke. "You're being summoned by the gamerunner."

Valeria sat up, surprise in her emerald eyes. "Do you know why?"

Her Help only shook her head and bit her bottom lip. "He didn't say."

Five minutes after changing into a more presentable dress and out of her silver nightgown, Valeria stood in front of Laurent's office. Her hand was raised and swayed above the door before, finally, she knocked.

"Come in." The two words, though welcoming, were clipped and tight.

This would not be a *good* meeting then. She released a breath before opening the door and stepping inside.

Sunset orange greeted her eyes as she looked around, taking in the brightly colored walls. Laurent sat behind a large desk, his gaze focused on the letter in his hands. A pair of oval glasses on his nose as he pursed his lips tightly.

He shot a brief glance her way. "Take a seat."

Valeria huffed and moved over to the leather chair across from him. She sat and splayed her fingers over her lap. Fidgeting, waiting for him to speak—to say whatever it was he needed to say.

After a minute or two, he set the paper down and took off his glasses before leaning back in his chair and folding his arms over his chest.

She averted her eyes when he only stared. "Have I done something?" She asked, hoping to break the silence.

Laurent scoffed, yet still refused to speak.

Valeria glared and rolled her eyes. "Spare the silence, please. It's late. I'd love to get some sleep before the next trial."

He blinked, then blinked again. "You realize what you've done, don't you?" She looked away from his angry gaze, but he heaved a sigh and started again, "Of course you don't. How could you when you've been hiding in your room the entire time?"

Valeria frowned and searched her mind for anything to say. She came up blank. "I'm sorry. I don't understand?"

He chuckled and leaned forward. "You've thrown yourself to the trolls, my dear. Everyone knows about the dragons now. And not even that," he went on, "The way you spoke to the Lord of Illusion? Not once in my fifty-one years on this earth have I ever seen someone speak to a lord that way." She fidgeted underneath his storming eyes. "Let alone the Lord of Illusion... You're lucky you're still alive."

"Haven't I heard." She mumbled. *Idiot.* She was a damned idiot!

Laurent tilted his head at her response. "I've given you time to mourn over your friend's death, but this is no way to deal with the pain. Not here, at least. You have to be stronger. This may be the Game of Lords, but trust me, dear. It is no game."

Sneering, Valeria crossed her arms and huffed. Bringing up Isaac had hit a nerve she was purposefully avoiding. How dare he?

"You think I don't know that? I've been fighting for my life since I've gotten here. People want me dead. People want me to be kind—they want me to be something that I'm not—that I refuse to be." He merely stared at her as she went on, "I am trying to do my best. I have failed at protecting Isaac. I have failed at many, many things, but I will not fail at how I choose to be strong. You may think caring for someone and hurting when that person is killed right in front of you is weak, but to me it's strong. I've fought battles that you couldn't—that you never will." She sat back and crossed her legs. "Everything I said to the Lord of Illusion was true, and if I die before killing him, then I'll make sure someone else does it for me."

"Are you done now?" Laurent pressed a grin on his face. Valeria shrugged, and he said, "Your attitude and persistence may not bother me, but you cannot spill the secrets of the games to the other con-testants. All of them, Valeria. I had to settle the entire estate down after you revealed the presence of the dragons. You cannot do that again."

She breathed a sigh, settling her heart as it raced inside her chest. "Everyone knows?" He nodded. "I—I didn't realize. I was so caught up with..." She closed her mouth, eyes drifting to the curtains behind Laurent's head. Isaac was too sensitive of a subject to talk about. She couldn't even say his name. "With everything that was happening in the moment." She finished, while shrinking into her chair.

Valeria wished it would swallow her whole.

Laurent's eyes softened a fraction. He pressed his hands onto the desk and looked down at the paper. "I'm sorry for your loss." He said. "He was a kind boy."

Valeria dropped her eyes to her hands and bit back the emotions that clogged her throat.

"Now that I've given you a mere warning, don't make me do it again." He said, "I've already broken enough rules for you, I won't do it again. If someone notices my spared kindness, it may raise suspicion." Before he finished, he added, "I have one more piece of advice for you, and let it be my last." Valeria forgot the aching in her chest and sat forward. "There will be another ball tomorrow night."

Gods. That meant the next trial was the morning after the ball. "So soon?" She asked. "The third trial was only days ago."

He nodded, a look of pain written on his face. "I'm afraid so... The lands overlooking the dropoff—look there, and you should find what you'll be facing."

"The dropoff?" She questioned.

With a glance, Laurent leaned over the desk to whisper, "Follow the main path from the front door of the estate. Follow it all the way to the gates. There you'll find the dropoff."

"What should I expect?"

Her mind was racing. Was it a jump the contestants would have to take and somehow survive? If so, how far would the fall be? Valeria didn't have the muscles in her legs to survive even a ten-foot drop. *Lords,* this was bad.

Laurent's gray eyes flared, and he pressed closer. "History."

28

The main door slammed shut behind Valeria as she trudged toward the gravel pathway. She'd never thought to follow the path, thinking it would only take her to the gates and nothing more. There was a persistent feeling of being trapped, unable to escape the inside of some kind of magical dome. Leaving her hopes of ever escaping the games useless.

Just like the angels inside of the forest, if there was some way for them to leave, Valeria imagined they would have done so by now.

She looked over her shoulder before throwing the hood of her brown cloak over her head. It was only the afternoon. Everyone was usually busy around this time, either training or coming up with some sort of scheme.

Precisely Flynn. He was always doing both of those things.

Four miles later, Valeria walked underneath a canopy of trees that covered the uneven road. A few rabbits and pixies crossed her path every now and then. Her eyes lit up at the tiny winged creatures as they floated past—fast as a lightning strike.

In the Court of Wind, it was rare to see such creatures. They seemed to appear in rather empty places surrounded by wood and dirt.

Valeria smiled and lifted her head. Dozens flew above her. She liked to think that they were shielding her from any wandering, hungry black eyes.

Around her, the forest was dark. Whatever lurked in the trees was silent, given she hadn't heard anything, nor had she wanted to take a peek.

After another two miles of walking, and pixies floating about, Valeria rounded a corner that led out of the forest. Up ahead, a shiny black gate stood, blocking her remaining path. It was where her brief journey ended.

To her right, a few twenty feet away, the ground descended into a steep drop-off. Valeria's eyes widened as she walked toward the cliff.

Her gaze traveled over the vast expanse of the land. Nothing but rocky ground and a few dead trees lingered out in the distance. Valeria dropped her gaze, examining the lengthy distance of the drop.

It was a few hundred feet, if not more. She took a quick step away from the edge. Breath quickening at the space between her and the bottom of the cliff.

Farther behind the gates, Valeria heard wheels turning and gravel crunching.

As fast as she's ever ran before, Valeria ducked into the forest across the road. She threw herself behind a bush and watched a carriage come barreling down the path. The gates began to open as it neared.

She licked her lips when an outrageous and stupid idea entered her mind. *No*, she would never make it through the gates without being caught. Even if the carriage was long out of sight, she wouldn't have enough time to escape by the time the gates closed.

The carriage sped through the opened gates, and not even a second later, they were closed. Snapping shut as soon as the edge of the tire was entirely through.

Valeria closed her eyes and swallowed the dying hope down her throat. When she was done, she ducked farther into the bush and caught the sight of five silhouettes through the window of the carriage. There was a gold and green emblem on the door.

Releasing a breath, Valeria glanced away from the royal carriage. Listening as it disappeared into the forest.

She waited for a few more minutes to pass before deciding that it was clear and crawled out of the bush. After dusting herself off, she crossed the road and stood over the edge of the cliff again.

Whatever Laurent had told her to look for, it could give her an advantage in the next trial. Whether it was the length of the fall to the bottom of the cliff, or something more. Something like... dragons.

She dragged her eyes over the rocks, searching.

When the chilly gusts of wind started drying her eyes out, Valeria sat and let her legs hang over the edge, despite the strong fear of falling.

Around thirty disappointing minutes later, she stood to her feet to leave.

She was turning back for the path when movement caught her eye.

Valeria faced the rocky ground and stared out over the dead shrubs and tall boulders. Deep in the ground was a cave of some sort. It looked small from where she stood, but would be the size of a large building if she were to stand directly in front of it.

The dirt beneath her feet rumbled, and she stumbled back. Gripping her cloak with a gasp, Valeria lifted her gaze again.

Her lips parted when she watched a large—no, large was not a good enough word to describe the thing she was seeing.

The enormous, thick, and long tail swept against the side of a boulder. A chunk of rock crumbled to pieces upon the blow.

Valeria fell back another step, her heart hammering viciously.

Shimmering red scales swayed back and forth as the tail shrunk into the darkness of the cave. Ripping and tearing into the rocks, destroying anything in its path.

Time passed slowly as she watched and waited until it was gone.

Nothing but the cold breeze kept her company. She waited on top of the cliff. Minutes passed, even an hour, but she never left. It was as if Laurent's words finally clicked into place before she turned away from the ledge.

Valeria had just seen a dragon.

A beast born in the first year of life. A beast that had been a part of the deep history of Laterra... Known to be extinct.

Trudging down the path she had come from, head buzzing, shoulders limp, and mouth ajar—Valeria heard a mighty roar that made the gravel shake beneath her feet.

The royal carriage that passed by earlier was now parked beneath the castle's main steps to the doors.

Valeria walked around it and worked her way up the hill to the backside of the estate where she would find the garden. She was moments away from entering the castle and heading up to her room so that she could change for the ball, when she spotted Flynn standing underneath the white gazebo.

His attention was focused on the princess in his arms, who pecked a kiss on his sharp jawline before turning to leave. Helena's eyes landed on Valeria.

Helena was first to glance away, flinging an unbothered smile toward Valeria before sauntering her way through the garden.

The Princess of Laterra stopped in front of Valeria and lifted her head. "Quite an evening, isn't it?" She asked. Chestnut brown hair swept back in a long braid, she was wearing yet another beautiful red gown.

Valeria bit the inside of her lip, bitterness sinking into her bones. "It is lovely." She lied, slightly bowing her head.

Helena's eyes lowered and scanned Valeria's rumpled clothing. Dirt was smeared across the knees of her tight black pants and her cloak was torn at the bottom, where it had snagged on a branch earlier.

She looked like a mess.

Helena grinned. "You've been busy it seems. I'll let you be so you can clean up." She turned toward the door as an official opened it, "I have plenty of things to do before the ball. I'll see you soon."

Then she was gone, and Valeria was left speechless. Not only with how the princess had continuously been kind to her, but because she had openly kissed Flynn. Anyone could have seen.

Did this mean that they were an item now? Together... *betrothed*?

Was Flynn truly going to live through these games, even if he didn't win?

Her face hardened when she turned and looked at him sauntering through the garden. She straightened her spine and marched, meeting him in the middle of the dirt path.

"Are you going to marry her?"

Flynn frowned. "How is that any of your business?"

She shook her head and sneered. "Stop being difficult. Just answer the question."

He shot a dazzling smirk, shoving his hands into the pockets of his black pants. "Of course I'll marry her if that is what she wishes. It'd be foolish of me not to." Flynn huffed when she refused to reply.

The words she wanted to say were lodged in her throat, rather, she kept them there. Afraid that if she said what she wanted, it would ruin everything. She'd already gotten close to Isaac, and now he was gone... She couldn't risk losing anyone else she cared about.

She hated to admit that she even cared for Flynn just by a little, because he could be the reason she was here. What did that make her? Unintelligent? Because none of this would be happening if it weren't for him...

He blinked. "Is there something wrong with that? You seem upset, perhaps confused... Wouldn't you marry the prince? Even if you didn't have a muscle in your body that ached for him? If it meant survival, would you? Honestly?"

"I cannot marry the prince, and no. I would never trap him in a marriage that wasn't made with love." She lied, only to convince him to change his mind.

Gods, why couldn't she let it be? Why couldn't she just be okay with him marrying the princess. It meant he'd be able to live...

He frowned and shuffled his feet. "Even if it meant death? You'd die before marrying someone you didn't love?"

Valeria bit the inside of her lips with a heavy breath. She couldn't tell him about how the prince would rather marry Flynn than her.

"I hope to die being exactly who I am. Nothing more. Nothing less."

"That doesn't answer my question." He stated plainly.

Valeria turned on her heel, anxious to leave. "I don't have to. Good-bye."

She heard a vicious chuckle before he wrapped his fingers around her lower arm and yanked her backwards.

Stumbling, she caught herself against his chest.

"First you want nothing to do with me, but now you question who I want to marry—who I *will* marry. What is wrong with you? Can't you ever make up your mind? *Truly*, Valeria. I try my damned hardest to understand you, but you've given me nothing, yet you want me to answer every question of yours. For *once* can you give me a break and tell me what is going on in that head of yours?"

All she could do was stare, not at his eyes, but anywhere else. Looking over his shoulder, Valeria took a step back and sighed. "I'm going to my room. I'll see you at the ball."

As she was leaving, sure that he would let her go this time, Flynn stepped in front of her, blocking the door. His eyes were darker than she'd ever seen before with black shadows swirling around.

"I don't know why you've chosen to hate me. I don't even know why I let it affect me, but I'm done." He towered over her, glaring. "I'm done trying with you. Our plans and alliance remain in place, but you've nearly driven me crazy. So... I'm done trying to be your friend. Good luck at the ball."

Flynn turned, opened the door, and left her standing alone in the garden.

29

T he past couple hours of Valeria's life seemed to haunt her at the third ball of the Game of Lords.

Haunting, as in the dragon she had seen earlier near the drop-off, would permanently never leave her mind. Especially with all the decorations for the night. It seemed the ball was going to be themed after the next trial.

Small glass dragons of all colors were placed on every event table inside of the castle. Her eyes ran across each one, taking in the details and filling her mind with dread. She nearly tripped over her long white gown as she stared at a large purple statue. The dragon's eyes were venomous orange, teeth as sharp as blades. Valeria gulped before lifting her gown and sauntering toward the ballroom.

Everyone inside the estate and under the king's order was there, filling the room to the cream floral walls.

She stopped beneath the threshold, gripping the fabric of her gown, crystals cutting into her fingers as she examined the dancing crowd in front of her.

Candlelight flickered from above, dangling from the golden chandelier. A man and woman sauntered past. Short golden hair flicked Valeria's nose as the woman swirled around in the man's arms.

Valeria bit her tongue and stepped farther into the room, scanning each face as she looked for Laurent. He knew what the next trial was; he knew and told her. Even when she had let everyone else know that they would fight against or for the winged beasts.

At least some of them would. The rest, well, they would die.

She relaxed her shoulders, loosened a sigh, and lifted her chin upon spotting Flynn entering the ballroom. A dramatic sway in his step.

He was drunk already? Valeria curled her lip.

He dragged his gaze across the room before landing on her. Swallowing, she straightened her posture, brushing a hand down her skirt as she held his hazy stare.

There was so much she didn't know about him. So much he has kept from her. And now Isaac was gone. He was gone, and despite how she felt about Flynn, he was all she had left.

Flynn raked his eyes down her form, taking in her floor-length white gown and the diamonds that dangled from it before meeting her gaze again, a smirk growing on his full lips.

The room began spinning when others brushed past her, twirling and curling their spines as they danced. She wondered if there were any seers in the room, tempted to find one and ask of her near future, when Flynn stepped toward her until he was only a foot away. His rough hand lifted between them and he bit his lower lip.

"Care for a dance?"

Valeria glanced around, searching for his wife-to-be. She cleared her throat. "Aren't you betrothed to someone else?"

His eyes brightened, and a humorous chuckle escaped his mouth. With a hand still between them, he said, "That doesn't mean I can't dance with the woman I'm in an alliance with. Does it?" She only glowered. He continued to smile. "Lords, you really don't like me... look, it's not official yet. I haven't even asked her." He bowed his head, nearly bending a knee when he said, "Please, let me dance with a pretty lady when we could both die tomorrow."

Despite everything else, the trial, the engagement, the death, and the supposed betrayal—Valeria took his hand.

And so they danced.

They were a tangle of black and white that brushed through the crowd of dancers. He twirled her around before pulling her back against his chest. That was when the violin slowed and the piano picked up. Hands on her waist, fingers gripping the fabric, Flynn's once bright eyes darkened as he stared down at her.

Valeria's breath hitched, and she failed to close her parted lips. She grabbed his hands from off of her waist and took a step back. Flynn lifted their arms and continued to move with the music, much slower than before.

"I have a question." He said.

She could feel his gaze wandering all over her face. She did the opposite and watched the flow of dancers over his shoulder. They kept her mind busy from having to think about who was currently holding her hands. Even if his cold fingers squeezed hers with an uncertain gentleness.

Caressing the backside of her thumb with his own, Flynn moved closer, their chests nearly grazing.

"What is it?" She asked.

Crystal blue eyes met her emerald ones when she finally lifted her gaze to his.

He tilted his head. "Why is it that you felt the need to search my room?"

Her jaw fell slack, eyes widening. He merely smirked.

Before he could point out her obvious guilt, she focused on her moving feet instead. "I don't know what you mean. I've never been in your room, nor have I ever wanted to."

He snickered, shook his head, then dipped her. Valeria gasped when he leaned over and drawled out, "Liar."

When he pulled her back up, an arm tucked around her waist, she pinched his shoulder. "It's not like I found anything interesting, anyway."

He bit back a smile. "You would think differently if I would've been there."

She rolled her eyes, scoffing when he tilted his chin to get a better look at her flamed cheeks. She asked, "Are you truly that obsessed with yourself?"

"Should I be?"

Then she smelled it, the liquor. It was pouring off of him, clinging to his clothes and breath. Valeria grimaced and tried to step away from him, but he pulled closer and spun her around.

"You're drunk." She stated.

"Not enough to stumble over my feet." As soon as he said it, she stumbled. He snickered and balanced her. "Unlike you."

Valeria glared at him.

With so much happening, a trial tomorrow, the princess sitting at the front of the room, and he was drunk? She ripped herself away from him, grabbed his arm, and pulled him to the side of the room.

"What is wrong with you?" Before he could reply, she started again, "The trial is tomorrow and you're drunk."

He blinked. A lousy smile spread on his lips when he glanced at her hand around his arm. "Is that a problem for you?"

Grinding her teeth, Valeria ran a free hand through her curled hair before closing her eyes and releasing a breath. "You don't know. Of course you don't know." Sighing, she grabbed his shoulder and pulled him closer. "Dragons, Flynn. They're a part of the next trial."

Flynn's mouth parted for a moment. She thought he might've shaken out of his drunken trance, but he only smiled yet again. "Flynn." She begged, then looked over his shoulder, where a table with drinks sat against the wall.

Pulling him with, Valeria stomped over to it, requested a glass of water, then handed it to the easily distracted man beside her.

"*Drink.*" She told him, holding the glass against his lips.

So he did. Though, not without staring at her over the rim. When he was done, she lowered the glass and set it on the table.

"I'm not a stupid drunk, you know."

She ignored him, searching for anyone that might've been looking their way. What would Helena think if she saw him this way?

Flynn leaned against the table. "I've only had three drinks, Val."

She refused to look at him after spotting the princess sitting at the front of the room, hazel eyes on her brother as he spoke. She huffed. "Three drinks too many."

"And you're the one to judge? The girl that doesn't want anything to do with me suddenly cares about how much I drink? Who I marry? And what's inside my room?"

Blood thrummed inside her ears.

She clenched her fists, squeezing back the anger as she hissed through her teeth, "I was only in your room because you are keeping things from me." She paused and stepped closer. "I have enough reasons to care about what you're doing, because you are the reason that I'm even here."

Quickly, he frowned and removed his weight from off of the table. "What?"

She pressed a finger to his chest and glared. "I know everything, Flynn. You switched my sister's name with mine. You are the reason I'm here, and I have every right to find out why."

His nostrils flared. He swatted her hand away from his chest. "I—"

Cutting him off, Valeria angled her body away from the people who started to take notice of their heated conversation. "Look, you said you're tired of my attitude toward you, but so am I." Flynn continued to frown, eyes wide and searching her face as she said, "This alliance or whatever plan you have to get us both out of here, that remains in place. That is the only reason I let myself be around you. No more games and no more lies. You got me into this, now you get me out of it." She grabbed another glass of water and slammed it against his chest. "Drink, because I'm relying on you. Not a drunken idiot."

His eyes flared before she turned and sauntered away.

She found herself in the hallway after some time. The statue of the dragon standing tall and proud in front of her. Teeth gleaming underneath the candlelight, scales shimmering against colorful gowns and suits that passed by.

The hallway was much darker than the ballroom since daylight came to an end and night fell. Perhaps that is why she chose it as the place to spend the rest of the ball. She couldn't stand the spiraling dancers and all of their chittering laughter. Or maybe it was just her need to hide from Flynn until her flusteredness passed. Either way, she didn't care. She was glad to be out of sight and out of mind. It was better than having a bunch of strangers constantly lingering over her shoulder, only interested in her presence in the games.

If Isaac were there, he'd be right by her side, quietly murmuring something about the way everyone was scouring around them, or making a joke about what Laurent was wearing for the night.

Valeria sighed and lifted a hand toward the dragon's snout.

She brushed a finger between the sharp teeth, feeling the smoothness of the crystal. It wasn't real. No, it was far smaller—far cleaner than the giant, bristly scarlet firetail she had seen earlier.

"They're much larger in person."

Valeria jumped and snatched her hand away from the statue. She turned, a fist upon her chest, catching her breath when she glimpsed the prince leaning against the wall across from her.

Prince Luther pressed off the wall. His eyes scanning the dragon, he said, "You wouldn't believe the height of the largest dragon that lived." He said while tucking his hands into his pockets. "The beast was giant. I'll tell you that."

The hallway light dimmed when he leaned over her shoulder. Valeria glanced passed him, peering into the ballroom. She didn't know if being seen with the prince would be good for her game. If anyone saw the threat that they already assumed she was, they wouldn't hesitate to try killing her tomorrow.

The prince moved into her line of vision, meeting her hesitant eyes. "No one cares." The hint of a smile tugged at his lips. "Being seen with me, I mean. Mostly everyone here knows of my interest in men. It's my father who refuses to see the truth." He scoffed, and then added, "He avoids the truth like it's a plague."

She pursed her lips and tilted her head. "I'm sorry to hear that."

"I'm not." He paused, examining the confusion on her face before starting again. "The less he knows, the better."

A prince that had secrets and a princess that was sneaking around with a Game of Lords contestant. What else could the kingdom be hiding?

"I assume you already know what the trial will be tomorrow morning?" She asked, hoping to get any sort of advice, or help.

He glanced at the statue before offering his hand. Valeria took it, and not a moment later he was tugging her through the hall and out the main doors of the estate. Her eyes skimmed through the darkness, lingering in the direction she had traveled early in the day.

Minutes passed as he stood and stared at the night sky.

The stars shimmered against the radiance of the full moon. He frowned and dropped his eyes. "I'm afraid there's not much I can tell you, nor that I can do to help you." She swallowed, staring at the small light that brushed against his chiseled jaw. He met her gaze before looking away. "There are far deadlier things in this world than what you'll be facing tomorrow. My only hope is that it'll be quick. Whatever happens, just let it be quick."

The last of his words were hushed. As if he was speaking more to himself than her.

Valeria turned away from him and stared at the sky, where small colorful lights flew in all directions, their bright hues left a trickle of colors behind as they danced beneath the moon.

Prince Luther brushed a soft finger against her wrist when he turned around, excusing himself. Valeria offered a small smile, although her gaze remained on the pixies. Letting herself believe that they were there out of comfort.

Making herself believe that everything would be okay.

That she would be okay.

Her legs trembled and throat bobbed, a tear slid freely down her cheek.

The night fell empty as the ball came to an end.

Valeria trudged up the stairs to her door, only to pause upon spotting Flynn resting against it. He ran his hands through his blonde hair before he saw her. She halted a step, then slowly continued toward him.

"What do you want?" She asked, too drained to argue. Her eyes were wet and cheeks were cold with undried tears. She was sure her makeup was smeared and running down her face.

"Are you okay?" He asked while pushing off the door and rushing to her side. "What happened?" His brows furrowed as he checked over her wellbeing. "I swear if it was Lance again I'll—"

"It wasn't Lance." She interrupted. "I've just... It's just been a rough night."

More like a rough month and a half.

Flynn frowned before taking a step back. He bit his lip, unsure of what to say.

Guilt pooled inside her gut. Taunting her—begging her to apologize, because the trial was tomorrow, and she didn't know if it would be her last night alive.

Just as Flynn turned for his door, she reached out and placed a palm on his elbow. "Flynn." She whispered.

He stopped and faced her, eyes wide, he asked, "Yes?"

She chewed on the inside of her lip, forcing herself to meet his crystal gaze. His lips parted, as if he wanted to speak, but craved to hear what she had to say first.

"I never thanked you."

He frowned. "For what?"

"For giving me medicine after the Forest of Angels. For defending me against Lance. For training me..." She stopped, feeling her heart sink into her stomach as the nerves on her face twitched.

Gods, please don't cry again.

Valeria licked her cold lips, and stepped closer to him. Examining the way his fist clenched at his sides, his searching—hesitant gaze.

Flynn's brows furrowed as she went on, "For sticking by my side after I've been anything but kind to you."

Before she let him respond, Valeria nudged past to get to her door. All she wanted to do was curl into a pillow and weep. Though before she could, Flynn put a hand on the door, stopping her.

"What?" She asked, drained from the games—from *everything*.

He pursed his lips and looked away. "I wanted to say... I miss him, too. You know? And I'm sorry. I should have tried harder to protect him."

That hard lump in her throat thickened yet again.

Flynn was the type of person she would have befriended in the Court of Wind, but since they had met under rather different circumstances, she'd only pushed him away.

It was for their own good, because this attraction—this feeling that clung and gnawed at her insides for him would only get her hurt in the end.

Valeria swallowed and faced the door before twisting the knob. "I'm not sure who you are Flynn, or what you have planned for us, but please—make sure that whoever did this to Isaac—whoever put him in here, gets what they deserve."

"I will." He said before they let silence fall upon them.

Valeria left him standing in the hall. She slunk onto her bed and stared out the window, watching the lights dance across the lake.

30

Carriages strolled the seven contestants down through the muddy paths and tunnels of Azrael estate. As Valeria was escorted through the tunnel and out through the other side of the mountain, she couldn't see a hint of light.

She watched out the window; the wheels bumping along the rocks. The sun filtered in through the small oval window at her side. Swiveling around in her seat, she peered out the other side where the land stretched for about several miles until a wall of dirt and rock sat in its way. Her eyes widened.

The drop-off.

Biting her lip, Valeria twisted her braid in her hands, wondering if she should have put it in a bun for the trial. Before, she had thought that the trial would start on top of the cliff, but somehow the carriages had taken them on a different path that led them straight down into the valley where she had seen the red scales of a firetail slink into a cave.

They'd be meeting the dragons face to face then. The simplicity she craved was a mirage in the treacherous world of the Game of Lords. She hoped for some sort of restraint on the beasts otherwise; she wasn't sure if she would last even ten seconds against them.

Each carriage came to a halt upon reaching their destination. A few moments later, before Valeria could take in her surroundings, an official yanked open her carriage door.

"Get out." He spat. Not giving her a chance to move before he reached in and yanked her out.

She tripped over her feet, fell the one-foot-drop to the pale stone and sucked in a sharp breath through her teeth.

The rush of icy air against her spine had her crossing her arms and hunching over. It was too cold for the near summer solstice that was supposed to arrive in just a few weeks.

The six other contestants stumbled out of their carriages, Flynn however stepped out calm and slow. His gaze fixated on her before glancing away. Valeria followed his eyes, finding Laurent stalking over a slump of a hill. He cursed when a pebble rolled underneath his boot.

The gamerunner stopped in front of the carriages, rubbed his palms together, and nodded over his shoulder. "Come with me."

One after another, they each followed him down the hill he came from. The land opened up, revealing stone and rubble. A few scraggly bushes lined the path as they trudged toward a set of tents.

Laurent picked up his pace when another burst of wind brushed past, rumpling his neat black suit. "We'll be staying in the tents for the time being. I imagine it will be a week or two before we travel back to the estate."

Valeria frowned, looking out over the vacant land. In the spot, miles away, where the scaled firetail had bashed into boulders before it shrunk into the dark cavernous cave.

They trudged closer to the camp. Officials stood, lingering around the tents. The largest tent was surrounded by not ten, not twenty, but nearly fifty officials dressed in their royal green and gold uniforms. Each holding a pistol at their sides. She noted how their eyes weren't focused on the seven contestants, but instead on the rocky hills of the valley.

"That's the king's tent." Laurent said after catching her drifting gaze. "The contestants' tents, however smaller, tend to be warmer, and have much more privacy." Laurent pointed over his shoulder.

Half a mile away from the king's tent, there were seven smaller ones. Only a few feet separated the single tents from each other. An official standing between each short gap of space.

Valeria attempted to throw the hood of her cloak over her head to block the gusting wind when her eyes landed on the back of Lance's auburn-colored-head.

If the dragons didn't kill her, Lance surely would.

"You can find your uniforms for the next trial in your tents. The officials will show you to your new rooms." Laurent ushered the contestants past, showing them the small rocky trail that led to their camp.

When Valeria passed him, he gave a tightlipped smile. His eyes squinting against the cool breeze, he dropped his gaze. "I'll try my best to make sure you are all taken care of."

She continued walking, as if he hadn't said anything else to them. She followed the short line of contestants. There were two contestants between herself and Flynn. Lance strode in the very front.

He stopped in place, causing Flynn to come to a sudden halt as well. With a grunt, Flynn shoved past, sidestepping Lance before he continued toward the camp.

Valeria froze in place as Lance's gaze landed on Laurent over her shoulder. Quickly, she ducked around him. Hoping he didn't notice her passing.

"Are the dragons here?" Lance asked.

Her steps faltered, Laurent took his time to reply.

Then, as she watched her feet crunch into the dry earth, Laurent spoke, "Yes... they are waiting."

Valeria let the words blur over the rest of her thoughts as she sucked in a soothing breath.

Standing on top of the rocky hillside, a valley of dead grass below. Valeria examined the tight black pants and shirt that sculpted her body. A hard cushion of leather armor curved around her waist and up over her chest. The material on her thighs was stiff. She tried stretching in the new armor before leaving her tent earlier, but she had been rushed out by an official who barged in, not caring when she screamed and thrashed in his arms.

He revealed little concern as he dragged her through the dirt, only letting her go once he reached the line where the rest of the contestants stood. They were all dressed the same, wearing the same leathers and black clothing.

At least she had gotten the chance to re-braid her hair.

Valeria reached over her back and double-checked her braid, making sure it was tucked tightly underneath her shirt. Anything that was loose could put her at risk of being snagged by snapping teeth, or hands that might grab and throw her toward a hungry beast.

Despite the rain and gray sky, the officials wouldn't let her wear an old raggedy cloak. Only the clothing that was on her back. At least she had her dagger. She could feel its wooden handle digging into her inner thigh.

They hadn't bothered to pat her down. It's not like she could kill a dragon with just a small blade, anyway. It wasn't for them; she reminded herself. Just Lance. Only Lance.

A small crowd of people stood behind her. She disregarded who it all consisted of. The king, his children, his people, they didn't matter.

The next hour of her life did, and making sure she survived was her sole concern.

Valeria fixed her sleeves, centered herself on the rocky hill, and focused on Laurent, who sauntered across the valley below. Dressed in black, he brushed a hand down his chest and smiled up at the crowd.

"Welcome to the greatest—most thrilling trial of the games!" He shouted.

An echo of yelps and whoops passed through her ears. She glared, adjusting her feet when a blast of wind nearly blew her off of the uneven stones.

"As we stand and wait for the winged beast, let's take a moment to remember the fallen." A few scoffs sounded from behind, but she ignored them, meeting Laurent's eyes. He offered up a small smile that she returned, though her lips shook as she pressed them together.

For Isaac, the brief silence was for him.

Valeria nodded her head at the gamerunner.

"Today, this hour, after centuries of wondering and searching—we have bred and raised a new generation of dragons." The crowd fell eerily silent. "Our seven contestants have a goal, and only one. Find a dragon, tame it. But be cautious. These beasts don't choose by chance. They make a choice based on their needs—their wants. They see through the walls of each person... they see what kind of soul you carry. If they disagree with your personality, they will unleash their golden flame."

Valeria gulped. She ran her eyes over the other contestants. Some were pale with fear, others a greenish hue.

Flynn was staring at his hands before he tucked them into his pockets.

Laurent went on, "Many of you will not be chosen today. In fact, I expect a majority of you won't be chosen, but that is not up to me. We don't have control of these beasts. They make the decisions today."

A rush of electric wind shocked Valeria, her toes curling inside her boots. It rushed up her legs, her belly, and all the way to her scalp. Suddenly, a current of fire flared, flaming from above.

Laurent didn't duck, but she noticed the way his knees wobbled when a mighty beast landed behind him.

The blood red dragon roared, casting a tower of flame above the gamerunner's head.

Laurent rushed forward, right toward Valeria. His eyes were wide as saucers when he brushed past. She didn't turn, she couldn't.

"Contestants!" It wasn't Laurent that yelled.

No, the tone was deadlier, stricter. It held more power.

The king stepped between the line of contestants. "Enter the valley. Become a rider or walk with the dead. This could be your new beginning or your end. It's time to play the Game of Lords."

Before the contestants could turn and take a glance at the crowd that would watch their ultimate doom or new life begin, another gush of wind blasted into their backs.

Valeria fell from the rocks, tumbling down onto the dry yellow field, and landed on her side. She hissed into the grass, her rib throbbing as she tried to stand up.

The others slid down on their hands and spines, rocks toppling down with. She watched Flynn remain standing on the hill. He turned and sent a deadly glare over his shoulder.

He didn't move.

"Flynn." She whispered with a hand on her ribs. He faced her, although his eyes were shaded with a swirling darkness. There was only anger in his narrowed gaze. "Breathe." She said, "Stay with me."

It took a moment to drown out the tension in his features, before his vision cleared and he trudged gracefully down the rest of the hill. Offering her a hand, she took it and slowly stood to her feet beside him.

Dusting herself off, she fixed her gaze on the rock she had fallen from. Then to Flynn, who was looking over her shoulder. A mix of colors and shock in his eyes.

She already knew what he was looking at from the heat on her back, the grass that shriveled up and turned to ash at her feet. Valeria spun around, slow, unprepared. She was entirely unprepared for what stood before her.

Violet scales, each one larger than her head, decorated the tall dragon that landed beside the smaller scarlett one. Its tail slithered back and forth, flicking the grass out of the ground. Leaving nothing but dirt underneath its length.

Valeria almost fell to her knees, but Flynn caught her elbow and held her up. "We do this together." His breath caressed the shell of her ear, just about distracting her from the enormous beasts that stood fifty feet away.

"Together." She whispered, straightening her spine.

The first contestant to take a step forward was Felix Caddel from the Court of Storms. A small voice cheered from behind, but her eyes never faltered from his catlike steps. His shoulders tensed when the red dragon swiveled its neck to look at him. Giant green eyes stared, nostrils flared. Steam vaporized through the air from its snout.

Flynn moved beside her. His hand was still gripping her elbow as they watched Felix prowl closer and closer.

What happened next was sudden, too quick to see how, or even why it happened. The red dragon lifted its head, opened its mouth wide, and a roar of flame enveloped Felix's body.

Valeria shrunk into her hands, blocking the heat from her face. When it was over, she opened her eyes and examined the spot where Felix had been. Only a trail of ash was left of his presence. A lump of black on the earth.

Valeria held back a cry of fear.

Flynn squeezed her elbow, but she failed to notice, because the violet dragon snarled.

"Val." He tried to pull her attention away. She only shook him off, stepping back.

No one moved.

Minutes passed as the remaining six contestants stared at what was left of Felix's body.

The crowd chanted, yelled, cheered.

Valeria looked over her shoulder. She watched the contestants. Examined their fear, their desperation to flee.

She turned back to the crowd and met the king's eye.

He lifted his lips into a grin. But all she did was stare. Let him see her. Let him see what he had done to these people—to these lives that he had taken. The lives that he was so selfishly playing with for his own greedy entertainment.

She'd kill him.

Another flame scorched her spine. Valeria removed her gaze from the king, catching how his dark eyes brightened.

Lance was laughing, bent over, cackling after shoving Vincent Brooks into the line of fire.

His body glowed underneath the flame before turning black and falling like dust into a pile of ash. She swallowed the bile in her throat and turned her glare onto Lance, who was wiping the laughter from his face as the red dragon approached.

The beast may have been smaller than the violet one, but its claws were still as large as a boulder. She watched it paw forward, straight toward Lance.

From her side, she noticed Flynns absence. Valeria turned and frowned. "Flynn?" She asked over the growling creature.

There were only two dragons, and five contestants left. What were her odds? How was this anything but pure cruelty? She'd never felt more like a mouse in a cage, trapped, only used for show.

And Lance was the lion, as he failed to show fear toward the dragon that towered above him. Its claws dug into the earth, gripping the dirt as it bowed before his body.

Valeria's blood chilled. She fell back a step, her heart sinking into her stomach.

How? How in Gods-eating Laterra was the firetail bowing to the one male she absolutely loathed?

She watched in silence. The entire crowd did as Lance lifted a hand toward the dragon's gleaming ruby scales. He brushed a hand down its leathery skin. A purr, granting access for Lance to climb over its shoulder and crawl onto its back.

He adjusted his weight comfortably on the dragon before lifting his gaze, a smug grin on his face.

"Look at that." He bragged. "You can call me the Lord of Dragons already."

The red dragon thrashed on its feet. Lance yelped and gripped the spikes on its back to keep his balance.

Valeria stood dumbstruck. Numb, despite the heat—the two piles of ashes only twenty feet in front of her. She was numb with burning, wretched anger. And where was Flynn? He'd left her alone after promising to stick together.

His plans were quickly going to shit

If there was only one dragon left to tame, then that meant... It meant it was either him or her. And if not them, then either the man or girl standing beside her.

Lance stalked off with his dragon, wings tucked in tightly at its sides, before spreading wide. A gust of wind blew the loose pieces of her braid back when the beast roared onto its hind feet. She watched in awe as Lance clung tightly to the base of its long neck, eyes wide and full of fear. Lance and the dragon lunged off of the ground.

The tan grass melded to the dirt when the firetail flew. Its large shadow crossed over their heads, flying toward the king and his crowd. She watched the red beast slowly descend, landing on top of the rocky hill. Its snarling growl rippled something deep within Valeria's chest.

She took a step back, entranced by its fire-tipped tail whipping toward her. She fell back, landing on her hands and watched Lance and his dragon look over the crowd from the rocks.

There was nothing but silence, and then... a hesitant moment later, a roar of cheers echoed across the hill and into the valley.

"Our first rider of the new generation of dragons!" The king shouted. His small eyes found hers over the slope of the hill. "Who will join him?"

Valeria never despised anything more in her life. Lance was winning.

A rush of unyielding fury was the only reason she stood to her feet and turned her back to the red dragon and its arrogant rider. She faced the larger, much deadlier violet beast. It snarled upon meeting her emerald gaze, dragging a claw into the grass.

Valeria didn't falter.

She brushed a hand over her hair, securing her braid underneath her shirt, and stalked for the dragon. She dipped her chin and focused on moving forward. Ignoring the buckling of her knees, she'd never felt such adrenaline. Her will to live—to survive... to win. She hadn't felt it before like she did now.

From her side, she found the blue eyes of Flynn, who marched beside her. She flicked a glance his way. "It's mine." She growled.

But Flynn continued alongside her, his gaze unflinching as he stared ahead at the dark beast that looked between the both of them. Its gaze considering, debating on which rider it wanted.

Valeria lifted her shoulders and prepared for a quick, fiery demise.

"Val, it's mine." He said.

She ignored him, only quickened her pace. The dragon stood taller, flaring its wings and bowing its head.

For her? Or for Flynn?

They were fifty feet away. So close. Yet so far from their alliance—their plans to win together. It wouldn't work. He couldn't take this opportunity from her. He had Helena. The princess.

"Flynn." She urged, as they got closer. "Go back, offer your hand in marriage to Helena."

"No."

Blood boiling, she clenched her jaw. "*Do it now.*"

"I can't." He said. Never missing a step, a beat, Flynn's steps grew wider.

Twenty feet. Only twenty feet to reach the bowing dragon.

"Please, Flynn." She begged. "Don't take this from me."

Flynn stopped. She followed. Although her eyes never strayed from the beast that bowed just a yard away.

"I'm not taking anything from you. Now let me get on what's already mine."

A wind so heavy that it raveled the grass beneath her feet and made the earth shake. Valeria met Flynn's narrow eyes.

The corner of his lip curled upward before he said, "Because yours is right there." He lifted two fingers to his forehead, turned, and jogged toward the violet beast. She watched him pat its purring snout and climb onto its spine.

When he was settled, they took off into a flight. Soaring over her head and landing right next to Lance and the red firetail.

She tried to remember everything she knew about dragons. Every piece of knowledge and information that Isaac had researched for her. Even the crumpled flower petal that was tucked inside her boot. She failed to pull it out when a white shadow landed in front of her.

The ground croaked and shook. A vibration of power made her knees buckle.

A memory of Lilith crumpling a note and tossing it into a blazing fire flashed behind her eyes. When she lifted her head and saw the white thorn tailed beast standing in front of her, she took that memory of her sister, and she took the ones that came after, and she forged them into that very moment.

She forged what used to be her past life—the days she'd picked flowers in the meadow behind her fathers antique shop... she layered the feelings from those memories into the one she was making in that dry valley.

And she sank to her knees.

31

G olden irises blinked, watching Valeria carefully—gently lift her head to examine the beast's scales and large white wings.

Her mind hollowed, lungs expanding, electric energy pumped throughout her already scattered heartbeat as she clawed a hand into the ruined grass. The dragon followed the movement with its eyes, a shallow breath fluttering her copper hair back as she pressed a hand into the ground to stand.

Despite the slight tremble of her knees, Valeria raised her chin and stared at the intimidating beast towering above her.

Over the sharp, thorny spine, she spotted Flynn swiveling around on his violet beast—blue eyes wide as he watched her from afar.

Valeria squinted, bringing her thick mental shields up, and holding them solidly in place.

"Alright." She muttered more to herself than to the dragon.

It tilted its head, tail stirring behind its legs, watching her with narrow golden eyes. Valeria cursed underneath her breath before reaching toward her boot.

Before she could grab the limp, dry Death Lily petal, a white paw stomped forward, stopping her, making the ground shake.

A small vibration traveling up her legs. "It's okay." She mumbled to the beast, who only stared down at her. Valeria lifted both of her palms, letting the dragon see that she meant no violence or fear. "See? I—I'm not going to hurt you."

Releasing a shaky breath, she held its eye. Unaware of what to think or even how to feel. Flynn said this dragon was hers, but there were still two other contestants left dragon-less.

Valeria needed to tame it before them.

She glanced over the white dragon's rigid shoulder, where Rob Johnson and Isabelle Callenfeer were standing. Rob was down on his knees, praying to the dirt and struggling to contain his tears.

But it wasn't him who Valeria was concerned about.

She saw Isabelle's determined glare. The younger girl trudged forward, eyes dark and centered on the whitetail that swept toward her. Isabelle stumbled back, but began her advance again, this time avoiding the swiping thorntail.

The white beast flicked its eyes away as if sensing the girl sneaking up from behind. It glanced back at Valeria before rearing up on its hind legs with an aggravated snarl.

Valeria fell back, landing on her hands. Cursing when her wrist twisted just too much. Though, when the dragon landed on its front legs again, wings flaring—it whipped its head back toward her. Blinking, slivered pupils dilating.

Her heart stopped when a breath of flame enveloped Isabelle's body from Lance's firetail, who was still sitting on the hill beside Flynn.

She snapped her gaze back to the pure white claws that prowled toward her. A low hum numbing the nerves in her body as the dragon stopped five long paces away. It held its head up, as if to strike.

Her face paled at the distance between her body and the dragon's teeth. Its enormous snout was nearly thirty strides high, staring down at her.

She forgot how to breathe—how to move when the dragon dipped its head. It leaned forward, first onto its ankle, and then on to its knees. Next, its neck was lowering down beside her body. Valeria couldn't believe it. She couldn't move. Nothing explained what she felt in that undying moment as the dragon knelt, bowed, and granted access to the most vulnerable part of its body.

When she took too long examining the edges of each shimmering scale, a growl vibrated down its neck and out of its leathery mouth. She released a breath, swallowed back her crippling fear, and reached up to grip a smooth white scale.

Climbing over a large leg, then up over its shoulder, took her merely an entire minute until she was sitting at the top of the beast's spine.

There was a moment of silence over the valley. Though, when her dragon turned to face the crowd—Valeria swore she could have seen a dark look glaze over the king's hardened face. Then she let her emerald eyes travel over the crowd, her body lurching left and right as the dragon began walking back to the hill.

She was dead. *Wasn't she?* There was no possible way that she had just lived through that. After everything... It couldn't have been real.

Valeria pinched her thigh before clinging harder to the dragon's scaley back. Keeping her grip tight in order to not slip off—she looked at her hands, then turned her head to watch the length of its white body move. The thorntail bashed into the grass, rippling the dry earth beneath its weight.

Gods. How did it happen? How had Valeria come from being a scared, innocent girl in the Court of Wind, to becoming a dragon rider? Let alone one of the final three contestants in the Game of Lords...

Lilith would never believe it. Her father would never—not in a million years believe what had just happened.

The climb up the hill made Valeria yelp when her body began sliding over a large shoulder. She gripped the nearest thorn and threw herself back into place. The dragon halted, tossing a look over its shoulder and huffed—as if annoyed.

Valeria furrowed her brows at the back of its head before looking over at the violet scaled beast holding Flynn on its back. She met his wide eyes, a small smirk blooming on his lips as he watched her.

They remained silent. Valeria was lost for words, but Flynn just smiled, nodding at her before he and his dragon faced the eerily quiet crowd.

Underneath the judging eyes of the king and his men, she lifted her gaze over the valley and searched for the gamerunner. When she spotted him, Laurent only stared. His eyes were wide and wild, mouth agape. Then he lifted his gaze to hers, and his lips only spread wider.

Valeria smirked through small, shaky breaths. Her chest was thrumming—beating so furiously she was surprised she hadn't passed out.

A clap exploded through the wind, brushing against her frozen ears.

That was when her eyes locked with the Lord of Sky's, who she hadn't seen standing in the crowd before. She frowned. He observed every detail of her face, expression falling flat when he realized who he was looking at.

She bit the inside of her lip and turned toward the king.

"Well, here I thought the rules were simple." He said. "So why do I see four alive contestants, yet only three are on beasts?" The king threw a sharp, demanding look at the four officials at his side. "Kill him." He pointed out over the hill where Rob Johnson was still on his hands and knees.

His rambling grew louder and louder as the officials stepped toward the cliff and readied their guns. Valeria's breath hitched. Her dragon growled, deep and unraveling. Steam escaped its snout before turning toward the king, who dropped his arm and walked back to his dais.

Rob Johnson lowered his chest to the ground, pressing his face into the grass. "For they don't know what they do!" He shouted. "Forgive them."

But his prayer was cut short when the first bullet was released from an official's pistol. Valeria closed her eyes and jolted.

When the second bullet was released, she didn't jump.

When the third and fourth were released, she opened her eyes and felt her body compulse, wanting and needing to do something. Her dragon stirred beneath her, just as Valeria's blood swam furiously through her veins.

Then, when the fifth bullet hit flesh, and Rob Johnson was no longer chanting, Valeria looked at the king, who was smiling and chatting with the Lord of Illusion.

Maybe there was some part of herself that she'd never experienced before that was hidden—buried deep within, but now it twisted and riled up, begging to be released. Maybe she had never been pushed so hard—felt so greatly, that the king's death was all she craved.

All of the officials standing at his side willingly and arrogantly, silent as they killed innocents whenever commanded to do so—deserved what Valeria wished so greatly to do. For Isaac, for Alexa, for Rob.

She would kill.

So when the white claws ripped into the rocks, shredding and tearing the boulders apart, Valeria held the king's staggering gaze, he snapped his hands toward her and the dragon she rode.

Valeria smirked when the white wings expanded around her. They flapped once, and then twice before she was airborne.

After releasing a breath of white-hot flame, and watching it simmer above the shocked crowd, she and her beast flew toward the mountains.

It wasn't long before a second pair of wings flapped behind her. She caught a hue of purple from the corner of her eye. Flynn clung tightly to his dragon's collar; they flew beside her, a smile blooming on his lips, eyes bright.

The wind bashed against her face, unrelenting and free. Valeria gulped before she was smiling as well. She'd never felt more alive.

Flynn whooped and shouted. She glanced over, eyes nearly shutting as the wind blew furiously against her. She watched Flynn tighten his legs, thighs hardening as he ever so slowly released his grip.

She almost yelled at him as he withdrew his arms from the violet dragon's spine. Flynn lifted his head to the clouds and threw his arms out.

She chuckled.

Flynn opened his eyes, his gaze wide and full of life. He shouted, but she failed to hear over the flapping wings. She only laughed.

If it was her last day in the game, she wanted to take something from it. She wanted to soar and fly. She wanted to feel alive. Running from the trial and into the mountains was the farthest she would take her short escape. A final moment of freedom. Even if it were to get her killed when she returned.

She didn't care. From what it seemed, neither did Flynn.

And so they soared through the skies, smiling through the wind. Watching the violet and white scales stir and mix together as the dragons raced for the mountainside.

A mighty roar trembled against her dragon's spine when it released a breath of scolding-hot flame. By the time they soared through it, it was nothing but a mist of warm vapor brushing against her cheeks.

Valeria's hair unleashed itself from her shirt and thrashed against her back.

They neared the cliff, and she closed her eyes, exhaling the pure adrenaline in her veins. She let herself feel. The air, the oxygen filling her lungs. The sting against her closed lids as she held herself up. The beating of her wild heart.

There were only three contestants left.

She prayed before they landed on the mountainside. Repeating the prayer she had heard from Rob Johnson. Whatever God he praised, she chanted his prayers against the wind. Hoping he could hear. Hoping he knew that she was listening—she was with him.

The landing was slow and rough as Valeria's dragon gracefully made her descent onto the side of the mountain. She had to cling tightly to a scale jutting out of the dragon's back in order to prevent herself from sliding off.

Her heart was thrashing inside her chest.

Hesitantly, she unclamped her thighs and slid down the smooth shoulder of the white thorntail. The dragon dipped lower, not expecting Valeria to get off.

Wind gushed against her back, pushing her closer to Flynn and his violet beast, who landed behind her. She turned, eyes wide, watching Flynn crawl over a shoulder and slide down the dragon's leg. He did so as if he'd done it hundreds of times before.

Flynn gave the dragon a pat on a large scale before he stepped away and faced Valeria.

She expected him to speak, but he didn't. He might have dragged his eyes up her body, scanning the way the black leather armor clung to her waist and legs. But she couldn't tell, because she was also surveying the way his armor shaped the muscles on his arms.

Her mind ran blank. She couldn't find the words to speak. Everything was growing hot—too hot.

Valeria had just ridden a dragon.

She swallowed, biting her lip as she held Flynn's full, undivided attention.

A *dragon*... she gave the white beast a mere glance before looking back at Flynn.

Her heart began to thunder harder and harder. Chest quaking when she remembered the way he smiled at her. His arms free, wind raveling his thick, messy hair... he could have fallen.

Eyes wide and vibrant, Valeria blinked.

He stood closer, a foot scuffing into the dirt when he paused for a split second, as if he almost let himself rethink his next decision. But he continued prowling toward her. Never faltering, not as his hands gripped the back of her neck and pulled her closer.

He didn't hesitate to lean down, and let his lips meld onto hers.

She tensed, unsure—indecisive, before melting into the feel of his cold skin. Adrenaline coursed through her veins. Digging a hand into his golden hair, she tugged him harder against her, needing him closer, *wanting* him closer.

Flynn groaned, throaty and full of desire. He bit at her lip, her knees wobbled, almost making her fall to the dirty ground.

She loosened her grip around his neck— *Flynn's* neck...

What was she even doing? Flynn wasn't right for her. Why was she letting it happen? Why was she enjoying it so much?

Valeria pressed her palms against his chest, he tried to pull her back in, but she was already shoving him away.

He dropped his arms and sauntered backwards, just a few paces, sure to leave a good enough space between them. Valeria's mouth parted, uncertain of what to say. She only stared at him. At his hungry, dark eyes. His swollen pink lips.

Her body trembled. The silence was lengthy enough to make her want to leave.

Flynn huffed, dragging a palm through his tangled hair. "Stop me."

"What?" She glanced at his clenched fists before meeting his shadowed eyes. "Stop what?"

Then he was moving again. First he slid his hands around her waist, then he pressed his solid chest into hers. She only stared up at his face, watching him lower his mouth down to hers, but stopping before they touched.

"Are you going to stop me?" He asked, dipping his head.

Then he kissed her slowly. And she didn't stop him.

They were a tangle of limbs and lips. Nothing else mattered at the moment. Only the passion of him on her skin. The taste of him in her mouth.

He tugged her closer, she grabbed at his hair, finally feeling the soft waves she dreamed so much about.

"We shouldn't—" She managed to say through their lips parting.

He kissed her again, longer and harder.

"Tell me to stop." He ordered, squeezing her hip. Valeria fell into him. That was when he chose to lean away, blinking when she ran her fingers over the nape of his neck. "Tell me to stop, and I will, but I won't listen to your excuses anymore. I know you're trying to convince yourself that this is wrong." He tilted his head. "But how can it be when it feels like this?"

He ran his fingers up her back, over her collar bones, and caressed her cheek.

Electric energy made her tremble against his body, bones aching at the forbidden look in his eyes.

Valeria had just flown on a dragon, through the heavens and clouds, but somehow there was nothing like him. Flynn felt good.

Even when her hair had been in a rattled mess behind her as she flew on the white dragon's back and she learned what it truly was to be free... to be alive.

This.

Him.

He felt right.

The rush of surviving and passing the trial—it filled her with this new awakening. This new life. This new world of things that she hadn't yet learned of. But now she could. She could live. She could make her own choices.

And *damn it*, she could kiss Flynn Adler.

Valeria didn't say anything... She didn't tell him to stop. She only stared into his heavy-lidded eyes and wrapped her fingers deep into his hair, slightly pulling on the ends.

Flynn closed his eyes and breathed through his nose before he spoke again, "Don't tempt me."

She furrowed her brows and tilted her head, too distracted by the pure need in her body to argue.

Searching her face, he must have taken in the way her eyes dilated, because he threw his head back and cursed. "Fuck it."

He kissed her again, harder than before. It grew heavier when she stumbled. Her back hit something hard, but he didn't let go. His hand left her waist, dragging up her side, leaving chills in its place, before he settled his palm against the tree on her back.

Warmth bloomed and spread in her chest, creeping farther down in her belly. She moaned and parted her lips, letting him taste the inside of her mouth.

"Gods, Val." He groaned.

She hummed in response, too distracted by his tongue that ran across her lips.

"I—"

She meshed her lips to his, shushing him. He placed a hand over her jaw, controlling their movement. Deepening the kiss before he dipped his head lower to her neck, kissing along her collarbone.

"*Flynn.*" She sighed, pressing off the tree to get closer.

He left a trail of kisses up her neck, moving a lock of copper hair over her shoulder as he kissed his way back to her mouth. But before he could place his lips on hers the dragons began to stir behind them.

Pulling apart, Flynn's lips lingered a breath away. Perhaps if she pressed a little closer...

No.

Valeria turned her face. She didn't look at him when she pushed away and stalked toward the white thorntail, even as his eyes closed and he held a faltering breath. He stared down at where she had been pressed against him. Shoulders falling, he sighed.

"Val—"

"We should go." She said, embarrassed of herself, for being so eager—for being so desperate for his touch.

The dragon huffed from atop the hill they landed on, the steam blowing her hair back. She met the beast's golden eyes, waiting for it to change its mind and devour her where she stood.

It would take a few days of training to grow more confident as a rider.

The dragon tilted its head, blinking, almost nodding for her to get back on.

She flushed and looked back over the mountain down at the camp below. Frowning when she noticed the black piles of ash that lay unmoving on the rocks beneath the red dragon.

Flynn reached for her arm, but she was already rushing up the hill to mount her dragon. "We need to go back."

"Val, just wait a second." He tried. Arm stretched as if she might slide back down to talk about what they had just done.

But that was exactly what she was trying to avoid, because she knew everything was different now. Where they stood, where she needed him to be, was no longer an option.

She needed him to just be another contestant, because if he wasn't—if he was anything more to her... she'd already lost Isaac and Alexa. She couldn't lose anyone else she cared for.

And Flynn was... well, Flynn was Flynn. There was no changing that.

Valeria kicked her heel into the smooth scales, and they pounced from the mountain. Still not accustomed to the rush of wind that threatened to blow her off, she glowered and hid her face behind the thorns, and waited for the solid ground to greet her.

32

Late at night, Valeria closed her eyes and failed to find sleep. A darkness crept toward her from the deepest, darkest pits of her soul. Threatening to take the last little bits of light that remained in the cavity of her chest—to grab, capture it, and drag the flickering light into the shadows within.

She licked her lips, flinching against the memories that were pulled from her mind.

Flynn.

She kissed him.

Though she wasn't entirely sure why. When he was the one to swap Lilith's name with hers. He was the one to give up on Isaac. He was the one that finished taking Alexa's life.

But... he was bright, where she was dark, and he was chaos, where she was calm. Valeria thought she might have liked that if it weren't for everything that brewed between them, pushing them apart little by little every day.

After the way she had treated him, yelled, cursed, thought about him... she didn't know when things changed, or even what she felt toward him anymore.

Valeria rolled on top of the flimsy mattress. The tent door flapped against the angry wind as she sat up and rubbed her knuckles against her drowsy-lidded eyes.

Sleep would not come, and she couldn't sit there drowning in the miserable thoughts that occupied her mind.

Standing to her feet, knees wobbling, she let her eyes linger on the dirty rug that covered the dry, rocky ground. That was, until something moved, catching her eye.

A shadow covered the entire far wall, moving across the fabric of her tent. A moment later, Flynn stood beside the door. Once he met her emerald gaze through the darkness, he pushed the limp door open and let himself in.

"I can't sleep." He said.

She nodded. A band of her copper red hair falling into her face as she played with her fingers. "Neither can I."

When she looked at him, all she could think about was the way his fingers traced her skin. Cheeks flaming, she hid her face.

Flynn gradually moved across the small tent, leaning over to avoid hitting his head against the flimsy ceiling. He stopped once spotting the dagger that she left on top of a pile of dirty black armor.

Picking it up, he said, "You should carry this on you at all times. In case..." He shot a glance toward Lance's tent. "In case someone comes with ill intent."

Valeria frowned and glanced in the direction he mentioned—where Lance was likely plotting her death. How he would do it. When he would do it... She licked her lips and stepped toward Flynn, grabbing the dagger from his hand and sliding it beneath her gown.

He leaned against the small wooden dresser, watching her underneath hooded eyes. "Quite a day."

Quirking her lips, she recalled the white dragon—Zakai. She learned the name after coming down from the mountain. "Very eventful." She replied.

The king wasn't too joyous when they returned, but he only had Laurent scold them, before disappearing into his royal tent.

The energy shifted when she lifted her gaze to Flynn's, holding his crystal-like eyes that softened. His attention drifted across her lips before blinking away whatever thoughts he might've had. Instead, the corner of his mouth crooked upward into a grin.

Valeria swallowed. "Why are you here?"

Flynn stepped closer. "I think we both know why I'm here."

She pressed her lips together, raising her brows. "If you think anything is going to happen, it's not."

"I know." He said, before taking yet another step.

Her feet were pinned to the ground, she was unable to move. Her heart pounded with scatteredness, nerves pulsing as his lashes casted dark shadows over his blue eyes.

"Look, Flynn—" She raised a palm to stop him, and was surprised when it actually worked. He dropped his gaze to her hand, the grin sliding off of his face. She chewed on the inside of her cheek before continuing, "This will never work."

"It doesn't have to."

She swallowed. "It's a terrible idea."

"It is?"

"Yes. It is."

"Hmm."

Valeria inhaled before releasing it slowly. "I think you should go back to your tent." She said quietly.

Flynn tilted his head, heat poured out of him and rushed over to her. It ran its hot hands across her skin, creating redness against her cheeks and over her chest.

"I just wanted to see you. That's all." He drawled, eyes narrowing as he examined her silver nightgown.

She shrugged and wrapped her arms around herself, suddenly vulnerable underneath his dark gaze. "Okay. You've seen me. Now you can go."

Pursing his lips, Flynn glanced around the small tent. "Why do you always push me away as soon as I get a step closer?"

It took a moment to reflect over his question, aware that she had been more ill-mannered than she had intended throughout the games, but it was all to protect herself from the pain she would feel if he were to be taken from her. Alexa and Isaac constantly reminded her of that.

She couldn't lose Flynn, even if she had partly made herself believe that she hated him.

"Like Saint Nyle said. We shouldn't get close to other contestants inside the Game of Lords. It'll only lead to heartbreak."

He scoffed. "I'd never let these games kill me, and I'd never let them kill you.'

"But you let them kill Isaac?" She asked. Her tone was soft, she wasn't accusing him, because it wasn't his fault, but he had admitted to giving up on trying to save Isaac.

"No. I didn't. If I would have known that that was the third trial, I wouldn't have used my advance to sit out of it."

Valeria felt her chest flutter when he looked back at her, as if he was hurt she would ever accuse him for Isaac's death. She said, "I'm sorry. I know it wasn't your fault."

Flynn let the moment pass, not wanting to focus on the what ifs, and buts. He looked as though he only wanted to focus on her. And she let him.

She examined the way he straightened his shoulders and brushed the heaviness off his back.

Valeria did too. She was tired of the darkness eating away at her.

Suddenly, Flynn moved until he was standing close enough that she had to bend her neck to meet his crystal gaze.

"What if I kissed you again?"

She choked. Surprised by his question. "I—you can't."

"Can't I?" He tilted his head.

Pressing her lips together she fought to shake her head. Heat burned over her skin, scorching her insides until they melted like butter. "What if I don't want you to?" She feigned indifference.

"I don't think I would believe you." He said, voice much softer than usual when he stepped closer, lifting his hand until his thumb rubbed against her jaw.

Valeria's breath hitched. "I—"

A muffled laugh escaped his nose. He observed the way she examined the blonde hair draped over his forehead. Forbidden messy, golden locks.

"Does it bother you? Knowing how badly you want to be touched by the very thing you despise?"

"*Flynn*." She whispered, dropping her eyes to his. Things throbbed inside her body. Things she had never felt before, only when she had kissed him earlier.

"Because it bothers me. Though I don't despise you." He paused. "It bothers me because I know *I can't* have you." He whispered, tracing her lips before looking into her eyes again. A soft smile played on his face. "You're so beautiful."

His compliment echoed in her ears. The way the words slid from his lips so gracefully.

"It bothers me too." She said, hating the way the words made her chest ache.

He only tilted his head, expression light as if he already knew how she would respond.

Licking her lips, Valeria pressed her jaw into his rough hand and closed her eyes. "What about Helena?"

He chuckled softly, ducking his head lower to meet her gaze. "What about her?"

Valeria huffed, eyes nearly rolled to the back of her head when his hand trailed up the underside of her jaw and rested against her neck.

"You have to marry her." She said.

The heat in her body dulled down to a familiar ache when reality settled in. Flynn's gentle smile fell.

"No, I don't." He said, hesitantly pulling her into his chest and wrapping his arms around her. She felt his lips skim against the top of her head when he whispered, "I don't have to marry her."

She had to swallow down the lump in her throat in order to speak. "Yes, you do."

Flynn must have seen the fear she was trying so desperately to hide. "Let's not think about that right now... I won't hurt you. I promise."

"You can't promise me that."

He backed away until his face was merely an inch from hers. He searched her emerald eyes, a look so sullen she thought he might give up everything for her right then.

"I can promise you everything, Val. I know I've been a dick, and maybe we haven't been on the best terms, but I have done *everything* in my power to make sure that you remain safe. I know I may have fucked up a few times. *Gods*, more than a few. But I would never.... *Never* let you get hurt. The Gods would hate to see me coming if you did."

Valeria chuckled at his furrowed brows and lifted a finger to smooth them down. They'd never been so close before—so soft spoken with each other.

A moment ago, Flynn had been so full of heat, but now he looked guilt-ridden.

His eyes softened. "I need you to know that I am not the reason you are here, okay?" She frowned, but kept her fingers on his troubled face. "I never switched your name with your sisters. If I did, I would have let you kill me a long time ago."

She blinked. "I never wanted to kill you Flynn. I just... I get angry sometimes."

"I know."

Flynn removed his touch from her skin, letting a stretch of space form between them. She longed to feel his fingers on her again, caressing her face, leaving a trail of shivers anywhere they grazed. She blinked to calm her body.

A silence passed before he spoke again, though the words he said hit Valeria like a rolling boulder.

"Let's leave together." He turned his face, as if afraid to see her reaction.

"Flynn." Her voice was quiet. She stood still, watching his back.

"Leave with me." He said again, reaching out this time.

Valeria's heart dropped. Her chest filled with utter heaviness while looking into his wide stare, he waited. Jaw clenched, Flynn dropped his hand.

Glancing between his palm and dreadfully handsome face, she quietly said, "But... Helena."

She didn't know why she let Helena linger so often in her mind, an anger of some kind lurked in her chest every time she thought of the princess and Flynn sneaking off during the balls. She wasn't dumb, she knew he had been all over the princess. Yet, she still cared for him in a way that she knew she shouldn't have.

Besides, he was delirious. There was no way they would make it—a ghost of a chance that they could leave and actually escape together. He was acting foolish—insane even.

Even if she wanted to live a life of running and hiding, she couldn't do it with him... No matter how torn up he looked, as if he knew it was crazy... Asking her to do something so insane, after everything she lost, Isaac, Alexa... She could not—nor would she run.

She would not be a coward.

Upon seeing the look in her eyes, the drop of her brows, the frown quickly growing on her face, he loosened a breath. "No, you're right. I—I shouldn't have asked. I wasn't thinking."

When he looked at her, sharp and unwavering, Valeria got lost. She traveled through the darkness of his blue eyes. Wondering, just for a moment, what it would be like to share a life with him.

She saw her hand in his as they ran through the forest. Two beasts flying far above them as they ripped wanted posters from the bark of the tree's. He turned back and smiled at her, she laughed.

And then the moment passed.

It wasn't real, and it never could be. Because she would not leave.

"I would never ask that of you." His tone was gentle, calm. So unlike the cool, smoothness she was used to hearing from him.

Words vanished on her tongue when he glanced at her hammering chest where she was tightly clutching her hands together.

Trying her best to remain standing, unfaltering to the crazed thoughts that ran through her mind. She let herself appear serene, unbothered even. She needed to make him believe that this wasn't affecting her as much as it truly was.

"Look at you." He said. She dropped her arms to her sides, a confused frown sliding on her face. Before she could open her mouth, he started again, "You make it seem so easy to hide what you feel. Whether it's your feelings for me or whatever. I know what I asked was rash, but I'm not clueless... I'm not. And despite how much you want me to believe that you don't care for me, I don't. Not after that kiss." She sucked in a sharp breath, but he continued, "I know I'm irritating at times, and *hell* so are you, but I see the way you look at me. I see the way your thoughts betray you."

Valeria's chest pounded, but she hid her surprise with a glare. "I feel enough for you to not want you dead. There. Is that what you want to hear?"

Flynn smirked, narrowing his eyes as he stepped closer. "I want to hear you admit the truth."

Her face heated as she held his unblinking stare. "The truth?" She walked toward him and came to a stop beneath his gaze. "I wanted to kiss you—I *enjoyed* kissing you." She bit her lip in order to hold back from admitting she wanted to do it again.

In fact, she wouldn't mind doing it that very moment.

Instead she asked, "It was just a kiss, right? It meant nothing." Something shifted in his eyes, his breath was long and heavy, fanning against her feverish face. "I wasn't thinking, and neither are you since you've come in here."

He scoffed and crossed his arms. "You could have pushed me away."

"I did." She argued.

"Not hard enough."

Valeria sneered, her frustration only growing heavier as she glared at him.

His nostrils flared, refusing to look away.

She pursed her lips, eyes retreating from their locked gaze first. She stared at his chest, where his loose white tunic crinkled in the slight breeze the tent door let in.

"This conversation is useless."

"Is it really?"

"Yes." She spit and spun on her heels to march back over to her mattress. She began fixing the bedding, anything to keep her body busy.

"And why is that?"

"Because nothing will come of it. You will marry Princess Helena, and I have to win. However you feel about me, whatever it is that you think will happen—will not. It cannot. Besides, you've done too many awful things—things I will never forget."

Like killing Alexa.

305

Finally, Flynn looked away. He closed his eyes and held his breath. All the while, Valeria continued making her bed, even puffing up her pillow, trying her best to ignore the man at her back.

A quietness filled the tent. One of understanding. The kind of silence that crushed lovers' hearts and left them scavenging for the pieces.

Valeria finished patting the mattress down and slowly sat on the corner. She rested her head in her hands, managing to set her tired gaze back on Flynn, who never moved from his spot in the dark corner.

He was staring at her, hands at his sides, shoulders held straight back, mouth slightly parted. There wasn't a single emotion on his face. He frantically hid the parts of himself that he never let anyone see. Anyone, but her.

Why her?

"I never wanted any of this," He whispered.

She glanced away from him, and at the flimsy knot that tied the tent doors together. "Neither did I."

He flinched. "I'll marry Princess Helena then. I'll ask her tomorrow, and then..."

"You'll leave the games—officially become a prince. I know."

A beat of silence, then a splatter of rain above their heads broke it.

Flynn looked up at the ceiling of the tent, where it quickly puddled with rainwater. "You'll win. I'll make sure of it."

She pressed her hands together and forced a small laugh. "I wouldn't bet on it."

"I would."

He left a moment later, leaving Valeria to sit in her own silence.

When she was sure he wasn't coming back, she fell back on her bed, closing her watery eyes. A boy with disheveled blonde hair and arrogant blue eyes, who remained close, yet too far to reach, filled her dreams.

33

It wasn't long before the news of Flynn and Princess Helena's engagement was traveling around the camps the following day. Apparently, someone had spotted them out past the valley and standing in a dewy meadow when Flynn dropped to his knee and asked the everlasting question.

Valeria didn't let herself linger on their conversation last night. Her mind was occupied with worrying about how she was going to survive with just herself and Lance left. Now that Flynn was engaged to the princess, he would no longer be competing in the games.

By marrying into the royal family, Flynn ensured he would no longer be put in harm's way. Helena would not want her future husband to be killed, especially in the Game of Lords.

Lance prowled behind a group of officials guarding the king's tent. Valeria had her eyes set on him the moment he appeared from his tent. Sitting on a boulder overlooking the valley, she tightened the leather straps of the black armor on her thighs. Now that she was a dragon rider, her superiors expected her to wear the training gear at all times.

Dragon rider.

The title still left her dumbfounded. It felt like a dream... rather, a nightmare. How she landed in these circumstances—Valeria didn't think she would ever realize the full extent of why Zakai chose her for a rider.

Even Laurent had looked at the dragon as if it were out of its mind for choosing her. She remembered the way his eyes widened upon watching her and Zakai bond after the trial yesterday.

She wondered what Lilith would think, often finding herself imagining what her older sister would say after watching Valeria fly through the skies on the white beast for the first time. She would yell at Valeria, scold her about tightening her grip, then ask when it was her turn to go for a ride.

Valeria grinned while picturing her sister's cheerful laugh.

Soon. Soon she could go home.

Standing from her position on the rock, Valeria swiftly followed the path Lance had taken into the king's tent.

Earlier, the king had invited everyone—even the contestants—inside his castle-like tent for supper. Laurent explained to Valeria and Lance that the event was a result of the princess's unexpected engagement earlier in the morning.

"In your leathers I see." Laurent stood at the entrance. His gaze sweeping over her form before crossing his arms behind his back and leading her down the makeshift hallway made of green draped curtains.

She snickered and examined Laurent's dark blue suit. He carried a cane in his left hand, a metal flask in the other.

As the hall opened up, and the curtains turned to wood, creating a wide dining room, Valeria gaped. There was a long table in the center of the room, decorated with all sorts of flowers and colorful stones. A few servants lined the left side of the table, surely waiting for any commands from the king, who had yet to enter.

"Haven't you heard? It's mandatory that I always have my armor on now." She replied. Although her eyes never strayed from the nearly full table. Almost every seat was taken.

"Yes, of course," Laurent said before he turned and examined the few remaining chairs. "Would you like to sit beside me tonight?"

Valeria pursed her lips. "I'm not required to sit somewhere else?"

As a contestant, she felt strangely odd about sitting at a table full of royals. Let alone the king.

Laurent chuckled. "Of course not." He pressed a hand against her arm and motioned to the two open seats beside each other. "Come."

She could feel multiple eyes following—watching her trail after the gamerunner.

When she sat with Laurent, the attention drifted past her and over to Lance, who had just taken his own seat beside the Lord of Thunder. Valeria grimaced and watched the curly haired lord smile proudly at Lance. The waves of his hair looked as if it was made from gold, the way the light reflected off of it, complementing his tan skin and green eyes.

The Lord of Thunder chuckled, making the table tremble with electricity.

The famous highlord's presence reeked of pride and vain righteousness. Lance, being the cruel man he was, made Valeria wonder how the Lord of Thunder treated his court. Was Lance always so cruel? Or did his highlord train him—teach him to be ruthless before the games?

Valeria shook her head as the king and his family strode down the makeshift hall. She'd worry about Lance later.

Her gaze lingered on the king's boot-covered feet.

When she lifted her eyes and searched upon the king's family entering behind him, her stomach dropped.

Valeria's hands froze as she folded them together on top of the table. Her breath caught in her throat, watching Flynn cross the room. A group of officials in front of him, escorting him as if... as if he were royalty. She gulped and tried to tear her eyes away, until they landed on his arm that was wrapped around Princess Helena's waist, a shimmering diamond on her ring finger.

The sight made Valeria swallow. She wanted to leave.

Blinking, she moved her gaze onto her hands.

Flynn, her ally, her closest chance to getting out of the games, was engaged. Engaged to someone he didn't love.

Something ripped inside her chest. Her heart started to hammer, claw its way up her throat, begging her to go to him, to tell him she changed her mind—that she would leave with him, just then. She would go with him.

For weeks, Valeria tried to ignore the growing attraction she had toward Flynn. She burned any thought—any emotion of yearning every time he would flutter into her mind. Yet, since the kiss, she felt as if something was being stolen from her. A chance of something more—of a life that she would never get the chance to experience.

And even though Flynn might've been the reason she was even in the games, Valeria couldn't help the anger that simmered just beneath her skin as she watched him pull out a seat for Helena before taking his own.

She watched him lean over in his seat and smile at the princess, his eyes darting toward the king only for a split moment before he sent a playful wink to Helena.

Valeria looked away, grimacing. Bitterness coated her tongue, filling her mouth.

"Careful now."

She bit her bottom lip harder than intended, listening to Laurent. "I'm tired of being careful." She whispered back.

Laurent chuckled from beside her, tapping her knee with a finger as he settled into his seat. "If anyone were to speak about the way you were just looking at the princess, the king would have your head served on a silver platter."

Valeria scoffed but straightened her shoulders. "I know... I'm just exhausted. I want it to be over already."

He frowned. "Are you talking about dinner? Or the games?"

"Both."

With an airy chuckle, Laurent leaned back and crossed his arms. They remained silent as the officials lined the wall, positioning themselves behind the king, who sat in his large throne-like chair.

The four highlords and highlady were sectioned throughout the long table, Lance being with his own.

Valeria searched for the Lord of Sky, who she found seated closer to the king. Her eyes narrowed when she noticed the way he was looking at Flynn. Flynn was three seats down, seated at the opposite end of the table as her. He was unaware of the Lord of Sky's inspecting gaze.

The highlord clenched his jaw, tilted his head and raised his brows. Flynn only chuckled at something the princess was whispering into his ear.

Perhaps her highlord was upset that a contestant from his court was to be married into the royal family. Or maybe he wanted Flynn to win? Valeria wasn't sure. She darted her eyes around the table until she finally settled on the king once again.

His long golden hair was tied back, not a single loose hair in sight. The king reached for a glass and brought it to his lips, taking a mere sip of the clear liquid. His eyes roamed around the table until he met Valeria's unfaltering stare.

She nearly choked when he set his glass down, a smirk growing underneath his straight nose, green eyes never flinching away from hers.

Despite the fear that crawled up the back of her throat, Valeria held his gaze.

Even as he reached for a butter knife and lightly tapped it against his glass goblet. A high-pitched ring sounded around the room, bringing everyone's attention to the king, who finally removed his eyes from Valeria.

She shrunk into her chair, reaching for her own glass, hoping it was filled with something more than water. Perhaps a drink so strong that it would erase her scrambled thoughts and growing migraine. She wanted a heavy liquor. Something to fill the black void in her chest.

Valeria swallowed the surprisingly tangy juice with a shake of her head. Before she could set her glass down, Laurent poked her thigh beneath the table. She looked down to find the small metal container in his palm.

He glanced at her, wiggled his brow, and looked away before she reached over and grabbed it from him.

A few short moments later, after the king began his speech that she didn't care much for, Valeria was feeling slightly lightheaded as she finished her third glass of the mysterious liquor in Laurent's metal container.

"As most of you may know by now, my eldest daughter is engaged!" The king shouted with a smile.

The room filled with cheers and the thumping of numerous empty glasses beating against the hard surface of the table. A few men stood from their seats to give Flynn a pat on the back, who smiled bashfully. Even the lords stood and congratulated him, all but one.

Saint Nyle, the Lord of Illusions, remained sitting in his seat across from her. Taking a swig from his glass every now and then, his eyes landed on hers.

She glanced away quickly, finding herself focusing on Flynn yet again.

Valeria couldn't help but wonder what it would feel like to be in Helena's place. The princess had everything... A life, confidence, control.... Flynn. What would it be like to live in the princess's shoes for a day? To not worry about whether she was going to die soon?

"I would like to formally announce that with my daughter's new engagement, Flynn Adler will be removed from the Game of Lords. Leaving only Lance Whitlock and Valeria Rox to perform in the final trial together." The king raised a glass, and others followed. But Valeria's eyes never strayed from the king, who shared her stare over his goblet.

She only pursed her lips and reached for the metal container beneath the table before lifting it to her mouth and chugging.

Saint Nyle chuckled.

Over the loud laughter and chatter, Valeria couldn't remove her eyes from Flynn, who was staring straight at her. He could have been examining the colors of her soul for all she cared, because he was looking at her. And that's all that mattered.

His gaze tangled with hers in a silent dance of temptation. There was a palpable tension that thickened with each passing moment. She knew if she were to say the words, to give him the confirmation that he needed, he would jump across the table and take her into his arms.

She could tell by the way his eyes flickered with darkness and light. How he dropped his chin and tilted his head. The conversation they had in the tent was only the beginning. Flynn wanted her to leave with him. To leave the games and everything behind. To be on the run for the rest of their lives together.

Around them, the guests chattered amongst each other, unaware of the silent exchange between their blue and green eyes. The world swirled around them as Valeria held his unrelenting gaze.

Yet still. Neither spoke. Only stared and traced each other's skin, hoping to remember the other's features before one was married and the other was dead or crowned as highlady.

And as the night wore on and the conversations rich with excitement continued around them, Valeria remained locked in Flynn's silent temptation.

34

Valeria jumped from Zakai's back and landed hard in the dirt. Both of her fists pounding into the ground as she let out a small cry.

She lifted her head and searched for any observant eyes. Much to her relief, nobody seemed to be concerned about her training today. She'd been in the valley practicing how to mount the white beast all morning.

Zakai shook her long, thick neck and stomped a hind claw into the ground before turning away from Valeria.

It had been a week since the king announced Princess Helena's engagement to Flynn. A week since Flynn and Helena jumped into a carriage and strolled away together to the kingdom, where Valeria assumed a wedding would shortly take place.

She'd been alone ever since that day.

The last time she had spoken to Flynn was inside of her tent, when he asked her to leave with him... when he nearly begged to taste her lips again. It wasn't just the adrenaline rush of riding a dragon for the first time.

He *wanted* to kiss her.

Valeria scoffed and pushed to her feet. She didn't bother wiping the dirt off of her leathers, knowing that she would only fall once more when she climbed back up Zakai's shoulder.

Leaning back, Valeria tried to meet the dragon's golden eye. The last time she attempted to mount Zakai without the dragon's consent, she had been thrown ten feet away, leaving a deep gash up the length of her thigh. After that, Valeria changed training destinations.

Any boulders or rocks of any sort were over a mile away so that she couldn't land on them if she were to be thrown off again.

She was thankful to have time to train with Zakai. Lance's red firetail was nowhere to be found. Apparently, the beast couldn't be too concerned with training or being around humans.

She didn't blame him.

Valeria whistled and flicked her hair back. Zakai spun her neck around, peering down at her with sharp eyes. Resisting a flinch, Valeria lifted her chin and swallowed.

"I'm going back up." She said.

Zakai snorted and dropped her head, granting access to her thorny back.

Valeria closed her eyes and released a breath before trying again. She gripped the top of Zakai's ankle and began to climb.

She'd been lucky the first time she mounted Zakai. The adrenaline dealt her a massive amount of strength to climb Zakai's leg without falling. Now, excluding the risk of dying or competing against others, Valeria was incapable of climbing past Zakai's shoulder without slipping on one of many rough white scales.

She gripped the sharp edge of a blade-like scale, pulling herself up and pushing with her legs. Almost out of breath, Valeria began to slip. Though, before she could, Zakai chuffed and dropped to her belly. Valeria fell a short distance down to Zakai's lower leg.

Zakai slightly rolled onto her side, giving Valeria effortless access to her winged back.

She glanced at the dragon's face, pursing her lips. "Thank you." She whispered before climbing over Zakai's shoulder and sitting in the proper seat on her spine.

Zakai stood to her feet, careful not to knock Valeria off. She flicked her wings, creating a waft of wind that blew Valeria's hair into her face.

Pawing into the dirt, Zakai let out a gravely breath.

Valeria patted Zakai's back. "No flying today, Z. I'm afraid I don't have the strength to hold on tight enough anymore."

The beast bowed her head in understanding. When she did so, Valeria spotted a group of figures walking out of the backside of the king's tent.

She recognized the shape of the king's golden crown on top of his head, and the gamerunner, Laurent, who strode beside him. The four others she could make out as officials, only because they stood behind the King of Laterra with pistols in their hands.

The king stood confidently on top of the rocky hillside overlooking the valley, listening to whatever Laurent was saying.

Valeria turned her head, glancing at the sky, making herself appear as if she were unaware they were even there. She kicked a heel into Zakai's side. "No flying, but perhaps walk around a bit. Closer to the hillside." She added.

Zakai huffed, but listened and began walking toward the hill where the king and Laurent stood.

The king dropped his arms and lifted his crowned head. She could feel his intimidating stare as they trudged closer.

Keeping up her oblivious performance, she squared her shoulders and brushed a hand over Zakai's scales. "Can you hear what they're saying?"

If there was one thing Valeria had learned about riding a dragon, it was the bond and all that it implied. Dragons could not speak out loud—not the language of Laterra at least. But they could communicate mind to mind. As if there was a thought flowing through Valeria's head that wasn't her own.

She didn't know it was Zakai the first time the dragon had spoken to her. It happened the night before Flynn left, after she was escorted out of the king's tent and sent away. She had wandered down the hill and found Zakai asleep.

Needing to refresh her mind and forget about Flynn, she woke the dragon and requested a flight through the clouds.

"Hold on tight." Zakai had said.

Valeria heard the words float through her mind and thought it was a God of some sort before Zakai leapt into the sky and Valeria nearly rolled off.

That was when Zakai dropped back to the earth and landed. *"Didn't you hear me?"* The beast had shouted in her mind.

Zakai didn't speak through Valeria's mind often, but when she did, it was always a command or attitude-filled response.

Now, as they strolled through the valley, Valeria clinging to a sharp scale, her braid slowly untucking from the back of her shirt, she wasn't frightened when the white beast finally answered her.

"The humans speak of an engagement, games, and a wedding. Why does it concern you?" Zakai asked.

Valeria rolled her eyes before she sent a glare at the back of Zakai's head. "I care because my life and possible death is in the king's hands."

A small flame burst out of the beast's nostrils when she stopped walking and turned her head.

Valeria looked into Zakai's golden eye, her sharp pupils dilated. *"Your life is my responsibility, human girl. Not another. You are mine. No human will kill you. King or not."*

Valeria narrowed her eyes and frowned. "I apologize. I'm not sure how this works." She said. Zakai began walking again after giving Valeria a long, intimidating look. "What are they saying about the games?"

Zakai didn't respond. She only lifted her neck and stared at the king, who was now watching them intensely. He angled his head to the side and whispered something into Laurent's ear.

Laurent dragged his attention onto Valeria and frowned. He stared at her for a moment before saying something back to the king.

"What was that about?" She wondered aloud, since Zakai hadn't answered her previous question.

Stubborn beast.

"The crowned one speaks of death—of murder." Zakai said.

The words sent chills up Valeria's arms. She glanced away from the king's gaze.

"Do they know we can communicate this way?'

Zakai didn't reply. Instead, she stopped in place and looked left, then she looked right.

No.

The king, Laurent, the officials—they didn't know, because they'd never bonded with a dragon. She'd never read about the deep connection between a dragon and its rider in the history books. So, all of it had been quite a surprise, and one she still hadn't grown used to.

Valeria took a deep breath and readied to slide down Zakai's side.

This time, when she landed in the dirt, she didn't fall to her hands. Her feet remained planted to the ground when she lifted her head and shared the king's sage green glare.

"There's been a change in plans."

"What?" Valeria asked. Her voice was much higher than normal as she stared at Laurent with widened eyes.

He flicked a glance to Lance, who stood unbothered beside his tent. "The king wants the both of you to perform the last trial in the kingdom."

Valeria kicked at a loose pebble and shook her head, confused. "And what about the dragons? I can't leave Zakai."

"They will fly ahead and meet us there. They are loyal to the crown. They are loyal to their riders. Where you go, they go."

She'd forgotten that Laurent knew more about the winged beast than she did. The letter she'd stolen from the Lord of Sky's office was proof of that. Laurent was the one to know about the eggs, and the Lord of Sky was the one to hand them over to the crown.

There was so much Valeria still didn't understand.

"When do we leave?" Lance asked this time. He sent a menacing look toward Valeria. A small smirk growing on his lips. "Will we be traveling together?"

Valeria straightened her shoulders, shooting daggers at him with her narrowed eyes.

Laurent licked his lips, sighing. "We leave tomorrow morning. It'll be about a day's trip—and no," He looked at Lance. "You both will travel separately. We don't need anyone being killed and winning the Game of Lords outside of the king's sight. He would like to witness the event."

Lance scoffed and turned back to his tent.

"For now, I need the both of you to pack your necessities. We're heading to Azrael estate in two hours. I expect the both of you to be ready to go by the time the carriages arrive."

Valeria turned her gaze to the sky and huffed. *More traveling.* The last thing she wanted to do. She just wanted the games to be over, whether she lived or not.

Laurent motioned to two officials, and they jogged over. He pointed a finger at Valeria and Lance. "Keep an extra eye on these two, will you? They're antsy for the games to end."

Lance ducked inside his tent with a growl. Valeria did the same upon meeting one of the officials gazes.

For a brief moment, she wondered if Jonathon knew the officials by name. Was he friendly with them? Did he go to a tavern and drink with the others when their shifts ended? And if he did—did they keep in contact? Did they keep him updated on what was happening inside the games?

Did Lilith still marry him after he told her the truth?

Valeria shook the thoughts from her mind and began packing up what little clothing she had.

When she stuffed the remaining pieces of her armor into the brown sack, something black and shiny slipped and fell from beneath her pillow.

Quickly, she dropped to her knees and picked up the small onyx dagger.

She recognized it instantly. All those times she'd watched it twirl between Flynn's fingers before he threw it into one of the many targets inside the training room. Or when he'd drop his hand where he kept it tucked into his belt every time he felt threatened.

He'd given her his dagger.

Valeria tucked it underneath the strap on her thigh, right next to the one she had used to slice open Lance's ankle.

Valeria stepped out of the carriage. Her eyes shifted from Lance's back and up over the castle stone walls of Azrael estate. Her chest ached when she stepped through the main doors.

Lance prowled up the checkered stairs and disappeared into the contestants' hallway, heading toward his room quarters.

She bit her lip and ignored the throbbing underneath her ribs.

She was alone. Besides Lance, who was somehow always there, taunting her.

After a few weeks, eighteen people were gone. Seventeen of them—killed. Flynn being the only one to make the princess fall in love with him and find a way to survive the Game of Lords *without* winning.

He was free. He could live his life however he wished now.

Valeria sighed and followed far behind Lance, making her way down the oddly silent hallway.

Isaac wouldn't be in his room at the end of the hallway... Flynn wouldn't be in his across from her.

Her steps echoed off of the widely parted walls as she walked. She came to a stop beside her door, eyes tracing the curves of her fingers before she turned and faced Flynn's.

It took a mere moment of debate, before she walked across the hall and stepped into his old room. The faint smell of spring water stung her nostrils.

She glanced around the room. Someone had made the bed and taken everything that made the room familiar out. She noticed the emptiness of the dresser.

It was clean. There was nothing in it. Nothing besides the dull smell of Flynn's past presence.

Valeria sauntered over to the plain mattress and fell to her knees. She reached up underneath the bed and lifted the mattress. The hole was still there, unstitched and gaping open. Wincing, she leaned forward and reached until her arm was deep enough to feel inside the cut open mattress.

Then she felt it.

Something light weight, yet rough and crisp. Valeria grabbed the thin paper and pulled it out.

It had been folded in half, with a name written in messy cursive writing on the front.

Isaac.

Bewildered, she stuffed the paper into the belt of her pants before rushing to the door.

When her own door clicked shut behind her, she raced over to the bed and sat. Ripping the letter free, Valeria flipped it open and began to read.

I wish things could be different, For you. For Valeria. For everyone. I tried, but everything led to one outcome... she was going to end up getting hurt either way. But her pain will be temporary. It's for the best. And I know you'll be okay. I'm sorry, Isaac. I really am. I wanted to tell her the truth. But, God's... she is so difficult. She's stubborn and keeps pushing and pushing. I'm glad she does though. I'm glad she's strong-willed. I'm glad she hates me. That's the way it needs to be. Otherwise, none of this would work. I love you. And I hope the best for you, lad. Good luck. There has to be a loophole somehow, and I'll find it. I promise.

— Flynn A.

P.S. Val is finally going to train with me.

Valeria closed the letter and blinked.

Flynn wrote this letter to Isaac as if they were brothers. Sure they spent a great amount of time together while Isaac was still alive, but this showed just how close they truly were. She hadn't realized how much Flynn was hurting. Her pain had been too distracting.

A tear slipped from her eye; she quickly flicked it away with her thumb.

She'd been awful to everyone. Flynn lost Isaac as well, not just her.

And now they were both gone, and both out of her life.

Valeria tried her best to contain the sob that racked through her body, but it clawed and ripped its way out of her throat. She brought her knees up to her chest, hugging her legs. She let herself cry, she let the tears slip from her eyes.

And she let the pain burn in her belly—burn until it was imprinted on her skin. Red, and aching. She would never forget Isaac... Flynn... Alexa... For they had tried their best to live, but the games had taken that from them.

Flynn wasn't free, he was just trying to survive. And if Valeria were to live, he had to marry the princess.

It wasn't a choice he wanted to make... It was protection and survival.

There was no one left to hear or even care when she cried into her legs.

After a few minutes her door burst open and Jacky's familiar long caramel hair appeared from the opening.

Jacky rushed across the room when she saw the tears that streaked down Valeria's face.

"What's wrong?" She asked, kneeling in front of her. "What happened?"

Valeria couldn't summon the words to speak. She could hardly catch her own breath.

Jacky pursed her lips and pulled Valeria's trembling body into her arms. "It'll be okay, hun. Everything will be okay."

Valeria shook her head, because no. Nothing was okay.

Nothing was ever going to be okay.

35

The first person to greet Valeria after she stepped out of the cold carriage and onto the hard concrete below the king's enormous castle was the prince of Laterra, Luther. He opened the door, offering her his hand before taking a step back, giving her space to take the massive kingdom in.

Valeria lifted her eyes up, up, and up until she could view the very top of the palace. She could see the officials looking down at her, keeping an eye out for any intruders or potential assassins.

The prince gave a pitiful smile before he turned, striding for the large entry doors.

She glanced to the left and watched Laurent open the door to the carriage in front of the one she rode in. Lance pounced out, cursing at the warm, fresh air that greeted him.

"That was the longest Gods-eating ride ever." He said.

Laurent lifted his lip into a snarl. "Watch your tongue, boy. Or the king will have the officials cut it out."

A few minutes later, they trailed in a line up the steps to the towering castle. Laurent strode just in front of her, accustomed to the line of townsmen who watched far past the gates. Their eyes, wide and full of interest. The steel gates rattled as they pushed closer, trying to get a better look at who was entering the castle.

Her eyes darted every which way, taking the lavish kingdom in.

The city of Jerume surrounded the palace, where bustling carts, giggling children, and busy men and women walked about.

Valeria wasn't aware the kingdom was so vast. She'd never looked it up in the papers or cared to research the royal family.

If she had known how large the kingdom truly was, she might have prepared herself better.

Shroom people flew past, much like pixies, but bigger by an inch. Their heads shaped like brown-topped mushrooms, their black beady eyes never blinking as they flew around with their velvet-like wings. The beak on their jaw, opening to eat the bugs that buzzed above.

She felt a grin grow on her lips as she watched them go.

The smell of roses and strawberries hit her nose when she took another step. Then, pulling her from a short-lived distraction, someone yanked her forward before she could enter the castle's main doors.

The official began patting Valeria down, starting from her chest and to her feet. Once he reached her thigh, she fidgeted underneath his hands. She felt his rough fingers rub against the two dangers hidden beneath her leather strap when he narrowed his eyes and almost tore the skirt of her gown up.

Laurent turned, recognizing the panic in her green eyes.

"Enough." He commanded, his tone bitter and full of disgust. "She may keep her weapons. I'm sure she's not foolish enough to make use of them on anyone important. Especially around thousands of officials." Laurent motioned toward the opened doors, raising a brow. "Now let her pass."

The official bit down on his bottom lip, before dropping the skirt of her gown and shoving her forward.

Valeria choked out a yelp, stumbling into Laurent, who allowed her the time to straighten her gown before pulling her to his side.

"Stay close."

She didn't feel like arguing, so all she managed was a nod and dropped her gaze to the floor.

Upon entering the royal castle, the maids and nurses greeted them. Women and men stood in a line, watching Valeria and Lance slowly stride farther into the brightly lit room.

Jacky stood at the end of the line, a soft look in her eyes once she spotted Valeria. Of course Jacky worked for the king, but it still didn't fail to surprise Valeria to see her standing there, blending in with the other Helps.

She had just cried in the woman's arms last night.

Valeria took a deep breath and followed Laurent through a hallway. They turned down two more before entering a broad room. She never took her eyes off of the black rug beneath her feet.

"Welcome to Jerume." Laurent whispered over his shoulder.

Finally, she lifted her head and gazed up at the people that filled the room.

The throne room was crowded, and she and Lance were the main attraction.

Curious eyes lingered on the back of her neck, the side of her face, judging the way she stood in front of Lance, who was tall and proud behind her.

Lance cleared his throat and Valeria stepped to the side before he could shove past her. She felt him stop beside her, a catty grin on his lips when he bowed.

That was when she noticed the others bowing with him.

She stood above the crowd, facing the king on his throne, whose dark eyes were focused on her upright form.

"*Valeria*." Laurent scolded. "Bow."

Only after a reluctant second did she listen and bend at the waist.

"Rise." An unfamiliar voice echoed through the quietness. "Please, give the king your utmost attention."

She felt the attention drift from her and on to the front of the room where the king sat on his dark stoned throne.

"To the people of my court who may be puzzled about the two unfamiliar faces here... I'd like to introduce Lance Whitlock and Valeria Rox. The remaining contestants of this generation's Game of Lords." There were a few gasps around the room. "I thought it might be fascinating to bring them to the city of Jerume, where the first games started. Don't you agree?"

The king smiled brightly, the crowd yipping and cheering.

Assholes.

She restrained the rolling of her eyes when the king dragged his gaze back to her.

Instantly, he frowned, tilting his head. "I felt it was pointless to introduce the both of them together, given only one of them will live, but I couldn't contain myself. Why not enjoy ourselves and have some fun this year??

Again, the crowd snickered and laughed.

Clenching her jaw, Valeria glowered. Her heart pounded. She could feel her blood thrashing through her veins, begging to be released.

She imagined the way the king's face would turn bright red, and then a dull purple after strangling him with her bare hands. Not only for herself, but for Alexa. For Isaac, and Rob Johnson.

For everyone he had killed.

The king would die. She would make sure of it.

An hour later Valeria was walking through the royal palace with Lance and four officials at their backs. The king sauntered in front of them, his footsteps loud and filled with authority.

She watched him move with a certain type of grace. The king of Laterra should have died centuries ago, yet there he was. Nearly three hundred years old, walking smoothly through the corridors of his home.

"Move with haste. I have much to reveal to the both of you." He spoke over his shoulder, never looking back as an official opened a door at the end of the corridor.

Two of the officials grabbed Valeria's arms, while the others focused on Lance, who stood beside her.

The king noticed the hold the officials had on her and chuckled. "They're just making sure you don't run off."

Valeria rolled her eyes when he wasn't looking.

Lance groaned and stomped his foot. "Where are we going?" He asked once the king led them into a dark stairway. When no one answered, he tried again, "Gods, can we just start the final trial already? This is nonsense, dragging us all the way up here."

It felt as if they had been walking for miles by the time they reached the top of the stairway.

"You're proving to be more of an annoyance than anything, young man. I could have you removed, and she can be the only one I present the extraordinary gift to."

Lance choked on his saliva before releasing a breath. "I'm going to kill her soon. Why show her anything at all? Why must we tease her with what's going to be mine?"

Finally, after averting her gaze, she heard the king come to an abrupt halt. His shoulders slouched when he turned and glared at Lance. His green eyes flickered to the officials that had a hold of Lance. "Take him away." He commanded.

"But—" Lance tried.

"Fill his mouth with a rag as well."

Valeria kept her gaze on her feet, listening to the scuffling happen beside her. Lance tried to argue back before his words became muffled. And then there was a thrash, and his body went limp. All she saw was the way his knees buckled, nearly hitting the ground before the officials yanked him back.

Valeria flinched and finally looked. Lance's unconscious body was being dragged down the stairs, then finally out through the doorway they had come through.

"The contestants this year are quite odd—quite futile. You would agree, wouldn't you?" The king asked, gaze still remaining on where Lance had been dragged out of the stairway.

She could feel his cold dark eyes graze over the side of her face.

Valeria licked her lips and nodded. Her fingers slightly trembled before she hid them behind her back and followed after the king once again.

The officials released their grip on her arms and stepped away, pressing their backs against the stone wall and staring straight ahead. The king noticed, but didn't seem to mind as he pushed open a small wooden door, letting bright light trickle in through the narrow opening.

Coming upon a patch of green grass, Valeria squinted. "What—" She paused, unsure before finally building the courage to speak. "What is this place?"

The palace walls stood tall around them, blocking the view below. She lifted her face and stared up at the open sky. They stood outside, yet it felt like another world—another universe. As if a land of great wonder were above the castle, just sitting on top of the palace. The kingdom and everything below it was unaware of the beauty that existed above them.

The king smiled over his shoulder, then turned. "This is the center of Laterra. Some believe it is the middle of the world. *Here,*" he paused and motioned forward. "Here is where the immortal power lives. It is powered from this very spot in Laterra. The only spot."

He stepped to the side, letting Valeria move closer to the ledge she hadn't seen before. Her eyes widened when she saw what he was grinning at.

A black pool swallowed up the garden. Purples and golds swirled around inside of its darkness, lighting up the inside by a little.

She took a step back, heart stammering inside her chest.

"I—" She gulped. "What is that?"

The king smiled, and raised his brows. "The beginning and the end. It is everything."

She bit her lip, failing to meet his eyes. The darkness drew her in, her blood thrummed as if begging her to jump in.

Come closer. Come closer. The blackness seemed to whisper.

She begged the Gods that he wouldn't throw her inside of it. Wherever it led to, she didn't want to find out.

He chuckled and grabbed her arm, his grip tight and full of control. "Take a closer look. Feel the blood beneath my skin. Make it make sense, Valeria."

The king shoved the sleeve of his coat to his elbow and placed her fingers on his wrist. His veins throbbed against her skin.

Valeria's eyes moved from the beating black pool and onto his wrist, where he clasped her fingers.

"Don't you feel it?" He drawled. When she looked up, she noticed his eyes fluttering shut, as if the blackness had some kind of pull on him.

Ripping her arm away, she remembered who it was exactly that she was touching. Who she was standing so close to—too close to. She was touching the King of Laterra, and he was letting her.

His eyes flickered open. She watched the swirls of blackness dance around in his green gaze as he looked at her. The same kind of black that trembled and roiled beside his feet.

"You're starting to understand, aren't you?"

Valeria glanced at the black hole, then back to his swirling pupils.

"That's it." He mumbled, barely stepping closer to her frozen form.

She mumbled something to herself while glancing at the murky blackness that bubbled and made her skin *crave* to melt into it. She wanted to climb into the black abyss and let it control her. Let it give everything back that she had lost.

Shaking her head, she took another step away from the king.

Because, no. She wouldn't let the power draw her in.

"The abyss." The king started once he saw the expression on her face. He smirked. "This, Valeria. This is where you will go if you win the Game of Lords." He pointed at the black abyss again. "This is your future."

She stumbled back. "N—no."

He pursed his lips, nodding. The swirls of black were now absent from his eyes. "It is the only way to become a highlady. If Lance does not succeed at killing you—This is where you will go. And I've already warned you already. I will not have another highlady in my courts. If anything, I'll make you my bride. You will give me a son. One much stronger than the one I already have."

Her hand brushed against a flower, stinging the tips of her fingers. She cursed and turned away. "That—You can't do that."

The king frowned and stepped toward her, farther away from the black murky abyss. "I can, and I will if you win...Give it up. Let Lance win."

Her stomach dropped when she met his gaze, where darkness thrived and relished. Where hatred built, and entertainment grew. He was enjoying this—enjoying the thought of her struggle—of her choice to live or die.

It wasn't fair.

Valeria shook the pain from her fingertips and squared her shoulders. "*No.*"

"You've lost quite a lot. Don't you think? Why not give up? Why keep trying?" He asked.

She held her breath before she could answer. "Because I have a family who cares about me."

He looked as if someone had just slapped him across the face before his eyes cleared with a new sense of arrogance. "And you think you'll see them again if you win?" A chuckle, and then, "You innocent, darling thing, that is not how the game works."

Valeria furrowed her brows.

"If you win, it means you lose everything, but are granted eternity. You do understand that, don't you?"

"You lie." She spat. Unable to hold back the anger simmering in her gut.

He parted his lips before taking another step closer. Smile dropping into a frown as he hissed, "You dare accuse me of lying in my own kingdom?"

She thought about it for a moment. A brief moment, where she debated her choices and the outcomes. Then she thought, how would Flynn handle this situation?

Finally, Valeria gave the King of Laterra a curt nod. "What more could I lose? As you said before, if I win, I lose everything I've ever cared about. If I lose, I die." Quirking her brow, she said, "I'm not risking much by assuming that you lie."

He didn't reply, only released a slow, pent up breath.

She examined his stance. The slight tremble of his fingers, as if he was holding his composure... his anger.

Let him lose control, let him be the one to make the first move.

She'd survived through enough the past few weeks. She'd lost enough.

"You are going to die. I will make sure of it." He whispered.

"Then kill me."

The words that left her lips were not of her own. She hadn't even realized she said them until she noted the king's reaction.

A sinister smile bloomed on his aging face "When the time is right, I will."

Valeria growled underneath her breath. Her chest hammering with each inhale and exhale.

She flicked a look at the officials holding the door, who lingered, sharp eyes examining the way the king stood over her. Then she inspected the pistols in their readied hands.

Closing her eyes, she breathed, releasing it through her nose until her heart slowed to a normal pace.

Slowly, her mind calmed, and her muscles relaxed. It would all be over soon. There was no need to rush anything.

The king snapped his fingers in her face. "Take Valeria to her quarters. I'm through with her for now."

He turned and sauntered back through the garden and into the dark stairway. Leaving her with the officials, who grasped her wrists and tugged her backwards, dragging her behind the king, whose cape brushed against the dusty stone steps.

She didn't try to escape.

When the door to the garden was closed, Valeria swore she might have heard someone or something whispering in her ear.

Come closer. Come closer.

36

The last trial of the Game of Lords was approaching, and Valeria was on a mission to uncover any details she could about it. By doing so, she would have knowledge of how her life may begin or end tomorrow afternoon.

The king weighed heavily on her mind. He threatened her. He was going to kill her.

She swallowed and followed a small group of maids and butlers down the hall until they rushed into a room. They hadn't noticed her following them for the past ten minutes, too focused on their tasks and terse conversations.

Valeria picked up on a sole part of their conversations, only because it had been about the royal wedding. She wasn't sure when the event would take place, and she hadn't even seen Flynn since that night he'd stared at her over the table, while holding onto the princesses fingers.

Before the door shut behind Valeria, hushed voices sounded as though they were arguing in the hallway. Instantly, she recognized who they belonged to.

She stepped back out into the long, elegant hall. The cream walls, almost orange like the sun, walnut wood bordering the doors and marble floors. She turned around and faced the prince and princess with a sheepish smile.

Prince Luther stopped mid-sentence and looked at her with parted lips. "Valeria...Hello. What are you doing down here?"

She shrugged, sending a glance down the hall, joints beginning to ache with lack of sleep. "Exploring."

Helena stepped forward, frowning. "You're not training for the trial tomorrow? Lance is already in the arena preparing with the firetail."

He was? She hadn't known.

Valeria pursed her lips, managing to hold back a shaky smile. Did they know what their father—the king thought about her? Did they know he was planning to kill her, whether she won or not?

"Actually, I prepared well before leaving Azrael estate. Though I'm sure Lance needs all the practice he can get." She forced a tight-lipped chuckle.

The prince narrowed his eyes. "Well, I'm certain you'll do marvelous tomorrow."

Grinning, they studied each other for a brief moment until Helena cursed beside him, throwing her hands back. "*Gods*, I have to go. The florist brought back the wrong flowers for tomorrow afternoon. I'll have to see you later." She reached up on her tiptoes to plant a soft kiss on her brother's cheek before running off. Not forgetting to throw a quick apology over her shoulder to Valeria.

Prince Luther remained smiling down at her, soft and full of comfort. He offered his elbow, and she took it. They began walking down the hall, passing several open doors filled with busybodies and panicked cooks.

"Is it always this hectic?" Valeria asked.

He chuckled while pushing a door open at the end of the hall. He let her pass through first before following. They stood on a balcony that overlooked the large city of Jerume.

The land was nothing but dead grass and dry dirt. Over the city border it was vacant. Arakanath Dunes stretched from the northeast, ending just before the Forest of Many Wonders and the towering mountains that stood hundreds of miles away.

Soft wind brushed her curled red locks back over her shoulders when she looked down at the people. Her eyes traced the buildings, mountains, and trees before she finally faced the prince, who was grinning down at his father's land—his kingdom... his future.

"My sister is to be wed tomorrow."

Valeria's mouth fell open as she searched for the right words to say. "But I thought the final trial was tomorrow?"

"It is." Her brows narrowed, and he sighed. "My father thinks it'd be best if Flynn and the winner become immortal together. After the wedding, he plans to take Flynn to the abyss."

Her heart stopped, slowly filling with dread as her eyes began to widen. She failed to let the smile remain on her face. "He—he wouldn't force Flynn to do that, would he?"

The prince laughed sarcastically and crossed his arms on top of the railing. "Trust me, he would." When he paused, Valeria examined the drop of his hazel eyes, the pout on his full lips before he spoke quietly this time, "Last spring I was forced into the abyss. Apparently I had come of age, and was ready to begin my journey of immortality." She remained silent. He clenched his hands into fists and blinked. "My sister, Helena. She tried to stop him, but... well, we're twins, right?" Chuckling harshly, he finished, "She went in after."

Valeria was silent. She didn't know what to say. Before, she wasn't sure if the royal twins shared the same immortal blood as their father, but now, here he was admitting everything. She debated asking more, needing to know if they hated him as she did. Why was the king doing this?

The prince started again. "I like to imagine that my father wasn't always cruel. That maybe he was once more human than he is now... but to experience and witness the things that he has done to innocent people? To the citizens he is responsible for? He views the world as a stepping stool... I won't be like that. I swear I won't."

He was speaking more to himself than to her.

Valeria bit her lip and played with her fingers. "He showed me." She whispered.

The prince swiveled his neck, eyes hardening. "What? What did he show you?"

She bit down harder on her lip, failing to meet his panic-filled gaze. "The abyss. He took me to it yesterday. He—" She paused, swallowing. "He has *many* plans for me if I win."

Some far worse than death, she failed to add.

Cursing underneath his breath, he ran both of his hands through his slick brown hair. "Lords, Valeria." He shook his head. "He's planning something."

Valeria looked around and prayed that no one was listening. If the king knew what they were speaking of, he would have them executed immediately.

Prince Luther paced back and forth on the balcony before he finally came to a halt in front of her, dropping his hands at his sides. "You need to listen to me, okay?"

"What?" she breathed. Heart pounding much faster than before.

He grabbed both of her arms and looked deep into her eyes. "Don't win." She tried to object and shake him off, but he only tightened his grip. "Don't win tomorrow."

She almost cursed at his insanity, until she saw the genuine fear behind his eyes. It was deep, dark, and desperate. He peered down at her. The desperation crawled out of his gaze and seeped into hers, begging, pleading for her to agree.

Here he was, a prince, an immortal, asking a normal human girl to do something. To give up her entire life for him. And for what? What did he know that she didn't?

"Okay." She said, "I'll let him win."

The prince's eyes brightened by a fraction before he dropped her arms and stepped back. He blew out a breath, closing his eyes. When he looked at her again, there was a smile on his face. "Thank you."

Valeria decided to have dinner by herself, spending it alone inside the room she was provided as she gobbled down her steak and veggies on top of the golden silk sheets. An hour later, after she finished dinner, she found herself wandering through the back of a dark courtyard.

She'd only been in the castle for a day and a half, the entire time she occupied herself by exploring different parts of the kingdom. Yet, she still hadn't seen all of it. Every main hallway led to different, smaller halls, and thousands of doors.

Luckily, she was able to find a Help that showed the way to the courtyard she had been looking at from high above through the window in her room quarters.

Valeria watched the full moon shine against the deep purple sky. The stars flickered and fell over the kingdom, illuminating the glass tables and flower covered gazebo.

She left her room in hopes of finding Flynn, who had been lingering in her mind ever since the game changing conversation with the prince.

He was going to become immortal, and there was no stopping it.

Valeria's head was heavy, along with her heart.

Everything was falling apart.

The plans she made with Flynn were no longer practical. She needed to tell him in case he didn't know. In case the princess hadn't explained the entire truth about tomorrow, and him being thrown into the abyss.

Valeria sighed and crossed her arms.

Once upon a time, she was free. She had been able to make her own choices. Once upon a time, she had thought for only a small, brief moment that she and Flynn could have something better outside of the games... but no. None of it was real. Everything that she once wanted was out of reach, never to be touched. Never to be experienced. Never to be *loved*.

A light, airy chuckle pulled Valeria from her thoughts.

She swiveled on her toes, finding the princess running across the small garden a few feet away. Valeria's chest thudded before she rushed toward the shadows to hide. Then, when her gaze trailed after Helena's giddy form, she spotted Flynn just past the roses, facing the bright city firelights.

She almost stepped out from the shadows when she spotted him. That was until she recognized the way his eyes lit up upon seeing his fiance.

Valeria shrunk back into the darkness, watching him pick Helena up and spin her around, all with a beautiful smile.

She'd thought she felt hope die before, but as her eyes traced the way Flynn's lingered down on the princess—the way his hands held Helena's small waist and squeezed, the remaining hope in her chest flickered out.

Valeria's eyes fluttered shut, and she released a breath.

She let go of the what ifs, and reached for the uncertainty of tomorrow.

Lance was going to win, and there was nothing she could do about it.

The prince never said he would save her, and she didn't expect him to. She didn't expect anyone to. Even if she did win, the king would still decide her fate.

37

The arena went wild when Valeria and Lance trudged from beneath the cement steps and out onto the rocky field.

She took in the screaming and chanting faces. Even the children shouted down at her and Lance after they stopped in the middle of the field. Some threw flower petals onto the gravel, while others threw their unfinished meals at their feet.

Most of the food landed near Valeria's, while roses of every color covered Lance's toes.

She grimaced and waited for Zakai to show, to make out what she might think of the trial and these people.

Were the citizens of Jerume aware she had a dragon?

Valeria arched a brow at a younger woman, who leaned nearly her entire body over the cement barrier that separated them. She tilted her head, examining the way the woman cursed and swore, even so far as to flip a certain finger in her direction.

Frowning, she turned away, distracted by the breeze that grew into a heavier gust.

A slight smile bloomed on her lips when she looked at the clouds and watched Zakai dive from the skies and land on all fours beside her. The white dragon lifted her neck and let out a mighty roar. Fire blazed above the arena.

The crowd fell into silence.

Valeria glanced back at the woman who had been cursing at her with old vile words. Then she lifted her lips into a smile. One that spoke volumes. One that would let the people know she had little care for their unnecessary hatred. Because these were her final moments before the trial began, and she would not let herself falter. Not for a second.

Lance strode for the red firetail. It may have been considerably smaller than Zakai, but the flame-red scales on its back and green eyes made it appear much—*much* deadlier.

It didn't help that the firetail behaved just like him. Lance was cruel, but his dragon was even worse.

She wasn't sure what she and Lance were supposed to do. No one had informed them about what the trial consisted of. The Helps and officials had sent them out into the field without another word. Laurent wasn't anywhere around when she was getting her armor on and makeup done by Jackie, who met in her room earlier that morning.

Jacky dusted Valeria's eyelids with a light brown color and her cheeks with an even lighter shade of pink. She hadn't complained when Jacky worked on her face. If anything, she was relieved that she wouldn't pass on to the next life with black shadows beneath her eyes.

A bell rang across the arena, and the ground shook when Valeria turned around and watched Lance ride off on the back of his dragon.

They coasted around the stands, causing the audience to chant and shout. Valeria swiveled around, watching as they landed on the wooden stands far above. His dragon reared back and blasted a flame toward her and Zakai, who chuffed at the smaller firetail.

Valeria swallowed and sauntered toward the white beast. "Let's not keep them waiting." She said.

Zakai's nostrils flared, the steam brushed against the front of Valeria's body as she neared. Before she could jump onto Zakai's wide ankle, Zakai dropped to her stomach and let Valeria climb up her shoulder, taking her rightful seat on her thorny white spine.

"Shall I kill those who curse and shout?" Zakai's words sneered inside of Valeria's mind.

She bit back a smirk. "No. Not unless you want me to get killed sooner rather than later."

She couldn't tell Zakai the truth. *How could she?* The dragon would never let her lose, but she had no other choice. Zakai could easily end both Lance and his firetail this very moment if Valeria were to ask, but she just couldn't.

"What is it that you hide, human girl?"

As Zakai spread her wings, Valeria secured her grip before they leapt into the air, ascending toward Lance and the firetail.

"What do you mean?" Valeria asked over the gusting wind. Zakai could effortlessly hear a hillside crumble from miles away, hence Valeria wasn't concerned about her hushed voice.

"I sense your thoughts. The beating of your heart. You're scared." Zakai said. *"What is it that frightens you?"*

Valeria stiffened like a rock as they landed beside Lance and his beast on the thick wooden post. She swallowed, clearing her throat before answering. "The king has plans for me... to harm me if I win."

The wood crumbled beneath Zakai's claws. She snarled and extended her long, white neck. *"He does not know of your true intentions. He does not read your soul as I have. You are pure, pure as first snow. That is why I chose you. That is why I will help you."*

Her copper red braid fell over her shoulder as she released a breath through her nose. She didn't have anything left to say or even ask. Zakai had been in her head—read her mind, her heart, and her soul. Yet, here she was, a vicious beast telling a small human girl that she was pure when she felt anything but.

Valeria sighed and leaned back, her eyes landed on Laurent, who emerged from beneath the stone steps and strode toward the middle of the arena. She peered over Zakai's neck and watched Laurent hold a small object that she could not recognize up to his neck.

He cleared his throat before shouting, "Welcome to the Game of Lords!"

The entire arena exploded into a rally of cheers and cries.

She winced at the noise ringing inside her ears.

"Today is the final trial." He paused for a moment and let the crowd gather themselves.

Slowly, the arena became quiet. Only a few twenty remained shouting, but Laurent didn't seem to mind when he turned toward Valeria and looked up. She was too far away to read the expression on his face when he began his speech.

"It is also the day that the lands of Laterra will gain a new lord or lady. As you can see," Laurent flicked a finger up at the dragons on the post before he continued, "many of you may wonder what the new court will be named. And it'll only be a few more hours until you'll find out just what it is. Although, it should be easy to assume."

Valeria already knew the names of the new house, court, and the name that Lance would have after she let him win.

He would be Lord of Dragons from the House of Embers, and ruler of the Court of Ash.

She only hoped he would look out for the townsmen who had built it for him.

Lance was already staring when she turned her head, glancing his way. He was leaning back with narrowed eyes. She hadn't noticed the brown saddle that he sat in until now. It wrapped around the firetail's chest and under its belly. Holding Lance in place.

The saddle explained why Lance hadn't been training as much as her. Why train when a saddle could be made instead? It almost felt unfair, but she had to give it to him. She hadn't thought to ask for a saddle. She's only learned how to ride bareback. Thankfully, Zakai made sure she knew how to do everything that was important already. That way she wasn't completely hopeless.

Valeria rolled her eyes and let her attention drift back to Laurent.

"Our remaining contestants, Lance Whitlock and Valeria Rox, will be performing on the back of their dragons the same way that the warriors from many years ago had trained for battle on theirs." The crowd made a series of oohs and awws before he spoke again. "The difference between our old riders and our new ones? The winner is not the one who manages to finish the challenge the fastest or the first. The winner is the dragon, and its rider that survives." Valeria's eyes fell to the back of Zakai's head, but she remained silent. "These dragons, these... *beast*. One may seem loyal, while the other may be a fighter. Whether the fighter falls first or the loyal. We have yet to find out."

She could feel the heat of Lance's brown eyes scratching on the side of her face. But she didn't bother to give him any notice. She couldn't reveal the fear that was currently climbing up her abdomen.

Valeria attempted to capture Laurents eyes with her own, but he only bowed to the excited crowd. He hesitated when turning his back, but whatever his second thoughts were didn't matter, because after a moment he finally left.

Another person she wouldn't get the chance to say goodbye to.

Confusion stirred inside her mind with what his speech entailed.

The winner was the dragon, and its rider that survives.

Valeria swallowed her rapidly growing fear. While boiling anger formed in the pit of her stomach.

Prince Luther wanted her to give up? She agreed to sacrifice her life—to die on her own. She had already lost everyone and everything she cared for. And she was tired. So, so tired.

But to let Zakai give her life as well?

No.

No, she wouldn't let that happen. Regardless of what she had promised the prince.

Her bond with Zakai could not be broken, and she would not let the royal family and the Game of Lords be their ruin.

She was going to fight.

A length of time passed as she and Lance sat on the wooden stands, peering down at the crowd and inner arena. Valeria's legs almost grew numb by the time a few historians strolled from beneath the stone steps.

One walked with more confidence than the other, he held the same device that Laurent used to raise his voice.

The historian pulled his dark green tunic away from his neck before clearing his throat. He began reciting a few passages from the sheet of paper in his hand.

"The training of the strongest warriors was brutal and deadly. Each exercise began at the top of Mount Qeona, the largest mountain in Arakanath Dunes. While diving, their only hope of survival was for their dragon to break their fall before hitting the earth. Afterwards they would fly to the greatest height, while spiraling away from flame. They called this the Flight of Ashes."

The historian continued speaking, but Valeria's chest was hammering deeper into the pit of her stomach. She could hardly pay attention to the rest of the historians' words before he and the others turned and left the arena.

Her ears vibrated against the crowd's chanting and yelling that only grew heavier against the stone. She swallowed and bowed forward until her forehead was resting against Zakai's scales.

"Have faith, human girl. I have lived for decades. Do not fret over one insignificant trial."

Valeria lifted her neck and rubbed her hands down Zakai's thorny back. "You may be a century old with over a lifetime of experience, but I am barely two decades, Z. Remember that."

Zakai huffed and rolled her long white neck before turning her head, giving Valeria a mighty glare. *"Do not think that age has anything to do with strength. I see you. I. Know. You."* She paused, slitted golden eyes flicking toward Lance, who was sliding down the length of the red dragon's leg. *"Now, prepare for the Flight of Ashes. Get off."*

She wanted to do anything else but let go and leave Zakai's side, but Zakai's tail wrapped around the wooden pole behind them as she lowered herself closer to the beam so that Valeria could easily slide down without injuring herself.

Once she was on her feet, Zakai gave Valeria one last glance, full of nothing but pure, unworthy trust. Their bond was already strong, despite the little time they had known each other.

Still, Valeria didn't feel as though she deserved it. She didn't know if she ever would.

Lance stood a few feet away, glaring down at the arena where the firetail beside him was preparing to lunge.

She took a step back from the edge and watched Zakai tuck her wings into her side before her large white body fell face first down into the arena. It was the only way to exit without knocking Valeria or Lance off of the wooden beams.

Valeria peered over the edge to make sure Zakai was safe, when a rush of wind shoved her back. Then a bright white light blocked hers and Lance's entire view of the arena when Zakai flew straight up, up, and up. She bloomed like a newly sprouted flower. Rushing through the skies.

It ended far too soon before Zakai dove back down into the arena. Awaiting the start of the trial.

Valeria hadn't noticed when Lance finally stopped glaring at the side of her head, but she looked back at him and waited. When the firetail lunged down to meet Zakai at the bottom, Lance was no longer staring. Instead, he had his hands fisted at his sides, clenched his jaw, and narrowed his eyebrows as he glanced around.

She swallowed a grin and followed his line of sight. Where the dragons were no longer sitting and waiting for them to dive from the stands. She couldn't find Zakai, nor his red beast. Panic nearly arose in her chest.

The wooden beam creaked underneath Lance's feet after he took a step back.

Then, to her surprise, he looked at her. His brown eyes untroubled, undisturbed. "May the best rider win."

Tilting her head, "May the best rider win." She whispered back.

That was when Lance Whitlock shook his hands, tucked his head down and ran. He threw his arms out in front of himself before jumping. A loud yell left his mouth before his body disappeared from the beams and he was gone.

Valeria gasped and ran to the edge. She watched his body fall toward the rocky earth. Tempted to turn away and close her eyes in order to avoid the memory of his body splattering on the ground. Valeria choked on the wind when a flash of red drove straight underneath Lance. It happened so fast that the firetail had only been a dark blur that bolted before her sight.

The crowd went silent.

The ground began to shake, and then she realized they were cheering.

Valeria winced as the wind grew heavier.

She heard a chant, and then a small voice in her head yelling at her, telling her to duck.

She did, and when she rose again, she spotted Lance on top of the red beast flying high above her through the stands.

He swooped around on the red dragon. They almost seemed to float above the arena when they turned back and stared at her still standing on the beams.

"Now, human girl."

Her heart hammered, but she bit back the fear and kept her eyes on Lance. There was nothing but determination in her gaze.

"I said now—"

Valeria didn't wait to hear the rest of Zakai's commands, because she was already running. Her feet pounded against the wood, once, twice, and then a third time before she launched herself into the air and dove straight toward the earth.

Time slowed as her body fell.

The wind was ruthless and unrelenting, thrashing against her falling body.

She didn't want to watch the ground greet her. Her life would not end here. She refused.

"Zakai!" She yelled through the fall. "Zakai, now!" The air scratched against her throat as she screamed.

Forty feet. Her eyes widened. The ground came closer and closer to ending her.

But then, there it was. A flash of white light that darted from her left, from underneath the wooden stands. Valeria's body crashed onto the mound of Zakai's back. Her cheek scratched against the thorns and she latched her hands and legs onto whatever she could to hold on.

Zakai roared and began her ascent.

"*I'm giving you thirty seconds to get in your rightful position.*" Zakai said.

Valeria could hardly hear Zakai's words through her own loud, rushing thoughts.

That was until the beast roared again and she felt the steam that Zakai's flame left behind in its wake. Valeria lifted her head, watching the sky welcome her. She almost smiled until she glimpsed the same flash of red circling around Zakai's large, white body. The firetail nipped at Zakai's thorned-tail and she hissed.

Valeria slipped when she adjusted her leg in hopes of gaining her footing.

"Just like we practiced, human girl. Use my scales. Use your strength and pull your damned self up."

She didn't know how she did it. How she managed to find the will and strength to crawl in a diagonal line, straight up Zakai's back, who stretched her neck, whacked her tail, and dodged the snapping teeth and daggered claws from Lance's firetail.

But when she was finally seated at the base of Zakai's neck, just above her large flapping wings, Valeria tightened her grip, and lowered herself against the bashing wind.

"What happens when we can't ascend any further?" Valeria asked, sending a glance over her shoulder. She saw Lance on his dragon not too far behind, then the ground, which was quickly growing farther and farther away.

The arena was merely a black speck compared to the red beast that snarled and snapped its jaw below.

Her stomach knotted, and she nearly barfed at the thought of losing her grip and falling to her death at the height. She'd die from heart palpitations before her body could even hit the earth.

"I sense fear. Look up, never down." Zakai swung to the side, avoiding another bite at her ankle. She swept her thorn tail back and forth, finally landing a sharp hit to the firetail's chest.

Valeria yanked her head around to face forward. Her legs ached against the hard scales on Zakai's back.

She thought that she had enough practice, but it... it was too much.

Her mind was too busy racing to notice the way that Zakai ignored her earlier question. She blinked and blinked against the blasting wind.

It wasn't long before they flew into a thick cloud. The moisture clung to her hair and cheeks. Her makeup was sure to be dripping down her face already, but she didn't care.

Valeria took a breath, it was short, and did nothing to shake the tension from her spine.

They remained silent. Only the gray sky and misty winds could fill the empty void inside her mind. She clung tighter to Zakai's back when they twirled in order to avoid another lash from Lance's firetail.

Lance hooted and hollered, pumping a fist straight up before latching himself closer to the red scales. She looked back and watched a sinister grin grow on his taunting lips. They were much closer than before, Zakai was growing heavier the higher they went, while the smaller firetail grew faster.

Turning back in her seat, Valeria focused on her breathing and tight grip. She couldn't let go, not even for half of a second. Not unless she wanted to fall to her death.

The ground was long out of sight, only the white clouds surrounded them as Zakai flapped her large white wings harder.

"I must slow." Valeria heard the hushed, quiet words filter through her thoughts.

"What?" she asked. The muscles in her arms were thinning with weakness and they began to shake.

"I must. This will not end until we fight. They want one of us dead."

Valeria swallowed a rush of air down her throat and closed her eyes. "Do it." She said.

Zakai's wings faltered before she tucked them tight against her ribcage. There was a brief moment where it felt as if they stopped time together. She hadn't noticed the beginning of the fall until her braid flung past her shoulders and over her face. Stomach rolling, Valeria clenched her thighs against Zakai's sloped scales.

"Keep your head down—"

Zakai screeched and spun around. She spread her wings to catch herself from running into the red firetail.

Valeria clung for dear life. If it weren't for the blast of hot wind that pushed against her, she would have slipped right off of Zakai's spine.

When she opened her eyes and gained her frantic breath, Valeria gasped at what little oxygen she could inhale. Zakai's entire neck was black and ashy. Singed from the heat of the firetail's flame.

Then, as Lance and his beast flew higher above, Valeria felt it. She looked at her hands, burnt, red, nearly ash. She bit her lip, and failed to hold in a vicious scream of agony.

The sky expanded around them as Zakai flapped her wings and screeched. She failed to give Valeria any warning before tucking her wings, rolling, and blasting a blazing red flame at the scarlet beast above them.

Valeria didn't see if her flame had hit its target. She was too busy screaming and scratching at the white slippery scales that were now above her.

"Cursed, human!" Zakai shouted before rolling back over through the skies. Valeria plopped back onto her spine, releasing a mighty long breath. Her vision was blurry, her mind empty, her lungs light and fluttery. She wasn't even sure if she was still holding on.

"We must make a decision!"

Valeria raised her weak neck, looking above, where a red shadow danced and opened its wide mouth. She clenched her jaw, waiting for the blast of flame to envelope around her—to end her.

"The palace." She breathed.

Zakai went silent, only to dodge a roll of fiery flame. Valeria felt it sear the right side of her leather armor, melting her skin. She cursed and leaned forward, pressing her forehead into Zakai's spine.

"Take me to the palace. *Now!*"

Just before Zakai began tucking her wings back to her sides to dive, a blast of fire, brighter than any other, hotter than any hellfire—burned, scorched and boiled into Valeria's back.

Her leather covered back turned to dust and ash. She was naked, burning raw flesh that dripped from her exposed ribs and down what remained of her spine.

Valeria was no longer conscious when Zakai screeched and roared. The wind kept waking her, as if begging her to stay awake—to stay alive. It bit into her skin like tiny, prickling needles. Only pulling her flesh farther from her bones.

Her body fell alongside Zakai's as they dove straight down toward the heart of Laterra.

She was nothing but a fleck of dust, falling through the sky, the clouds looming above her, the firetail still on their tail, diving to kill.

The kingdom of Laterra grew larger behind her closed eyes. She felt the oxygen fill her lungs and then leave, as if working on its own. Whether her mind was there or not.

Zakai pulled her wings out, trying to catch Valeria's falling body. Valeria landed against the back of Zakai's wing. Scorched, dead flesh meeting burnt scales as she tumbled through the air and down the length of Zakai's back.

She opened her eyes as she fell through the sky. Understanding death as it reached up to claim her.

There was nothing left underneath to catch Valeria. Zakai was far above, screeching desperately into the air as she flapped her wings, only watching the wind carry her rider toward the royal palace.

A blackness washed over Valeria's mind, and then she heard the words that were not of her white dragon.

"Come closer. Come closer."

The city streets and homes crumbled with silence when a body fell like rainwater from the skies. The people of Jerume felt their attention being pulled—tugged toward the royal palace as a ripple of magic flared to life across the lands.

The abyss welcomed Valeria's torn, dying body with open, watery arms.

PART III

A Game of Immortality

38

The world stilled as Valeria sank into the black void of nothingness.

She traveled to a place where there was no sound. There was only an empty soul floating about, searching for something more. Something that it could perhaps cling to until death came to drag it away.

The absence of her physical body didn't make her frantic or scared, yet she somehow knew just where she was and where her old body was being taken.

The abyss took her old parts and began repairing something new. A worthy, delicate skin that would fit her much better than the old one had.

She envisioned a large, black starry hand reaching down into her essence, stirring an aura of colors around. As if she were soup in a pot that boiled over a stove.

It spoke to her with soft, kind words. Caressing her being with comfort and the strength that kept her from letting go. It told her stories of the past—of the ones that came before.

The ones that took bits and pieces of the abyss's life. It's power.

She didn't want any of it. She tried to whisper back, but with no physical body, with nothing but a white and purple aura that floated around the blackness, she remained silent.

The hand reached further into her essence, running a gentle finger over the colors.

"*Breathe.*" It seemed to say. "*Take the bits and pieces I've been greedy with. Take the parts of my being that I've saved for you. The lucky star. The one who will end all evil.*"

Then, as the finger orbited around her, stirring and weaving her strings of life back together, Valeria breathed.

39

A beast landed before the black abyss, just inside the garden that dried up and turned yellow quicker by the second. The water was still rippling from when Valeria hit its surface when a pair of feet landed on the gravel.

They stepped closer to the edge of the black pool, waiting, searching for any signs of life beneath its surface.

Lance glanced back at Oziah, the firetail, a frown etched onto his face before he faced the abyss again. He had never seen something so wicked, so vile, so full of... darkness. He didn't know how deep the water or whatever was rippling in front of him went.

She could have hit her head at the bottom of the pool and died. She could be drowning right then, for all he knew.

Lance almost turned back to claim his victory as the last remaining survivor in the Game of Lords when something emerged from the middle of the abyss.

His eyes widened, and he tried to take a step back, but he fell, catching himself with his hands as he watched the woman stand inside the black pool.

Her stare was of liquid death.

There was nothing but a burning rage in her emerald eyes. Valeria strode from the depths of the abyss, hair dripping wet, black droplets sliding down her cheeks, and grinned.

"What—" Lance stuttered, scooting back on his arms. "You should be dead." He glanced from the sky and back down to her completely healed body that stood above the black pool. "I—we... You were burned. You were dying." He grasped at the gravel beneath his fingers.

Her smirk grew wider, eyes narrower.

"Lance." She drawled, standing above him with the grace of all the angry gods as she tilted her head. "I cannot be killed," she declared. "Not anymore."

He crawled, trying to fathom what he was seeing—*who* stood right in front of him. She was no longer the small, fragile girl she had been moments ago. She was no longer his competition.

She was the Lady of Dragons.

"Go. *Leave*. Before I change my mind and kill you myself."

Lance stuttered in a breath. His chest shook when he rose to his feet and bowed his head. He couldn't look her in the eye before he turned around and ran toward the firetail, who was staring over his head at her with a bright, awestruck gaze.

"*Eternal*." It whispered into his mind. "*She is the eternal being. The blessed one.*"

He didn't hear the rest of the beast's words before he jumped onto its back and gave him a hard kick in the ruby red ribs. "Go! To the east!" He yelled.

The east, where he would find the Court of Storms and his little sister, who waited desperately for him to come home.

So Lance and the firetail flew. They avoided the watchful eyes of the officials—of the royal family—and he escaped the Game of Lords.

He didn't look back once.

40

The black pool, once still as ice, now simmered and bubbled. Valeria was uncertain what she was seeing when she turned her attention from Lance flying off on the back of his dragon and watched the abyss drain.

It was shallower by a few feet, much emptier than it had been when she fell into it moments ago. Valeria engulfed the air, filling her new lungs with fresh oxygen.

She was alive.

With a shaky exhale, Valeria closed her eyes and let herself feel the warm breeze that slowly dried her dripping wet hair. After rubbing a hand across her face, she examined the black, inky water staining her fingers. Valeria's legs felt lighter, her blood ran colder, and her hair felt thicker.

A shadow stirred in the corner of her eye, pulling her from her thoughts. She swiveled on her toes, expecting to find a fight, when she spotted the familiar black hair that belonged to the Lord of Illusion, Saint Nyle.

Saint Nyle grinned, stepping out from the dark doorway.

The grass beneath his feet crumbled. What was once green and luscious was now yellow and dead.

"You look different. Are you going to have my head at your feet now?" His eyes were focused on the black water that dripped from her unbraided, messy hair.

She couldn't believe what she was seeing, or rather, *who* she was seeing.

Squaring her shoulders, a warmness encased her body. Ignoring the unusual heat, she wiped a dead flower petal off of her black armor. "Someday I will. Right now, I have more important things to do."

Tilting his head, a grin sliding on his sharp face, he said, "I see." He took a step closer, and she might have imagined it, but his eyes flickered from a familiar blue and into a light yellowish green color. She swallowed, feeling uneasy, and bit the inside of her lip. "Would you like me to escort you to the royal wedding?"

Valeria snarled and began walking. She sent a glare his way before brushing past his shoulder and entering the stairway door.

He walked alongside her as they descended the round staircase. "Do you hate everyone that you meet? Or is it just me?" He asked, although his voice remained light and humorous.

With a huff, she took her next step. Then, after a few hundred stairs, they reached the bottom, and she trudged for the exit into the main corridor of the palace. Despite her annoyance, Saint Nyle continued to follow close behind.

"I hate the circumstances I was forced into." She didn't bother turning her head to look back at him when she answered his questions. "And yes, I hate you. I have a passion of hate in my entire body for you, because if it weren't for you, Isaac would still be here." Her voice was plain. She held her spine straight and continued down the empty hall. Ignoring the way Isaac's name made her chest ache.

He chuckled and brushed a hand through his raven black hair. "That's understandable."

She didn't have enough focus left for the wretched man beside her, so she picked up her pace and jogged through the large throne room doors, only to find that it was empty.

Sighing, she continued searching down each hallway, each room and had yet to interrupt Flynn and Princess Helena's wedding. Surprisingly, Saint Nyle remained by her side the entire time.

"Why are you not at the wedding?" She found herself asking after they rounded a corner.

If it was already over, and Flynn had already married the princess... Valeria wouldn't let herself think about it.

She could feel the heaviness that flowed through her veins as she burst through another large door.

The Lord of Illusion suddenly appeared in front of her. She skidded to a stop, swearing underneath her breath.

"I have more important things to take care of." He said, clenching his jaw. She watched his throat bob and his blue-green eyes narrow. "That way." He nodded to the left, at the widely set grand doors. They were decorated with different colors of roses, greens, blues, golds, it was beautiful.

Valeria lifted her chin, swallowing back the bile in her throat.

"Don't go far." She told him, marching for the doors. "I have much planned for you."

Without turning around, she could hear the arrogance in his voice when he said, "I'll be waiting."

Before she kicked the doors open, she thought about how she might have Saint Nyle killed. She could make it quick like he had for Isaac, but

370

the mountain of pain he caused for several people that loved Isaac? She wanted to make Saint Nyle beg for mercy—to crave death. She longed to watch the life leave his eyes just like she had seen it leave Isaac's.

The royal ceremony came to a halt when the doors bursted open, slamming against the officials guarding them. Every head turned toward the noise, finding Valeria, who stood on the center of the red rug that led to the altar. Blackness dripped down her face from her hair. She looked like a mess—an vengeful, angry mess.

Her gaze could have thrown a thousand daggers across the room.

Valeria's chest grew lighter with every breath as she began walking down the aisle toward Flynn and Helena, who stood at the front of the room below a dripping candle that floated above their heads.

She snarled, letting her eyes drag away from Flynn's messy blonde hair and on to the king, who met her stare. The corner of his lip curled, he tilted his head with a grin.

"Just in time." The King's voice filled the room, making it shake like a rumbling mountain. "Welcome to the royal family, Flynn." Although the king spoke to Flynn, whose eyes had yet to find her throughout the room, the king's gaze remained on her. "Prince Flynn of Laterra."

Instead of the guest cheering loud and happily, it was silent. Uneasiness filled the great hall, all the joy fled out the open door behind her. Because she was not supposed to be there. She was supposed to be dead, her body lying somewhere in the mountains beneath the rocks and dirt.

Valeria licked her teeth and stopped once she reached the end of the aisle. That was when her eyes drifted up to Flynn, who had finally realized why everyone was silent.

He watched her, his gaze softened and lips parted.

"Val." He mouthed, although she wasn't sure if she imagined it or not.

His usual messy blonde hair was neatly combed back, and his white tunic shirt was tucked into his blue pants instead of pulled out carelessly. He didn't look like himself. She hadn't seen him for weeks, and here he was... so not himself anymore.

He was a prince.

He was married, and not to her.

She bit her lip too hard before taking another step closer, letting her eyes scan all corners of the room again. The prince stood to the left of the altar, a few feet behind Helena. He reached a hand out before dropping it back to his side, squinting as he breathed heavily through his mouth. Then, he shook his head at her.

She glanced away.

She was here for Flynn. No one else. Nothing else.

They didn't matter.

A gentle voice cleared their throat before beginning to speak. "Why are you here?" Princess Helena dropped Flynn's hands and stepped toward Valeria, her eyebrows drawn together as she pulled her golden skirt up. "Take a seat, please. Let us finish the ceremony."

She almost chuckled... almost. Instead, she bit back a smile and squared her shoulders. "I cannot."

Helena stepped back, a hand to her chest as if in shock. "I have been nothing but kind to you, and here you are, interrupting my marriage? I am the Princess of Laterra. You must do as I say."

Valeria then let herself chuckle.

Before she could reply, the king stepped out from behind the newly wed. Flynn dropped his eyes to the ground and held his hands in front of himself, allowing the king to pass.

All while avoiding her eyes.

"All is well, Helena. We may celebrate your marriage this evening, after I take care of your husband and... the girl."

Valeria held her ground, his words only making her eyes twitch. She clenched her fists and sighed. "We are well taken care of. There is nothing else that we want, nor need from you."

Flynn finally faced her, a frown etched onto his handsome face. "Val, what are you doing?"

She ignored him, too angry to rip her eyes from off of the kings. "This ends here. You will leave Flynn alone. You will leave the citizens of the courts alone. Stop the killing. No more games. No more forcing eternity on others."

First the king frowned, and then, slowly, so slowly, the wrinkles around his eyes formed and he laughed.

When he was done, he lifted a hand, flicking it toward the far door. "I apologize for the sudden interruption, my guests. But you may leave now. The celebration will continue later this evening."

One by one, the guests behind Valeria stood to their feet and left in a hurry out the large doors. They were quick once they realized a group of officials were pointing their pistols at them, hastening their pace.

Valeria and the king continued to stare at each other, while the others stood and watched in a daze.

The grand doors slammed shut behind the last guest, and the king suddenly spun on his heel. He prowled around her, his eyes harsh and angry. Her gaze never left his as she turned and traced his steps.

"So, you have won the Game of Lords." He said, but she only lifted her lip into a snarl. The king smiled, running a finger across his grin. "And you think that makes you the Lady of Dragons? You think that we are to bow at your feet now? Haven't I warned you enough? You. Will. Die."

She blinked, and then blinked again before tilting her head and letting the new, thicker blood swim and boil beneath her skin. "And how might you kill me?" She lifted her arm, flipping it over before she pulled the dagger from her thigh and sliced a long line down the underside of her wrist. The leather sleeve of her armor divided in half, exposing the black blood that began to puddle and drip down the length of her arm.

The king jolted back upon the sight of her blood.

Inhaling a deep breath, he marched over, yanking her wrist toward his chest and leaned over to get a better look. He examined the skin that quickly healed over, the black blood that dried. Then he looked up into her eyes, where blackness swirled.

"How?" He hissed underneath his breath.

"It was mine to take."

He squeezed her wrist tighter, baring his teeth. "That is impossible. I gave no such thing. How have you done it? No one has survived after going in alone."

She snarled, trying to yank her arm free, but he was too strong. "I wasn't alone." A moment of utter silence passed as she watched his face drain of all color. She waited for the king to catch his breath.

When he took too long to reply, she stepped around him, covering her wrist up with her split open sleeve. "Flynn." She called and watched him lift his head, meeting her angry eyes. "Come with me."

Flynn bit the inside of his lip and shook his head. He shot a glance at Helena before stepping toward her. "Val, my loyalty is with the crown. I'm not coming with you."

Valeria squinted, and gulped down the heat that rose in the back of her throat. "They are going to turn you, Flynn. Can't you see? They do not care about you... They never will. This is all a part of their plan."

She pointed a sharp finger at the princess. "She does not want you. This entire wedding was just a plan to turn you. They only wish to make you another immortal."

His usual sparkling eyes grew dark when he glared down at her. "You should've stayed in the arena. You should have listened to the king. You have no right to show up here uninvited."

Where there once was a seed of hope, that she watered hourly, sometimes daily, it was now empty. The small glow that she felt in her chest... it was gone.

She watched Flynn latch his arm around Princess Helena's waist and pull her into his chest. Helena sniffled back a tear, spreading her hands over the back of his neck, where Valeria had once touched—had once caressed.

Scoffing, she took a final step back. "So, this was your plan? You get out unharmed, you don't lose anything, and you leave me behind?" She spit at his feet, turning toward the small crowd of highlords that stood in the corner of the room, feeling the king's harsh glare on the side of her face. "His entire plan was to let me win, and he was going to marry the princess, so that we could both get out together. He wanted me to win."

"Val." Flynn warned. "*Enough.*"

Her eyes scanned over the faces of the highlady and four highlords, then the prince and a few other people of royalty she had seen in the papers.

She was hardly aware of the words that she spoke, given her heart was pounding too loudly in her chest. The temperature of her body was rising drastically as everyone looked at her with weary eyes.

She thought she might explode if it weren't for Prince Luther, who took a step out from the side of the room. He walked slowly, safely with his arm outreached toward her until he was standing in front of her.

"Let me escort you back to the arena. Before this turns into something drastic, something unneeded at my sister's wedding." His eyebrows narrowed when he finished, and he tilted his lips to one side. "*Please.*" He silently urged so that only she could hear.

The prince grabbed her arm and began pulling her past the king when a hard hand gripped her shoulder, holding her back.

"No." The king growled. "You are not to announce yourself as the winner until the boy's body has been found," the king warned.

She gasped, her vision becoming blurry as the king summoned two officials over to her side. All she felt was a sudden dull pressure on her ribcage.

He sent the prince back to his spot in the side of the room, his words cruel and filled with hatred.

Glancing to the left, down at her hip, she saw the official's pistol pressing against her side.

Gulping, Valeria tried to inhale a heavy breath.

Lords.

Lords.

Lords.

What was she supposed to do?

She looked away from the pistol and up at Flynn. He was petting a hand down the length of Helena's long brown hair, although his gaze was on hers from across the room. Valeria only shook her head, mind running blank with betrayal.

He won. He planned everything, and yet there he was. He was not going to save her, even when she had tried to do so for him.

She never resented anyone more in that moment, watching a frown grow on his full pink lips.

A sudden shove into her back had Valeria toppling down to the floor, the armed officials were quick to wrap their hands around her arms and hold them against her spine. Her cheek smashed against the cold floor, she ground her teeth together, knowing her chances of survival.

Even if she was immortal the king would still find a way to harm her, to possibly even kill her.

A pair of booted feet stepped up to her side before the king knelt and peered down at her sweaty face.

"Where is the boy's body?"

He was talking about Lance.

She could tell him the truth, where Lance was, but he would only find a way to kill her now and then hunt down Lance to announce him as the winner. Besides, Lance was probably too far gone now, and that red beast of his would never let anyone harm him. Not without getting its vengeance.

Valeria bit her tongue, dropping her forehead to the stone floor beneath her.

The king growled before he glanced up at the officials. "Break ribs until she decides to speak." He demanded.

She sucked in a sharp breath before she felt a piercing strike sink into her already bruised ribs. Valeria coughed and spat, trying to regain her breath as she struggled against the pain.

Before she could swallow down another breath, the official kicked her again, this time in the stomach. She tried to roll away, coughing and gagging into the floor.

The king closely watched her struggle. He dug a hand into the thick, long locks of her hair, pulling her head back, exposing her neck. He leaned in closer, whispering, "If he is, in fact, dead, it should bring you no harm to answer. Where is Lance Whitlock?"

She was moments from spitting out the truth when the grand doors bashed against the walls. Pulling against the strength of the king's grip on her hair, Valeria turned her head and watched the Lord of Illusion saunter down the aisle toward her and the king.

"There's no reason for all of this, your majesty. Lance Whitlock's body has been found and is currently being taken to the arena." Saint Nyle didn't bother to look at her. He only picked at his fingernails, smirking down at the king. "Would you like me to send word to the gamerunner? Let him know to start making plans for her celebration?"

The king sat back on his heels, silent. He pressed his lips together and debated the Lord of Illusions words. She hadn't realized he released her hair until she heard his feet scuff against the floor and he stood.

"Very well. I'll have my messenger bring a note to Laurent. No need to have you running all around doing the work of a slave."

Saint Nyle simply nodded and dropped his hands to his side. "And what of the new highlady? Should I send her back to the arena?"

The officials pulled Valeria to her feet, she tried her best to meet Saint Nyle's eye, but he would not pull his gaze from the kings.

The king snapped his head toward her again. She could feel the way he dragged his dark eyes down her trembling form, a moment of hesitation on her covered wrist that already healed over due to her new power-filled body. He blinked, tearing his attention from her and settling it onto the front of the room, where Flynn and the princess remained.

"I'll keep her with me for the time being. We don't need the latest highlady running off, do we?" His throat bobbed; he feigned a cough.

Saint Nyle nodded, pursing his lips.

Then, finally, he looked at her. When his turquoise gaze met her heavy-lidded emerald one, Valeria's breath hitched. He grinned before stepping away from the king and sauntering to the side of the room, where he stood with the rest of the highlords and the Lady of Wolves.

The king faced Helena and her new husband. "Flynn, you'll need to come with me. We have much to do now that you are a part of my family."

The arrogance in his tone was nauseating to Valeria's ears. She managed to bite her tongue when Flynn smiled and let go of Helena. He trudged down the five steps, meeting the king face to face. His crystal blue eyes did not falter from the kings when he bowed.

"I am grateful to be a part of your family, your majesty. Words fail me. I fear I cannot show enough thanks."

Gods. Valeria gagged and turned away. Even with the official's strong grip on her arms, she couldn't help but be disgusted.

Though, she still prayed to each of the Gods for the ground to swallow the black abyss whole before the king could throw Flynn into it.

Flynn stood before the king, his black cape falling over his shoulders before he straightened it behind his back. "May Helena come with us? I'd hate to be separated so soon after our marriage."

Valeria's heart broke little by little with each word that left Flynn's deceitful lips.

How could he?

She scoffed and stared at her feet. Unable to look at him when her stomach grumbled and growled with betrayal.

Helena walked down the steps to stand beside her new husband. The king shifted on his legs, he looked between the both of them, considering his daughter's gentle smile.

"Father, I would love nothing more than to join you. Please, I'll stay back and let the two of you speak. I only wish to watch."

The king swallowed, his eyes brightening before he asked. "Is that so?" Helena nodded. "Very well then. You may come."

And so the king led Flynn, Princess Helena, and Valeria to the top of the palace, where Valeria wasn't sure if the king would find his precious black pool of magic.

41

V aleria couldn't fathom that she was traveling through the same
dark hallway she had just wandered through with the Lord of
Illusion only an hour ago.

The king had a tight grip on her arm as he trudged a pace ahead.
Flynn's presence warmed her back while he and Helena lingered close
behind.

"Hasten yourself, will you?" The king mumbled, tugging on her arm.

Valeria stumbled forward, catching her footing before she could fall.
A hand grabbed the shredded leather material on her back, balancing
her. She thought she might have imagined it at first until a warm finger
skimmed across her spine, then fell away too quickly.

"Might I ask where you're taking us?" Flynn asked, acting as if he
hadn't just saved her right in front of his wife.

There was a hint of a smirk in the king's voice when he spoke. "Why
don't you tell him, Helena?"

Helena remained silent. The only noise she made was a few guttural
huffs as she pushed herself up the steep steps of the stairway they entered.

Their footfalls sounded off of the narrow walls. Valeria stayed beside
the king, focusing on the way her thighs didn't burn with the excessive
use. Usually, she would be bent over, heaving up her guts with all the

exercise she had been doing. Add the final trial on top of it, and she might have been dead.

But now, she felt as if she could run a thousand miles and still have the energy to run another thousand.

Valeria rounded the steps, doing her best to avoid tripping into the king. Even though the thought had crossed her mind to shove him over the railing once they were high enough. She swept the idea away once she remembered his daughter was climbing the stairs just behind them.

She would be imprisoned for life, if not killed on sight, if she murdered the king in front of his daughter.

"I have a few questions before you decide to take me to my likely death." She muttered. Tired of letting the thoughts run through her mind like a current breaking free.

The king paused mid step, then continued onward, tugging at her arm as he went. "Might as well. I could use a bit of entertainment after the week I've had."

She tilted her head and glared at his rigid back.

Clearing her throat, she asked, "Did you know the contestants were being attacked by your officials this year?"

Flynn choked behind her.

"Are you okay?" Helena asked, rubbing Flynn's arm.

Valeria rolled her eyes, but kept her steady attention on the king.

"I did." Was all he said.

"And?"

He paused on the steps before turning his head with a curled lip. "And it hurried the games along. I have much use for those dragons. The faster the games end, the quicker I can claim the dragons of my own."

Valeria laughed and tried to move past him, but he squeezed her arm roughly, causing her to bite back a curse. "You believe the dragons will listen to you?"

"Of course. I rule all of Laterra. Including the beasts."

He was unaware of how the dragons lived then. Valeria only smirked when they proceeded to climb the stairs. If she were to die in a few moments, then it'd be best if he were clueless about Zakai before she blew him to bits of ash.

"Is that all? I'd love to move things along now."

She took a moment to glance back at Flynn and Helena. He was staring up at her, blue eyes narrowed and lips pursed tightly together. They shared a brief look that made her confusion grow.

Flynn's eyes were glossed over, as if he were worried for her.

She took a breath and faced the king again. "I actually have another question... You plan to kill me now. Don't you?"

The king merely scoffed once they reached the top of the stairs and opened the door. "The abyss does not gift power twice to the same vessel. If given another opportunity, it takes as much life as it wants."

She swallowed, praying that the abyss had shrunk completely. If she were to be thrown back in, it would be the end of her story.

Whether Flynn and Helena heard her questions and the king's response, their silence revealed nothing.

Instead of letting her growing worry show, Valeria covered her voice in false confidence. "Good luck." She purred.

The king halted, looking at her with squinted eyes before pulling her forward and out into the dead garden. There were a few spots on the ground where her black footsteps had stained the yellow grass and dry gravel from before. Valeria stared at the marks when the king kicked fresh dirt, covering them so that Flynn and Helena wouldn't see.

No one had seen the black blood spill from her veins when she slit her wrist open to taunt the king. He blocked her from view when she had done so.

Valeria slowed, taking the time to measure out her next few steps from the door and to the abyss. Flynn, Helena, and the king sealed her only exit, but it was worth a shot to try and flee.

Otherwise...

She glanced at the sky and hoped that Zakai could hear her thoughts from wherever she was. But no, her dragon was probably far gone by now. Mourning the death of a friend that she had known for only a short amount of time. She couldn't wait to find her again, to let her know that everything was okay. That was, if she escaped.

If the abyss didn't take back what it had just given her.

"I actually have a few questions of my own." The king suddenly said, his voice made the abyss ripple against its stone border. She looked back at him, thankful for the distraction. He brushed a tendril of blonde hair behind his ear as he peered down at her.

"Do you?" She asked.

"How did you live?" He shot his eyes to the side, revealing that he didn't want his daughter and son-in-law to know of her rushing black blood.

Valeria adjusted her stance and straightened her spine. The truth, or the lie. Which one would she give him? Which one would make him feel uneasy?

She licked her lips before answering, "It has a much needed use of me."

The king laughed with shock before taking a step closer. "And what use do the old Gods need from you?"

She strode closer to him, peering up at his sharp jaw and thin lips. Then she examined his dark, round eyes. He was just a man up close, nothing more. She could see the age in his hazy stare, the wrinkles growing deep on his face from a centuries old life.

"Your death." She said.

He snapped his head up. Swallowed and grabbed her arm again, much tighter than before. The blood puddled in her veins underneath his grip, her hand was numb by the time he started speaking. "Thank the lords there are no Gods anymore." He seethed.

Dropping her chin, Valeria held his harsh gaze without faltering. "You're wrong."

"I am not."

"Then what am I?" She asked, hoping to prod more at his annoyance.

The king examined her black armor, her mangled hair, before meeting her eyes again. "You're a useless being who found herself falling into a black pool and nothing more."

It didn't occur to her that the king had a power of his own until it was too late. A hidden, freezing shadow spread across her entire body before it wrapped around her throat and lifted her up until her feet were no longer touching the dry gravel.

She sputtered out a cough, eyes wide and tear-filled as she clawed at her neck.

The king smirked. A hand reached toward her, clenching his fists together so that his power wrapped even tighter around her throat. "You truly thought that you could speak to me in such confidence? Have you ever stopped to think about the outcome?" He stared up at her dangling form, her body thrashing and kicking. Trying her best to break free from his frozen shadows.

He was going to kill her.

She panicked and snarled beneath his tight grip. "Even your children hate you."

The princess and Flynn stood together, their eyes wide and frightened as they watched the king choke Valeria with nothing but three hundred-year-old rage filled power.

Her gaze landed on his furious face before his thin lips parted. The King of Laterra stood frozen, his voice stolen by the enraged shock. Her words must have struck something deep within his chest, because his eyes narrowed into sharp daggers.

The ground grew farther away as her body hovered higher and higher above the castle. Then, gasping for breath, her vision became blurry, the king launched her across the garden.

Wind blew into her ears as she flew, only to tumble and sprawl across the gravel when she landed. She reached out, scraping her fingers against the rocks to stop her flailing.

"*Val!*" Flynn's voice filtered into her ears before his rushed footsteps pounded into the ground toward her.

Valeria lifted her head, too weak to move. She watched him run for her, but her gaze drifted to the king who strode farther behind. Her jaw dropped when the king lifted his arm again, his steps only getting faster when Flynn reached her.

"Move." she whispered, her voice hoarse.

"What?" Flynn asked. "No. Val. Get up."

"*Move.*" she said, louder this time.

Before he could understand, the king whipped his arm out and Flynn vanished from her side. Thrown across the garden, Flynn yelled. She could only watch as his body finally stopped rolling, though his eyes remained focused on her. He reached out, watching her claw at her suffocated throat once again.

The King of Laterra stood beside her face, wrapping his power around her neck and lifting her high above the garden. "I'm sure my daughter hates you far more, since you've seemed to seduce her husband somehow."

Valeria kicked, hoping to knock him unconscious, but he threw his arm out again, and her body swung through the air before she hovered above Flynn, who was attempting to stand.

That was when she spotted it. Princess Helena, Flynn, and Valeria shared a panicked glance when they realized what the king had planned.

She dropped her gaze to the black murky abyss beneath her. All the king had to do was let her go, and she would be gone.

Gone from this world—from this land, and left for the old Gods to ruin.

Flynn strode two paces toward the king. She examined the furrow in his brow, the way his eyes begged and pleaded. She'd never seen Flynn look so fearful. She'd never seen how light his blue eyes could truly be.

"Please." Flynn said. He reached for the king's outstretched arm, attempting to bring it down—to bring Valeria down. "Please. Don't do this—" He choked, a guttural groan falling from his lips. He dropped his eyes.

Flynn's words broke off at the end, and Valeria's heart sank completely into the dark pit of her stomach.

The king jerked his chin, and used his free hand to reach into the scabbard on his thigh. The sword that sat on his hip was no longer there, the grip was in his hand, the tip of the blade... jabbed into the center of Flynn's abdomen.

Valeria tried to scream through the black dots that covered her dying vision. She managed a sob, and swung her body. She thrashed, wrapping her fingers over the frozen, shadowy rope around her neck. Nearly bending it as a broken cry left her throat.

"My daughter never needed a husband." The king said, twisting the sword deeper into Flynn's stomach, who coughed and gagged on the blood that puddled in his mouth. "Let alone a poor boy from the *filthy* Court of Wind."

Flynn pressed his lips together, his body began to shake with the pain. "Fuck. You."

Valeria watched Flynn slowly adjust his leg, planting it behind the king's ankle. Then she lifted her blurry gaze to the prince, who prowled out of the shadows beneath the castle wall.

She tried fighting off the haze, only to watch how it would end, but her body was growing weak. *How many times could an immortal die without coming back to life?*

Distracted by Flynn who was still attached to that damned sword, the king began to slice upward, toward his ribs. Flynn cried out, but kept his feet planted. His blue eyes darted over the king's shoulder at the prince who neared.

Then, before Valeria's vision went black, Prince Luther stood behind his father, reached over his shoulder, and yanked the sword from the king's grip and out of Flynn's stomach.

Before the king reacted, Prince Luther raised the sword and swung at his fathers back, slicing into his fathers spine, splitting the skin and bone into separate parts.

The King of Laterra lifted his gaze to Valeria one last time before his eyes rolled to the back of his head. He stumbled, tripping over Flynn's foot and wobbling around in order to manage his balance.

Slowly, the king's frozen power unwrapped around her throat, Valeria began to fall.

Just before the king found his footing, Valeria, mid-fall, kicked off of his back as hard as she could, sending him straight into the abyss.

If she was going back in, she was going to take him with.

The king struggled, grunting and cursing as he fell. Though before Flynn could move out of the way, the king wrapped an arm around his legs and pulled.

Flynn shifted his remaining strength toward Valeria. He grabbed her falling body and pushed. He shoved her far, far away from certain death.

Only to find his own.

The princess reached out for Flynn, almost grabbing his hand before the weight of her father took him down. Flynn fell, the king atop him, straight into the black, murky waters.

Valeria screamed.

Her mind ran hollow.

She heard nothing, felt nothing, saw nothing but Flynn's golden hair floating beneath the black, thick abyss.

"*No!*" She rasped, her throat dry and aching. If it weren't for her immortal strength she surely would have been dead.

Tearing at the gravel, she crawled toward the edge of the abyss, planning to throw herself in.

"Stop." Helena barked, dropping to her knees beside Valeria. She pressed a hand on her back, holding Valeria in place. "He can't die in there. He's not immortal yet."

"I don't care." Valeria cried. Her chest shook as she sobbed. Tears dribbled down her face and landed in the abyss, creating white sparks of energy that evaporated as soon as they appeared.

How could everything go so wrong?

She hated herself for pushing him away all those times before.

"There's nothing we can do." Helena whispered, brushing Valeria's hair out of her wet face. "It's up to him to come back up."

Sobs wracked against her body. She felt small. She felt weak. She couldn't do anything but stare down at the abyss and *hope* that Flynn would come back.

He had to come back.

"Flynn." Valeria whispered in a hushed cry.

"I know." Helena stood and began to walk toward her brother, who lingered behind Valeria.

Prince Luther held the sword, looking down at it. A clear water lined his eyes. His mouth was set in a gentle straight frown. His chin, though, began to wobble.

"Will he come back?" The prince asked his sister.

Valeria heard Helena pat her brothers back, before she gripped the handle of the sword and pulled it out of her brother's hands. "I don't know."

The Prince wasn't asking about Flynn, Valeria knew that. He was asking about their father. He had expressed so much resentment for the king, but Valeria would have never thought he wanted him dead.

Just like she'd done during the third night of The Vanishing, Valeria contemplated her choices. She could have gone after her father that night, she could have said goodbye.

Now, she debated diving into those damned black waters. She could pull Flynn out, it might kill her, but she didn't care. Not when Flynn was down there, floating somewhere in the in-between. Someplace unknown.

She called out for him, chanting his name through her mind before finally, she began to pull herself to the edge.

"Valeria, don't."

She ignored the princess, only pulling harder against the rigid stones.

"Valeria—"

Valeria twisted her neck to look over her shoulder at Helena. "I'm going in for him." She growled, but was cut off when a deep voice sounded from below her.

"Don't you dare sacrifice yourself for me."

Relief flooded through her body, soaking into her core as she looked down and gasped.

There he was, floating above the waters. Golden hair an inky mess atop his head. Flynn smirked when he met her eye, though it was darker than before.

Before any of this.

She examined his healed chest, his cut shirt, the skin underneath was stitched over. As if he hadn't been wounded at all. He dragged his arm through the thick waters, lifting it until something gold shimmered against her tear-filled eyes.

"Prince Luther." She whispered, unable to remove her gaze away from the object in Flynn's raised fist. He held the king's crowned head up. "Look away."

"Why—" A wretched, broken sob fell from the princess' lips. She covered her mouth and dropped to her knees.

Flynn dragged himself out of the abyss and dropped the king's severed head back in.

"How?" She asked. The dread in her body warmed only by a little when he wrapped his wet arms around her, pulling her close.

She hadn't realized how hard she was shaking.

Flynn lifted a long dagger from the leather strap on his thigh.

She nodded, and let herself sit in his tight hold. Though the princess' cries broke the shaken silence, Valeria felt the remaining cold power lingering on her throat drip, and drip, filling the blackness below.

The abyss took something back for the first time in five hundred years.

From once being small, to growing larger and larger. The black pool was almost full by the time Flynn helped Valeria stand up, holding her shaking body still.

The King of Laterra was dead.

42

"**M**y father is dead, and I am to blame."

The vast throne room was full, yet never felt emptier without a king to sit on its throne.

The four highlord's and highlady sat around the long walnut table. The prince and princess occupying the chairs at the heads of the table. Helena rested back in her seat and sighed. Looking far more stressed than her brother, who had just finished informing the entire room he had killed his father.

But he didn't? Why was he taking responsibility for the crime they all committed? The prince may have made the first attack on the king, but she had kicked him into the waters, Flynn had cut the king's head clean off. They all shared equal guilt.

Though if she hadn't shown up at the wedding—if she would have waited until it was over—she could have pulled Flynn away and he would have still been human. He wouldn't have this horrible blackness flowing through his veins.

And it was all because of her.

Flynn sat diagonally from his wife, eyes dimmed as he looked away from Prince Luther and scooted back in his seat. "The king's death is by fault of no one. The abyss was the one to take him."

The Lady of Wolves smirked, picking at her black nails, sending a look of knowing toward the Lord of Illusion, who smiled in return. His black hair swallowed the light that trickled down from the ceiling.

Valeria stood beside Laurent, who crossed his arms behind his back and released a breath.

"It was me." She said, feeling the guilt weigh off of her shoulders with the short admission.

Guilt was a heavy thing. The way it clung to her bones and threatened to clog her throat. It'd been growing throughout her entire body ever since she waited and waited for the king to reappear and walk out of the black pool. She thought she had imagined it a few times. When he didn't, and Helena's cries persisted, Valeria felt it. It had covered her like a freezing blanket of snow.

The Lord of Sky nearly shoved out of his seat to face her, when Saint Nyle pressed a hand on his arm to hold him in place.

"We speak without judgment here, Slater. Keep the peace. From what I hear, no one is guilty of the king's death yet. Only two people have admitted to being guilty, but neither has given a reason."

The Lord of Sky, now known as Slater, sat back and pursed his lips. He shook Saint Nyle's hand off of his arm with an annoyed huff.

"She was the last one to be seen with the king in an altercation. How does that leave her unresponsible for his death? For all we know, she could have shoved his body into the abyss." He challenged.

Prince Luther pushed out of his chair and leaned over the table to growl back at the Lord of Sky. "I was the one who shoved him into the abyss. *Me*. I killed him."

"Lie." Valeria mumbled.

He snapped his head in her direction. "Lie?" He chuckled. "Did you not see what I had done? Was everything I told you not enough? His power would still be ruling Laterra if I had not stolen the Sword of Eternity. If I didn't—he might still be here..." He scanned the length of the table.

No one seemed to be concerned with his lengthy admission.

The prince slammed his hands onto the table, knocking a few candlesticks and glass flutes over in the process. "Why isn't anyone angry? Why isn't anyone threatening to have me removed from this damned place?" He shouted, eyes nearly bugging out of his head. Valeria thought she might've seen a drop of spit fly across the table when he yelled.

A chair screeched against the stone floor as Helena stood abruptly. Her face morphed into one of anger and sadness. She focused on her brother. "Sit down, Luther!"

The prince faltered, his chest hammering up and down, in and out, as he breathed.

The entire room fell silent. Even the Lady of Wolves folded both of her hands into her lap and waited patiently for the princess to speak.

Helena stepped away from the table, pointing a finger at her brother. Her cheeks were stained red from mourning her father.

"You know... you know exactly whose fault this is." Valeria stopped breathing. Helena was going to blame her, rightfully so. "Stop acting as if it is your fault, brother. Because if it is your fault, then it is equally mine."

Luther fell back into his seat, eyebrows furrowing as his face paled. "Helena... no. I didn't mean it that way—"

"Let me speak!" She yelled, her high-pitched voice ringing against the walls of the room. "I am just as much at fault for his death, because I wanted him dead as well. I have longed to see the life drain from his eyes for months."

Prince Luther's chest shook as he covered his tears. "I—I..."

Helena wiped at her eyes and turned away from the table. "It is not as if these people care. Why must we question anyone? We all wanted my father dead."

Valeria licked her lips and glanced around the table, watching as everyone seemed to agree. Some nodded with understanding, others with pain, and the Lady of Wolves with anger.

"So must we argue over who is guilty? When all of us are?" She asked, her voice nearly breaking.

Flynn sat silently in his seat, staring at his hands. He hadn't said anything since he walked out of the abyss. A darkness was draped over his shoulders, he couldn't even look her in the eyes.

Did he blame her?

Valeria craved to snatch a fist full of his blonde locks, rip his head upward, and make him understand the pain that his wife was in. She had watched her father die. Yes, Flynn may have been half-dead when he fell into the abyss, but Helena would never see her father again. If he cared so much for the princess, then why was he being so heedless?

He saved you. He loves—

The words vanished as soon as they came. Valeria shook her head and focused on the Counsel of Lords. She couldn't focus on Flynn anymore. He was a married man. A Royal man, and she didn't need to make an enemy out of the princess.

The Lord of Fire leaned over the table, a gentle hand raised as if he was waiting his turn to speak. Helena nodded her head, and he started, "Excuse me, your royal highness. But if we do not find someone to blame, then the entire kingdom will seek vengeance. It will be utter chaos. The citizens of Laterra have lost a king, and if there is no one to blame, they will question us." Black hair fell against his shoulders, complimenting his dark complexion.

Helena swallowed, forcing a smile. "Of course..." She paused and shot a glance at her brother. "Any ideas Luther?"

He lifted his head from his hands and bit his lower lip. "Perhaps it was an accident? We can blame it on the dragons if anything."

Valeria's heart raced.

The highlord's and even the highlady agreed, all sharing a look around the table.

"Perhaps the violet one? Flynn? Where is your beast, anyway?" The Lord of Illusion offered, shooting a smirk at Valeria.

She growled, eyes blazing.

Before Flynn could speak, Valeria stepped forward, blood beyond boiling. "No. The dragons are not to blame. Besides, they belong to no one."

Prince Luther straightened his spine and hardened his stare, inspecting her. "The dragons belong to the kingdom."

She rushed toward the table, leaning over him. "I am the Lady of Dragons. They *belong* to me."

Luther slouched, watching the way she bared her teeth. "Not quite yet, Valeria. We could easily have that altered. Besides," he sent a look at someone over her shoulder. "My father wasn't wrong about seeing Whitlock's body first. No one has provided proof of his death. And until then, there is no winner of this year's Game of Lords."

Valeria released a breath, cooling her bones before shoving off of the table and trudging back to Laurent's side. He gave a comforting smile and brushed a hand against her elbow.

"I have seen Whitlock's body. He is as dead as it gets. If that means anything to you, Prince Luther." Laurent said.

Quirking her lip, she crossed her arms and shifted on her feet. Lance was truly dead then. He hadn't managed to get away. What did that mean of the firetail?

The prince clenched his jaw before giving a curt nod. "Fine. But she has still not been announced as the winner. The dragons remain in the kingdom's possession."

Flynn finally lifted his eyes to meet Valeria's. He swallowed before glancing toward Helena, who was still processing everything. Her hazel eyes watched her brother across the table.

"If we blame Ignar, will she be killed?" Flynn asked.

Helena met his crystal eyes and frowned. "No. Not unless the people of Laterra agree otherwise. We will have a few townsmen' hunt the beast down, but a battle between a dragon and a few men? They wouldn't stand a chance against the smelting flame."

Valeria found herself nodding in agreement. The memory of her skin melting off of her bones flickered through her mind. She grimaced, scrunching her eyes closed.

"What happens next then?" The Lord of Thunder asked. He was staring at his folded hands on top of the table. Lance's highlord had been silent the entire time, often running his hands through his curly blonde locks or scratching at his golden brown skin.

Saint Nyle leaned back in his seat, crossing a leg over the other. "I could use a drink." He muttered.

Valeria rolled her eyes. She remembered the vow she made. How she promised to kill him—to have his head at her feet. He had taken Isaac from her. All for a foolish trial that hardly made any sense.

The Lady of Wolves slapped a hand against his knee and chortled. "After today, yes, please. Let us all meet at the Black Tavern in a few hours."

Utter disbelief flooded Valeria's mind. After the intensity of the entire discussion they all shared together, they wanted to drink at a tavern as if nothing happened? Valeria thought she was going to be hanged, for God's sake.

"Something bothering you?" Saint Nyle asked after he stood from his seat, brushing his hands against the wrinkles on his black pants.

Valeria's lips thinned and she raised her brows. "I'm just a tad confused. So you've settled on harming the dragon's reputation instead of blaming someone for the king's murder? And now you all plan to drink in what—in celebration?"

Saint Nyle flashed a grin before disappearing and reappearing right in front of her. She gasped, falling back into Laurent's chest.

"Gods, Nyle." Laurent scoffed. "You'll give me a heart attack before my time is up."

Saint Nyle apologized, but Laurent only scoffed and turned to leave the room.

The Lord of Illusion waited until the others were gone, bowing to the prince and princess as they left. Flynn was the last one to leave. He held her gaze until the door was shut between them.

"Now would be the perfect time to have my head at your feet, don't you think, darling?"

Valeria shoved at Saint Nyles' chest and he smiled.

"I've killed one too many men this week. Let's reschedule for tomorrow." She huffed.

He lightly gripped her arm, making her come to a halt before she could leave. She flung her fist at his chest and growled when he caught her wrist mid-blow.

"You've been quite violent toward me. I think there are a few things I should fill you in on before you decide to go through with your vow to kill me."

With a curse, Valeria rolled her eyes and spit at his feet. "That is a vow I will not break. I've killed a king. What harm could come of killing a highlord?"

Yanking her closer, he snarled. His breath smelled oddly familiar. "Listen, before I do something I'll regret, would you?"

She paired his glare with one of her own. "Make it quick."

"It is not me who you'll be listening to."

Her world crumbled to pieces when she heard a quiet voice filter into the room. Silently brushing off the stone walls as hushed words fell into her ears. Not sure if she was having a nervous breakdown or if the Lord of Illusion was casting one around her, Valeria gasped for a breath when she heard the voice speak her name.

"I'm here, Valeria. I'm here... I'm alive. I'm here." Isaac's voice was thicker, and much deeper than before... when she had last seen him.

She pressed a hand to her mouth and cried.

"Stop." she whispered.

Saint Nyle must not have heard her, because the voice continued to remind her that he was there, and she could only sniffle into her hands. "Stop." She said again, interrupting Isaac, who continued speaking throughout the room. She couldn't see him, but she could certainly hear him clear as day, as if he were truly there. As if he were still alive. "Stop!" She finally shouted.

Saint Nyle blinked, and Isaac's voice fell silent. "What's wrong? Why are you crying?" He panicked.

Valeria slashed at his face, tears dribbled down her cheeks. "Stop, you Gods-eating bastard!" He jumped back when she swung with all of her might toward him. She clawed, kicked, and screamed at the Lord of Illusion. "He's dead! He's fucking dead, and you killed him! Now you're tormenting me with his voice?" She pounded into his hard chest, ignoring the confusion on his face. "You're an awful person! Just awful!"

That was when he grabbed both of her wrist and tried his best to hold her still. "Stop, Val! Stop!"

She kicked between his legs. Saint Nyle groaned, releasing her wrist.

With free hands, Valeria punched him square in the jaw, surely leaving a bruise. She was reaching for the daggers on her thigh when he lunged at her, sending them toppling to the ground.

"I said to fucking stop!"

Unable to move, Valeria gathered saliva on her tongue and spit into his blue-green eyes. Saint Nyle cursed and sat up. He vanished, then reappeared farther across the room.

She was beginning to stand on her feet when something heavy and invisible slammed against her chest, weighing her down. Valeria clawed at her black armor and groaned as she landed back on the floor.

"Let me go." She cursed and kicked.

Saint Nyle gained his breath before he trudged over to her. Kneeling down beside her struggling body when he spoke, "I was not tormenting you."

"Get your ridiculous illusions off of me! Let me go!" She yelled.

"That voice you heard... it was real."

Valeria felt her heart ache and throb. She would kill Saint Nyle. She'd start by wrapping her hands around his throat and—

"Isaac is alive." Saint Nyle said.

She froze.

Valeria lifted her head and stared straight into his eyes. "*What?*"

He ignored the paleing of her skin and stammering expression as he stood and began to saunter slowly around the room. "Not only that, I know where he is."

Valeria slapped the stone floor, her palm stinging as the sudden sound vibrated off the walls. "Tell me." She hissed. "Tell me where he is."

Finally, he stopped. A hand rubbed against the little stubble on his chin. He looked as if he was nearing his mid-twenties, just like the Lady of Wolves. They appeared so young, but she knew he was well over two-hundred years old, older even.

"I will." Saint Nyle paused before staring back at her. "If you agree to break your vow."

"What?"

He chuckled, dropping his hand from his chin. "Break your vow to kill me."

Valeria pushed against the invisible weight on her chest, but it wouldn't budge. "I will break it if—and only if—you prove that Isaac is alive and well."

Clicking his tongue, the Lord of Illusion blinked and sauntered over to her. "We have a deal."

As soon as he reached her, the weight vanished from her chest and Valeria engulfed a deep breath. She coughed a bit before standing to her feet. Saint Nyle extended a hand for her to seal their agreement, but she held both of her arms against her chest.

Shaking her head, she asked, "How will I know that you're not just throwing another illusion around me?"

He smirked, but pressed closer. "You may ask Isaac a few questions, just to be certain he's real."

She scrunched her face before sighing and taking his large hand into her own.

"Take me to him."

43

Saint Nyle pulled Valeria against his chest. She inhaled, shaking, when she found his turquoise eyes searching her emerald ones. His lips turned up at the corners.

She examined the way his eyelashes fluttered against the lightness of his irises. His rigid jaw clenched as he looked back and forth between her gaze. He was like a black raven, his darkness resembled an onyx stone, his rosewood skin glowed underneath the candlelight. He was a shadow in the midst of light. An unwanted darkness that hovered about, making her squirm.

"Must we be so close?" She whispered, unable to meet his intimidating gaze.

His smile only grew when he leaned closer, brushing his cheek against hers as he whispered in her ear, "If I am to summon Isaac's soul, I need to borrow some of that black magic running through your veins."

She scoffed, tempted to yank her arms back. But Isaac... She'd do anything to see him again. "Fine." She closed her eyes, letting him run his palms down the length of her arms until he grasped both of her hands in his.

"It'll only take a moment."

Her blood seemed to thicken when he closed his eyes. She opened hers and examined the sharp edges of his face. His eyelashes brushed against the unblemished skin on his cheek as he focused. She traced the shape of his straight nose, her mind calming as she inspected every part of him.

The Gods carved him to perfection.

Valeria almost stomped on her toe to stop the invading and unwanted thoughts when her body became rigid. Some sort of solid, thick energy formed in the pit of her stomach before growing heavier and heavier.

She puffed out her cheeks and held back the bile that threatened to fill her mouth.

Soon the watery thickness swam up and up throughout her entire body until it reached her shoulders. She stumbled over at the uneven weight in her body when Saint Nyle pulled her harder into his chest. He leaned over her, balancing her weight against him.

Valeria yanked and pulled, but he simply tightened his grip.

"Calm yourself. I'm only borrowing. I cannot take anything from you, nor do I want to."

At his words, she relaxed into his chest. Anticipating the appearance of Isaac.

After everything she had been through, seeing her friend's face was all she wanted. It was all she needed.

If he was alive, truly alive—Valeria couldn't contain the joy that grew in the back of her mind.

Gods, please. Let Saint Nyle speak the truth.

Let Isaac Bushman be alive.

"There." Saint Nyle whispered, as if he had seen something in his mind.

She wondered how his magic worked. How much power did the abyss give to him when he won the Game of Lords two-hundred and fifty years ago?

Gods. Valeria cursed and watched his expression focus. He was the first lord to win the games.

What was it like back then? How did he win? What were the trials? What about his family?

She chewed on her lip, running her eyes down his chest to where he held her hands. He must've had no family besides a few friends here and there. Unless he had children of his own? Were the high-lord's even allowed to have offspring?

There was still so much that she didn't know.

He was one of the oldest immortals, possibly even the oldest now that the king was dead. Unless the king had transformed others in secret. She wouldn't be surprised if he had.

"There he is." Saint Nyle said, louder this time. His turquoise eyes flickered open.

Valeria's lips parted.

She watched his eyes fill with a hazy gray, as if a storm had formed inside his mind. They were no longer a normal blue-green shade. His eyes were one color. He looked as though he were possessed by a demon from the pits of Hel.

"Nyle." She cursed and tried to step back. His grip remained firm. He stepped with her. "Your eyes." She muttered.

"He's here." Saint Nyle said.

Valeria tore her widened gaze away from him and searched around hurriedly.

"Isaac?" she asked, voice echoing around the empty room. "Isaac?" She tried again once she failed to receive an answer. Eyes narrowing, she bumped her chest into Saint Nyle's. "He isn't here, you filthy liar—"

"Valeria?" A small voice asked from beside her.

There have been many moments in Valeria's life where she thought her heart might have stopped. Too many to count throughout the past couple months, at least. But then, as she turned and found Isaac's curly black hair that was braided against his scalp, and his dark brown eyes that smiled back at her with a new shimmer of life, Valeria's heart truly... *truly* stopped.

Her knees gave out beneath her and she crumpled to the floor. Saint Nyle kept his hands over hers as she balled them up against her chest and failed to find the words to speak. She didn't care, or notice how the highlord crouched down so that their power-linked hands wouldn't part.

"Valeria," Isaac's voice filled her body with utter joy, reigniting the pumping of her black blood. "Look at me." The young boy said.

She attempted blinking back the growing tears as she leaned toward his extended hands. He ran a palm down her cheek, wiping away a warm tear with his thumb.

Isaac chuckled and blinked the tears out of his own eyes. "I've missed you." He said with a wobbling chin.

Once she gained her breath and calmed the trembling of her body, Valeria let herself thoroughly examine his body. "You're okay?" She asked quietly.

Isaac only nodded as he continued to wipe at his face. "I'm fine."

Saint Nyle squeezed her hand and coughed. "I hate to ruin the moment, but keep it quick. The wyrmhole is shrinking."

Valeria dug her nails into his fingers and was left unsatisfied when he merely smirked.

"Nyle says you have a few questions for me... to make sure I'm real?" Isaac asked, frowning.

Valeria swallowed. "Yes, I'm sorry. I just—I can't trust him. If you're alive like he says, I... I can't erase the memory of your lifeless body in the grass." Her voice cracked as she recalled the moment she'd spotted his hollow eyes across the field. "I thought I'd never see you again."

Isaac shot a glare at Saint Nyle before he moved closer to Valeria. Dropping to his knees and placing his warm palms on her shaking shoulders. "Look at me," He said, and she lifted her head. "I'm alive, Valeria. I'm alive. Just let him explain everything. You can be angry, you can even hate him, but let him give you the truth." He glanced at Saint Nyle, who closed his eyes to focus on the connection through the wrymhole. "Now quickly, ask me something only you and I would know."

Valeria searched her mind for anything that only he would know. She thought over and over through every memory with him. When she remembered something—a short spark of a moment with him...

"What did I tell you the night before your final trial? Can you remember?"

Isaac narrowed his brows, dropping his chin to his chest as he fought for the memory.

Worry grew on her expression when an entire minute passed, and he still had not answered.

Adjusting her knees, Valeria shifted her gaze onto Saint Nyle. His eyes were open, watching Isaac, then he flicked them onto hers once he realized she was watching him. He only frowned and shrugged.

Isaac snapped his fingers and jumped to his feet. "Your mother's name. She shares your name, doesn't she? I remember perfectly. It was after you told me about—"

Valeria grinned so widely that she thought her teeth might crack. She shushed Isaac, but continued to smile up at him.

Pushing to her feet, she laughed. "I believe now. You're real. It's you."

Isaac flushed after realizing he had almost blurted her secrets about Flynn in front of Saint Nyle. She had gone on and on about how much she despised Flynn that night. Little did she know how much she would grow closer to him after Isaac's death.

"I wish I could hug you." She muttered, sending a glare at the large hands wrapped around hers.

Saint Nyle squeezed harder. Warning her to hurry up and say goodbye to Isaac. She felt the little bits of power surging out of her palms. Valeria paled and would have sunk to her knees again if it weren't for Saint Nyle holding her up.

"*Now*." He cursed. "Say your goodbyes now."

Isaac rushed over, trying to help hold her up, but his hands traveled straight through her arm, as if he were a ghost. Valeria swallowed a cry.

"I'll see you again," Isaac said, slowly fading away, back to where his physical body was waiting.

Valeria removed a hand from Saint Nyle's and reached out for her friend. "Wait! I don't know where you are. Where can I find you?" Her throat was hoarse and dry as she watched him flicker in and out of the room.

His mouth moved, but only silence fell from his lips before he became a shade of colors. Purple and black shadows floated and waved in the middle of the throne room where his body had just been

Valeria ripped herself away from the Lord of Illusion and grabbed at the remaining colors, hoping to latch onto whatever was left of Isaac. Before she could reach them, they vanished, what remained was merely a trickle of dust.

She choked on a sob, gulping it down.

"Bring him back." She commanded.

Saint Nyle was on his knees behind her. His head slunk against his chest and arms draped to the floor, looking like a fallen angel. Valeria scoffed and stomped toward him.

"Where is he?"

He rolled his head back and blinked. "He's safe."

She ripped a dagger from her thigh, holding it up to his throat in an instant. "Take me to him now, or else."

Smirking, the highlord lazily smiled and reached up to press the dagger deeper into his skin. "Be my ruin, darling." He drawled. "Slice me apart, bit by bit, but please. Spare me for a few more hours. I need a drink."

Valeria ripped the dagger away when he let go and slid it back underneath the strap on her leg. "Just tell me where he is so I can leave."

The smirk fell from his lips as he slouched to his feet. Her power must have drained him of his own. "He's safe in the House of Cards. There's no need to rush. I can have him in a carriage over by tomorrow morning."

Her chest caved and she released a breath she hadn't realized she was holding. "Will it be safe? With the king dead and everything?"

Saint Nyle pursed his lips, running a hand through his onyx hair. "Listen, Val. You're alive. Why don't you appreciate that for the rest of the day, and then tomorrow you can ask all the questions you want? But for now, let us drink. Let us celebrate the death of the cruel king, and feel alive just for the night."

He trudged past her, heading straight for the grand doors.

Valeria stood in the middle of the empty throne room for a few more minutes after the Lord of Illusion left. She stared at the bare throne at the head of the room, imagining the king she killed staring back at her, a taunting smile on his thin lips.

The cruel king. The only name she would remember him by.

Shaking her head, Valeria turned, leaving that room, that king, far, far behind.

44

Two months passed into the middle of summer, when the birds and bees, the pixies, gnomes, and selkies came out of their natural habitats and joined society.

Valeria Rox stared down at the Court of Wind from atop the highest mountain, Vayu Peak.

Zakai bathed in the clear creek a mile away. Her white scales had turned brown from their extensive flight to the west. The skin where Lance's firetail had scorched her was slowly healing over. The scales were tender and peeling, and the heat of the sun in the Court of Wind wasn't making the thin wounds feel any better.

Over the hill, Zakai chuffed and flapped her wet wings.

A grin fell on Valeria' lips as she dragged a hand over her long, copper red hair. It was to her hips now and made riding through the winds tougher than usual.

Valeria fixed her messy braid and scanned her eyes over the village of people she used to know.

It never looked so small, given she had never seen it from so far away.

A finger pointed farther out, past her father's old shop and the House of Air. It pointed to the darker, murkier side of the Court of Wind. The south-side.

"See that building?" The curly-haired boy asked. Valeria glanced at Isaac, who was too distracted by the view of his homeland to notice the way she smiled at him. "The brown one with the green roof. I used to spend my free hours up there whenever I had the time to do so. My mother would always be ridiculously mad when I'd come home late." He chuckled, dropping his hand as he recalled the memories. "I used to think the view from up there was so beautiful, but nothing compares to this."

She couldn't agree more.

Valeria pointed to her father's home. The small, sturdy blue house just off of the main city street. A mile past the market. It sat perfectly in the sun, the city river running underneath the concrete bridge in the front of the small home. Her eyes stung when she watched and waited to see if her father might come hobbling out of the front door.

He never did.

"That's my home." She said before dropping her hand. "I never thought I'd see it again."

Isaac frowned and turned to take a step back. He faced the mountain before beginning the trek back to the river, where Zakai was waiting. "It's good to be alive." He whispered.

That word... *alive*. It sounded bittersweet in her ears, because... well, because she would always be alive. For decades and decades. Possibly even centuries if no one bothered to kill her.

"I hope someday Slater will let you come back."

Valeria dropped her head and removed her gaze from the old blue house she used to call home. "Me too."

The Lord of Sky wouldn't allow her to go back to his Court and live out her immortal life, because she was supposed to be declared a highlady. Specifically, the Lady of Dragons, in a few days.

They'd waited to announce her as the winner of the Game of Lords, because they needed to blame the king's death on the dragons. And if she were to be lady and owner of the beasts, the citizens of Laterra would have her head severed from her body.

Valeria blinked and pursed her lips before finally deciding to catch up with Isaac.

She was only dropping him off so that he could pack his things and move out of the court with his family.

Since everyone knew that he was a contestant in the games, they'd recognize him and wonder why he was alive if he were not a lord.

To cover their tracks, the rest of the royal family and highlord's decided to do what was best for them and their individual courts.

She and Isaac would never be home. They didn't have a home anymore.

At least, she didn't. Isaac would find and make one with his mother and baby brother.

She would have to wait to see her sister. And her father... she wasn't even sure if he was still alive.

Valeria turned her head to the sky and released a sigh.

If she would have known that this was her destiny after the Game of Lords, she would have let the angels inside of the forest kill her. She would have let Lance kill her. She would have let *anyone* kill her.

Isaac stopped beside the warm river and splashed water onto his face. His skin glowed. He never looked healthier. His body had filled out since the first time she saw him. He'd been working out and eating more ever since he escaped the games.

"We should get going." Isaac said.

Valeria cleared her thoughts, breathing through her nose. "Zakai!" She called.

Zakai snapped her head up from beneath the water. It sizzled and vaporized when the beast sneezed and shook her neck.

"It's time to go."

"I can only go as far as the gates." Zakai said.

"That's fine." Valeria gave Isaac's shoulder a pat before stepping around him and marching up to Zakai's side. "Let's go."

Once they were both on Zakai's back and diving in slow swirls down the mountain to the inner hills of the Court of Wind, Valeria felt Isaac rest his head against her leather back.

Valeria Rox smiled at the sky.

Releasing her grip from Zakai's thorny scales, she wrapped her fingers around Isaac's hand that was latched around her waist.

She felt peace.

"Don't forget your hat," Valeria said after pulling it from the brown baggage that was strapped to Zakai's chest.

She had the necessary halter made a few weeks ago when she tried to fly with extra luggage throughout the kingdom and it fell into piles across the dry city.

415

Isaac thanked her when he reached over and snagged the tan ivy cap from her hands and tugged it onto his head, covering his neatly braided scalp. "You're sure you can't come?"

There it was, the question and offer that she had been avoiding ever since they left Jerume.

Saint Nyle had sent Isaac to the kingdom by carriage, and they'd only spent a few days together before Slater found them. Angry that Isaac had somehow escaped the games without his knowledge, Saint Nyle talked the Lord of Sky down, and they settled on the agreement to relocate Isaac and his family.

She grinned before giving Isaac's shoulder a shove. "I would love to, but I have to start heading back if I want to make it in time for the ceremony."

It was a two-day flight through the mountains to get back to the kingdom.

Isaac pursed his lips and released a breath through his nose. "I know. I just thought it wouldn't hurt to ask." They shared a brief look, his eyes light and happy, hers dark and heavy. "I'll try to find a way to visit you, Val. I promise."

Her shoulders fell, she pulled him into her embrace. "I will too... promise."

Isaac squeezed her harder into him, burying his head into her neck. "Thank you." He whispered.

Valeria tried to pull away to question him, but he wouldn't release her just yet. She rubbed a hand down his back and squinted her eyes toward the main gates of the Court of Wind. Watching them swing open.

"You don't have to thank me for anything." She muttered.

Isaac finally pulled away and stared into her confused gaze. "Yes... I do."

He began to step back, but Valeria's attention was focused on the tall woman who stood beside the gate. The woman's dress brushed against her ankles and she held a small child to her chest.

"Talk to Flynn." Isaac said. "He'll tell you everything."

Valeria's eyes landed on Isaac just as he turned and found his mother waiting for him at the gate. He froze in place. His shoulders lifted higher and then lower as he panted out a shaken breath.

"Mama?" Voice trembling, completely forgetting Valeria behind him, Isaac dropped his shoulders and ran into his mother's arms.

Tears blurred over Valeria's emerald eyes as she watched the small family bury themselves into each other's arms. Isaac reached over his mother's wrist to plant a soft kiss on his baby brother's head. He lifted his eyes for just a moment to find hers behind the closing gate.

Valeria lifted her palm and waved.

45

The entirety of guests stood from their seats as they watched Flynn Adler exit the throne room.

His wife, Princess Helena, wrapped her slender arm around his as they walked together.

Once they were outside of the room and the doors were shut behind them, only then did Helena remove her arm and step away. A grim frown was planted on her ruby red lips as she stared up into his crystal eyes.

"Valeria is back." She muttered, easily recognizing the way his gaze brightened at the mention of the copper headed girl.

Valeria had been gone for a week, taking Isaac back to the Court of Wind.

His body flooded with relief, because he feared that if she hadn't returned, he'd have to jump on Ignar's back and fly off in search of the girl he had grown fond of.

Helena snatched his wrist into her hand, digging her long, painted nails into his skin. "She must never know the truth, Flynn."

He blinked and let a tender smile flourish on his lips. "Of course. You have nothing to worry about."

The princess searched his face, looking for any slight change in his expression as he smiled back at her.

Finally, before she turned to leave, Helena chirped, "Very well. Let's keep it that way, *husband*."

The smile on his face fell when she turned around. "No problem, *wife*."

Later, Flynn found himself sitting over the castle wall, where the view to the west was wide open. The greenery of the trees and mountains relaxed his mind as he pulled an apple out of his brown pants pocket and cut into it with a knife.

A gust of wind blew his white tunic open to reveal the smoothness of his chest underneath.

Flynn slid a piece of apple from off of the knife and into his mouth.

He didn't need to turn around to see whose footsteps were striding up behind him as he chewed and swallowed.

The unusually heavy wind, and the sound of leathery wings flapping, was more than enough to let him know that the girl with the fiery attitude and freckled cheeks was indeed Valeria, who stood behind him.

"Need something?" His tone was sharp and unbothered, as if he couldn't care less about the girl at his back, when, indeed, he'd found himself always thinking about her. How her wide emerald eyes stared into his, or how her hair appeared pink when she stood underneath the moonlight.

Valeria scoffed.

He imagined her crossing her arms and rolling her eyes while he grinned down at his apple.

"Is there something that you're not telling me?" She asked.

"Always." He chirped.

A second later, he felt a slight kick to his ribs before she stepped up beside him. Not bothering to crouch down to his height, she was too busy looking out over the vacant land. The Forest of Many Wonders.

Only hunters and a few brave souls found themselves wandering into the forest during the months of autumn. Some had never returned, rumored to be eaten by a troll or river beast.

Valeria kicked at a rock and they watched in unison as it tumbled down the steep hillside.

The sun barely peeked over the green mountains when she spoke again. "I need to know if you were the one who saved Isaac." Her voice was hardly above a whisper.

He glanced up, watching as she fiddled her fingers together. Her eyes darted down to him before glancing away.

Flynn threw the core of his apple over the hillside and tucked the dagger underneath the strap on his belt.

"It's complicated, but in a way... yes. I did."

She bit her bottom lip, nodding. "And how did you convince the Lord of Illusion to do so?"

He'd never found himself speechless by anyone else before, but Valeria—the way she always questioned him, when no one else had ever tried to or would ever imagine to. Flynn rested back on his hands and squinted at the sunset.

Fire red.

The same color as her hair.

"We're close friends." He said, heart pounding when his thoughts turned to mush.

He couldn't tell her the truth. Because if he told her the truth, then everything would be ruined. All of his plans, all of his actions and scheming, would be for nothing.

A flock of birds flew from the garden over the castle walls. Flynn watched the wings turn a dark shade of purple as the dying sun beat against their feathers. When he looked back at Valeria, the wings were black again—their natural color.

"You just so happen to be long-time friends with the first-made highlord?" She questioned, sharp tongue and even sharper eyes staring directly into his.

He could see anger booming from her small body the longer he remained silent.

Valeria ran a stressed hand through her messy unbraided hair and shook her head. "A boy from the Court of Wind. *You.*" She chuckled sarcastically. "Excuse me if that doesn't make any sense, because how in the Gods does a boy make friends with a highlord who is centuries older than him? I'm just a tad confused. And quite literally, tired of all of your lies."

Flynn knew he was already making an ass of himself, so all he managed was a shrug and pursed lips. "I haven't lied to you, ever. Like I've said before, I just haven't told you all of my secrets. And I bet it drives you mad that you don't know everything about me. Doesn't it?"

Valeria kicked dirt at him, ruining his perfectly white tunic. He grinned.

"You wanted me to run away with you—to leave the games and live the rest of our lives together in hiding. Was any of that real? Did you truly want that? Or were you only trying to get into my pants?"

His throat bobbed as he swallowed. "How many times do I have to tell you, Val?" He pushed himself to his feet, absolutely annoyed with the woman that stood in front of him. Annoyed with the wind that played with her hair and brushed against her face. Everything that touched her, moved a part of her that he couldn't. "I've never lied to you. Not unless it meant protecting you."

With every word that left his mouth, Flynn inched closer to her. His face narrowed as if he could intimidate the infuriating girl that stood a foot shorter than him.

She growled, lifting her chin. "You're lying right now."

Flynn cursed, throwing his hands into his rugged blonde hair. "You're ridiculous!" His shout echoed down the hill, over the trees.

Valeria stepped back, eyes squinted as she watched him try to regain his composure.

"What is it that you think I'm lying about?" He finally asked, dragging a palm down his face.

Licking her lip, Valeria prowled closer and closer until her finger was digging into his hard, muscled chest. "Who you are, Flynn." His eyes widened. The corner of her lips tugged upwards as she watched his expression drop. "I know who and what you are."

Everything fought against him. The wind, the dirt, and even the way her eyes locked with his. She nearly pushed him over the edge of his own mind.

Flynn swallowed and clenched his jaw. Before he could say anything else, she jabbed her finger harder into his chest, then turned and sauntered up the hill. Disappearing around the corner of the outer palace wall, Valeria was gone.

46

C eremony day arrived.

Jacky woke Valeria up and sent her to a massive, elegant room to bathe and dress for the ceremony first thing in the morning. Then, Valeria ate breakfast by herself at the lonely table in the great hall of the palace, where she was joined by a few of the servants and officials.

Time passed slowly after that. She'd spent a few hours in the garden reading before she gave Zakai a visit, annoyed that she was informed to avoid riding today in order to keep her makeup and royal black, skintight dress from being ruined.

A servant came to her as she was sitting in the dried-up meadow with Zakai. That was when she was dragged back to the palace.

The servants and officials surrounded her when she was escorted to the vast throne room, where she would soon be announced as the Lady of Dragons.

She found herself bowing before the Crown Prince Luther and Princess Helena, who stood tall on the steps to the king's throne.

Valeria prayed for the ceremony to pass quickly. She was not in the mood to drink and play into the highlord's and royal family's performances.

She was tired of pretending.

Holding Prince Luther's gaze, she stood to her full height and forced a smile. Examining the lack of his father's crown on his head. He had been pushing his coronation off for as long as he could.

"Valeria Rox, as the last standing contestant of the sixth annual Game of Lords, I, the Crown Prince of Laterra, announce you as this year's winner."

She didn't flinch when her chin sunk into her chest and he tapped her left shoulder with the Sword of Eternity. The same sword he had swiped through his father's back.

Luther then handed the sword to his sister, and Helena tapped the blade onto Valeria's right shoulder. The only weapon in the world capable of killing an immortal. The only weapon made by the abyss.

Lifting her gaze, Valeria nodded her head at the princess.

"As winner of the Game of Lords, I hereby announce you, Valeria Rox, as the Lady of Dragons." Helena raised her chin and waited for the servant beside her to place a thin silver crown into her palms. She held it up and let the other highlord's and highlady examine the fine silver artistry.

Together, as one, Prince Luther and Princess Helena placed the dragon shaped crown on top of Valeria's head.

"Lady of Dragons. Ruler of the Court of Ash. You are now responsible for the care of your people."

A ballroom bathed in dark colors of scarlet, violet, emerald, and gold greeted Valeria's eyes as she dragged herself through two oak doors. There were no lights or candles to brighten the room, only the glowing, colorful pixies that flew past her like tiny strikes of lightning.

She felt a grin blossom on her cheeks as she watched the small creatures take flight all around the room. Glancing upward, she noticed the absence of a ceiling. Where wood and stone should've been, the night sky and stars sat high above.

Tripping over her long emerald gown, Valeria removed her eyes from the stars and focused on the royal guests dancing around the room in their beautiful, elegant dresses and suits.

It was absolutely unthinkable.

The memories of each ball, each night she had been dressed like a queen only to be riddled with anxiety the entire time inside of Azrael estate. Now, the ball she stepped into was not about the trials and bets... The ballroom and the people that surrounded her, were there *for* her.

She was the Lady of Dragons.

Valeria fixed the mesh of golden lace that sat on her wrist. She inhaled and adjusted the tightness of the corset around her waist and brushed a finger over the feather material that was currently tickling the base of her neck.

"I'd assumed you'd be more comfortable at events like this by now." Laurent muttered from beside her. He was fixing his own white tux sleeve. Valeria giggled when she imagined what kind of joke Isaac might have made about the gamerunner's outfit. "Do you like the color? Since the night is about you and your dragons, I'd decided to match no one else but your very own beast. Zakai is her name, correct?"

Valeria nodded and offered him a hand. He accepted it with a sheepish grin.

"So, what's next for you?" She asked as they joined the slower waltz the other dancing couples moved to.

Laurent glanced over her shoulder. His gray hair was down, complimenting the neatly trimmed mustache above his thin upper lip. "I haven't gotten that far. I suppose I'm no longer needed for the games... not for another fifty years at least, and I imagine I won't be around for those."

Her hair draped over her shoulders in a spiral of curly flame when Laurent spun them around to the beat of the piano. The music filled the silence as she let his words settle in deep. He wouldn't be around, but her... she surely would.

"But you have a home here, right?" She asked, trying her best to avoid the topic of life and death.

"I do."

"You know, I might be pretty lonely in such a large estate all by myself... perhaps you could join me in the Court of Ash?"

Laurent slowed his pace before his pale face turned bright and pink. He smiled. She had never seen him look so happy before. He leaned closer, pulling her into a hug. Surprisingly, Valeria closed her eyes and sighed into his chest.

"I'd love to join you."

Because why else would he stay in the kingdom? In a castle where no friends were to be made, nothing but the piling history of his ancestors that lived the same life he was currently living.

And of course, why stay at Azrael estate? When it was going to be abandoned for the next fifty years until the next Game of Lords contestants would fill its halls and rooms.

Laurent pulled away, holding both of her arms in his hands as they slowed their dancing. "I always knew it would be you." He whispered.

Valeria released a breath and patted his elbow. "No, you didn't."

They laughed together before parting ways.

She spent a few minutes resting against the polished cream walls, examining the dancers that blurred into colors of all sorts. A few smiles and laughs filled her ears and eyes before she made way to exit the ball.

After tonight, she would no longer be known to the world as Valeria Rox.

After tonight, she would never be a normal girl again. She hadn't realized the last time that she actually felt normal, anyway. Because it had been months since she'd been the girl who lived inside the Court of Wind.

Normal was her older sister, Lilith, brushing her hair, braiding it tightly down the length of her back as she blabbed about the current boy she was seeing into the mirror.

Normal was hearing the jingle of the bell as she stepped into her father's shop and he already had a basket clean and ready for her to pick flowers down by the river with. Normal was her family. Normal was her innocence.

Normal was gone.

Valeria stumbled into the wall, her dress shrank tighter and tighter around her waist. She grabbed at her throat, trying to catch her breath as she pushed herself off of the wall. The torches that lined the walls hardly lit the hallway. People brushed past her with eager grins on their faces, excited to be a part of something special. Something that she should've enjoyed, because *Lords*, wasn't she alive? Wasn't that everything she had fought for?

The torch flames flickered against her eyes before she felt a cold brass handle against her sweaty palm and pushed it open, falling into the unlit room.

She searched for some kind of light, but quickly became unbothered when the tightness of her dress continued to shorten her breath. She was bathed in complete darkness as she rushed across the room and leaned against a desk.

Her breathing grew heavier when she clawed at the strings on her back. She pulled the knot apart and the relief of her loosened corset expanded her lungs. Deeply inhaling, Valeria closed her eyes and relaxed against the table.

A scuffle sounded from the doorway and she turned her head just in time to see Princess Helena and Flynn enter the room. The princess shut the door until it was almost completely closed, then quickly, she backed away from him.

Valeria slowly, but silently crouched to the floor, ducking behind a large accent chair. She gulped down another breath before releasing it against the cloth of the chair. Hoping she was silent enough to stay hidden.

"You said too much to my brother, you damned fool." Helena spit, and Valeria would have gasped if it weren't for the possible truth that could come spilling out of Flynn or Helena's lips any moment.

Flynn leaned back against the door, his arms crossed. "I only said what was needed. He doesn't know anything. He's just as clueless as your father was."

Helena scoffed and raised her fist before dropping it to the brass door handle. "I do not care. When you are with me, you need not speak so much. I will handle everything." Flynn rolled his eyes. "I have no use of you for the rest of the night. I'd rather you just leave me alone. Find someone else to bother for the time being." Before Helena left, she swifty faced him and stood on the tips of her toes. "Stay far away from the girl. Understand?"

They didn't share hurtful looks when Helena opened the door and marched into the hall.

Why did they marry? Did they not fall in love inside the games?

Valeria glanced at the wrinkles on Flynn's navy-blue tux.

He pushed off of the door, running a hand through his hair before brushing his knuckles down the fabric on his chest. As his fingers skimmed over the expensive material of his tunic, the dark blue color changed—altered to a pure black.

If it weren't for the chair keeping Valeria steady, she would have fallen on her ass at what she saw.

Flynn turned around to face the door. She watched him place a gentle hand on the doorknob and dip his chin.

Her chest shook as she released a slow, uneven breath.

When Flynn lifted his head and twisted the brass door handle, his hair was no longer shaggy and blonde.

It was black. Black as midnight—black as a raven's feathers.

He turned, shooting a grin over his shoulder and into the shadows, where Valeria was hiding behind the chair. And then he turned and sauntered into the hall.

Shoulders falling, she pushed to her feet. Lips parted in shock, not in surprise at who Flynn was, but at the certain truth he had just laid out in front of her.

How he controlled the games. How he was the strongest player. How he saved Isaac...

She understood it then, as she rested her gaze on the man through the darkness.

He saved Isaac after she begged, pleaded, and bargained with him. He had lied to her about everything.

Valeria sank into the chair, staring at the closed door the raven-haired man just walked through. She blinked, letting her mind place the scattered pieces together.

Flynn Adler was Saint Nyle, the Lord of Illusion.

ACKNOWLEDGEMENTS

The Game of Lords would not be the same without a few people who have helped make it possible.

Thank you so much, Abbey my very first test-reader who really helped me get this book started. I wouldn't have been so motivated to finish it without your helpful comments.

Thank you, Hope Arnold, for believing in this book, and even pushing me to have it traditionally published. (If I had the patience, I may have even gone that route.) Your beta reading comments, and advice have truly helped shape this book. I can't thank you enough.

I can't fathom what I would have been doing with my free time as a stay-at-home-mom if it weren't for my own mom who told me she was writing a book. She reminded me of an old passion of mine that had died out over the years. As an early teen I had written and started novels, but I could never finish them.

Now, here is The Game of Lords, a book that wouldn't have ever been written if I didn't remember a dream of being chased through a forest by angels and read a few of my most favorite books.

The process of getting this book published was long and really tested my knowledge and patience. I wanted the book to be out, but I hadn't realized how much went into the publishing process. The cover, map, formatting, ISBN's. All of it held me back, and I'm glad it did. Numerous rounds of editing have gone into it because I couldn't publish it as soon as I wanted, and now this book is something so much more to be proud of.

Thank you to everyone who reached out and offered to make up a cover!

For my mom, thank you. You have been my biggest supporter since day one. Every word I've ever written, whether it was for an unfinished projected, or something I scrapped, you have supported it. My biggest critic, but the most help and truth that I could ever ask for. The Game of Lords, Valeria, Isaac, and Flynn would not be written, formed, and created if it weren't for you. It is your push that made me pick up my old laptop and start outlining. I love you.

And finally, to God, thank you. Every prayer has been answered when it came to writing this book. Every publishing worry, editing worry, art worry, has been solved because you chose to answer my prayer.

Thank you.

About the author

Sandra is a stay-at-home mom, with a strong passion for stories, whether she is reading or creating them. Though she didn't attend college, she did focus on writing and world building for books that she would soon create in the future. Her passion for writing began when she was twelve years old. Sandra wrote online and had a few stories become popular. In high school, she was homeschooled and started three or four novels, though a single one was never finished. After having her son, she found the time and motivation to finally work on her dream.